A Knowing One

Book 4 of the Branwell Chronicles

Judith Hale Everett

Evershire Publishing

Published by Evershire Publishing, Springville, Utah
ISBN 978-1-958720-98-1
Library of Congress Control Number: 2023907190

A Knowing One is a work of fiction and sprang entirely from the author's imagination; all names, characters, places and incidents are used fictitiously. Any resemblance to actual people (living or dead), places or events, is nothing more than chance.

To Diane,
for your unflagging support and encouragement.

To my readers:
Make sure to read the Author's Note in the back for historical
information on concepts and events described in the story.

To get *A Near Run Thing* for free and to learn more about the Branwell Chronicles series, go to judithhaleeverett.com, or scan the QR code below:

A
Knowing
One

Chapter 1

THE VIEW FROM the drawing room window of Wrenthorpe Grange was one usually certain to bring contentment to Tom Breckinridge's breast, for it was of a tidy garden abutting the well-kept Home Wood. Even in this unseasonable June heat, the prospect was neat and refreshing—evidence of the diligent care of a thoughtful master. The same care by the same master, Sir Joshua Stiles, had changed the fortunes of the Breckinridge family the previous year, when Sir Joshua had married Tom's mother, Genevieve, and provided her the happiness and security she deserved and had long been without. Such dutiful stewardship spoke to Tom's soul, for he had spent his formative years also without security, and had vowed never to subject his dependents to anything approaching the neglect which he and his sister and mother had suffered at his profligate late father's hands.

Unfortunately, the view this morning was unable to produce its usual soothing effect upon him, for it was marred by the presence in the room of Tom's sister, Lenora, and her newly betrothed, Lord Helden. Tom had endured three weeks in their nauseating company, as well as in that of his still newlywed parents, and it had stretched his patience to the breaking point. Even now, as Tom gazed intently out the window trying to regain some part of his natural sangfroid, Lenora and Helden snuggled on the sofa, their billing and cooing continually grating on his pragmatic nerves. He was firmly of the opinion that such exhibitions ought to be restricted to more private hours, and not aired for the benefit of patently unappreciative relations.

Lenora, of all people, thought Tom, ought to be sensible that he would dislike overt displays of sentiment, having frequently observed his incomprehension of all things romantic. But if he was fair, he must admit that, until now, his habit had been generally good-natured toward such inclinations. Doubtless, to her mind, his usual carefree and quizzical manner had suddenly and inexplicably vanished upon his removal from London, leaving in its wake a cynical, stern figure whom she could not recognize. But though Tom acknowledged this, he would not address it, for he could not bring himself to admit the truth underlying the matter.

"And what, pray, has given you so sour a look, Tom Breckinridge?"

Whirling, Tom found himself alone with Lenora, Lord Helden having silently and mysteriously vanished. His sister gazed sardonically at him, her back straight and her eyebrows raised inquiringly.

"If you do not know by now, dear sister," retorted Tom, returning her gaze with an imperious one of his own, "then you are even more of a ninnyhammer than I took you for."

She blinked slowly, tipping her head to the side. "If you mean that your sensibilities are offended by the sight of your dear sister in love with an excellent man, then one cannot help but wonder at so unreasonable an irritation."

"It is not only you and Helden, Nora, but also Mama and Sir Joshua," replied Tom testily, avoiding her latent question. "The two pair of you are as revolting as any pack of heroes and heroines in those horrid romances you are forever reading."

She tutted. "You cannot have been so foolish as to imagine that newlyweds such as Mama and Sir Joshua should not be at least somewhat silly, especially after having discovered that they are soon to welcome another child."

"No, but need they be so silly in my presence?" retorted Tom.

Lenora raised her brows again. "You will forgive my saying that your tone smacks of selfishness, Tom. This is their home."

Huffing, he turned back to the window, crossing his arms. "And what is your excuse, Nora? You are merely betrothed. May I expect your disgusting displays to increase upon your marriage? Perhaps I ought to avoid visiting you at Helden Hall altogether."

There was a slight pause before she said, "I believe you are jealous."

Tom swung about, opening his mouth to refute this ridiculous notion, but Lenora forestalled him with a shrewd look.

"You are jealous, sir," she stated, rising and striding to him, "and you only are to blame, for Diana would have you the moment you offered for her. One is only left to wonder why you have not done it."

"One need not wonder at it, Nora," he said gruffly, a sneer marring his handsome features. "Any gudgeon can tell that it would be a gross presumption for me to do so."

"Tom, how can you be so vexing?" cried Lenora, letting fall her dignified manner and scrutinizing his countenance with real concern. "You are acting so oddly!"

"Indeed he is," put in another voice, and they turned to see their mother, Lady Genevieve Stiles, enter the room. She looked from one to the other of her children. "Does he deny it?"

"Yes, I do, Mama," snapped Tom, but at her look of mild reproach his shoulders slumped and he ran an agitated hand through his already unruly dark hair. "I beg your pardon, Mama—and yours also, Lenora. I have been behaving badly, and there is no occasion for it."

"Except perhaps this horrid heat, into which you will take yourself. It cannot be healthful to be always riding out in such weather, for it puts you in such a temper. Poor Helden and Sir Joshua are continually in a quake with wondering at what next you will say to them. Are we all so unpalatable that you prefer to go outside to be baked?"

"Yes," was the blunt answer.

Lady Stiles took his hand, pulling him away from the window to sit with her on the sofa. "Forgive me, Tom. I have been too caught up in my own happiness to tend to those around me. I ought to have made your comfort more my concern. But I will make up for it now by owning that I think all is not well with you."

"Certainly I am not well—I have a touch of the sun," said Tom with forced lightness.

But Lady Stiles persisted. "No, no, my dear, do not dissemble. Lenora is not the only one to have remarked the stark alteration in your manner. Will you tell us what is the matter?"

In answer, he sat back against the cushions, pressing his fists into his eyes.

"He is envious of our situation, Mama," said Lenora helpfully, "for he fancies himself unworthy to achieve it."

Irritated anew, Tom stood from the sofa and stalked back to the window. "By all means, believe my hopes to be blighted. I daresay you will not be very far from the truth."

As Lady Stiles regarded him with a furrowed brow, Lenora joined him again at the window. "What are you talking of, Tom? Scarcely a month ago you very nearly asked Diana to stand up with you a third time at the Colderbeck's ball! You sent her flowers and trinkets and took her driving everywhere around Town, and she welcomed it all with delight! It is an understood thing that you will make her an offer. What has happened to make you despair? You—you did not have a falling-out?"

Tom chewed the inside of his lip. It was not his policy to bare his soul to anybody, but he also knew his mother and sister well enough to recognize when he had been cornered.

With a grimace, therefore, he said, "She has another beau, Nora."

"She has any number of beaux, Tom. Don't be a saphead. She has preferred you to all of them for months! Or are you blind?"

"I see more than you know, Nora," he said, rubbing the back of his neck. "It's this Popplewell fellow that's come out of nowhere. It's as plain as day she cares for him more than me."

Lady Stiles sat up. "Who is Popplewell?"

Lenora, who had been staring stunned at Tom, turned toward her mother with an incredulous laugh. "Good heavens! He is merely Diana's childhood playmate, Mama, separated from her for some years. What a cawker you are, Tom! Diana is only glad to be reunited with him—nothing more, depend upon it."

"I'm no cawker!" retorted Tom, nettled. "Diana adores him. Her eyes light when he comes into a room, and she delights in every trifling thing he says. She even admires his frippery clothes—for he's a Bartholomew baby if ever there was one. It's enough to make me itch to draw his claret!"

"Which you know well you ought not to do to Diana's friend, or you will be in the suds," Lenora said, joining her mother on the sofa.

"And he is heir to a viscountcy, which you can be sure Mr. Marshall is more keen on than my paltry portion," added Tom belligerently.

"Especially when it attaches to such a disagreeable object as yourself," replied Lenora.

Tom grumbled something about Job's comforters and swung back to the window, while Lenora, at a look from her mama, begged his pardon and turned primly away.

Lady Stiles went to her son, laying a hand on his arm. "Perhaps it is not so very unaccountable of Mr. Marshall to prefer an intimate family friend to you, who have known Diana but two seasons, but it is shocking all the same. What a horrid inconvenience, to have this Mr. Popplewell come on the scene so suddenly. A future viscount! It is a daunting prospect, to be sure, but it is my belief that there is nothing in it to make you go off into the dumps."

"Nothing? The heir to a viscountcy, and one to whom Diana is prodigiously attached!" ground out Tom. "If that is nothing, then I must beg your pardon for having overstated the case."

Lady Stiles was undaunted. "I cannot believe that Miss Marshall has become cold to you, my dear. Are you certain that you are not refining too much upon a trifle?"

If Tom was at all uncertain of this, he was in no mood at present to own it to his mama. He was tired, hot, disillusioned and irritable, and he wanted to go home, to his estate at Branwell, where love was not an issue and romance was never in the air. He told his mother as much as he began pacing restlessly about the room.

She returned to sit beside Lenora on the sofa, sharing a look half-annoyed, half-laughing with her. "I wonder that your brother can have attached any young lady with such an unromantic disposition, Lenora. He has his looks, to be sure, but it is an unnatural young lady indeed who does not wish to be courted with some degree of romance."

"I now perceive that has been my mistake, Mama," Tom said sarcastically. "I have been at a loss to explain Miss Marshall's sudden desertion, but you have hit upon a very cogent possibility. I have had it coming, I apprehend."

"Now Tom!" Lenora said reproachfully. "Do not be provoking! It is not as though Diana has rejected you."

"No, for I have not offered for her, but I might well save my breath, for if the last three weeks of our stay in London are anything to go on, she would rather have Mr. Popplewell."

"Next you will say that we been deceived in her, for she is a mercenary and wishes to be a viscountess."

"Never!" cried Tom furiously. His mother and sister gazed blandly back at him and he had the grace to blush, slumping into a wing chair. "Forgive me. This wretched heat! My head is aching fit to split."

"I do not doubt it, my son," said Lady Stiles gently. "Pardon us for teasing you; we should know better. Though I do not believe I have seen you so wound up since you were in shortcoats and your papa would not give you a pony. Do not eat me! I am very serious. You threw a dreadful tantrum and Badeley and Matthew both were obliged to carry you off to your room—after you kicked your papa in the shins. What a horrid little boy you were then—but never after, Tom. Never after that day did you afford me a single cause to believe you would not grow up to be just the fine gentleman you have done. I could not be more proud."

Tom, still hanging his head, gave a grudging smile. "Even now, when I have enacted such a scene? Even though I have no sensibility, and am not romantic enough to attach a young lady?"

"Always, Tom!" said his mama with determination. "I beg you will forget what I said earlier. A gentleman need not be romantic, precisely, to attach a young lady—I have seen it often and often. There is much more that a lady looks to find in a husband, which you do possess! Steadiness is paramount, as are high principles."

Tom made a face. "So I am a dull dog. Thank you, Mama."

"Nonsense. I know whereof I speak, young man, for your father was all that was charming and romantic, but his unsteadiness nearly lost us our home, and all his principles went by the wayside as soon as a gaming table was in sight." She nodded smartly. "A lady may wish for romance, but what she truly wants is security and companionship."

"It is unfortunate that the lady in my eye wants them all."

"Nonsense, for Miss Marshall is a rational young woman, and if she does desire a more romantic manner, she at least has not shown the least disinclination for your company—indeed, I am much mistaken if she has not sought you out, Popplewell or no Popplewell." She paused, wrinkling her nose. "What a name. If she does marry him, it will serve her right."

"I will not go so far, Mama," said Tom, a bit of his native humor showing in his eyes, "but I will own that it beats me how anyone could wish to be allied to someone named Popplewell."

"It certainly is not a very dignified sort of name," giggled Lenora. "I must own that I should not like it. But more importantly, Tom, I assure you that Diana does not wish to take a name such as Popplewell."

"It doesn't much matter what she wishes if Mr. Marshall steers her toward his choice," said Tom, his smile vanishing.

"Now Tom!" Lady Stiles remonstrated. "Do not go back into the sulks. You know as well as I that he could not force her to marry where she does not wish it. Indeed, he is a most indulgent father, and would not wish her to be made unhappy."

"But Popplewell does not seem to make her unhappy," pursued Tom doggedly.

Lenora would not allow this. "They are like brother and sister, Tom! Surely you must see it—if you have not, Mr. Marshall must have."

Tom shook his head. "He shows it oddly, then, Nora. Diana has been at Brighton half the Season—"

"I am well aware of that, Tom. They have gone for her father's health—Diana says they always have gone to Brighton when he is poorly, for it is not ten miles from their home, and he will go nowhere else. But I do not know what that has to say to anything."

"It has everything to say to it," said Tom, suddenly exhausted. He passed a hand over his eyes. "Her father's health has never been better, or I'm a simpleton. He goes to Brighton, and carries his daughter with him, to follow Popplewell."

Both Lenora and Lady Stiles regarded him keenly.

"But how can you be certain?" inquired Lenora. "Mr. Popplewell's estate is near Brighton, to be sure, for they are neighbors. Are you sure he also has gone to Brighton?"

"Dead sure," said Tom. "I was present when he announced his intention of removing thither a fortnight before we left Town. And not two days later, Mr. Marshall discovered his rheumatism had become so insupportable as to require the sea air and Indian Vapor Baths of Brighton."

The ladies were silent for a moment, pondering this.

At last, Lady Stiles spoke. "Dear me. He is, then, either a great invalid or Mr. Popplewell has done something immense to gain his favor."

Tom snorted. "You forget that he has done nothing less than become heir to a viscountcy, Mama, and to a very tidy fortune, if my information is good. Add that to his already snug estate and he becomes quite a million times more eligible than my humble self."

"Oh, no, Tom!" cried Lenora. "I cannot believe Mr. Marshall to be so insensible as that. Your estate is nothing to scoff at, you know. That is, in a few years it will be excessively profitable, and surely he may judge that you are an excellent manager and will take very good care of Diana. Besides, it is how she judges that matters, and she does not want a title and a fortune, depend upon it! She has ten thousand pounds of her own, and she is just the sort of kind, generous-hearted person who would want to put it to good use, I am persuaded."

"You comfort me exceedingly," remarked Tom wryly. "I am now no better than a charity case."

Dismayed, Lenora went to him and knelt beside his chair. "Come, now, Tom, no more of these blue devils. You must be calm and rational. Perhaps Diana has been distracted by Mr. Popplewell, but I can assure you that she thinks very highly of you—Do not look at me in that odiously cynical way! I had a letter from her only last week, and if she mentioned how well she liked Brighton it was only to urge me to visit her there, and to mourn the loss of her time with her friends—all her friends, Tom. She most specifically requested that I remember her to you, and I am much mistaken if she did not hint that she would be delighted if you were suddenly to appear there, or at Findon when they are returned home."

Tom merely humphed.

"Well, my love," Lady Stiles said briskly, sitting up and clapping her hands. "It seems to me that there are only two courses open to you. Either you love Diana or you do not. Which is it?"

"It is not that simple, Mama," Tom muttered, rising and going once more to the window.

Lenora's lips pursed in disgust. "I never fancied you to be so poor-spirited, Tom. You appear already to have given it up!"

At his stormy silence, his mother said soothingly, "Perhaps it is not simple, Tom, but you must own that your present manner is excessively inert, and does you no credit."

Tom cast her a deprecating look. "I apprehend that I ought not to have sought your advice."

"I beg your pardon," she said, "but you must be brought to a sense of your own stupidity. It seems to me that you have allowed Mr. Marshall and his *protégé* to intimidate you. Lenora is correct—it is unlike you, Tom, and you will pardon my also saying that if you continue to approach the situation with such lassitude, you will end very unhappily."

Tom's jaw tensed and he muttered, "It is not as though I wish to let Diana go, Mama."

"Ah! A breakthrough!" cried his mother, taking him by the hands. "If you do not wish to let her go, then you must pursue her to the end."

"But neither do I wish to make myself odious to her, if she prefers another." He blew out a sigh. "It would be much simpler if I knew her sentiments."

"My dear Tom," said Lenora, taking his arm, "as one of Diana's fast friends and privileged to know her innermost thoughts, I am ready to swear that she continues to prefer you above anyone, even Mr. Popplewell. Do not hesitate to resume your pursuit!"

"I trust we shall have her here with you within the summer," put in Lady Stiles, "acting in as nauseating a manner as either of us."

Either from fatigue or relief that his anger had burnt out at last, Tom smiled weakly. "If Diana does choose me over Popplewell, then I suppose even that will be possible."

Chapter 2

IT HAD BEEN excessively relieving to Tom's spirits to discuss the matter of Diana and Popplewell with his mother and sister, and he meant to show his gratitude in a much improved demeanor. He was so changed a creature when he came down for dinner that evening, therefore, that his mother and sister exchanged significant glances, and Lord Helden and Sir Joshua lost all their dread of being alone with him again over port.

Much as his altered manner refreshed the company, it did nothing to revise his resolution to remove to Hertfordshire without delay, and when he retired to his room at night, he ordered his bags to be packed. The following morning he said his goodbyes, making his apologies for his irascible behavior of the past few weeks, and after felicitating Lenora and Lord Helden very sincerely and promising to return for their nuptials in the autumn, he hastened away to the staid comfort of his fields and plantations, his barns and cattle.

From the age of thirteen, Tom had been master of Branwell Manor—a once prosperous estate wasted by his reckless father. While in temperament exactly opposite to his father, Tom did take after him in his striking good looks—a fact greatly lamented by himself and his mother, for they neither of them wished to remember Bertram Breckinridge with any degree of exactitude. Perhaps this was the cause of Tom's early determination to restore the estate; by doing so he should go a long way toward separating himself from his father's likeness. It had taken several years of frugality and hard work, but between them, Tom and his mother had paid all his father's debts and invested in the estate, and Branwell Manor was now on the verge of prosperity once more.

Tom arrived home late in the morning, and before entering the house he went to see after his greys, who had been brought by Matthew, his head groom, back from London in easy stages, and had arrived in very good time and in fine fettle. He was so pleased to be home that he bethought himself of an issue to discuss with the gardener, and that accomplished, considered he may as well go about the farm before he had changed out of his travel-stained garments. Ordering his mare to be saddled, he rode at a trot between the fields, inspecting the winter wheat that stretched in a green haze to his left and right, and basked with relish in the security of familiarity and order.

He was master at Branwell, ordering things as he chose, and there was no need of wondering at how his worth compared with that of anyone else. It was measured in black and white—or in green and brown, as the crops grew and yielded their plenty, or the cattle reproduced and were sold off and tallied as gains on the record sheets. It was measured in the acknowledgment of his tenants as he rode by, and the farmhands who doffed caps, and sowing women who curtsied to him on his way. Here, Mr. Popplewell and his viscountcy meant nothing, and Tom was comfortable in his place.

He rode past newly plowed fields that awaited the summer crop, and toward the barn that rose up beside several sheds where farm implements and fodder were stored. Arrived at the barn, Tom dismounted and strode to where his land agent was readying a cart of barley and clover seed to be sown in the near field.

"Good afternoon, Burke!" said Tom, casting an expert eye over the seed bags. "The East Field seems a bit dry. Can we divert water from the river? Have you checked the trenches?"

"Aye, sir. And it's good to see you back. A few trenches are blocked, but I've set Ramsey and Pratt to clearing 'em."

"Perhaps it's for the best we didn't invest in pipes."

Burke smiled. "Home but an hour and it's straight to business, is it? Very well. Aye, pipes are a deal of expense, sir, but it looks as though they can wait. Mighty dry this season."

"Yes. We would have had to wait 'til next year anyway, if we had decided to put them in."

"Aye, sir." The land agent noted something on his board and looked it over. "How was London?"

Tom tapped his whip against his thigh, finding this departure from security annoying. "Dashed waste of time. Glad to be home."

"What's this?" said Burke, glancing keenly at his master. "Never say your young lady has throwed you over?"

Tom looked sharply at him, then recalled that Matthew had been home nearly a month, and had apparently imparted all the news of his master's doings in Town. Resigning himself to the inevitable, therefore, Tom answered, "I've not met that ignominious fate, precisely.

However, there is no saying how long I shall hold out in the lists."

"The lady's other beaux didn't seem to have put you out before, if I may be so bold, sir."

"Perhaps not. But I find I compare pretty poorly with a belted lord."

"A belted lord, is it?" Burke narrowed his eyes, regarding his master with something like disappointment. Then he huffed, shaking his head. "That's it then. Nothing to do about a trumped up nob taking your young lady out from under your nose."

Irritated, Tom glared at him. "You know nothing about it, Burke."

"No, not a thing, sir," replied Burke blandly, "but that as long as I've known you there's been none could keep you down, nor none you'd take nay from. Just look what you've done with this farm, and the whole estate! You've got more backbone than a great whale, I'd have figured. Fair jiggers me to find you ready to slope off so easy."

"It's nothing like that," Tom retorted, swiping his whip at an insect that had landed on the bag of seed before him. "I know about farms and estates. They're a far cry from a lady's affections."

"P'raps," said Burke, eying him askance. "But I'll wager ignorance never stopped you before. It's a fact I learned my first day at Branwell—that Mr. Thomas Breckinridge never backs down from a challenge." He pointed a thick finger at Tom's chest. "If you'll pardon my saying, sir, you'd best keep up the chase—if you've any liking for the girl, as I suspicion you do—or you'll never forgive yourself."

At that, Burke walked off to consult with some of the field laborers, and Tom blew out a sigh, wondering if there was any place on earth safe from the mention of matrimony. Shrugging off the conversation, he mounted his horse once more and rode out toward the paddock. There he met Matthew, who greeted him with pleasure.

"All's well, then, sir? Your sister is better, I trust."

"Oh, yes. I left her cozily planning her nuptials. Dashed silly business. I saw the greys came along fine. How are those new Herefords settling in?"

Matthew, accustomed to his young master's single-minded ways, smiled and shook his head. "Going along like winking. We'll have prime bulls this autumn, and plenty of cows to breed. I've had to move the Leicester sheep to the next meadow, though. The rams had taken to butting through the wall. Burke set some men to repairing it, for it was an old wall, and weak."

"Good." Tom gazed out into the paddock at the herd of cattle grazing along the far side. "If you're done here, you may accompany me back to the house. I'd like to discuss whether we ought to consider moving to dairy breeds rather than butcher breeds."

Indicating his willingness to ride back with his master, Matthew followed him to the horses. He had been with the Breckinridges since before the old master had got himself killed on the hunt, and had stayed with the family through all the lean and hard years, working at everything from groom to butler to gardener. He flattered himself that he had sometimes stood in a position of counselor, and now, he attended to Tom as he went on about the advantages of dairy farming until they had reached the stables and dismounted.

"I'd wager you're the youngest gentleman in the county to know all the ins and outs of dairying versus butchering," he observed.

Tom glanced at him, his brow furrowed. "What's that to say to anything?"

Matthew shrugged. "Naught but you had an early start, sir. Times I wonder if it weren't too early."

"I'd have pushed my nose into your business at fifteen whether my father had broke his neck or not, Matthew," Tom informed him.

"Aye, and welcome. While other young gentlemen are off to Oxford and getting up larks, you're set to be a prosperous landowner at one-and-twenty."

The furrow on Tom's brow deepened. "And yet you seem to fancy it a bad thing."

"Not at all, sir," said Matthew placidly. "I only wonder at your being so bent on business. It's not often you put up your feet and let those, as have the right, to do your work for you. It's what you pay us for, after all, sir."

Tom snorted. "I'd be dashed bored if I sat around like some fine gentleman while you did all the work. I've been enough in London to know I'd rather throw myself in the river than prance about ladies' drawing rooms prating about nothing! That is why Branwell does so well, Matthew. I'd far liefer get my hands dirty with improvements than fly away for pleasure and expect that the rents will come pouring in, as my dear father did."

"I know it, sir, and you're a better man for it," said Matthew. "You've done wonders here, and will do—that's just it, sir. You've plenty of time."

They had reached the house and Tom dismounted, handing his reins to Matthew. "What on earth are you driving at, Matthew?"

The groom scratched his nose and looked off over the fields. "You've no call to hover about the estate, sir, while life passes you by. There's plenty of us as will look after your interests, and gladly, while you're away. If you've a lady in your eye who's playing hard to get, go after her. The estate will keep."

The groom touched his hat to his master and led the horses to the stables, while Tom, beginning to believe that his personal life was an open book, entered the house by the side door, removing his soiled footwear in the corridor. As he hung his greatcoat on its peg, his thoughts were diverted into pleasanter channels by the delightful scents of baking that wafted to him from the arch that led into the kitchen.

Popping his head through the arch and inhaling rapturously, he inquired, "What is that heavenly smell, Sally?"

The plump cook was in the act of removing a pan of Bath cakes from the oven and she jumped, only just avoiding the disaster of tossing all the cakes onto the floor. Regaining her equilibrium, she scrupled not to cast a reproving look at her master, for she was another who had been in service to the Breckinridges all Tom's life.

"Shame on you, sir! How dare you come up on me in that sneaking way! It'd served you right to have no cakes with your nuncheon."

Tom slipped into the kitchen. "Ah, Sally, you divine goddess! I beg your pardon with all my soul. Bath cakes are just the thing for my sad nerves. How did you guess that I was out of sorts?"

"You'll not touch a one, Master Tom," adjured Sally, slapping his hand away from the pan of cakes. "Not 'til you've washed up like a gentleman."

"But Sally, you've no notion how I'm put upon," pursued Tom earnestly. "Sitting by for two weeks while Lenora and her Lord Helden cuddled and cozed—and my Mama and Sir Joshua are no better! Then I come home to be lectured by Burke and Matthew on marriage—I tell you, I'm at my wits' end!"

Sally chuckled. "Bath cakes won't fix what ails you, sir, so you needn't pull that face. I know your wheedling ways—have done since you were knee high! Burke and Matthew have the right of it—what you want is a wife."

"Not you, too, Sally!"

"The place needs a woman about—and not another servant, mind you, though a few new maids will do wonders! But all in good time."

"Done, Sally! I've meant to hire a cookmaid these three months, but I've been busy with—never mind. I'll get another maid. You know I'd do anything for you!"

"Then bring home a wife, sir," said Sally, with a nod of her mob-capped head. "I'll be spared your shenanigans then."

"I'd marry you in a heartbeat, Sally my love," retorted Tom, inching toward the pan of cakes, "only you've rejected me twice."

Sally whisked the pan out of reach. "A six-year-old knows no better than an eight-year-old, sir, but a man of one-and-twenty knows better than to trifle with his cook."

Tom crossed his arms over his chest, sitting on the corner of the wooden slab table. "What if I did bring home a wife, Sally? Would you truly be glad of it?"

"I would, sir, for though Mrs. Reedy is a fine housekeeper, there's no substitute for the mistress of a house. If you'll pardon the liberty, this place has been too long without a proper mistress, for Mrs. Breck—that is Lady Stiles was obliged to leave it for the Cottage years back, and though it was all for the best, I'd dearly love to see the house put to rights just as the land has been."

Tom averted his eyes, considering this. "Thank you, Sally. I, too, should like things to be all fit and proper here, but there's only so much a man can do, if a lady doesn't return his admiration." He raised his eyes to hers and added, "Or if her father doesn't care for the match."

"What's the use of that handsome face of yours, then, I'd like to know?" Sally said, turning to place the pan on the oven top while she stacked the cakes on a platter. "It may seem like a curse to you, Master Tom, but it goes a long way to a girl's heart, and when a girl's heart is lost, there's nothing a father can do about it. Now you go along and wash up like a Christian and let me alone to get your tray together!"

"You're a wise woman, Sally," said Tom, standing to place his hat over his heart in contrition. She nodded, satisfied, and went about her work, but as soon as her back was turned, he plucked a cake from the platter behind her.

As though sensing this depredation, Sally looked back in time to see him pop the cake into his mouth. Crying out, she snapped her towel at him, but he fled, laughing, into the corridor and through to the entry hall, only to skid to a halt mere inches from his butler, who stood with a look of longsuffering on his dignified countenance. Slater was relatively new to the household, having been employed by Mr. Breckinridge only six months.

"Welcome home, sir," Slater intoned, his gaze flicking ever so briefly to his master's stockinged feet. "I trust your journey was pleasant."

"Reasonably so, thank you, Slater," replied Tom around his mouthful of cake, as he handed hat and gloves to the servant.

"You'll forgive my taking the liberty of reminding you, sir, that after a journey of any length, a gentleman enters his home through the front door, so that his servants, who are trained to observe his arrival, may," he coughed, "do their duty."

Tom smiled rather like a guilty schoolboy. "Am I a sore trial to you, Slater? I beg your pardon for offending your sensibilities, and I give you my word I shall endeavor not to do so next time."

Slater seemed to take this with less than full confidence. "Certainly, sir."

Leaving the retainer to his disapproving thoughts, Tom ascended the stairs to his room, but not before he caught a muttered, "A mistress would never allow such goings on," float up from the entry hall. Sighing, Tom continued to his room and undertook his ablutions, changing out of his traveling clothes and into the comfortable raiment of a country gentleman. Then he descended once more to the library, where he found a tray with an assortment of cold meat and fruit awaiting him on his desk, and he grinned at the lone Bath cake that reposed primly in the center.

"Your point, Sally," he murmured, and settled to his nuncheon as he ran an eye over the post that lay in a pile next to the tray.

This could not keep his attention long, however, for his mind continually wandered to his recent interactions on coming home. It was not every day his staff took him in hand, for he was, and had been for years, master here, and was well-respected for it. But Matthew had accompanied him on his latest sojourn to London, and had seen enough of Miss Marshall—and Tom's admiration of her—to set them all in expectation of a change, and Tom supposed they simply could not get the certainty of it out of their heads.

Their impatience both nettled and pleased him. Most people—servants and gentlefolk alike—would not expect so young a man to settle down. Tom had only just attained his majority—an age where most young men had scarcely begun to sow their oats—but he had never been like other young men. Fate had made him master of a broken house at a tender age, and necessity had forced him early into manhood thereafter. But though his mother had often remarked that he had been born dutiful, he knew himself somewhat better, having instigated some larks outside her knowledge that were downright foolish. And though it was well-known that he liked nothing better than to quiz his closest friends and relations, his humor or fun hardly ever exceeded reasonable or rational bounds.

Perhaps that did make him a dull dog, Tom thought, scarcely to compare with Mr. Popplewell—he who had every hair in place and not a speck on his tightly molded coats and breeches, whose neck cloths were immaculately tied, and whose shirt points came up so high that he could barely turn his head. It was a devilish annoying habit, to Tom's mind. If Popplewell had spent years with only one maid, as Tom's family had, he would comprehend just how much work there was to be done in the laundry. Tom was dashed if he understood how a man could waste his maids' precious hours of washing, starching, and ironing by running through neck cloth after neck cloth only to attain the perfect effect. It was what made Tom deprecate dandyism as a blasted reckless use of time and money.

As Diana had shared his opinions on the matter on more than one occasion, he couldn't imagine what made Popplewell so mightily interesting to her. There was the likelihood that the man was excessively romantic, which Tom supposed counted for something—but even Lenora, who had been addicted to romance novels, had cast aside such foolishness when she had fallen in love with the penniless Lord Helden.

As the evening fell, Tom had begun to believe that perhaps Lenora was right, and Diana thought of Popplewell as a brother, and the cursed fellow was only interesting to her father. Tom couldn't guess what a lazy, smiling, foppish dandy could excite in Mr. Marshall's mind when compared with himself. Tom was principled, dash it, and he was proud to be so. So what if it made him a dull dog.

But as he drifted off to sleep that night, he dreamed of Miss Marshall, whose eyes sparkled as she conversed with Mr. Popplewell on the fripperiest of subjects, and when he interposed a comment on the best way to mend a ditch, she turned blank eyes to him and said, "Dear me, Tom, you are a dull dog," and it mattered to him very much.

Chapter 3

Two days later, as Tom yawned over the accounts—which were admittedly as dull as they were impressive—Slater brought in the post on a salver. Tom thanked him and, feeling too fatigued of mind to continue with charts and numbers, sorted through the letters and bills. He set aside a letter from Lenora—no doubt an effusion over her happiness and outlining all her plans with Helden to restore the Hall—and took up one in an unknown hand that had been posted from Sussex.

He broke the wafer and spread it open, reading the signature at the bottom: Mrs. Frank Marshall. He blinked. The letter was a very civil invitation for Tom to join them at their estate at Findon for a house party. He gazed at the letter for some minutes, visions of insinuating himself into the bosom of Diana's family, earning her entire affection, and winning over Mr. Marshall to his cause dancing in his mind. But then Mr. Popplewell suddenly appeared with his dazzling smile and intricate neck cloth, and annihilated the delightful scene at a blow.

Tom got up and poured himself some brandy, sipping at it as he considered the letter. Mr. Marshall, he knew, was unimpressed by his prospects, but Mrs. Marshall had always been a friend to him. Even when Mr. Popplewell had been present, she had been at pains to show Tom to advantage, and Tom was grateful for it. Mrs. Marshall was much like Diana—lively and conversable, with a humorous eye—and she seemed more interested in her daughter's happiness in marriage than in the possible profitability of such a match to herself.

He was inclined to believe that Mrs. Marshall would not invite him for a house party if she did not believe Diana to have a partiality for him—one generally did not invite guests from far off counties to house parties without sufficient cause. He could not imagine that she would expect him to come all that way merely to make up her numbers at table, or to play companion to the odd lady. No, he flattered himself that she must consider him to be an eligible match for her daughter, and was giving him the opportunity to prove it—if not to Diana, perhaps to Mr. Marshall.

He eyed the invitation. If his mother were here, she would say it was providence, and he would be a gudgeon not to take it. She need not have worried; he would not hesitate to accept it. What troubled him was the probability of Mr. Popplewell's having also been invited, and the uncertainty of his own success in direct competition with his rival. However, with his mother's exhortation on lassitude ringing in his mind, he quickly resolved that Popplewell's proximity was of no consequence. He would go, for he had determined to pursue Diana until her choice was made, and Popplewell could watch his own back.

Putting down his glass, he returned to the desk and penned

a response to Mrs. Marshall, expressing his obligation to her and gratefully accepting her invitation. As he rang the bell for Slater, a wry smile crossed his features, for here was just the thing to heighten the servants' expectations, yet there was no telling what the outcome would be. No matter. He would take Matthew's advice and leave behind the work on the estate to disport himself at Findon and do his possible to prove to Mr. Marshall and his daughter that, whatever his opinions of romance, he was no dull dog.

He immediately set about preparations for his journey into Sussex, but it was not to be expected that he should find no cause to reconsider, being as he was a responsible landowner with many irons in the fire. Going out on the day appointed for his departure for one last inspection of the farm, he was informed by Burke that he anticipated no interruption of the heat in the coming days.

"It mightn't amount to much, or we may lose the harvest," said Burke philosophically.

Tom pursed his lips. "It's a dashed awkward time for me to be haring off to Sussex."

"Beggin' your pardon, sir, but your staying won't do a mite o' good for the weather," said Burke stolidly. "Those new seedlings are at the mercy of God, not you, sir."

With a reluctant smile, Tom said, "Still, it'll worry me no end not to know what's going on here."

"With all due respect, sir, it'll worry me no end for you to stay only to get under my feet and fret yourself to flinders over a little heat. No, I'll thank you to go on to Sussex and leave the farm to those as can stand the huff."

"May I remind you, sir," said Tom, assuming a dignified air, "that I'd been managing well enough for some few years before I hired you."

Burke snorted. "No need. I'm reminded every time I look and find you one-and-twenty and not five-and-thirty—for that's how old you pretend to be, sir." He turned to survey the nearest field. "What think you of the Ransome plow? It's been used to good purpose at Histon in Cambridgeshire. I think we can't do worse than give it a try."

Tom, appreciating the compliment latent in this speech, allowed the land agent to win the round. "I've heard devilish good things about the Ransome, and goodness knows we've yet to make up from the Year Without a Summer. I'm agreeable." He clapped Burke on the shoulder as he turned away. "Take good care while I'm gone."

Tipping his hat to some women who had come into the barn, their sowing bags slung over their shoulders, Tom went out and remounted his mare, turning her out onto the lane that led back to the pastures behind the stables. At the fence, he met Matthew, who was to accompany him to Sussex.

He dismounted and they stood side by side watching the paces of two young colts who had been turned out to run in the pasture. "They've promise, sir," remarked Matthew.

"Indeed, they do," replied Tom with feeling. "That's five this year—almost double our luck last year. It's an excellent return, but perhaps I may look out another stud at Tattersall's, to further improve our stock."

"A fine notion, sir, on our way back through Town," said Matthew, moving toward the door to the stables. "We'll send for young Jed to meet us, to go back with the horses."

"And why not stop in at Tatt's on the way to Sussex?"

Matthew smiled. "No need to tempt fate, sir, and be late to the house party."

"Have you no patience, Matthew?" said Tom in a rallying tone. "A look in at Tatt's would do no harm, if we are already to be in London."

"It's all one to me, sir. But nature can't work on nothing. A seed won't sprout what isn't planted."

"Drat you, Matthew!" huffed Tom, switching his whip at a bush. "What do you know about it?"

"I know enough, sir." He tipped his hat and walked away to ready the curricle for the journey, while Tom went in to supervise the packing of his trunks.

They took a leisurely way to London, to save the horses, and the drive was uneventful. On their way through London, Tom, whose pride never rode him too closely that he couldn't see the good sense in his servants' advice, chose to give Tatt's the go by. Staying the one night in Town, therefore, they arose next morning betimes and set out on the Brighton road by eight o'clock. Tom was not one to aspire to emulate the Prince Regent, who was known to have made the journey from London to Brighton in less than five hours. On the contrary, because he wished to have his own horses with him at the house party, Tom and Matthew took another two days to reach Findon, which was short of Brighton by only twelve miles.

He arrived punctually to his time, and with plenty of daylight to admire the fine Georgian mansion that had replaced a crumbling Elizabethan manor some twenty years previous. A groom came to accompany Matthew and the horses to the stables, and after having been shown to his room on the first floor by the attentive housekeeper, Tom changed and presented himself in Mrs. Marshall's saloon at a quarter to six o'clock.

"There you are, Mr. Breckinridge!" cried Mrs. Marshall warmly. "Kittering said you had arrived. You must pardon me for my absence—I was in the rose garden. I trust your room is to your satisfaction?"

Tom assured her it was and thanked her for her kindness in inviting him, and greeted Mr. Marshall, who shook his hand rather perfunctorily. Resolved not to be daunted, Tom asked after his health and was rewarded by a fairly detailed summary of the effects of rheumatism on the healthiest of frames, and the beneficial effects of Indian Vapor Baths, the best of which were only to be had at Brighton. When at last civility allowed Tom to turn away, Diana had risen from the sofa to give him her hand.

"How good it is to see you, Tom!" she said as he bowed over her hand. "I declare it has been an age since we left Town. It was the greatest bore. Brighton could hold no pleasure for me after London!"

"Now, Diana, that's a taradiddle!" remonstrated her father in a bluff tone. "There were ever so many of your friends at Brighton."

"Reggie is not ever so many of my friends, dear sir," she said, with a pert look. "I left the best of my friends behind me."

Taking courage at this, Tom smiled, saying, "You were sorely missed, Diana."

She blushed, reclaiming her hand. "But here you are now, and we can have a comfortable coze."

Tom admitted that was exactly what he wished, and allowed her to lead him to the sofa.

"You are very obliging to listen to Papa bore on about his ills," said Diana, when they were seated. "He is a dear, but I cannot imagine that he is so very affected."

"No one would to see him," said Tom judiciously. "The Vapor Baths must be exceedingly effective."

Diana smiled at his diplomacy. "It was a trial to me to be wrenched away just as Lenora's affairs were becoming so interesting! Were it not for the post, I should have died of suspense! But it has all worked out wonderfully, like a romantic novel. Do not you agree, Tom?"

"I must," said Tom, much struck by her view of the matter. "I think even Mrs. Radcliffe would approve of the outcome, coming as it did after so tortuous a journey."

Diana laughed. "You never read Mrs. Radcliffe in your life, Tom Breckinridge, and I will not allow you to be an authority. If you were, you would know that hardship is the food of love."

"With that I cannot agree," said Tom, with a raised brow. "How often in history has a promising love story been quashed at the first sign of trouble? Look at Cleopatra and Mark Antony. Or Heloise and Abelard. Hardship quite literally killed them."

"But their stories only prove my point," insisted Diana. "Their love was tested so excessively that it became strong enough to outlast death!"

Tom shrugged. "At least one may assume so, if indeed love exists after death."

"Of course it does! And so shall Lenora and Lord Helden's love prove," she persisted.

With all his cynical leanings, Tom was not proof against the martial light in her bright eyes, and he relented, bowing to acknowledge her superior understanding. Mrs. Marshall, who had been watching them both with a tiny smile on her lips, suggested then that she ring for dinner and she was universally seconded. Tom was allowed to lead Diana into the dining room and was seated beside her at table, and so enjoyable was the conversation from all sides that he had begun to believe that fate had truly sided with him.

Scarcely had they begun the second course, however, when the sound of a carriage on the drive set them all to blinking in astonishment while Mr. Marshall grumbled at the temerity of a visitor to arrive at such a late hour. Kittering, who had circumspectly withdrawn at the first sound of an arrival, returned presently, and Mr. Marshall threw his napkin on the table and demanded of the butler to tell him who was so uncivil as to thrust himself upon them in the middle of dinner.

"It is Mr. Popplewell, sir," said the butler with a respectful bow. "He offers his apologies for having come before his day, but trusts that you will forgive him."

"Popplewell!" cried Mr. Marshall, his ire forgot. "Bring him in, Kittering, bring him in. We stand on no ceremony with Reginald. Old family friend, welcome at any time. Assure him, Kittering."

Bowing again, the butler retired and within a few minutes, Mr. Popplewell appeared at the door, his many-caped greatcoat covered in dust.

He smiled sheepishly. "Too good of you to take me in under the circumstances, Mrs. Marshall, Mr. Marshall. But I'm devilish grateful. My own guests took it into their heads to take themselves off a day early and I've been kicking my heels—dashed dull it's been with nothing for me to do. The prospect of drinking my port in solitary state was the last straw—determined then and there to come here and be done with it. Beg pardon for having interrupted you at dinner."

He was greeted with a chorus of admonitions not to trouble himself over anything, to take a seat, and to think himself one of the family, while Tom felt his insides turn to a lump of clay. Mr. Popplewell, however, declined to join them in all his dirt, claiming to have baited on the road, and retired to his room to change and refresh himself, promising to meet them all in the drawing room after dinner.

The conversation resumed, but as it almost exclusively involved "dear Reggie" and his lovably ridiculous starts, Tom thought the ladies could not withdraw soon enough. But he was made to repent this wish when he was left alone with Mr. Marshall to be regaled with anecdote after anecdote of Popplewell's perfections from childhood to manhood. It was with the greatest self-command that he managed not to set his host at odds by revealing his own opinion of "dear Reggie's" charms.

At last they adjourned to the drawing room, and as Popplewell took some thirty minutes longer to present himself, they all embarked upon a game of whist to pass the time. Tom was partnered with Diana, and partook freely of her smiles, though he was unable entirely to enjoy them. His suspicion that as soon as his rival walked into the room, he, Tom, would fade into the background, and "dear Reggie" would engage all the Marshall's attentions and solicitude rather dampened anything like delight he could feel.

As it transpired, however, his supposition was not quite right; Popplewell settled himself with the apparent intention of monopolizing Diana, but fell victim to Mr. Marshall's anxious interest. Thus, "dear Reggie" was the sole recipient of Mr. Marshall's conversation, while Mrs. Marshall and Diana succeeded in spreading their attentions very equally between the two young gentlemen. While Popplewell made many attempts to turn the conversation to more open subjects, Mr. Marshall was continually drawing his young neighbor into a discussion of politics, and Mrs. Marshall very obligingly joined with them. This afforded Tom several opportunities to snatch semi-private words with Diana, and his spirits began to improve. By the time the ladies rose to excuse themselves for the evening, he was of the opinion that, even though Popplewell was undoubtedly Mr. Marshall's favored choice for his daughter, Mrs. Marshall yet stood his friend, and Diana was, as Lenora had asserted, quite partial to him.

As Tom would rather poke out both his own eyes than stay to be scorned by the other gentlemen, as soon as the ladies had expressed their intention to seek their couches, he did likewise. He was only slightly put out when Popplewell did the same, for then Mr. Marshall found it expedient to come along behind and the whole group trooped out into the corridor. Mr. and Mrs. Marshall accompanied the young people to the second floor, where the male guests were to be quartered in one wing and the female guests, with Diana, in the other. As Mrs. Marshall bethought herself of something she must say to Diana and escorted her to her door, this precluded any attempt by either young gentleman to make private speech with her, and they both took polite leave of their hosts at the landing.

Suspecting that to subject his companion to frigid silence, even for only the length of a corridor, might betray his none-too-friendly feelings, Tom stifled that temptation and instead civilly expressed his delight in finding an acquaintance at Findon.

"Oh, one often finds me at Findon," replied Popplewell carelessly. "It is as a second home to me, and the Marshalls as my own family. They have known me forever."

"So I understand," said Tom politely, refusing to be intimidated. "I suppose you think of them as near relations."

Popplewell laughed. "Mr. Marshall, perhaps, could be seen in the light of an uncle, and dear Mrs. Marshall an aunt, of course, for they are both so very generous and obliging, but Diana—" He stopped in front of the door to his room, lifting his quizzing glass and polishing it with an air of unconcern on the sleeve of his coat. "Diana is nothing like a relation to me."

As Tom's door was across the corridor, he stayed to face his companion, a polite smile pinned to his mouth while his eyes measured Popplewell. "Yes, well, it was excessively kind in them to invite me," he said. "I stand in no relationship to them other than as Diana's very good friend, you comprehend, and I intend to make the most of this opportunity to further my acquaintance with them."

"Certainly," replied Popplewell, with the utmost cordiality. "I should think less of you—indeed of anyone—who did not. Perhaps I might be of help to you, as I know them so well."

"So very obliging of you," said Tom.

"It is nothing, I assure you, Breckinridge. Good night."

Tom returned the civility and went into his room, thinking as he sat before his dressing table that Popplewell had misjudged his man. For all Tom was a country bumpkin and a nobody to the Marshalls, he did recognize a challenge when he heard one.

Chapter 4

THE FOLLOWING MORNING, Tom entered the breakfast room in time to interrupt Popplewell and Mr. Marshall in discussion of the plans for the day. The gentlemen had apparently settled upon riding together, and it was quickly apparent that Tom's participation had not been considered until that moment, for Mr. Marshall made a rather convoluted speech regarding the shortage of proper mounts in his otherwise well-stocked stable that ended in a feeble offer of his second-best hack. On his best behavior, Tom accepted this invitation with a very good grace and steeled himself for much awkwardness. The ride, however, was pleasant—despite the weather being so very warm, and Popplewell making offhand comments upon Tom's perspiring person while his own shirt points suffered no detrimental effects.

When the gentlemen returned and had changed and repaired to the drawing room to look in on the ladies, Popplewell's solicitude for

Tom ceased abruptly, being applied entirely—and more amiably—to Diana. Tom hardly blinked as Popplewell swept him aside to take the place beside Diana, for he had inured himself to such snubs this morning. As "dear Reggie" engaged her in lively conversation, Tom determined that he was not so badly off, for he was left to the care of Mrs. Marshall who, though not her daughter, was a fine companion.

"You are not accustomed to our warmer clime, Mr. Breckinridge," she observed, after having discovered how the gentlemen had spent their morning. "I hope you did not find the ride disagreeable."

Tom assured her he had not and, patently ignoring the bursts of animation which frequently came from Diana's direction, complimented his hostess upon the scenery hereabouts and inquired more particularly into some of the landmarks which he had observed while riding.

"Yes, there is the Cissbury Ring quite close by, and I am told, though I am not at all sure I believe it, that on a clear day and from the top of one of the hills one may see Bramber Castle far off to the east. Perhaps, if the weather cools, we may get up a party to visit one of these sites."

Still stoically disregarding Diana's evident pleasure in Mr. Popplewell's conversation, Tom expressed his delight in this prospect and inquired of Mrs. Marshall when the other guests were due to arrive.

"They will trickle in over the next day or two," she said. "Among them, you will find some of our London acquaintance, for Iris and Athena will be coming, and Lord Greenbury, whom I believe you met in Town."

Tom was pleased that he would not be entirely at the mercy of Mr. Popplewell's altruism, for he did know Lord Greenbury—a decorous and staid individual who stood to inherit an earldom—though only slightly. But the Goddesses he knew rather better, for they had been in Lenora's circle in London, and he had been much in their company. Diana, Miss Iris Slougham, and the Lady Athena Dibbington—daughter of Lord Gidgeborough—were so named because they all bore the names of Greek or Roman goddesses, and had been inseparable since their very close births. Both these facts had much to do with the excessively strong friendship between their fathers, which was emulated—though not to so great a degree—by their wives, and thus their children.

As it transpired, Lady Athena and Miss Slougham arrived together, as dissimilar as an ice maiden and a social misfit could be. Lady Athena was tall, elegant, and coldly beautiful, with a raised brow for any circumstance or utterance she considered untoward. Iris nearly always wore a vague look, which was only accented by the indistinctness of her pale prettiness and reddish-blond hair, and though she tried valiantly, she could not open her mouth but to utter something shocking.

"How glad I am to be out of that carriage," said she as they entered the drawing room upon their arrival. Tugging at the ribbons of her bonnet, she pulled it off and tossed it aside, moving forward to exchange embraces with Diana. "The last ten miles seemed to be so full of potholes as to turn me to jelly, and no thanks to my corset, I declare my bosoms nearly bounced away."

"Iris," said Lady Athena, her expression pained. "Your brains must be jelly as well, for you have not perceived that there are gentlemen in the room. How do you do Mrs. Marshall? Mr. Marshall. Diana."

"Oh, I beg your pardon, Mr. Marshall," said Iris, coloring. "But you know me well enough to—"

"It is not only my father," murmured Diana, her lips twitching as she came forward to embrace her friend, "but also Tom Breckinridge and Reggie Popplewell. Recollect, Iris, this is no family gathering, but a house party."

"Oh, dear," whispered Iris, looking around, eyes wide, to see Tom and Mr. Popplewell standing near the window and the pianoforte respectively, their expressions polite and smiling. Tom's face was, perhaps, a bit pink, but Popplewell came unabashedly forward to take Iris's hand.

"Charming to meet you again, Miss Slougham," he said, almost grinning.

She reclaimed her hand as quickly as she could, stammering something indistinct before turning to rush from the room. She was caught at the threshold, however, by her father, who had, at his wife's insistence that she must recover in solitude from the disaster of her daughter's belated first Season, consented to be their escort. He had justified his acquiescence with the professed intention of providing essential support to Mr. Marshall at the house party, but his secret desire—plain to all who knew him—was to enjoy some time away from his overbearing wife.

"Now, now, Iris, what is all this?" he said a trifle testily, bringing her back with him into the room. "Here a bare minute and already mortified yourself? I thought you learned how to command your tongue, at least, in London."

"It was nothing, sir," said Diana, hastening forward to take Iris by the arm and lead her to the sofa. "It is already forgot, is not it, Tom? Is not it, Reggie? You see, sir? You remember Mr. Breckinridge and Mr. Popplewell."

As the prior acquaintance was acknowledged, Diana applied herself to soothing Iris who, through the habit of frequent experience, was able fairly quickly to regain her countenance, though not her tongue. Tom wondered if she had experienced a setback since last he had seen her, for she had been in a fair way to holding a decent conversation at that point. But as Miss Slougham had not been the despair of her harassed parents for nothing, he supposed it was nearly inevitable that she should suffer a relapse at some point.

The other guests, who came the following afternoon and evening and were unknown to Tom, were exceedingly friendly, and the party augured to be lively—if not precisely well-matched. There was a Miss Silverdale, a genteel girl—though being only just out, she tended toward simpering and giggling—while Mrs. Ridley, who at three-and-twenty was already the widow of Mr. Marshall's second cousin, was possessed of the disastrous combination of considerable spirit and the allure of an experienced woman.

The gentlemen were at least as dissimilar. Mr. Daniels, just down from Oxford and willing to be worshiped, took for granted Miss Silverdale's tittering attentions. In contrast, Lord Greenbury—evidently invited in the stead of Lady Athena's admirer, Lord Foxham, whose attendance could not be secured—applied himself with painstaking civility to any female who wandered within his orbit. And Mr. Holt, if he spoke at all, could tell anyone who would listen all there was about hunting but not much more. It was Mr. Popplewell alone who seemed both willing and able to make himself agreeable to any and all of the members of the party, particularly the young ladies—not to exclude the daring Mrs. Ridley. Even Lady Athena unbent somewhat toward him, a circumstance which did little to recommend him to Tom.

The remainder of the party consisted of the elder generation: Lady Silverdale and Mr. and Mrs. Throckmorton—all very ready to sit by and allow the young people to enjoy themselves.

As Mrs. Marshall was neither so dashing as to throw a party every evening nor so dull as to expect that her guests would become acquainted through mere talking, she provided herself with a list of diversions ready to be consulted at need, and allowed the whims of her guests to dictate the flow of the entertainment.

With several young people in the group, the general desire was for air and exercise, but the weather continuing hot and dry, they quickly found they were obliged to confine themselves to the manor, for travel further afield became too fatiguing. Mrs. Marshall, having prepared for just such an eventuality, consulted her list and declared a boating expedition on Findon Pond, which was near enough to walk to but cool enough to provide some hours' enjoyment. This program was greeted with delight and relief, for more than one of the guests had come to Findon solely to escape the prospect of a summer spent staring at various persons across the polite confines of a drawing room.

As the party made their noisy way down to the pond, Tom found himself escorting Miss Silverdale, but the circumstance did not rankle, for Diana was gallanted by Mr. Holt and not Popplewell, and was walking just before him and Miss Silverdale. Mr. Holt was recounting in great detail one of his better runs with the Quorn the previous year, to which Diana was listening politely, but as his talk was interlarded with a great many cant terms, and Diana did not have brothers, Tom doubted whether she understood the half of what was being communicated and fancied she could not be feeling much enjoyment.

He was therefore surprised when Miss Silverdale remarked sapiently, "It sounds to me as though Mr. Holt draws his coverts too quickly."

He turned with raised brows to his companion and inquired, "Do you hunt, Miss Silverdale?"

"Oh, yes—that is, I did with my brothers, just on our own estate." She blushed and tittered, "Once I came to grief following them over a stile, and they threatened never to take me again, but when my father found out about it, he said I was a right one and told them the only way to cure me of such folly was to continue to take me. However, I blush to tell you that it was many more times I was thrown at a regular stitcher."

Tom, at first stunned that Miss Silverdale—tittering, simpering Miss Silverdale—knew what a regular stitcher was, let alone had been thrown at one, now was revolving a plan, and gazing thoughtfully at her, said, "Shall we come up with them so you can hear?"

"Oh, yes, shall we?"

Nodding, Tom quickened his pace until he and Miss Silverdale had drawn up with Mr. Holt and Diana. Leaning forward to speak across his companion, Tom said, "You were there, were you not, when Assheton-Smith over-ran his hounds?"

This stratagem worked to perfection; Mr. Holt animatedly launched into the story and while Miss Silverdale attended with great interest, Tom slipped behind and took Diana's arm, leading her ahead.

"You're a sly one, Tom!" murmured Diana, a dimple—which he secretly found bewitching—peeping in her cheek.

"Not sly—compassionate. Only a monster would have allowed him to prose on to you all the way to the pond."

"Then I am beholden to your humanity," she said, smiling.

"Or at least to Miss Silverdale's unaccountable love of the hunt."

She laughed, stealing a glance back at Mr. Holt and Miss Silverdale, who were deep in discussion behind them and continued so all the way to the pond, where two boats were being readied at the short dock. Lady Athena and Mrs. Marshall declined to enter them, declaring themselves disinclined to embark upon the water, and receiving a grave offer of protection from Lord Greenbury. But the others scorned the notion of sitting tamely on the blankets which had been laid out beneath the large poplars that skirted the pond and made a scramble for the boats.

Mr. Popplewell, who had squired Iris to the dock, had already handed her into a boat, and he turned to call out, "Here, Diana, Miss Slougham wishes you to accompany her."

"But what of you?" Diana inquired archly.

"I naturally wish to be with you, my fair one," said Popplewell, extending his hand to her.

Tom stood in stoic silence as Diana let go his arm to take Popplewell's hand and smilingly allowed him to seat her in the boat. During this process, Tom was utterly overlooked until Iris glanced up and saw him there.

"You must come with us, Tom," she said matter-of-factly. "There is no room in the other boat."

"Oh, yes, Tom," said Diana, still distracted by the business of getting settled. "Do come with us."

Tom eyed Popplewell, who was jeopardizing the exact creases of his cravat by helping to stow a picnic hamper beneath one of the seats in the boat, and considered the merits of remaining on the shore with Mrs. Marshall and Athena. Diana, however, added an encouraging smile to her invitation, and he concluded that he had much better go with her, be it with Popplewell in a boat or to Jericho in a basket, and he stepped into the boat, taking the remaining seat.

The other boat shoved off, Mr. Holt at the oars, and Tom watched as he struggled, apparently at a loss without four legs beneath him. Mrs. Ridley and Miss Silverdale called out encouragement as his boat wobbled this way and that, gaining little ground, but while Mr. Holt did his best to heed their suggestions, it was to no avail. Mr. Daniels, jovially stigmatizing him as a waste of good limbs, threatened to take his place, to which Popplewell shouted his approval, and Holt, showing his quality, grinningly told Daniels that he had better change places with him, else they would all be grassed.

The change was made, though not without some shrieks from the ladies and a show of athleticism on the part of the gentlemen, for the boat wobbled dangerously as they shuffled past one another. But to his credit as a sportsman, Mr. Holt managed this well enough, and once Mr. Daniels had seized the oars and was dragging away, he paid strict heed to his example, vowing to take his place on the return.

Tom laughed and cheered them on with everyone else in his boat, but then they all fell silent and it was with some dismay that he discovered them all to be looking expectantly at him.

"Do you intend to take us out, then, Breckinridge," drawled Popplewell, "or do you feel safer here at the dock?"

Tom, recognizing only then that he had sat in the oarsman's seat, made a grab for the oars, knocking one loose in his haste. Before it drifted away on the water, however, Popplewell lunged for it and, smiling maddeningly, pushed it back toward Tom. Tom tried not to mind Diana's giggles and Iris's disconcerting stare as he hastily secured it and pushed away from the dock, pulling them swiftly across the pond. As they came to where the other boat now drifted carelessly in the overhanging shade of some trees, he couldn't help but wonder if it was simply his lot to feel foolish whenever in Popplewell's company.

The oars safely stowed, the ladies delved into the picnic hampers that had been secreted beneath the seats and distributed sandwiches and bottles of cold lemonade to their companions.

Diana dangled a hand in the water. "Even the shade is hot," she said plaintively.

"Yes," Iris sighed, eying the water longingly. "I wish I could jump into the water, but I should be obliged to remove my gown or it would be all in a tangle."

"Now that would be something," said Popplewell with a roguish smile.

"Reggie!" cried Diana, blushing and glancing quickly to her equally rosily blushing friend.

But Popplewell's expression was instantly contrite. "I beg pardon, Diana, and most especially Miss Slougham! I spoke without thinking. What I meant was that I sympathize with that wish, for it would undoubtedly be refreshing to cool off in the water, which would be something in such hot weather. But of course it could not be done, nor could I imagine you would wish to in this company."

Diana's countenance showed she was less than mollified, which pleased Tom not a little, but the errant hope that Popplewell had irretrievably sunk in her estimation was soon dashed, for Popplewell turned the subject to unexceptionable ones and her expression lightened, and presently she was laughing again.

This pleasantry was interrupted by a screech from the other boat, and they craned their necks to see that their companions had also been wishing to avail themselves of the water for cooling. Mr. Daniels, himself spattered with water, was in the act of splashing Mr. Holt in the face, and Mrs. Ridley, seated beside him and receiving more than her share of the droplets, shrieked again and laughingly urged Mr. Holt to avenge her. Miss Silverdale, meanwhile, looked with an uncertain smile from one party to the other, gripping the handle of her sunshade as though it were a lifeline.

Popplewell gave a shout of laughter. "Now there's a good notion," he said, looking back at Tom with a glint in his eye.

"Only if you intend to take your own again," said Tom promptly, nodding toward Popplewell's immaculate coat.

After brief consideration, Popplewell shrugged. "I dare not risk my valet's ire. Shall we go back then?" he suggested, standing to change places with Tom. "It is my belief that Mrs. Marshall and Lady Athena will have tired of sitting on the bank, and have been wishing us back this half hour and more."

Before they had gone far, however, the other boat drew level with him and Holt, at the oars once again, called over to him. "And you thought to leave us behind!"

Popplewell eyed him cannily. "Up for a race, Holt?"

Mr. Holt hesitated, evidently struggling between a sportsman's thirst for a challenge and a recognition of his own inferiority at rowing, but Mr. Daniels took the choice out of his hands, voicing his assurance that Holt, as his pupil, was the sure winner.

"Oho, then! Shall we make a wager?" said Popplewell. "First rower to the dock gets a sovereign from the loser!"

"Done!" cried Mr. Daniels, turning to encourage Holt to show that lofty-guts how to row a boat.

But Mr. Daniels' tutelage had not been quite enough, for Popplewell easily won, pulling up to the dock several lengths ahead of his opponent. As the other boat slid up, it looked likely to ram the dock, and Tom leaned out to help guide it in at the same time that Popplewell, inexplicably, stood up to celebrate his victory. The boat, which had scarcely dipped when he had changed places with Tom earlier, wobbled precariously, and as the ladies screamed and clutched at the sides, Tom was pitched into the water.

The ladies cried out, watching the surface of the water with shock and concern, but Tom rose almost instantly out of the water, which came only to the middle of his chest. He spluttered and, after a cough or two, accepted Popplewell's extended hand.

"I'd say you're rather better off than the rest of us, you dog," said Mr. Daniels, jovially assisting Popplewell to pull him onto the dock. "You're no longer feeling the heat."

Tom shook his head, feeling more than a little like a dog as droplets flew from his hair. "Not at all. I f-feel famous! You ought to try it!"

"Not I," said Popplewell, smiling a trifle too broadly for Tom's liking. "Pinder would have my skin. But as you've no valet, Tom, a good ducking is of no consequence to you."

He turned with the others toward the shore, and Tom, stripping water from his coat sleeves, was left once more striving not to feel foolish, which was hardly made easier by Iris hastening back with a blanket to wrap about him.

Chapter 5

TOM WAS WELL aware from their meeting in London that Popplewell was a friendly fellow, but it soon became apparent that he possessed skills that found wonderful scope within the confines of a house party. He was an excellent storyteller, as evidenced by his recounting to Mr. Marshall and the other elder members of the party the race across the pond, in colorful detail, complete with the ducking of Tom at the end. Tom would normally have had no trouble in seeing the humor in the story, but after his inauspicious beginning and end in the boat, the raucous laughter from Popplewell's audience rankled. Determined, however, not to allow his pride to get the better of him—or at least not to let Popplewell get the better of him—he forced a smile and even laughed, offering at the end of the recital, "It was so refreshing that I offered to do the same by Popplewell as he had done by me, but he unaccountably refused the treat!"

This brought on even more laughter, and a bright-eyed look from a dimpled Diana, which effectively silenced the twinges of irritation. His spirits were further soothed the next minute when he overheard Lady Athena, who had watched the interlocutor with hooded eyes and a disapproving look, murmur to Lord Greenbury, "It is these sorts of frolics that make country house parties so vulgar, do not you agree? It was wise in us to remain on the bank, I am persuaded."

His lordship, who had been attending to the story with some amusement, quickly lost the smile that was on his lips and, instead, nodded sternly in agreement. Tom thought he had never been more in charity with her ladyship, or Lord Greenbury, in all their acquaintance.

He could not, however, derive more consolation from this circumstance, for it seemed that only with the superior Lady Athena was Mr. Popplewell unlucky; no amount of reverential talk could completely unbend her, nor elevated wit lighten her condescension. But even Tom was not entirely acceptable to Lady Athena, whom he suspected tolerated him merely out of respect for his sister Lenora. It fell to Lord Greenbury's lot to entertain her ladyship, for his station made him the only proper male companion, in the present company, for the daughter of an earl.

With everyone else, Popplewell seemed able to walk the fine line between high spirits and impudence, thus preserving his reputation as a right one with the gentlemen and a delightful companion with the ladies. In this he was assisted by his excellence in discerning character—he could one moment charm the tittering Miss Silverdale into simpering hero-worship and the next make himself agreeable to the awkward Miss Slougham with easy chatter. He could trade hunting anecdotes with Mr. Holt and even bring a reluctant but admiring smile to Lord Greenbury's lips.

It was well that Tom was generally counted to be a congenial companion, for anyone so overshadowed would otherwise struggle to be at ease, but Tom, though it was difficult to show himself in a good light when Popplewell was by, was not so poor-spirited as to give up. He had come to Findon with a purpose, and as Diana had thus far not singled out either he or Popplewell as the owner of her affections, Tom still had cause to believe he was high in the running.

On Midsummer's Eve, the sky was blessed with clouds, and with the sun thus screened the consensus among the group was to take an outing to Cissbury, to try for a glimpse of faeries dancing on the mounds. Tom instantly offered his curricle for the expedition, in the hopes of being allowed to take Diana up with him and remind her of his excellence as a whip. But as the numbers dictated they were better off to take three carriages, he contented himself with being merely in the same vehicle with her. It soon became apparent that Popplewell was also to be their companion, however, and Tom's annoyance was palliated only by his delight in Diana's choosing to sit beside himself. Thus, he began the drive in good spirits, firmly telling himself that he had nothing to be anxious over and amiably chatting about a fascinating observation he had made on his journey thither.

"Have you ever noticed that the sheep on the west of the river Adur are all white-faced and horned while those on the east are hornless and black-faced?"

Popplewell, seated opposite them with Miss Silverdale, said, "No, for how could anyone care? Come now, Breckinridge, you cannot expect even sweet Diana to be interested in such stuff! Indeed, upon reflection, I cannot find I know a single person who would be."

This elicited a titter from Miss Silverdale, and Tom, smarting under the very insecurity he had sought to suppress, said stubbornly, "The tapster in Washington, whom I consulted regarding the phenomenon, told me the breeds have been so delineated since time immemorial."

Diana put a soothing hand on his arm. "Reggie knows not whereof he speaks, Tom—or he does not know his company as he ought— for I have often observed this singularity in the local sheep and have been fascinated by it."

"I've known you since you were in leading strings, Diana," replied Popplewell, "and you cannot deceive me! You may have observed it, but are bored to tears by the mere mention of sheep, only you are too generous to say so."

"The four-year gap in our acquaintance has weakened your memory, then, Reggie," retorted Diana tartly. "For I was always a very selfish creature, incapable of such generosity as you are so obliging as to impute to me. I will have you know that a young lady is generally excessively interested in any creature—particularly soft, gentle ones like sheep—and while a few seasons in Town may be enough to erase such a fascination from some minds, it was insufficient in my case."

Popplewell laughed. "Very well, I cede the point. Diana wishes to immolate herself upon the altar of good breeding, Breckinridge, so by all means, carry on with your agricultural lecture."

Tom, disliking this speech as much as could be expected, stiffened, but Diana abused Popplewell as a wretch, incapable of understanding the meaning of the term "good breeding," and turned pointedly back to Tom, requesting earnestly that he ignore the oaf across the way and continue his very interesting conversation.

Tom did so—a little belligerently, and with a louder tone than was necessary—while clinging to the small proof in this interchange that Diana did not find him dull. But it was hard work, for Popplewell and Miss Silverdale carried on their own conversation with many a smirk and sly look that undermined his confidence, and made him question whether Diana—whom he did know to be exceedingly generous—had not been merely trying to spare his feelings.

As soon as the group had descended from the carriages and begun the climb up the hill, Tom's place at Diana's side was supplanted by Popplewell, whose adroit observation of what looked to be faerie footprints leading off the path brought all the younger ladies—excepting only Lady Athena—clamoring about him. Lady Athena walked serenely past on the arm of Mr. Slougham, who was with Lady Silverdale their chaperon for the outing, and did not deign to look down.

The other ladies, however, were engrossed by the slight indentations in the undergrowth, which did, with a stretch of the imagination, resemble tiny footprints. As the gasps and giggles ensued, Tom was utterly forgot, Diana, her hand in Popplewell's arm, being also held spellbound by his wild assertions and suppositions.

After some minutes, he was saved from grinding his teeth to nothing by Mrs. Ridley, who took his arm with a knowing smirk. "It is all nonsense, of course, but you must own it a delightful diversion to think what mischief could, even now, be brewing in those little minds."

"Whose little minds?" inquired Tom, frowning.

Mrs. Ridley laughed, a rich and musical sound that put Tom in mind of an opera dancer with whom his father had been acquainted. "That I will not scruple to say, though I do not mean our dear Diana's, to be sure. Let us pretend, for civility's sake, that I refer only to the invisible. You must own that the workaday world does lose some of its dullness when one considers that fae creatures may be blamed for whatever mishaps might occur."

Tom looked at her askance. "Are you in expectation of mishaps, ma'am?"

"Dear me, no," she said demurely. "But if a wind should come along, say, and whisk the hat from your handsome head, rather than drat the wind like a dead bore, I should swear that a faerie had taken a fancy to your headgear and meant to abscond with it. Or, if a certain person seems always to be just outside my reach, rather than curse my ill luck, I should imagine that the faeries have some devilry planned, and that perhaps it would be better that I join them. It is very much more fun that way, you see."

Tom stared at his companion for a long moment, then turned back to regard the group clustered around Popplewell, which had begun slowly and laughingly to move along.

"Some persons have a talent for drawing attention to themselves, like flies to honey," mused Mrs. Ridley by his side. "It is devilishly provoking, but not impossible to counter, Mr. Breckinridge, I am persuaded, especially given your fine face and figure. To make one's own conquest, one must simply fight fire with fire." She cast him a provocative look. "When in Rome?"

Tom was utterly taken aback, and for a moment he doubted the conclusion her words had brought to his mind. "What do you mean, ma'am? For I assure you, I do not have the pleasure of understanding you."

"My dear Mr. Breckinridge," she said, smiling and shaking her head indulgently. "You need not fear me. I know why you are here, and I know what it is you wish, oh so desperately, to achieve. But you will pardon my impertinence in suggesting that you are not doing so very well on your own. What you need is a partner—a compatriot to shore up your chances."

"But what could you—erm, a partner possibly do?"

"A great many things, I assure you, sir," was her purring reply.

Though she was correct regarding his lack of significant progress, he was not the least tempted by her suggestion. He had considered her almost on sight to be an unprincipled woman and could not listen to her with any degree of respect—particularly not after this speech. Indeed, his chief thought was that he did not like the direction of this conversation, nor did he appreciate the tone of her mind. However, his response—which may well have affronted her, lowly principles or no—was forestalled by Popplewell's group rejoining them, and as soon as Tom was able, he detached himself from Mrs. Ridley.

Unfortunately, this landed him in Mr. Holt's clutches, and he was obliged to take part in a one-sided discussion of the ease of hunting grouse versus pheasant. Tom, whose interest in shooting had been severely hampered by his father's reckless waste of his own wild-life, found it a struggle to pay even civil heed for a few minutes. He was saved from utter distraction, however, by a stunning similarity between himself and Mr. Holt which burst upon him.

With something like excitement, he said, "Grouse are much the same as Lancashire cows. They breed so quickly, but their meat is inferior. I'd much rather have a herd of Norfolk cows, though they do not produce half the offspring."

Mr. Holt looked much struck and replied after a thought-ful moment, "I wager you're right about that, Breckinridge! Can't say I know much about cows, but I'd take a pheasant any day over a brace of grouse! Better meat and a devil of a lot less trouble. Tiresome hunting grouse—requires too much energy by half."

"Well, that's why I raise cows, so I need not worry about hunting them."

"That's devilish clever!" cried Mr. Holt, and he would have gone on in praise of Tom's sagacity, but that Popplewell's voice cut in.

"Going on again about livestock, Breckinridge?"

Tom turned to find Popplewell lounging against a ruined wall at the crest of the hill. Popplewell shook his head and continued, "The two of you together could put a bishop to sleep."

"No, Popplewell, only think," said Holt eagerly, "if you raise the things in a pen, you need not hunt them! Far less fatiguing—"

"And a dead bore!" Popplewell pushed away from the rock and came up beside them, surveying the landscape that spread out before them. "The point of hunting is the challenge, Holt. I should have thought you, of all people, would know that."

Again, Mr. Holt looked much struck. "Well, certainly, there is that. I'd sooner wish to cut off my leg than leave off hunting altogether. I only meant that when one is fatigued, one need not bother hunting if—"

"Yes, well, you couldn't hunt if you cut off your leg, at any rate," said Popplewell, glancing between them with a satirical eye. "Pay me no heed, however. I am the first to admit no initiation into the mysteries of livestock breeding. Ask him about sheep, Holt. He knows a devil of a lot about them."

"And rightly so," came a welcome voice, and Tom turned about again to find Diana gazing quellingly at her "dear Reggie." Tom's irritation, which had come perilously close to anger, was instantly soothed at the sight of her coming to his defense, and all the heat in his head went to warm his heart.

"Some persons have profitable interests, Reggie," she went on, coming to stand beside Tom, very much like a companion-at-arms. "And though one person finds them uninteresting it does not follow that everyone must. Indeed, I find livestock vastly interesting, and am dying to learn more about it. Shall we, Tom?"

With that, she took Tom's arm and, chin high, swept away with him. Tom went with her meekly—though the look he cast back at Popplewell was nothing like meek—and when they had gone far enough to be out of earshot, he thanked her for coming to his rescue.

"Pooh," she said, marching steadily on. "Reggie has lively spirits, and can be the kindest gentleman imaginable, but he is often thoughtless. I must apologize for him."

Tom took this in good part, playing it off for her sake. "I daresay it is as you say, and some persons simply cannot appreciate mundane considerations."

"But they must consider them," she said, with spirit. "Else how will they live? I must own I worry for Reggie's estate if he cannot be serious sometimes. He would do better to attend to you when you speak of sheep and such. I am persuaded it would do him good."

Much enjoying the direction of this conversation, Tom warmly agreed with her, offering to give an agricultural lecture to the assembled party at any time, at her command.

She laughed, glancing archly up at him. "And you would, too! But it would not do, and you know it." She sighed. "I wish you knew Reggie as I do, Tom. You would like him prodigiously, I am persuaded."

Tom's spirits fell as mercurially as they had risen. "Do you think so?"

"Oh, you could not fail to do so," she said, looking thoughtfully ahead as they continued on a track that wound along the side of the mound. "He was my favorite companion as a girl. He is older by two years, but he always took me birds-nesting with him, and let me keep the best ones. He also was very kind to me before I was out. He practiced my dance steps with me, and taught me the waltz."

"That does redeem him, certainly," allowed Tom dryly.

She looked up at him, seriously. "But it does, Tom. It pains me to have you both at odds. Reggie is the dearest friend—nay, more. He is—" She paused, apparently searching for the words.

"Like a brother to you?" supplied Tom, not unhopefully.

"No, not that, precisely," Diana said, and Tom tried not to wilt next to her. He suddenly wished no longer to be having this conversation, and perhaps the faeries heard him in their mischievous way, for just then he and Diana came upon Iris and Mr. Daniels standing under a tree, he speaking smoothly to her and she in obvious distress.

They stopped short at sight of this surprising tête-à-tête, and Mr. Daniels' voice came to them over the quiet air, pressing Iris to go with him that night to the pond, to try how refreshing the waters could be by moonlight. Iris did not reply but she hardly need say a word, for her posture expressed all the horror in her mind. Diana started forward, Tom on her heels, but before they had gone two steps, Lady Athena swept into view, bearing purposefully down on her hotly blushing friend.

"How dare you, Mr. Daniels!" she cried, coming up to Iris and clasping her arm. "For shame! To solicit a gently-bred female to such an assignation!"

Mr. Daniels, stammering terribly, attempted an apology, but under Lady Athena's basilisk stare at last burst out with, "But it was her suggestion—at the pond!"

Her ladyship's eyes darted to Iris, who looked so absolutely chagrined that the matter was apparently instantly plain to her friend. Athena's chin went up and she looked imperiously down her elegant Grecian nose at Mr. Daniels. "Only a vulgar mind could impute such a thing to Miss Slougham. I have no doubt her words—if they referred to anything close to what you claim—were entirely innocent, and it was the workings of a crude—nay, a diseased mind that put upon them the construction you have chosen. Mrs. Marshall shall hear of this, sir, I warn you. Good day!"

With that, she sailed away, Iris on her arm, and Diana flew forward, pausing only long enough to look daggers at Mr. Daniels before hastening to catch them up. Mr. Daniels, stunned, watched them go wide-eyed and positively flinched when Tom came up to him.

At the look on Tom's face he immediately put up his hands in a defensive posture. "It was her idea, I tell you! Popplewell told me so—she—she wanted you all to take a dip in the pond! I thought—I thought—"

"What do you mean, you thought, you cod's head?" growled Tom. "You could not have thought, or you should have known, in an instant, that Diana's friend could never be a—a dashed lightskirt! What kind of a gentleman are you? The girl is simply honest, and expressed the regret that we could not avail ourselves of the water to cool off—a regret I recollect perfectly you seem also to have had."

"Oh," said Mr. Daniels lamely, and he hung his head.

Tom, seething that Popplewell was behind this effrontery, demanded to be told exactly what that gentleman had said, but upon the repetition of it, he was obliged to admit that the words in themselves had been innocuous enough. His mind whispered, however, that with just a touch of encouragement to such an overgrown boy as Mr. Daniels, they could easily have been misconstrued. It was not difficult to imagine that Popplewell, with his excellent judge of character, had guessed as much, and in his "high spirits" had made a little joke.

That absolved Daniels of some part of the blame, but there was no point in confronting Popplewell over suppositions. Bridling his temper, therefore, he read the quaking Mr. Daniels a lecture he would not soon forget, and extracted from him the promise of presenting an abject apology to Miss Slougham as soon as they had returned to the house, and then to give her a wide berth for the remainder of the party. Sending the poor young man on his way at last, Tom set his jaw and marched back along the track, exerting all his good breeding to suffocate the desire to throttle the high-spirited, impudent, 'right one' Popplewell as soon as he laid eyes on him.

Chapter 6

As he was a well-bred young man, Tom's efforts to command himself were not in vain, and the outing was not marred by the awkwardness of attempted murder. Indeed, upon returning to Findon Place, the members of the party—excepting two—declared it to have been the most delightful outing of the week. Iris declined to comment, having scarcely recovered the countenance required to remain sheltered by Diana and Athena within the group, and dared not risk loosing her treacherous tongue. Mr. Daniels, observing Lady Athena anxiously lest she defame him to Mrs. Marshall before he could make good his escape, took the first opportunity afforded him to corner Iris and deliver his apology. That accomplished, he went directly to Mrs. Marshall to give her the sad tidings of an ailing relative to whose deathbed he had only just received a summons. Mrs. Marshall took his explanation without question and released him with her good wishes for a safe journey, expecting that she should be put in full possession of the facts of the matter soon enough.

Little notice was taken of Mr. Daniels' speedy departure, perhaps because the majority of the company—the ladies at least—were too caught up in Popplewell's latest story: a retelling of his similar fantastic discovery of faerie tracks near a ruin by his home. As Tom tried not to listen from behind a newspaper at the window, he became of the opinion that a man could be too expressive, and risked being mistaken for one who had taken to the stage. The notion of Popplewell having missed his calling appealed greatly, and Tom was lost in contemplation for some minutes of how changed his fortunes would be if Popplewell could be persuaded to tread the boards. But upon the recollection that even actors could inherit titles, Tom was obliged to give up this pleasant reflection and resign himself once more to the present.

He could not console himself that his situation was a promising one. Popplewell, with all his excessive expression, seemed the planet around which the young ladies revolved like satellites, and Tom could not ignore that Diana was one of their number. Indeed, over the proceeding days, all the young ladies excepting only Lady Athena seemed to come to the conviction that Mr. Popplewell was the most amiable gentleman in creation, and Tom was little surprised that after only a sennight the ceremonious appellation of 'Mr. Popplewell' had been all but dropped. 'Reggie' was the hero of every hour, and the more so as he managed somehow not entirely to eclipse the other gentlemen. Mr. Holt and Lord Greenbury evinced no jealousy of him whatsoever, the former because he wasn't, as he put it, in the petticoat line, and the latter because his efforts among the female sex had never been crowned with much success.

But Tom did feel jealousy, and he wondered if it had been foolish to rely on his mother's and sister's advice to pursue Diana. They had been so certain that she preferred him, and while she did not keep him at arms' length, neither did she do so with Popplewell. It was a devil of a position, and Tom chafed at it. But he had come and must stay, holding out hope that the constant interactions of the house party would settle things between himself and Popplewell, allowing the emergence of a clear winner at last.

Mrs. Marshall, ever resourceful, could have secured another gentleman to fill Mr. Daniels' place within a day or two, but this proved unnecessary as Reggie was fully capable of entertaining two damsels at any one time. Popplewell's chief companion was Mrs. Ridley, a circumstance which at first seemed eminently propitious to Tom's success, for Mrs. Ridley was an absorbing companion and took much of Reggie's attention away from Diana. But after only a brief period, Tom was made to be excessively uneasy, particularly when Mrs. Ridley cast him conspiratorial glances behind Reggie's back. This habit could only mean one of two things: that Mrs. Ridley had misguidedly taken it upon herself to avenge Tom, or that she had guessed that, at Cissbury, he had meant to refuse her offer and she was so affronted that she had flown to the camp of the enemy. As either of these possibilities boded ill for Tom's comfort during the remaining days of the house party, he found it difficult to dispel his gathering foreboding.

To add to his concerns, Diana had not been very much relieved by Popplewell's increased attentions to the other ladies in the party. Her responsibilities during the house party spread her pretty thinly at all times, for she was a conscientious hostess, taking care that Iris was unmolested as well as prudent, Lady Athena was occupied, Lord Greenbury happy, Mr. Holt entertained, Miss Silverdale with an agreeable companion, and the elder persons comfortable. Mrs. Ridley scarcely required her attention, so resourceful as she was, but Diana still found time to spend with Popplewell, which time seemed wholly enjoyable to her.

It was a constant source of annoyance to Tom to see the light come into her eyes while she talked with Popplewell, especially after she had endured a more than usually grueling hour of entertaining. The suspicion that Popplewell, in being "more than a friend" to her, was in reality her one true source of comfort served to throw Tom into the dismals, and he took to wearing a grave face.

"My dear Tom," said Diana one afternoon, coming to find him in the library where he had gone to brood over his wrongs. "Whatever can be the matter? You trail a thundercloud wherever you go!"

Unable and unwilling to acquaint her with his true grievance, Tom could not return a satisfactory answer.

Diana, perhaps taking his silence for serious distress, took his arm and led him out to a bench on the veranda. "I never feel blue when I sit in the sunshine, and here we are with more and to spare! We must allow it be useful." So saying, she closed her eyes and turned her face to the sun's rays, smiling contentedly.

Tom, his worries not so easily dispelled, nevertheless did not counter her, for her counsel necessarily provided him with her companionship. He therefore followed her example, turning his face up to the sun, but he did not close his eyes as she had done, watching instead her face from the corners of his eyes. Diana Marshall was not a beauty, having neither dark or light hair but something in between, and with features that were pretty without being striking. To Tom, however, who had known her for over a twelvemonth and had seen her in so very many situations, with ever so many variations,

Diana was lovely. Her honey-brown hair glinted in the sunlight, her dimples peeped as she placidly smiled, her slightly plump figure was deliciously pleasing, her delicate hand felt so right resting on his arm. He could not imagine, sitting beside her now and watching her breathing and smiling and simply being, that he could ever be satisfied with another woman at his side.

The realization set his heart racing, and he felt all at once that he must make a declaration—that he must tell her the feelings of his heart now, before anyone came to interrupt and the moment was lost. He opened his mouth—but Diana opened her eyes the same moment and looked at him, her blue eyes earnest.

"Tom, I have been meaning to say something to you, oh, for days!"

Tom's heart began to thud in his chest, and he swallowed. "What is that?"

She turned on the seat to face him, releasing his arm and clasping her hands tightly in her lap. "I wish to thank you for what you did for Iris."

"Oh." He felt the heat flash in his face and he hoped, foolishly, that she had not detected it, and willed his heart to slow its ridiculous thumping.

"She was terribly mortified!" Diana went on. "You can have no notion—or perhaps you had, for whatever it was you told Mr. Daniels, he could not begin to express his horror at having misunderstood her—not only that, but to have assumed what he did!" She shuddered eloquently. "I do not think I shall ever forgive him! However, he did beg her pardon, and if he does not now believe her to be entirely innocent, I have greatly mistaken the matter. He fell all over himself in his apology to her! It was—well, it was your doing, and I could not go another hour without telling you that I am excessively obliged to you!"

She sat with hands clasped, her blue eyes gazing earnestly into his own, her lips turned up in a delectable smile. All Tom could do—the circumstances having turned out so very differently than what he had only minutes before envisioned—was nod and disclaim and declare himself her servant. She blushed and smiled and averted her eyes, saying something about his modesty, and he took her hand and kissed it.

Abruptly she stood, shaking out her skirts. "That must be enough, Mr. Breckinridge, for my mother will scold me for subjecting my complexion to the harmful rays of the sun and will say that I have ruined my chances at a good match."

"I cannot imagine that could be so," said Tom, standing up quickly beside her.

She lowered her eyes, fiddling with the button on her gloves. "Come now. Even you would not like the lady you chose to marry to neglect her complexion, I am persuaded."

Tom blinked. "I would not mind it. Why should I mind it? I never give a thought to my complexion."

"It is different for a man," she said, but she smiled in satisfaction as she brushed a speck off his coat lapels and straightened his sleeve where her hand had rumpled it. "Now I must go speak to Cook about dinner, but I expect to see a lighter expression on that handsome face of yours, Mr. Breckinridge."

With a coy glance up at him, she was gone, and Tom, reeling a little, sank back onto the bench, considering the disparity between the conversation he had hoped to have and the conversation that had taken place. Upon reflection, he was inclined to believe that his situation had improved, for though she was not now accepting his proposal of marriage and demonstrating her indisputable preference for him over "dear Reggie," she had certainly provided him much needed encouragement.

That evening, as on many of the sultry evenings heretofore, Mrs. Marshall provided for the entertainment of her guests by setting up card tables with new packs of cards. Before Mr. Daniels' defection, the party could seat four tables at whist, and on the more active days when everyone was tired, this had been a welcome way to pass the evening. But now that their number was diminished, they were obliged to turn to round games, a notion which failed to excite those of the elder generation but which appealed strongly to the younger members of the party. Speculation was a favorite, as was *Vingt-et-Un*, and more than once the noise of the game brought murmurs of surprise from those more staid members of the party who had chosen not to be involved.

No matter what game he played, however, Mr. Popplewell could be counted on to become the life and soul of the party, winning or losing both handsomely and extravagantly, making wild bets at one moment and devious ones the next, and generally being noisier than anyone else. Tom watched him, at first with his usual irritation at the ease with which he manipulated an entire roomful of people, but then more closely, as he caught hints at just how clever Popplewell could be, particularly with cards. He noticed the carelessly elegant flick of his wrist when drawing out cards, and the practiced manner he used to shuffle the deck. The more he watched, the more he was convinced that Popplewell was a seasoned player, and it remained only to guess what his reasons were for hiding it.

For hide it he did. Even when playing whist he had been accorded only a bland commendation by Lady Silverdale, herself no mean player, who when paired with him had been obliged graciously to lose nearly every other game. Tom considered that, without having witnessed those endless nights of play at his own home—when he would sneak out of his room to spy on his father's friends, the men his mother called "devils in sheep's clothing"—he would not have recognized the signs. Such reflections were inevitably disturbing—as was anything that brought a remembrance of his father or his father's friends. But after much rumination, Tom could not find out any darker motive for Popplewell's deception than the wish to appear more modest than he actually was.

Tom himself was not entirely averse to cards, but whether from higher principles or a disgust of all forms of addiction which invariably took from a man all decency and loyalty to family, home, and duty, he never bothered to apply himself to a skill that was of no use outside a drawing room or club. He played well enough not to embarrass himself at social gatherings, but he could never hope to successfully hide a card up his sleeve, much less plant it in the deck, as he suspected one of Popplewell's skill could do.

But Tom did enjoy round games, for though these often involved betting of some kind, it was such a modest sum that anyone could play without a tremor to their conscience. Thus, invigorated by the refreshment of finding what he guessed was another flaw in Popplewell's character, Tom threw himself into the game of lottery tickets that was now in its third round.

Tonight, as on many other a night, Diana was not beside him, but she was across the table from him, which afforded him an excellent view of her bright eyes and dimpled smiles. She had taken five tickets for, said she, "I am determined upon winning this round, and not even Reggie can better my odds!"

Popplewell instantly bet against her coming within three of the value of any of the prize cards, at which she got a dangerous glitter in her eye and took the bet. Tom, who had taken only three tickets, also took the bet, and added his own that he would win the smallest prize. A spirited exchange of bets ensued between the other guests, Diana and Popplewell vying to stake the most fish, at which Tom, fortified by his exchange with Diana earlier in the day, experienced only a few twinges of jealousy. Even these could not dim his enjoyment, however, for no sooner were they felt than they were soothed by a quick, warm glance from Diana, whose secret smile thereafter he congratulated himself was at least partially of his making.

The bets were laid, the cards turned up, and Popplewell gave up a loud groan upon perceiving that he had lost a huge sum of money—nearly a pound—for Diana had won the two larger prize cards and Tom the third. There were many other cries of dismay or joy, for the betting had been fierce, but the foremost sentiment among the players as they exchanged their fish for winnings or paid their losses was delight. Even Lady Silverdale, who had joined them for the round to put her considerable skill at cards to the test, declared herself pleased by the game.

Diana triumphantly counted her sixpences out, announcing that she had doubled her takings in the last round, and dropped them rather loudly into her purse for Popplewell's benefit.

"That was a lucky risk you took, Diana," he said, putting his lighter purse back into his coat. "I would not have taken you for a Don—or in this case, a Donna."

"And what is that, pray?" inquired Diana primly.

"It is a knowing one at cards."

"You flatter me, sir!" replied Diana airily. "Tom is quite the Don, too, for I declare if he has not won more than he staked as well."

Tom smiled and patted his pocket complacently. "A lucky guess, I assure you. But I've quite reversed my fortunes this evening, thanks to the two of you. Obliging of you."

Popplewell handsomely waved Tom's obligation away, but his beneficiary did not miss the glint of calculation in his eye as he turned away to offer consolation to Mrs. Ridley, who had also lost.

The arrival of the tea tray put an end to cards for the evening, and Diana being stationed at her mother's side to help dispense the tea and muffin, Tom fell into conversation with Miss Silverdale, who was lamenting her lack of prowess at card games.

"But recollect, your talent lies on the hunting field, ma'am," said Tom.

She sighed. "You are very kind, sir, but I am persuaded that is nothing to the point, for you must have seen that Mr. Holt played very well."

Tom would not allow this. "A game of chance! Everyone's fortunes varied widely from round to round, and not because of skill."

"My mama tells me it is otherwise. She arose a winner in her first round at play, and she ascribes it entirely to her skill at cards."

"Perhaps there is some room for skill, but it does not ensure success, I am persuaded. Diana did not win the first two rounds, though she did the third. With due respect to Lady Silverdale, it seems certain that victory at lottery tickets is almost entirely by chance."

Miss Silverdale blushed, smiling gratefully at Tom, and turned the subject by evincing a sudden keen interest in sheep.

When the ladies rose to retire for the evening, the gentlemen stayed behind as usual, Mr. Marshall and Mr. Slougham lighting their pipes and attempting to draw Lord Greenbury and Mr. Popplewell into a discussion of politics. Their exertions met with only marginal success, for while Lord Greenbury felt it his duty to evince his opinions on the weightier matters of the day, he had few to offer. Popplewell avoided their lures altogether by proposing a game of billiards to Tom and Mr. Holt. Tom thought to take the opportunity of endearing himself to Mr. Marshall, but after bravely offering some observations on the shocking price of grain due to the Corn Laws, his efforts were met by a stern lecture on the solidarity of the King's loyal subjects against French villainy. Not deeming it wise to press matters, he accepted Popplewell's proposal and joined the billiard game.

Popplewell seemed unable to participate in any competition without placing a bet, however, and when the stakes at the billiard table threatened to empty their purses, Tom announced his intention of seeking his bed. As he laid down his stick, Popplewell quizzed him for being a wet blanket, pressing him for another game, but Tom was firm, asserting that he had no skill in the game and had only played to pass the time. He sought to forestall any further attempt to sway him by turning away to take his leave of the other gentlemen, but on his way from the room, Popplewell put out a hand to stop him.

"Holt and I are going to play cards in the library—as billiards is not your game, you are welcome to join us. We could play at hazard, or faro. What say you?"

Tom, reflecting that his purse would be as empty playing cards as billiards, especially considering Popplewell's apparent skill at cards, civilly declined, pleading fatigue, and excused himself to his room. But the following morning, meeting a heavy-eyed Mr. Holt in the breakfast room, he inquired how the game had gone.

"Popplewell's a devil, I tell you!" he said cheerfully, reaching for the coffee. "Had me up until nearly three, all so he could win my last shilling. Played for shilling points, you see. Won everything I had on me."

Assimilating this, Tom expressed his sympathy and inquired what experience Holt had in card play.

"Oh, the usual. Play at parties and at the club, but never win much. Don't much see the point in gambling. M'heart's not in it, I suppose. Better to mount a hunter than to bet on one, m'father says, and he's right."

Pleasantly surprised, Tom revised his opinion of Holt's intelligence and inquired whether he intended to play against Popplewell again.

Holt shrugged, taking a swallow of coffee. "Might as well. Nothing else doing in the evenings. Besides, don't want him to take a pet. Get over uneven ground as easy as you can, I say."

Obliged to reverse his earlier revision, Tom nevertheless smiled and turned the subject to racing—in which he was reasonably versed—while filing away what he had learned against a later date.

Chapter 7

THE FOLLOWING DAY was Sunday, and the entire party went to church. Findon church was just beyond the borders of Findon Place manor, and could be reached by an easy walk of about half a mile. Even Mrs. Throckmorton and Lady Athena declared themselves amenable to such an easy walk, and joined the group in their Sunday finery ready to inspire the local villagers with awe.

The church, a small but neat building hailing back to the fifteenth century, stood in a grove of trees which gave it the feel of a druidical mound surrounded by sylvan solemnity. The members of the party seemed instantly sensible of the change in mood, and by the time the church door was reached, they were more absorbed by their own sensations of awe than by the notion of instilling it by their presence in others.

The sermon was a good one, to Tom's taste, being imbued with less hellfire and damnation than his own brimstone preacher liked, and more encouraging to the storm-tossed soul. The parson, a kindly old gentleman with bright green eyes and a pate wreathed in snowy white curls, needed only wings to elevate him to the personification of an elderly cherub. He greeted each member of the Findon Place party with undiluted pleasure, thanking them for sharing his humble sermon, and wishing them well for the remainder of the stay.

Mrs. Marshall was caught up for a time in the pleasing task of bestowing the favor of introductions on her village friends. She presented Lady Silverdale, Lord Greenbury, and Lady Athena to the various smiling ladies of the neighborhood—who insisted they came up to her merely to inquire after her health and with no notion of putting themselves forward to such exalted persons. Tom was obliged to wait until these introductions were completed, for Diana refused to leave Athena behind, and he never considered going back to the house ahead of her. Popplewell, it seemed, had had enough of spirituality for one day, and had walked to the lych gate immediately the service was ended, expressing his intent to Tom to return directly to Findon Place.

"I will tell you, Breckinridge, I can't stand this sort of thing—all sorts of persons I don't know ogling and bowing and scraping for my attention. Makes a fellow shiver, and almost puts him off wearing his best dress!"

Tom smiled pleasantly. "It will be a sore trial to you when you are a viscount, I'm afraid. But perhaps you ought to have a middling suit made for just such an occasion, to disguise your true station. I am persuaded your problem would then be solved."

"That's a devil of an idea," said Popplewell, "but I daresay Pinder wouldn't like it. He'd never bring himself to dress me in it." He glanced about and, perceiving Diana at Lady Athena's elbow, pursed his lips.

"She'll be some time, I'll wager. Don't know how she can stand it, but that's a female, all over."

"I beg your pardon, sir," said Mrs. Ridley, having come up to them, "but I am a female, and I dislike this sort of thing as thoroughly as you do." Turning to Tom, she fluttered her lashes and said, "Coming, Mr. Breckinridge?"

Tom declined, saying, "I am persuaded I should bring down Mrs. Marshall's wrath upon my head if I abscond with you. We are short a gentleman as it is, you know."

Mrs. Ridley looked as though weighing whether or not to attempt to persuade him further, but at last simply said to Popplewell, "Shall we be off?"

With a final glance at Diana, Popplewell cast a brilliant smile upon the widow and offered his arm, tipped his hat to Tom, and bowed his way through the throng. Tom watched them go without regret. Though he also did not much like to do the pretty, country strangers were more to his taste than either Popplewell or Mrs. Ridley. He considered it rather foolish to count the slight discomfort of being obliged to mingle with strangers not worth the chance to take Diana back to Findon Place on his arm.

As it transpired, he was honored to take not only Diana but Lady Athena on his arm. Lord Greenbury, though he had waited quite as long as Tom to see the civilities through, was claimed by Lady Silverdale—who had tired of awaiting the close of Mr. Slougham's discussion with Mr. Marshall and the vicar—and his other arm was naturally taken by Miss Silverdale. Tom's feelings upon being obliged to share Diana with an earl's daughter were less than delightful, for he had never much liked Lady Athena, with her superior airs and cool civility, and he fancied she returned the sentiment. But as a gentleman, and as Diana's admirer, he knew well that his duty was to support and entertain both Diana and her friend as well as he may all the way back to the house, and he resolved, with real gallantry, to do so.

However, his magnanimity was utterly misplaced, it seemed, for no sooner had they passed through the lych gate than Lady Athena said, "Do you intend to accept Mr. Popplewell, Diana, or are you simply leading him on for your own pleasure?"

Tom stiffened, and he felt that all the air had frozen around him, but then he perceived that it was not the air at all, for Diana had stiffened at exactly the same time.

"Good gracious, Athena," she cried with a forced little laugh, "what an odd creature you are! I should never have expected such a question from you, for such insensibility generally belongs to Iris."

Tom, wishing to become invisible between his two charges, looked sideways at Diana in time to see the quelling glance she directed at her friend, but Athena was apparently unaware of its meaning, for she continued loftily on.

"I really cannot comprehend your reasoning in keeping him on tenterhooks, Diana. He is an old friend, to be sure, and his faults must be known to you, but that is nothing when his attentions to you now are so marked. Indeed, the ease of long friendship must make courtship more pleasant, for it alleviates so much in the process that otherwise would be disagreeable."

"If you imagine courtship to be disagreeable, Athena, then I cannot wonder at your concern," replied Diana tartly. "But you may depend upon it that you are in the minority. I happen to look forward to courtship."

Tom flinched inwardly at this, unable to determine whether she meant courtship in general or specifically with Popplewell.

"Certainly one would have to be a simpleton," said Athena imperturbably, "to believe you to find Mr. Popplewell's advances the least awkward, my dear. And it is as it should be. He is an excellent catch, particularly considering his impending viscountcy, and your father approves of the match. But you must cease your dithering and act."

Diana's steps had quickened, and she all but dragged Tom and Athena down the path. "I cannot imagine what it is you would have me do, Athena. It is for the gentleman to make his proposal, after all."

"But it is not so simple, Diana, and you know it very well. A gentleman must be given encouragement, or all too soon he may lose interest. You ought to be busier, my dear, or he will find another object more agreeable to his advances."

"You are always to be depended upon to dispense excellent advice, Athena," Diana said in an admirable imitation of Athena's cool civility. "Perhaps I shall even find cause to put it to good use; however, it is time we leave off this subject, for I am persuaded Mr. Breckinridge has been wishing it at Jericho. What think you of Lenora's engagement to Lord Helden? Is it not delightful?"

Tom had been wishing Athena's conversation at Jericho—or more preferably, himself—for it had left his emotions excessively unsettled. It seemed apparent that Athena took Diana's eventual engagement to Popplewell as fact, and Diana had not contradicted her. This could only mean that she did not prefer Tom, as he had been made to believe yesterday, and he berated himself for a fool for even imagining it. But as they continued toward Findon Place, the ladies chatting civilly of the benefits and risks to Lenora's upcoming nuptials, Diana's grip remained firm on his arm, and the warmth of her many glances up at him afforded him the courage to reconsider.

For the remainder of the walk, therefore, he weighed Athena's

statements and Diana's responses this way and that, and at last determined that it was entirely possible that Diana's anger at Athena had
not been merely because Tom was a spectator to a dialog she had
rather he did not hear. On the contrary, Tom came strongly to suspect
that the fierceness beneath her careless answers could very well have
arisen from resentment at the assumption that Popplewell was her
choice. This conclusion naturally relieved his feelings to the degree
that he was able to again put aside his doubts and, as Diana had yesterday requested, to assume a lighter expression on his handsome face.

After dinner, the cool of the long summer evening drew the
company outside, and while the elder generation assembled on the
veranda, the younger set took to wandering about the lovely pleasure
garden. As groups and pairs formed and made their way into the
gardens, Tom was the happy man to whom Diana attached herself,
and his earlier conclusions were further confirmed by her suggestion
that they leave behind the others and take the rather lengthy walk
beyond the groves and around the pond.

They had scarcely reached the end of the garden, however, when
Popplewell came down a side path with Mrs. Ridley on his arm and,
guessing their proposed route, begged leave to join them.

"For I've been over these gardens a score of times, and Mrs. Ridley
would have me believe she is a great walker," said Popplewell.

"I am a great walker, sir," said that lady, with an arch look. "At least
with a fine, strong gentleman to support me."

With what patience he could muster, Tom added his assurance
to Diana's that they would be welcome, and as the four continued
on into the grove, he remarked with meticulous civility on the glorious weather and the beauty of the scene. The others did not appear
much moved by his efforts, for they remained quiet until Mrs. Ridley

said quite suddenly, "So you are to be a viscount, Reggie—my felicitations. Was this sudden elevation a surprise, or was it not entirely unexpected?"

"It was somewhat of a surprise, ma'am," Popplewell answered readily. "I knew the present viscount, Lord Belstone, as a distant relation, but never dreamed of succeeding to his dignities, for he is still in his prime, and there have long been two others before me in the succession. To be sure, it is rather too much to hope that a man one hardly knows will die simply to oblige one. I need not have caviled, however, for the previous heir—a distant cousin—was a cavalry officer who survived the Peninsular Wars only to be carried off quite recently by consumption in Paris."

"And the other?"

Popplewell paused. "That one was less obliging, to be sure. It was my father, who died last autumn."

"Oh, dear!" said Mrs. Ridley, a lavender-gloved hand pressed to her mouth. "How odiously thoughtless of me not to have guessed. Pray, allow me to offer you my heartfelt condolences."

Popplewell took these with a bow of his head, and after a brief silence he went on, "My previous modesty did me the further disservice of keeping me in almost total ignorance of my future estate. It is as large as I don't know what, as profitable as I don't know how, and in a county to which I have never had the privilege to go—Devon."

"Devonshire is excessively romantic," said Diana, taking up the subject with more enthusiasm than Tom deemed necessary, "or so I have heard, for I also have never been there. But I have an acquaintance from Exeter, who tells me it is quite beautiful, if very wild. The coastal regions are as excellent for sea-bathing as any in Sussex, I hear. Sidmouth, at least, is very well spoken of—as modern and delightful as Brighton, but quite without the crowds. I should like to go there."

"Then you shall, Diana," said Popplewell, bestowing a dazzling smile upon her. "As soon as I am so fortunate as to be made viscount, you will be my guest at Reeve Place and we may get up a party to go to Sidmouth."

"I hope I shall be one of the party," said Mrs. Ridley. "I find suddenly that I long to visit Devonshire."

Popplewell expressed his pleasure in the idea and then, as if recollecting Tom's presence, wheeled to face him. "You would, of course, be included in the invitation, Breckinridge, should you wish to join us."

"I'll not trouble you, Popplewell," said Tom, with a smile that rivaled Lady Athena's for cool civility. "I cherish no yearnings for sea-bathing."

"But Tom," said Diana, her eyes dancing, "sea-bathing is a most healthful exercise. My father goes at least twice a year to Brighton precisely for that purpose. Perhaps you may find it agreeable to your own constitution."

"Oh, yes," put in the widow, her gaze sweeping Tom's person. "Only think of the benefits to be had when one surrenders oneself to the sea."

Tom's acute discomfort at this remark was relieved by a sudden conviction on Diana's part to rest on a bench in the shade of an elm.

"You go on, Reggie, and take my cousin to the pond," she said sweetly. "I feel certain she will wish to be shown the frog spawn on the far side, for it is just the sort of thing she should like, and we did not go there in the boats."

Mrs. Ridley, oblivious to any slight in this remark, declared herself indefatigable and allowed Popplewell to lead her away down the path through the grove, leaving Tom and Diana to contemplate in somewhat ruffled silence the cool verdure surrounding them.

"Some persons simply do not know how to behave with propriety," said Diana at last.

Tom readily agreed. "Popplewell certainly is careless with his invitations."

"Reggie? Oh, that was nothing—a mere instance of thoughtlessness. He simply did not consider the obligation he should be under. I was speaking of my cousin."

Tom wisely agreed with her, though taking exception to much of this speech. "Mrs. Ridley is...an interesting woman," he offered.

"To the male sex, certainly," said Diana, a hint of acid in her tone.

"Undoubtedly!" Tom said emphatically, but his agreement was met by heavy silence, prompting him to turn his head and remark the alarming stiffness of her countenance. "That is, to a certain sort of male," he amended hastily.

Diana cast him a searing look. "I most sincerely trust you are not of that sort."

"She is excessively alluring," explained Tom, looking through trees to the pond and watching as Mrs. Ridley, bending to see to what Popplewell was pointing in the water, uttered a little shriek and teetered artistically, so that Popplewell was obliged to snatch her into his arms. Tom shook his head. "Too much of a good thing, I'd say."

"A good thing?" sputtered Diana.

Tom blinked. "To be sure!" Almost instantly, however, he recognized the necessity of retrieving the situation. "What I mean to say is, every man wishes for his wife to be alluring, but—but not to every Tom, Dick, and Harry. At least—in my case, I'd wish her to be alluring to one Tom—but not every—" One look at her heightened complexion and his own color deepened. "I beg your pardon!"

Flustered, he returned his agitated gaze to the couple by the water, who had only just drawn apart, and attempted a further explanation. "I cannot imagine what can have been her husband's sensations. Dashed if she's not just like Potiphar's wife—"

Diana glared at him. "Alluring?"

"Not to be trusted!"

Diana sniffed, "I own I wonder how many gentlemen would do as Joseph, and 'get him out,' should she come upon him alone."

"I always thought that was a waste of a good coat," replied Tom, but at Diana's shocked look quickly clarified, "What I mean to say is, it would be best to steer wide and clear at the outset—to avoid the business altogether."

Diana regarded him with a fulminating eye. "That would certainly be the wisest course."

Backed against the ropes, Tom felt it was high time he diverted attention from himself. "If that is the case, your dear Reggie seems none too wise."

"It is not that at all," said Diana peevishly, peering at her childhood friend as he plucked a flower and gave it into Mrs. Ridley's hands. "Merely, he is very friendly and obliging."

"Excessively friendly and obliging," agreed Tom.

"You do not know him as I do, Tom! He is only ensuring her comfort, depend upon it." At Tom's significant silence, she drew herself up. "I have known Reginald Popplewell anytime these fifteen years. I believe I may claim to know something of his character."

"But you had seen nothing of him for some time," he pointed out. "What if during those years you were apart his character underwent a change?"

"I cannot imagine it would be so material a change as to result in his being taken in by a scheming widow," Diana answered, pursing her lips. "Reggie was at Oxford, where he was most studious, and my father says he learned enough to be up to every trick."

Tom, comprehending this slang term rather better than she, could do no other than agree that Popplewell was quite shrewd, especially in regard to females, and Diana continued heatedly, "If you had heard how tenderly he attended his father in his last illness, you would not make such ridiculous—nay, ungentlemanlike suggestions. My father holds him in deep affection."

"I do not doubt it," said Tom.

Diana regarded him narrowly. "You need not think it so very exceptional. He loves him for his father's sake. My father and Reggie's father grew up together, their estates being so close—Ashurst is not ten miles away. Papa attended his deathbed, and promised to keep a weather eye on Reggie."

Keeping his belief that Mr. Marshall had his own motivations for keeping dear Reggie under his eye to himself, Tom merely murmured something that could be taken for agreement.

"I wish you will not be so detestably smug," said Diana, visibly consternated. "Anything could happen to a young man just coming into a double inheritance. His father simply wished to avert danger if he could."

"But I entirely agree with you, Diana," protested Tom. "It is not detestable to agree with a lady."

"You do not agree, you mock me. You have come to your own conclusions regarding Reggie and will not hear a good word for him, and it pains me excessively." She stood, smoothing her dress. "But pray, do not regard it. If you are rested enough, I am ready to go on."

Seeing he had pushed her too far, Tom got quickly to his feet beside her. "No! No—that is, I am ready to go on. But I do not mean to mock." He took her hands in his own and sighed. "Diana, you are right that I have made my own conclusions regarding Popplewell, but now—" He hesitated, knowing she would not like the truth, but having no wish to lie outright. "Now you have made the matter more clear. I shall no longer conjecture what is Popplewell's character or his relationship with your father."

She stood for some moments, her brow furrowed, until he said coaxingly, "I own I have cherished a wrong idea of him, but you have made me understand him better."

She looked up at him and he smiled encouragingly, tucking her hand in his arm.

Sighing, she relented. "Very well, Tom." They continued through the grove to the pond and she added, "I wish you will cry friends with Reggie."

"Well, as to that," Tom began, but the tightening grip of his companion's hand on his arm prompted him to change his tack. "I assure you, Diana, if Popplewell does not become my friend, it shall be through no fault of mine."

He was rewarded with a dimpled, if wry, smile.

"I believe you are the most complete hand, Tom," she said tartly. "Perhaps you have more in common with Reggie than you would like to admit."

Merely smiling, Tom earnestly hoped not.

Chapter 8

THIS CONVERSATION GAVE Tom to understand that though Diana did not appear to be in love with Popplewell, she held for him the same fierce loyalty she did for all her fast friends, and with it a fond blindness to all their shortcomings. She had been quick to see and to point out the faults of her cousin Mrs. Ridley, with whom she had never been intimate before the house party, but in the same breath she excused or denied Reggie's faults—though they were as glaring to Tom as were Mrs. Ridley's. This partiality could be seen by an outside observer as admirable—but Tom was no outside observer. The more he saw Popplewell at work, the more strongly was he convinced that, no matter his own feelings in the matter, Diana must not be allowed to fall in love with her dear Reggie.

For Tom felt no scruple in styling Reginald Popplewell a hardened flirt, and he would not at all be surprised to discover him to be a gamester. The two defects too often went hand in hand, for they both required a thirst to win at any cost, and a disregard for the consequences to himself or anyone who was so unfortunate as to get in the way. If Popplewell were merely a common flirt, Tom would feel nothing more than disgust. But the deftness with which dear Reggie played upon the ladies' emotions like puppets on a string convinced Tom that he was possessed of a deeper, immoral stain on his character. Tom had seen the like in many of his father's friends—and in the end, in his father himself. It showed in the effect dear Reggie had on every lady in his orbit—young and old—and in the evidence of his hidden skill at their card parties, and his readiness to enter into odd bets.

If Diana were to fall for Reggie's wiles, it did not admit of a doubt to Tom that she would be as unhappy as his own mother had been after her marriage, when her husband's charm had worn away to reveal a selfish, vain, and intemperate man. Diana could have no idea of Reggie's being anything but her high-spirited friend, for she was very innocent in the ways of men, having been, through the excellent guidance of her mother, kept from the company of the worst of them. But Tom had grown up in the company of a man whose latent menace was well hidden by suavity and charm, and had detected such signs in Reggie who, similarly to Tom's father, had insinuated himself into the best drawing rooms in Town with as much ease as he had captivated his present audience.

It would be unnatural for the Marshalls to suspect Reggie of insincerity, as he was their intimate and long-time friend, and it followed that their guests would be equally unwary. Lord Greenbury and Mr. Holt were disinterested at best, and the other young ladies—with the exception of Lady Athena—had already fallen under Popplewell's spell. Even her ladyship's indifference did not prove her to have penetrated Reggie's act, only to be unmoved by it.

It seemed that Tom was the sole possessor of doubts regarding Popplewell's character, which put him in the unenviable position of wishing to open his companions' eyes without any real prospect of being able to do so—for who would heed him? He had no material evidence of Reggie's duplicity, besides a handful of slights and snubs aimed at himself, and other observations and deductions based on past experience. But these would not withstand the scrutiny of an audience predisposed to like the accused. Tom was obliged to resign himself to the fact that, unless Reggie became careless, there was little hope of Diana or her mother or father ever perceiving his high spirits for what Tom feared they really were.

After the confinement of Sunday, the young people expressed a desire to drive into Worthing for a change of scene and to give the shops their custom. To this, the elders of the party readily agreed, for it would mean another day of quiet for those who stayed behind, and Mrs. Marshall put into use whatever system she had devised to assign chaperons for the group. Duly accompanied by Mr. and Mrs. Throckmorton, therefore, the young people all piled into three carriages and descended upon the unsuspecting good people of Worthing.

Leaving their chaperons at the Sea House Hotel to secure a private parlor and cold nuncheon for the party, the young people set out along the esplanade toward the Steyne park, which Diana told them was in almost exact imitation of the one in Brighton.

"I suppose they think to make Worthing so much alike to Brighton that sea-goers will find nothing to regret in choosing the one that is less crowded."

"A fine notion," said Popplewell, surveying the surroundings, "if only Worthing were worth the notice. But it is quite a speck compared with Brighton, and they cannot imagine that the creation of a Steyne park and an esplanade in imitation of their betters will draw any visitors of note."

"But it has drawn us!" cried Miss Silverdale. "That must count for something."

"Only because we cannot get to Brighton and back within a day," replied Popplewell, with a look that made Miss Silverdale color and simper.

Lady Athena, on Diana's arm, observed, "It certainly is not an arresting town—indeed, it is hardly a town, but more of a village."

"Pooh," said Diana. "It has grown immensely even since I was a child. There is a new hotel on the Steyne that is quite as fine as the one in Brighton. But even so, I prefer quaint old buildings like the Sea House."

"I fear there has been a great expenditure of funds and energy for naught," declared Athena. "As long as the Prince Regent patronizes Brighton, there is no chance of Worthing's competing with it."

"I cannot like the Prince Regent," said Iris. "He is vulgar and fat."

Tom smiled but Miss Silverdale gasped. "You mustn't say such things, I am persuaded, Miss Slougham! Whatever will people think! He is our Regent, and must be accorded respect."

"Exactly so," said Popplewell, taking Iris's arm with a mischievous look. "Every little fish must pay its duty to the Prince of Whales, for without such largesse, particularly from the school of Parliament, his Highness would not be half so large."

Even Lady Athena allowed this to be clever by relaxing somewhat the disapproving line of her mouth. They continued their tour around the Steyne, past the grand new Steyne Hotel, and on up the high street, looking into many of the shops which were plentifully provided with various articles of interest to young ladies and gentlemen who wished to be parted from their money. The group necessarily split up, a gentleman with each lady, and when Popplewell turned to offer Diana his other arm, Tom prepared to be annoyed at not having been paying attention, for it seemed he would now be at the mercy of Mrs. Ridley.

But Iris let go Popplewell's arm and seized Diana's, saying, "Diana and I shall go together, for there is an unequal number of gentlemen and ladies, and Mrs. Ridley has been winking at you."

"You horrid girl," cried Mrs. Ridley, laughing. "I had no notion I was being so indiscreet! I should happily have gone with Mr. Breckinridge, but that Reggie promised to show me a delicious little hat shop hereabouts, and it would be excessively disappointing not to see it."

To Tom's delight, Popplewell did not demur, going away on Mrs. Ridley's arm and leaving Diana and Iris to his care.

"Was she truly winking, Iris?" inquired Diana, incredulous. "There is no end to my cousin's shamelessness, I declare! But it is all of a piece. And I would not have it any other way—what a cozy grouping we are!"

Tom agreed, smiling a trifle foolishly. "Where to, ladies? I am at your service."

"No hat shops," said Iris decisively. "I shall not have the stomach for it. Delicious, indeed! I hope she gets indigestion."

Diana giggled. "Reggie likely will. Have you any objection to going down the market street, Iris? I find there are such interesting things to be had in the market stalls, though my father does not like me to patronize them."

"I've no objection, for I am of the opinion that if gentlemen so greatly dislike ladies' visiting establishments that are more rough or rude, then they themselves should not be forever visiting them," observed Iris.

Tom, smiling over the wisdom in this remark, nevertheless attempted to explain such lapses in his fellow men by saying "In my experience, it is only that they cannot justify their own rude inclinations to satisfaction, so they see nothing for it but to refuse the privilege to anyone within their control." He gestured expansively down the street. "But I see nothing so horrid in a few market stalls, beyond their containing nothing you really wish to buy. However, I give you my word as a gentleman that if you are accosted by a vendor too importunate for your kind hearts to withstand, I shall stand ready to defend you."

Iris and Diana, expressing their immense pleasure in this amiable declaration by each taking a proffered arm, turned with him into the market street and enjoyed the greater part of an hour wandering among the stalls and admiring the wares. Tom proved nearly as tender-hearted as the ladies, being very little use in keeping them from purchasing several trinkets that they could very well have done without, and they laughingly told him so at the end of their spree as they balanced the last of their several parcels in his arms.

The time was then only wanting a few minutes to two o'clock, so they turned their steps back toward the Sea House Hotel. As they walked down Chapel Road, Diana stopped to admire a reticule in a shop window, pulling Iris with her. Tom, uninterested in reticules, gazed about, thinking of the nuncheon that awaited him and wondering if there would be preserves for the cold beef. As he considered the merits of raspberry versus blackberry, his attention was caught by a couple just exiting a building down the side street whom he quickly recognized as Popplewell and Mrs. Ridley. They were deep in conversation, pausing more than walking, and once Popplewell took Mrs. Ridley's arm and drew her very close, almost into an embrace.

But Tom could not see them clearly enough to discern the nature of the interaction, and it was over before he had wits enough to draw Diana's attention to it. She and Iris were still admiring the reticules, and when Popplewell and Mrs. Ridley stepped onto Chapel Road, they hailed their companions without hesitation, forcing Tom to stifle his suspicions that they had been up to no good.

They met the others of the party at the hotel, where the proprietress, a Mrs. Hogsflesh, had provided a magnificent repast, complete with cold beef and ham, cold pork pie, a pyramid of peaches and nectarines from local succession houses, apricot tartlets, warm bread, and blackberry preserves. Having decimated this feast—while admirably biting their tongues on any reference to the provenance of the ham—the party retired to the beach in front of the hotel to admire its evenness and to wish they could dip their toes in the lapping waves. A welcome sea breeze dissipated the heat of the afternoon and they wandered along the beach until they came upon a sign advertising Aquatic Excursions. Upon inquiry of a strapping gentleman in a frieze coat with a greasy kerchief knotted about his throat, they learned that he would, for the bargain price of a few shillings, row them out three or four miles from shore to gaze back upon the fine prospect of Worthing set against the rising downs and verdant forest.

Having still some coin rattling in their pockets, the gentlemen declared it the dearest wish of their hearts to treat the ladies to a boat ride, and the deal was struck and the boat launched laden with passengers. The party being so large, Mr. Holt offered to take one of the long oars and the boatman readily agreed, pleased with the notion of retaining his fee while doing half the work. But as soon as Holt took his place at the oar, a disagreement ensued.

"What do you think you are about, Holt?" cried Popplewell,

pointing at the offending party. "Do you mean to ruin our outing by taking us in circles? It won't do at all!"

"It is no such thing," interposed Diana, before Holt could utter a word in his own defense. "He did very well on the pond, once he had learned, and will no doubt do very well on the sea."

"But the sea is entirely different than a pond," pursued Popplewell, appealing to the boatman. "Is that not so, good fellow?"

The boatman was obliged to own this was so, and Popplewell, ignoring Holt's affronted expression, declared, "I spent a shilling of my own on this voyage, and I won't have it gone to waste through the upstart pretensions of this paddler!"

"Will you be taking his place, then?" inquired Tom pleasantly. "You did win the rowing contest on the pond."

Choosing to ignore this, Popplewell crossed his arms and looked a challenge. "Five to one we end beached in ten minutes."

At last finding his voice, Holt took the bet and everyone resumed their places to await events. But it seemed Popplewell's disgust was misplaced, for Holt dragged so strongly and steadily at the oars that the boatman had trouble at first keeping pace, and after adjusting his stride, laughingly congratulated his swell companion on throwing a smut in that one's eye.

The boat ride was all that was delightful to everyone but Tom, who not only had been unable to find a seat near Diana—for Popplewell had taken the only seat next to her—but no sooner had they got onto the rolling water than he began to feel ill. He had never in his memory, he realized, been out on a sea-going vessel, and he thought it very unfair that he should have no inkling before now that he was prone to seasickness. It took all his strength to concentrate on the bright blue of the sky, the rough wood of the boat, and the soothing sea spray on his clammy face—anything but the rise and fall of the waves—to keep from casting up his accounts in front of everyone.

The view from the sea was all it had been promised, and Tom thought the others should never stop exclaiming and wishing they had brought their sketchbooks and pencils. Staying in one place on the rolling water was somewhat better than moving swiftly along, but it nevertheless was a great relief to Tom when the party soon fatigued of the exercise of looking and gave the signal to the boatman to take them in to shore.

As soon as his feet touched ground again, Tom's sickness left him, and he uttered a silent prayer of thanksgiving that Popplewell had not noticed the pallor of his face and drawn it to everyone's attention. Indeed, no one had seemed to notice, so caught up were they in admiration of the sea and sky and view, and it was all they could speak of on the walk back up the beach to where Mr. and Mrs. Throckmorton anxiously awaited them. Time had flown while they had been on the sea, and being expected back at Findon for dinner, they were obliged to scurry about, gathering themselves and their innumerable purchases into the carriages. Within a very few minutes, therefore, they set off northward, highly satisfied in the day and leaving various inhabitants of Worthing hoping for their early and open-handed return.

Their arrival at Findon Place was hailed with gratitude, for Mrs. Marshall had charged one of the footmen who had attended the party with the task of procuring enough mackerel for dinner, and her cook had been champing at the bit to receive it so that all the other dishes would not be kept waiting. This seemed to have been accomplished in the nick of time so that the cook, relieved of the likelihood of splitting a blood vessel, settled down to her task with alacrity. She scarcely uttered an oath until dinner had to be set back a quarter of an hour due to Lady Athena's toilette taking somewhat longer to complete.

When the ladies had left the gentleman at their port, Mr. Marshall again tried to pidgeonhole Popplewell in a discussion of politics, but somehow he ended with Lord Greenbury instead, while Popplewell changed his seat for the one beside Tom.

"An excellent day, eh, Breckinridge? Who would have thought Worthing could be so worth our notice?"

Tom smiled perfunctorily. "You are in good spirits tonight. Was the day so excellent for you, Popplewell?"

"It was, it was. It is not as though I have never been to Worthing before, but today seemed particularly fine. Did not you think so? The sun so bright and the sea air so refreshing."

"And the company so well suited," supplied Tom helpfully. "I hope Mrs. Ridley found something she wanted in the hat shop."

Popplewell rubbed his nose. "Well, as to that, there wasn't a thing in the shop but what was downright dowdy. She was prodigiously disappointed, for she had set her heart on a new hat, so I took her to a little place I know of around the corner—on that street we met you at the end of."

"Ah. No doubt Diana would know of it."

Popplewell looked for a moment as though he thought this highly unlikely, but all he said was, "You did not seem to enjoy our little voyage very much."

Irritated, Tom said, "I have never been out to sea before."

"I see," said his companion, with all too much understanding for Tom's comfort.

"The sun was so bright on the water that it hurt my eyes," he said.

Popplewell smiled and nodded sympathetically.

"And I got a splinter from the wood on the side of the boat," Tom added, wishing his companion would not look so smug. He downed the contents of his glass and turned the subject. "Unfortunate you mistook Holt's prowess at the oars, Popplewell. What was the figure it cost you?"

Popplewell merely laughed. "Oh, a couple of sovereigns. But it was well worth it! I didn't fancy taking up the whole afternoon rowing out to sea and back again. What a dead bore! Thought I'd put a bee in his bonnet and speed the whole process along."

"Worked like a charm," said Tom, gazing stonily at him.

"Yes, didn't it? And you were so—erm—blinded by the sun's light on the water that I had Diana all to myself." He polished his looking glass with a lazy smile. "Altogether an excellent day."

Setting his jaw, Tom stood. "I believe the others must be ready to join the ladies. There was some talk of music during dinner, and I, for one, do not wish to keep them waiting."

"I've no doubt of that, Breckinridge," said Popplewell, rising and slapping his shoulder with maddening camaraderie. He turned to their host and said, "Seeing as how the port is gone, sir, may I suggest we adjourn to the drawing room? Miss Silverdale mentioned music, and Breckinridge here finds himself in need of soothing."

Chapter 9

NATURALLY, TOM'S OPINION of Popplewell's character was not much altered by this interlude. He might have spent the remainder of the evening in high dudgeon had not Diana's playing—which was capital—and the bright looks she continually cast him throughout served to soothe him as Miss Silverdale's singing never could do. But as Popplewell rose at the end of her performance to guide the perfectly capable Diana to a seat beside his own, and kept her in smiling spirits until the music ended, Tom was made to gnash his teeth until Popplewell allowed himself to be prevailed upon by Mrs. Ridley to make up a table of whist. This did not bring Diana to Tom's side, however, for Lady Silverdale wished to commend her performance, and so Tom was obliged to nod and agree to everything Holt said while eying Popplewell's flirtation with Mrs. Ridley with righteous indignation. This mood naturally hampered his enjoyment of the evening, and retaining at least a grain of sense, he took himself off to bed early.

Tom was not one to stay forever in the sullens, however, and he arose the next morning with renewed hope and determination. It was the last day of the house party, with a ball planned for that evening, and knowing it may be his final opportunity to fix his interest with Diana, Tom prepared for it with unusual care. He was not a vain young man and had been used to disregarding his appearance, for he believed that his handsome features and good figure were unworthy of consideration, being as they were a legacy from his dissolute father. He recognized that this attitude, however, was a grave handicap in the present circumstance, for he wished very much to display himself to best advantage but lacked the experience to do it with certainty. Popplewell employed a valet who would choose which coat he should wear with what waistcoat, and Tom wished with every fiber of his being to shine him down.

After a painstaking hour, Tom was obliged to leave off vacillation or be late to dinner. He put on a blue coat and, with a last critical scrutiny of his person in the large mirror, he looked himself in the eye and declared that he was a fine figure of manhood, slap up to the echo. If some small part of him continued to doubt, he managed to silence it with the belief that he was at least every bit as dashing as any gentleman there. Thus fortified, he descended to the drawing room ready to please and be pleased.

Upon his entering the room, however, Popplewell hailed him to come and explain a matter of farming to Mr. Marshall. "For he cannot believe that anyone in his right mind would attempt to farm such marshland as you have," explained Popplewell.

Tom, who could not recall ever having described his estate as marshland, said, "You are under a misapprehension, sir, for I merely must trench a few of my fields, and that only in spring."

"A wasteful enterprise, if you ask me," was his host's damping reply. "Just look at the fens in Lincolnshire—all that fuss and bother for nothing! You ought to learn from history, my boy, and save your money."

"With all due respect, sir, you entirely mistake the situation," pursued Tom. "My land is nothing like the fen country—well above water level and hardly so troublesome, I assure you. Only a few wet fields which are put to rights with simple trenching, and the trenches need only be re-dug every few years."

"What nuisance, all for a few acres of indifferent land," remarked Mr. Marshall, scandalized. "Depend upon it, my boy, you'll do better to put your resources into improving what good land you have."

"All land, in my opinion, is good, sir," replied Tom, his hackles up, "for any land may be improved, whether it is too dry or too wet, stony or clay. It is to one's credit to put one's money toward realizing the greatest gains, and even if I had inherited a marsh, I should have done what I could to drain it and put it to good use, and not counted the cost."

Mr. Marshall harrumphed, turning to Popplewell. "With such addle-pated notions, he'll be bankrupted within the year, mark my words."

"If you will allow me to contradict you, sir," said Popplewell, "Diana assures me that his policies, however revolutionary, have quite revived his estate."

Mr. Marshall paused, eying Tom with a raised brow. "Turned a profit, have you?"

"Not exactly—not yet," said Tom, annoyed to be obliged to admit it. "But it is only a matter of time—"

"Doing it too brown, my boy," said Mr. Marshall dismissively. "No good to hold out baseless hope. Everybody knows Bertram Breckinridge's estate was irredeemable."

Before Tom could formulate a suitably civil retort, Kittering announced dinner, and he was obliged to swallow his ire at so unjust a view on his prospects and follow his companions into the dining room. He was considerably mollified to discover that he was to be seated at table next to Diana, with Miss Silverdale on his opposite side. The improvement in his mood suffered a slight relapse upon discovering that Diana had been bespoken by Mr. Holt for the first two dances of the ball, but it was fully restored upon her disclosure that she had saved him the supper dance while Popplewell had merely secured a cotillion, and he was able to apply his ear with a very good grace to Miss Silverdale's chatter during the second course.

Indeed, when tempered by the knowledge of Diana's marked preference, Miss Silverdale's inconsequential talk struck him as lively and engaging—enough that he was moved to request her hand for the first two dances. This offer was accepted with alacrity, and Tom had nearly forgot his earlier affront when an unfortunate collision with an overeager footman caused him to spill gravy down the lapel of his blue coat.

"Oh dear!" cried Miss Silverdale, instantly calling for water and obligingly wetting her own napkin to dab away the offending liquid. But it was to no avail; the stain would not come out without more vigorous treatment.

Tom, looking up from Miss Silverdale's ministrations to find several eyes upon him—including Mr. Marshall's disapproving ones—felt heat creep up his neck.

Popplewell set the seal to his mortification by remarking kindly,

"It's for the best, Tom. The burgundy coat will do better with that waistcoat, I am persuaded. Give your blue coat to Pinder to clean. He will have it spruced up in no time."

With such unwelcome solicitude ringing in his ears, Tom excused himself to change his raiment, ruminating all the while over the perverseness of Popplewell's kind attentions this evening, which had served merely to increase Tom's discomfort and sink him in Mr. Marshall's estimation. With such heavy misfortunes to cloud his thoughts, he lingered over his toilet and did not reappear until the party had left the dining room and convened in the ballroom, where additional guests from the neighboring houses had begun to assemble. Thus hidden by the growing crowd, he achieved an unremarkable entrance, and made his way to Miss Silverdale's side to claim his two dances.

"My dear Mr. Breckinridge," she cried at his joining her, "how unfortunate for you! I devoutly trust your coat will be saved."

"I believe Mr. Popplewell's valet to be an excellent man," said Tom, "and to know just what he is about. I've no doubt he will save it, if it can be saved."

Miss Silverdale sighed. "I hope it will be. It is just the color to exactly match your wonderful eyes."

She tittered and blushed at her own forwardness, but though Tom suspected she had calculated on the color to heighten both her beauty and his interest, he chose to overlook it, for she had vindicated his fashion sense with her remark. Smiling triumphantly, therefore, he thanked her with sincerity, and led her into the forming set with more real satisfaction than he might otherwise have felt. Miss Silverdale was a lovely girl and he was pleased to partner her—if he could not have Diana.

After this set, Tom danced with Iris, and then found himself cornered by Mrs. Ridley, who drew him into conversation until the set had been made up and they could no longer hope to join in the dancing. This was all well to Tom, who had no desire to dance with Popplewell's flirt, and he was feeling quite in charity with her for rendering the event impossible, when she bent toward him quite suddenly and whispered:

"Mr. Breckinridge, may I speak with you privately? It is about Reginald."

Utterly taken aback, Tom knew not what to say, but Mrs. Ridley took his arm and led him toward the veranda, hissing, "If anyone asks, we will say that I was overheated. I am persuaded you will wish to hear what I have to say."

His curiosity piqued, Tom allowed her to guide him over the veranda and out into the pleasure garden, which had been hung with lights to guide its visitors through the gloom. Mr. Slougham strolled with Lady Silverdale down one of the walks, and Mrs. Ridley steered Tom the other way, to where a hedge grew high to provide a backdrop to a statue of Hermes the Messenger, who was so fleet of foot as to be held suspended above a reflecting pool. Two benches reposed in the shadow of the hedge, and she drew Tom to one of these, indicating for him to sit beside her.

"I know that you and Reginald have the same object in view," she began, turning so that her bosom, its white curves enhanced by an emerald-drop necklace that guided the eye downward, was fully facing him. "In light of the circumstance, I feel it incumbent upon me to renew my offer."

Tom leaned away from her, his gaze fixed on her left eyebrow. "In light of what circumstance? What object?"

"Marriage with Diana, stupid!" The lady gesticulated impatiently with one hand, the other coming to rest on the back of the bench behind him. "I am a great believer in fair play, and it has come to my attention that Reginald is not. Therefore, in consideration of the favor in which Mr. Marshall holds Reginald, I wish to help bring you onto a more equal footing."

Tom began to rise, saying, "You are mistaken, ma'am. I've no use for such machinations—"

But Mrs. Ridley gripped his arm with surprising strength, pulling him back down to the bench. "Only listen, Mr. Breckinridge!" Her eyes glittered with such intensity that Tom shut his mouth and did as he was bid. She continued in an urgent undervoice, "Reginald is *not* so very far above you, I am persuaded. He is only heir to the viscountcy, and may not inherit in Mr. Marshall's lifetime—for it is my belief his future title is what attracts Mr. Marshall, besides Reggie's being an old family friend. But without the viscountcy, Reginald is very much your equal, for you have an estate of your own, do not you?"

"I do, ma'am," said Tom, taken aback by the keen interest evident in her dark eyes. "However, it is not as profitable as Popplewell's—at least not to my knowledge."

Tom thought he detected a hint of disappointment in her look before she shrugged her white shoulders and averted her eyes. "One mustn't believe everything one hears, Mr. Breckinridge. Reggie certainly wishes everyone to believe he is rich, but I am persuaded that the true state of things may very well be contrariwise."

His scruples overborne by surprise, Tom blinked at her, inquiring, "How came you by this supposition, pray?"

The lady smiled. "I have a quick ear and, if I may be so bold, a keen understanding. By applying them both, I frequently discover interesting facts that are not generally known." She looked back to him from beneath her lashes. "It is one of my many talents."

Undoubtedly, in addition to making decent gentlemen exceedingly uncomfortable, thought Tom, edging away from her once more. He wished to be well away from this secluded place, this lady, and this conversation. Aloud, he expressed the sense of his obligation to her, assuring her that he had no notion what she thought he would do with her information, and again made to rise and take his leave. But suddenly she gave a little shriek, gripping at his coat lapels with both hands while staring in horror at the vicinity of her left hip.

"A spider!" she breathed, apparently too terrified to utter anything above a whisper. "Oh, Mr. Breckinridge, kill it, kill it, I beg of you! Oh, I cannot abide the horrid things! It has crawled under the skirt of my gown, just there on the bench! Cannot you see its hairy little legs protruding? Oh, kill it!"

Tom, who could see nothing very much in the gloom despite the feeble light of the lamps placed here and there, was prevented movement to more closely inspect the scene by Mrs. Ridley's panicked grip on his coat front. Taking her upper arms firmly in his hands, therefore—to hold her heaving bosom away from him as he leaned forward—he craned his neck to look over her shoulder at the place she had indicated.

He could see nothing, and was about to say so, when a startled gasp issued behind him. Turning, he saw Diana, who had come round the hedge and was gazing at him, aghast. He instantly released his hold on Mrs. Ridley and rose—at last successful in leaving the bench—and took a step toward Diana, only to be arrested by the appearance of Popplewell at Diana's side.

"Dear me, what have we here?" Popplewell inquired conversationally, taking in the scene with a comprehensive glance.

Prevented from making a full explanation of how he had come to be here, with Mrs. Ridley, by a desire not to disclose the topic of their conversation to its subject, Tom opened his mouth and shut it again. He felt uneasily that he had been sadly mistaken to have ever believed himself up to every trick.

"Tom!" uttered Diana at last. "How—after our dialog—"

"Mrs. Ridley was overheated," he blurted out, "and then there was a spider—"

"Yes, a spider," cried Mrs. Ridley, rising to the occasion. "That was it!"

Tom cast her a consternated look, for it all sounded shady, even to his ears. He turned back to Diana. "You must believe me, Diana. It is not what it seems."

Diana stared angrily at him, but also with desperate searching. He earnestly held her gaze, and after what seemed an age, she averted her eyes. "The supper dance will begin soon, Tom. You are engaged to me, if you still wish it."

"With all my heart," said Tom emphatically, stepping forward to take Diana's hand and pull it through his arm. "Come, I would not miss it for the world."

She went with him readily enough as he strode back toward the house, but her silence as much as his mortification prompted him, as soon as they were out of earshot, to attempt to dispel her fears.

"Mrs. Ridley tricked me, Diana. She drew me away, insisting she must speak to me privately, but now I am persuaded it was all a ruse."

"She used her extensive allure to cloud your judgment, no doubt," replied his companion acidly.

"Yes!" cried Tom, but when she set her jaw, he amended, "Perhaps not allure—that is, she is very persuasive."

This had little better effect, so he stopped to face her on the path. "Diana, you must believe that I would sooner take poison than seek Mrs. Ridley's company, particularly for what you doubtless imagine had been going forward."

She cast him an injured look. "I should never have believed it, Tom, but I saw you just now with my own eyes—seated there in the dark, with her locked in your arms!"

"She was not locked in my arms!"

"No? Then my vision must be sadly at fault, for that is what I saw!"

Tom prevented her storming away by taking her by the shoulders. "She brought me to that spot to tell me some Canterbury tale about Popplewell because she fancied I would wish to use it against him. I told her what I thought of that and was about to leave her when she grasped my coat and cried out that a spider had gone under her gown."

"I heard her shriek, to be sure," huffed Diana, her eyes flashing. "It begs only to be known what was the true cause."

Tom only just kept from shaking her in his frustration. "It was just as I have been telling you, Diana, I swear it! She begged me to kill the spider but clung to me like a limpet, and I was obliged to crane my neck to look for the cursed thing, and no doubt appeared as if in a passionate embrace!"

"That you did!" agreed Diana, but her gaze dropped and she was silent.

Tom let her go and pursed his lips at a new thought. "How came Popplewell to be with you?"

"There is nothing in that," she said, crossing her arms over her chest and lifting her chin. "He partnered me for the cotillion, which only just ended, and he accompanied me to find you for the supper dance."

Tom's eyes narrowed. "He led you right to us. A trifle convenient, if you ask me."

"What do you mean by that?" demanded Diana.

"Only that I am a great gudgeon," said Tom, glaring into the gloom toward the statue of Hermes. "This was a setup, plain as day."

"Nonsense!" cried his companion. "Only you *will* make Reggie out to be a villain! You do not like him—you never did—and so you see only bad in him."

"Not at all—that is, I don't like him, but it's nothing to the purpose, I tell you! Mrs. Ridley never saw that imaginary spider until you were just around the corner. They must have arranged a signal." He paused, arrested by Diana's thunderous countenance, and looked away again with a huff. "Perhaps you are right. Perhaps it was her plot to entrap me, and Popplewell was only a bystander."

"You can be certain of that, Tom," she said firmly. "Reggie is no more a scoundrel than you are."

"Well, I'm glad to hear I compare so favorably, after what you just accused me of."

"You cannot blame me after what I saw!" cried Diana. She growled in frustration. "Oh, even now I don't know whether I ought to believe you."

She whirled and stomped away, but Tom caught her hand, turning her about. "You must believe me, Diana! I would never pursue such a woman!"

"And why must I believe you, Tom?" she challenged, eyes glittering with angry tears.

"Because I—because you are—I only—" The whole of his frustrations that had built up over the past week overcame him, and too consternated to form the words, he threw propriety to the winds and showed her, kissing her hard on the mouth.

She stiffened, then for a glorious moment she melted into him, and his arms went around her as reason fled as quickly as propriety. Diana was his—all his—and Reggie and his meticulous shirt points and excellent valet and wealthy viscountcy could go hang. But the illusion was all too fleeting, for within moments she pushed him away, blinking and stunned, her bosom heaving and confusion only one of the many emotions crowding her face.

Stricken, Tom reached for her. "Diana, I—"

But he got no farther, for she dealt him a ringing slap and stormed up the path to the veranda, disappearing into the house.

Chapter 10

AFTER SUCH AN evening, coming after such a week, it was not to be expected that Tom would enjoy a peaceful night of repose. He tossed and turned in his bed, gazing into the darkness for what seemed like hours as scenes from the previous several hours replayed themselves in his brain. He was at turns a prey to extreme guilt and excessive mortification, for though it seemed that Mr. Marshall, Popplewell, and Mrs. Ridley had all conspired to make him appear foolish and unprincipled, in the end he had only proved them to be right.

He readily acquitted Mr. Marshall of trickery, for his part had been only to pay heed to Popplewell, whose comments had been singularly unhelpful. And while Tom was in no way inclined to believe Popplewell to be guileless, Diana's insistence that he was no scoundrel obliged Tom to allow—though grudgingly—that he could, reasonably, have been as innocent a pawn as himself.

With regard to Mrs. Ridley, however, Tom was satisfied that her performance had been anything but innocent. He could have wrung her neck when she had hopped up beside him and acted as though the story of the spider had been a clever tale he had made up on the spot. It was no wonder Diana did not believe him—though it smarted that she could think him so lost to all propriety. Her suspicion had wounded him to the heart, and then she had hit him—

But he had deserved nothing less—and probably much more. He could wash his own head for giving her that kiss. It was an infamous thing to do, and the more so in light of what she had been tricked into thinking him capable of. If only he had not lost command of himself—if only he had tried to regain his composure rather than allowing himself to be brought to such a height of insensibility—but it was no use wishing. He had done it, and he might as well be done for. She may never forgive him, and he had only himself to blame.

If he had ever regretted his similarity to his profligate father, it was now. After such an exhibition, he feared the likeness went deeper than his looks, and he would do everything to nip that possibility in the bud. To start, he would give Mrs. Ridley a wide berth. He was convinced that she had deliberately drawn him away with intent to do him harm, and he did not doubt that it was to his advantage to stay well out of her power.

Why she had fed him that questionable story of Popplewell's possible insolvency, however, Tom could not conjecture. If her chief aim in drawing him away with her into the garden was to compromise his honor—which he didn't doubt for a second—what good was it to make Popplewell's embarrassments known to him, particularly if Reggie was her accomplice? If he had not been, and she wished only to even up the odds between two rivals, how could she hope to succeed by next placing Tom in so damning a position, just when Diana would arrive to see it?

He could not reconcile any of it, and when sleep at last did claim him, it was to flood him with dreams of endless hedged mazes, where every path ended in a smugly smiling Greek god, and where all the players in last night's drama floated out of reach, offering faulty advice.

He arose next morning with a heavy head, and he nursed it with strong coffee and breakfast in bed. His spirits were not improved by the arrival of his blue coat, immaculately cleaned and pressed, by the hand of Popplewell's valet. After a bite or two of food, however, followed by a stern exposition to the mirror on his own shortcomings, he felt as prepared as ever to go in search of Diana, for the house party would be breaking up, and he must not delay in making an attempt at reconciliation.

He found her in the rose garden, alone, and gladly thanked whatever power—be it faerie or heavenly—that had contrived so promising a beginning. His relief was short-lived, however, for though he knew she had seen him, she did not look up as he approached and her silence when he reached her was chilly. He removed his hat and stood beside her like a chastened schoolboy whilst she cut blooms with a vigor that belied her outward calm.

"Good morning, Diana," said Tom into the cold silence.

"Good morning, Mr. Breckinridge," was the clipped response.

With a deep breath to diffuse a rising sense of alarm, he continued, "I am glad to have found you alone, for I have something that I must say to you regarding—what occurred between us last night."

"Very well," said Diana, her eyes fixed on the plants as she continued her work.

Tom cleared his throat and, deciding that prudence forbade circumlocution, dove in. "It was unpardonable of me to take advantage of you so. I ought never to have done it, and I most sincerely apologize. I could blame your charms or the violence of my feelings or the agitation brought on by the events of the evening, but it would be craven and selfish. I fully acknowledge that no gentleman—no principled gentleman—ought to allow such things to sway him from his duty to treat every young lady with respect and dignity, no matter the situation."

"Thank you," she said succinctly, without ceasing her work.

Tom shifted from foot to foot, turning his hat in his hands. "I will do anything to earn your forgiveness, Diana, even if I can never regain your esteem."

She paused at that. "You know what you must do, Tom."

"But I do not, Diana," he said, bending to look into her face. "Only tell me—I am at your service."

"You must behave as a gentleman," she said, glancing briefly at him. "From this time forward."

Exhaling, Tom said earnestly, "I give you my word, as a gentleman, that I shall never again press attentions upon you that are not—that you do not find—well, I should hope that someday—that is, I shall never do anything so despicable again."

"I would expect nothing less of you, Tom," she said, a dimple peeping as she looked at him askance. She shifted back, considering the flowers before her. "And what of Reggie?"

Tom stiffened. "What does he have to say to any of it, pray?"

"Everything!" she said, her dimple vanishing.

"Everything?" he repeated, incredulously. "We agreed last night that he had nothing to do with it!"

She returned to her vigorous clipping. "You insist upon misliking him, Tom, and I will not have it. He is my dear friend, and if your feelings are so very violent toward me, I wonder that you can continue to disoblige me in this!"

"Must I befriend every friend of yours, to prove my attachment to you?"

Diana dropped her shears into the basket of blooms by her side, taking it by the handle and moving swiftly toward the house. "I cannot give my heart to one who is blind to another's virtues," she said.

The retort that had begun to form on Tom's lips as he scrambled to keep up with her was forgot as he assimilated the meaning of this pronouncement. "Diana—do you—could you mean—" When she only looked down to dust the dirt from her gloves, he went on, "I recognize—that is I believe—certainly, I see that Mr. Popplewell is possessed of many virtues."

"Such as?"

Thinking quickly, Tom said, "He is very friendly and obliging."

"You must do better than that," she said, her blue eyes unyielding.

"He tells a good story," said Tom, a little strained.

"And?"

There was a pause. "And he can see faeries."

Diana gazed blandly at him. "You can think of nothing else, sir?"

"I am certain he is possessed of many virtues, but they are all unknown to me," said Tom, shrugging irritably.

She mirrored his shrug, lowering her eyes but not her chin as she stepped around him and resumed walking toward the house. "Then I suggest you make an effort to find them out."

"I do not see what purpose is served by my discovering a dashed list of Popplewell's virtues!" Tom called after her. When she did not stop, he hastened to catch her up, gesticulating with his hands. "He ties a devilish fancy necktie. He employs a clever valet who can get stains out of coats. He dances like a caper merchant. He has fine taste in women."

Diana stopped short, pausing a pregnant moment before turning to gaze searingly at him. "And he is the perfect gentleman."

"Well, that's beyond anything!" Tom uttered, slapping his hat against his thigh as his temper snapped. "I suppose you mean that he would not have kissed you as I did? Well, I wouldn't lay odds on it! Your dear Reggie is a flirt and a rogue and may well be a rake for all we know, but you'll never see it, for you're enamored with the picture you've saved of him from years ago! When will you see that time changes people? For it changes young men most of all, I may tell you!"

"Did it change you, Tom?" demanded Diana, stepping up to him. "Are you materially changed from your youth to today, simply for the passage of time? I think not! Indeed, Lenora has told me you are not. A man's character is fixed in his youth, as was yours, and as was Reggie's."

"If you think to compare him with me, I beg you will not, ma'am! Fate has led him in a widely different path from my own, and I'm much mistaken if he knows anything of want or hardship or sacrifice."

"How can you be so sure?" she cried. "You know nothing of him, Tom! When will you see—oh, it is folly to argue the point with you! Headstrong, obstinate, vexatious—I will not listen to you further. It can do no good!"

She hurried away down the path and Tom followed, but when he tried again to speak to her, she pushed him away, shouting, "Leave me alone!" and ran into the house.

Tom, of a sudden likewise inclined toward solitude, took off into the gardens, striding briskly down the paths until he found himself at the statue of Hermes. He glared at this stone god, and after debating for a tense moment whether the satisfaction of knocking the head off its shoulders would be worth the disapprobation of his hosts, Tom turned abruptly and struck out into the path leading through the groves and around the pond.

Walking had the wonderful effect of relieving much of his spleen, and he was soon able to turn his remaining energies to reflection. This was not pleasant, however. As had transpired last night, he was forced to own his fault in the interchange and, again, he deeply regretted his intemperate response. Diana had been right—he did not know Popplewell. Perhaps his own prejudices had colored his view and Reggie was a decent—if high-spirited and irritating—young man. It was the least he could do, if he truly wished to honor his attachment to her, to make a push to know Popplewell and not be the one to refuse him friendship, no matter how poor his character may be.

He had nearly finished the circuit around the pond when he perceived Mrs. Marshall coming to meet him. He had little doubt that she had been put in possession of all the facts leading up to Diana's present state of high emotion, and his shame was so great that he knew the impulse to throw himself into the pond rather than face her inevitable censure. He was making a desperate resolution in which hollow reeds played a part when she prevented him by waving and smiling as she came nearer.

"Mr. Breckinridge! Dear Mr. Breckinridge," she called as she hastened to clasp his hand. "I have been looking for you this hour. I beg a thousand pardons, for myself and for my child. You poor soul! What a bumblebath Diana has made of nothing."

Blinking in astonishment, Tom denied that Diana was in any way at fault, but was hushed by his hostess. "You will allow me to know my daughter better than you know her, Mr. Breckinridge," she said, threading her hand through his arm and leading him back toward the house. "She is an excellent creature, but in matters such as these—I fear her inexperience causes her to be a little short-sighted."

Utterly bewildered, Tom walked on with her in silence, until Mrs. Marshall said, "I feel I must reiterate my apology, sir, for placing you in so impossible a position. I ought never to have arranged things thus—but allow me to explain. Mrs. Ridley, bless her, is a bit of a dasher—but you are well aware of that already, I daresay. Mr. Marshall is on a crusade to retrieve his late cousin's honor by ridding the world of another well-born but ill-bred single female, and so requested that she be invited to our house party. I thought perhaps Mr. Daniels or Mr. Holt would do for her; however they neither of them seemed to catch her eye."

Still all at sea, Tom murmured something polite and correct and let her go on.

"That is why I must apologize to you, sir. I grossly underestimated her abilities—not to mention her propensities! I foresaw that she would go after Reggie—for every young woman does, you know—but I never imagined that she would try for you!"

"I presume that you heard something of what happened between us last night, ma'am?" inquired Tom, beginning to comprehend.

"I did," she said, in the same light tone. "I had it from my maid this morning, who had it from Reggie's man last night. Without those two schemers I might never have found it out, as my poor, silly Diana would not tell me what it was that had vexed her so. She has hoarded it all up in her bosom so that she may explode with great dramatics at the most inopportune moment, I fear. Indeed, I expect the occurrence at any time. She can be most provoking—but I assure you, it is all owing to the present situation, so you need not be anxious. She is in general a sensible creature, as you no doubt have come to believe."

She patted his arm comfortingly and Tom felt it incumbent upon him to say, "I beg your pardon, ma'am, but I do not comprehend how you can know the whole. If your information originates with Popplewell's man—"

"My dear Mr. Breckinridge, I know Reggie almost as well as I know my dear Diana. True, he was apart from us for many years, but he is still the same high-spirited, impulsive, ill-judging boy that he always was. His man worships him, and though his story was rather incredible, I got a pretty good idea of the true state of things—though, to be fair, Jennings, my maid, has quite a flair for the dramatic, so perhaps some of the high color was owing to her embellishment."

This news, though distressing in its way, was nevertheless balm to Tom's wounded soul, and he began to hope that all was not lost.

"I must explain, Mrs. Marshall, that I allowed myself to believe Popplewell was in on a scheme with Mrs. Ridley to entrap me," he said.

"It would not surprise me if they were," she said serenely. "But if he did have anything to do with it, you must not think it was done maliciously. He ever was a prankster, you know, and as an only child was the center of attention. And poor Mrs. Ridley never could pass up the opportunity to showcase her talents—which are more innumerable than even I apprehended."

Tom bit his lips. "She wanted more than to thrust a spoke in my wheel, ma'am. It seems she may wish to thrust one into Popplewell's also."

"Goodness! That would be odd behavior in an accomplice. But it is all of a piece with Mrs. Ridley, who I am more and more strongly persuaded is possessed of not one scruple when it comes to her own interests—whatever they may be."

Tom gravely agreed and they walked on in silence for a while. When they were near the garden gate, he stopped, eying the house with misgiving as his sense of shame returned. If Mr. Marshall had got wind of it—Tom dared not imagine the outcome.

"You need not trouble yourself over Diana, Mr. Breckinridge," Mrs. Marshall said soothingly, apparently guessing his sensations. "I was the only one to have seen her distress this morning, and I very prudently left her in the care of her maid. Mr. Marshall will know nothing of it, for though he is an excellent parent, he is not very astute in affairs of the heart, and if he had witnessed Diana's tears and connected them to you, he should very likely have thrown you out, if he did not feel himself obliged to fight you."

Much relieved at this near miss, Tom commended her good management, and thanked her for her goodwill.

"Certainly, Mr. Breckinridge," she said amiably, starting again toward the house. "I like to think of it in the way of an investment. May I tell you, sir, how very much I like you? I do not think any other of Diana's suitors has stood up to Mr. Marshall quite as well as you have."

"I?" inquired Tom, incredulous. "If he does not think me a gape-seed I am very much mistaken."

She chuckled. "That is neither here nor there. Mr. Marshall is a single-minded individual—suggestion is lost on him. However, he will move heaven and earth for the causes he chooses to espouse, including those of his dear child. Give him time and he will change his mind about you, depend upon it."

He thanked her again and, emboldened by her approbation, asked whether she thought it wise for him to attempt speech with Diana before his departure to Branwell that morning.

"Unfortunately, no," she said. "It will be some time before she is ready to think clearly again. Though it does you credit to wish to make amends immediately, it must wait. We remove again to Brighton almost directly, however, which should hasten the return of her senses. Mr. Marshall—ah—finds himself once more in need of the Vapor Baths." She paused, then bending her head toward him said carefully, "I hope you will pardon me for saying that I should not find it amiss—indeed, I should be very grateful to you—if you could find it within your power to follow us there—or perhaps to precede us there—rather than returning into Hertfordshire."

Tom stared at her as he grasped her meaning. Then, collecting his wits, he declared himself her servant and made it clear that Branwell was in good hands and that he would like nothing more than to see Brighton. "I have always wished to try a little sea-bathing," he declared.

She laughed. "Now that is a bouncer. But I must say, I do not believe you will find Brighton entirely irksome. It has much to recommend it, at least for a visit. One does tire of forever going there—but I believe I have good reason to hope that, if you should choose to visit us, the fascination will pall on Mr. Marshall."

They separated in the hall, and Tom, bowing gallantly, took himself off to the stables to inform Matthew of the change in plans.

Chapter 11

RETURNING FROM THE stables, Tom took the stairs two at a time and went to his apartments to supervise the packing of his trunks. This was done in a remarkably short time, and he was soon making his way back to the drawing room to take leave of Mrs. Marshall. She was not there, however, and upon inquiry, Tom discovered that she was believed to have gone out into the garden with some of the ladies. He went out in search of her, therefore, but had scarcely reached the garden path before he was met by Lady Athena, who actually looked nominally pleased when she saw him and stopped to speak with him.

"Mr. Breckinridge," she said in a tone less cool than usual. "I am glad to have met you before your departure. You go back into Hertfordshire today?"

"No, my lady," he said, bowing with the deference he knew she expected, "I have taken a fancy to see Brighton while in the vicinity."

Her brows went up, and something like a smile curled the edges of her lips. "Ah! Very sensible. It is a bustling place, to be sure, particularly at this time of year. However, I am certain you will find it pleasant, for everyone who is anyone will be there."

Tom, mistrusting her sudden civility, began to take his leave, but she forestalled him, saying, "If you are looking for Mrs. Marshall, I can take you to her. It is no trouble, for I have something particular I wish to say to you."

This pronouncement very nearly struck terror in his breast, but Tom manfully offered his arm and allowed her to lead him along the path.

After a moment she said, "You must have wondered at my speaking so improperly before you after church Sunday last. It gave you pain, I daresay, and I am sorry for it. But I do not apologize for my speech, for it was necessary, I am persuaded."

Uncertain how to answer this, Tom remained silent, but Lady Athena did not seem to require a reply.

"It is some time since I have been convinced of Diana's attachment to you, and I have not viewed it with approbation, for your situation even you must admit to be less than ideal for one of her fortune and connections."

Interpreting "connections" to mean herself, Tom let the affront pass and allowed her to go on uninterrupted.

"When Mr. Popplewell renewed his acquaintance with the Marshalls last autumn, and made one of their circle this spring, I was quite satisfied with his pretensions, for he is to be a viscount, after all. It is not precisely what I could wish for my friend, but it was better than—well, suffice it to say that I thought him all that was unexceptionable."

She was silent for some moments and Tom began to wonder if this was his cue to speak, but when he looked to her, she was gazing into the middle distance, as though deep in thought. Very slowly, as though for once in her life the Lady Athena was uncertain as to how to proceed, she said, "But there has been a development—that is, I have since been made to acknowledge—there may be circumstances under which one may be right in—in choosing personal preference over duty—that happiness in marriage may, possibly, not be left to chance."

Tom went so far as to raise his brows at this, but she took no note, merely walking on at the same decorous pace, though speaking now with somewhat more surety. "Some persons imagine I am insensible, but that is absurd. It is because I am sensible that I am careful, and particularly for my friends. I have watched with great interest Mr. Popplewell's attentions to Diana during the past two weeks and, perhaps more to the point, her response to them, and I do not scruple to tell you, Mr. Breckinridge—" She cast him one meaningful glance and went on, "I am now thoroughly of the opinion that he could not make her happy. Not as I believe you could."

Blinking, Tom made sure he had misheard her, but knew at the same time he had not. She paused significantly, and he apprehended she at last expected a response. Gathering his scrambled wits, therefore, he managed, "I do not know what to say, my lady."

"Very likely," she said, smiling in her way. "That is why I spoke as I did when you accompanied us home from church. Diana is too free with her smiles—she does not know the power a lady has to encourage a gentleman to believe himself her favorite." She looked at Tom, whose brow had furrowed at this. "Do not be anxious, sir. I know her well enough to assure you that her encouragement to you—such as it is—is genuine. However, it is not striking enough to discourage

Popplewell. He is, you will agree, one of those persons who think very highly of themselves and cannot believe they have a fault."

Fancying she was more intimately familiar with this type of person than she imagined, Tom merely murmured assent and she went on. "Thus, I felt it expedient to give her a nudge—a jolt, even, if you will. It was necessary to make her see what she has unwittingly led everyone else to believe: that Popplewell is her favorite and that you are merely the friend." She smiled complacently then, a fuller smile than she often wore. "It was effective. She was, you remember, most irritated at the notion of receiving Popplewell's proposals. It gave her to think, and if I am not much mistaken, she has acted accordingly."

As only that morning Diana had, in fact, as much as told him she wished to give her heart to him, Tom was much struck, and sought for words to express the sense of his obligation to her ladyship for her timely intervention. She waved his pathetic attempts away, however.

"My actions were for Diana's sake, sir, though I have been taught to respect you as a gentleman." They came to the turning that brought Mrs. Marshall into view and Lady Athena stopped, facing him with majestic condescension. "I wish you luck, Mr. Breckinridge. I trust you will not take my confidence lightly."

In a word, he assured her he would not, and bowing over her hand, he took his humble leave of her. She turned back the way they had come, leaving him a trifle overwhelmed and in need of a few breaths of air and the homely sounds of his hostess working among the roses to convince him that he was, indeed, awake. The Lady Athena, on his side! How very singular, and how very unanticipated.

He was obliged after only a few moments of reflection, however, to greet Mrs. Marshall, who was with Iris, taking cuttings of roses which she informed him were for Mrs. Slougham.

"She must remain in London this summer, for there is work going on at their country estate, and rooting a few rose bushes may keep her spirits from depression."

"Mama is cross that I did not get an offer," said Iris with a sigh.

"Nonsense," said Mrs. Marshall, wrapping another cutting in a length of wet linen. "She could not expect that you would make a match in your first Season. Neither Diana nor Athena have done so, and they both are through their second Season."

Iris colored faintly. "You are very kind. It is only that I am so odd, and she had great hopes at one time of my being off her hands."

"It may yet happen, my dear," said Mrs. Marshall soothingly. With a sly glance to Tom she added, "Some gentlemen merely need a little push."

Placing the last of the cuttings in the box by her side, she stood, dusting her gloved hands. "Now, Tom, if you would carry these cuttings into the house with Iris, I shall follow presently, for I gather that you would like to be on your way. But I must instantly speak to the gardener about aphids or before we know it, I shall be obliged to beg cuttings from Mrs. Slougham."

Tom of course agreed to this, picking up the box and offering his arm to Iris, who carried the basket with the spade and spare linen.

"You should not go away, you know," said Iris abruptly. "It would be rather stupid."

Unoffended by this manner that he had come to understand, Tom smiled and said, "I know it, and so I go to await the Marshalls at Brighton."

"You do? Why then, you are wiser than I knew." She blushed and said quickly, "That is, I knew you to be wise after a fashion, but you have lately been making rather a fool of yourself—oh dear." She looked helplessly at him and he laughed.

"I suppose I have, haven't I? But as we are being blunt, I hope you do not imagine me entirely to blame."

"Oh, not at all! Reggie has been quite horrid," replied Iris without hesitation. "He ought to be ashamed, the way he has baited and mocked you and generally made you to look no-how." She clapped her mouth shut and closed her eyes with a sigh. "My wretched tongue. Pray, forgive me, sir."

"You must not feel guilty, ma'am, for I did say we were to be blunt."

She smiled weakly. "True. However, I ought to have palliated it a bit. It is something I know so perfectly and yet I am never able to recollect in the moment. It is one thing to understand something, and another entirely to act upon it, do not you agree?"

Tom assured her he did and her smile brightened. "Truly, you have been a splendid sport, and have shown us all what a real gentleman is. Reggie has only gone his odious length, and he is, regrettably, very talented at it. It ought to have been more than a man can bear, to be sure. But you have borne it, and hip-hurrah for you. But Tom," she said turning earnestly to him, "why did not you make an offer?"

"For many reasons, foremost of which being that I did not know if Diana wished me to. She has been rather difficult to read."

"I suppose so, though I never had any trouble reading her. She is an open book to me."

Tom looked wryly at her. "If only I had your insight! But females are more perceptive than males, I am persuaded. However, that is at an end, for she has made herself much more clear."

"Then you no longer have cause to hang back," observed Iris.

"Unfortunately, I do. I have only this morning given her cause to hate me, and I do not know if I shall ever redeem myself."

"But she could not hate you! You cannot be so stupid as to believe that, sir!" She squeezed shut her eyes and added contritely, "If you will pardon my saying so."

Tom could not help but smile, saying gravely, "Of course, and thank you. I most certainly will try not to be. However, even if Diana does forgive me, I am still tied by the heels, for Mr. Marshall does not look kindly on my suit, and will not, I am persuaded, as long as Popplewell is in the running."

"He has ever been pig-headed, drat him!" She colored again but went quickly on, "I mean him no disrespect, precisely, but it is not as though a viscountcy will do him any good. Reggie may eventually take his seat in the House of Lords, but Mr. Marshall cannot hope to gain much from that. And another estate may add to Reggie's consequence, but it will not add a jot to Diana's happiness." She turned again to him. "For he will not make her happy, Tom! He is a flirt and a gamester, and Diana will never know peace again if she marries him!"

Tom was a little taken aback by her conviction; however, as he agreed wholeheartedly with her, he could do no other than say so.

She was satisfied and turned again to continue up the path. "It would be an excellent thing if Reggie were killed, I think."

"Pardon?" said Tom, astonished.

"What? Oh! No—oh, dear. I mean that he has been so odious that I wonder that he has not been called out. I should think that he has made other gentlemen than you very angry, and I cannot help but think that perhaps he may do so again, and then he may be killed, and all your troubles will be at an end—" Her hand flew to her mouth.

But Tom, finding her train of thought delightfully refreshing, laughed out loud, and Iris was able again to regain her countenance, and to join him in mirth.

When they both had sufficiently regained composure, Tom said, "It is regrettable that murder is not sanctioned in my case. If one could simply do away with one's rivals, the world would be a much friendlier place, and true love would go on unhampered, to be sure."

"More likely the villains would murder the good men and true love would languish with the fair maidens left to fend for themselves," opined Iris.

"But you are forgetting the murderous females," Tom pointed out. "They would have their share of the fun, so perhaps all the good women would simply join all the good men with God and leave the villainous men and murderous women to plague each other to death."

"Surely that is what will bring on the end of the world," said Iris. "But that is nothing to the point, Tom. You must make a push to rise in Mr. Marshall's esteem. Do you have any political influence?"

"No, none."

"A pity. Do you have any distant relations who may die suddenly and leave you a title or a fortune?"

"None of whom I am aware."

She shook her head. "Then you must rely on your own wits— and my good word. I shall extol your virtues to my father, who will undoubtedly write favorably of you to Mr. Marshall, for they are forever persuading one another to think differently over something simply by prosing on about it until the other can no longer stand it and changes his mind simply to get some peace."

Tom expressed his reservations to this idea, but she stopped him with a look. "I have determined to help you and that is the best I can do for you, for I am only a female with no beauty or accomplishments to lend me *eclat*. I must use what influence I can."

"Thank you," Tom said humbly, then determined to turn the

subject away from himself. "Do you remain in London, then?"

"Yes, as does Athena. Lady Gidgeborough has declared her intention to bear my mother company, so Athena and I will have one another to while away the time. It will be exceedingly dull after the Season."

They spoke comfortably of the limitations of Town and the unreasonable expectations of mothers until Mrs. Marshall met them. Then Tom, having said all he wished to say, took his leave, and promising to call on Mrs. Marshall when she should arrive at Brighton, went off to order his curricle.

Returning into the house, Tom met Popplewell in the entrance hall, giving instructions to the footman as to the disposition of his trunks in his own carriage.

"Ah, Breckinridge," he said amiably, holding out a gloved hand to shake Tom's. "It seems a shame the party is to break up after such an agreeable time together. I should have liked to have gone on in this way for a month."

Tom, not doubting this, smiled blandly. "But perhaps Mrs. Marshall should not have liked it so well."

"Perhaps not with everyone," Popplewell conceded. "But I need not repine, for I shall have the happy chance of seeing the Marshalls again, very soon. They follow me to Brighton, you understand."

Tom had not comprehended the matter in so exact a light, but he merely made a noncommittal noise and said, "Brighton is a large place. Perhaps you will meet other acquaintance there, as well."

"That is a certainty with me, Breckinridge. I grew up near there, you recollect. Everyone who is anyone finds his way to Brighton at some point." His tone became mildly bitter and he added, "It is an ever-changing scene that yet, somehow, remains the same."

Eying him steadily, Tom said, "You look forward to your impending removal to Devonshire, I suppose?"

Popplewell laughed. "It will be a change, to be sure. But I fancy I shall wish to keep Ashurst, my estate here, as my principle residence. The lady who shall become my wife, whoever she may be, may very likely wish to remain in the vicinity."

"Unless she is as wild to live in Devonshire as she is to visit," said Tom dryly.

Popplewell smiled wryly, looking down to adjust his gloves. "I own I am blessed to have so many prospects—too many perhaps. But that is what comes of financial security. It is a state that not every man can boast, I regret to say. It must be a great trial to you, for example, to anticipate the probings of your prospective bride's guardian into your finances." He put a hand on Tom's shoulder and said in an encouraging tone, "But this too shall pass. You will come about in no time at all, and will be too busy warding off the match-making mamas to regret the loss of the one lady whose papa is unwilling to entrust his daughter to chance."

If he had not received Mrs. Marshall's unalloyed approbation only minutes ago, Tom might have risen to the bait, but he merely smiled in much the same way as Popplewell and said, "I have no doubt I shall find a way into the heart of my chosen bride's papa, one way or another. It is not so great a stretch to believe that, when presented with a reasonable expectation of success, a doting father would not deny his daughter the wish of her heart, after all."

There was an almost imperceptible tightening around Popplewell's eyes, though his expression did not otherwise change. "No, not so great a stretch, to be sure. But then, one's definition of success may differ widely from another's, just as one's perception of a lady's wishes may be absolutely outside of reality."

Tom considered that, as things were, it would be more likely for the King to regain his sanity than for Popplewell to cry friends with Tom. Popplewell was like a cat toying with a mouse, only Tom was no mouse to be toyed with, but a man with excellent reason to hope for his desired outcome. If only he could bring Diana to see reason regarding her dear Reggie—that or find a way to fulfill her expectations without putting himself completely in Popplewell's power. Either one could be accomplished once he got to Brighton, if he played his cards right.

He smiled, putting out his hand. "How right you are, Popplewell. It occurs to me that I could learn a thing or two from a man like you. Perhaps I may make my way to Brighton one of these days."

Popplewell shook his hand, smiling somewhat condescendingly—perhaps disappointed by what he assumed was capitulation. "I hope you will! You would be very welcome at any time."

Tom did not wait to see him out the door, but went upstairs to collect his portmanteau and to direct the footman as to his belongings.

Chapter 12

A QUARTER OF AN hour later, Tom set out in his curricle with Matthew beside him. He was not disposed for conversation, his head being too full of the morning's various revelations to do anything else but sort them out, and merely guided his greys automatically south on the New Road from Findon toward Worthing and thence along the King's Road to Brighton. Matthew, no doubt having heard through servants' gossip something of what had transpired last night—and possibly even this morning—did not press him to talk.

It seemed evident that, while Diana was blind to them, the defects in Popplewell's character were glaringly obvious to both her bosom friends and to Mrs. Marshall. The encouragement he had received from them was enough, almost, to convince him to make Diana an offer as soon as she had forgiven him—if he could convince her to forgive him. But Mr. Marshall was still a problem. His promise to the late Mr. Popplewell that he should keep a weather-eye on his son proved he was at least cognizant of Reggie's aptitude for knavery, and in light of this, Tom considered whether he had mistaken Mr. Marshall's interest in Popplewell—if instead of wishing him to marry Diana, Mr. Marshall wished merely to keep him close and out of trouble, if not to benefit from his political influence. But if such was the case, it could afford Tom little consolation, for the circumstance did not erase Mr. Marshall's evident disdain for him. It seemed that no matter how Mrs. Marshall or Diana esteemed him, or how Tom comported himself or expatiated on his prospects, Mr. Marshall viewed him only as an annoyance to be tolerated.

But as Iris had pointed out, this was due largely to Reggie's interference, which Tom determined could be overcome. It would be no less difficult in Brighton, however, than it had been at Findon, for Popplewell would be just as large a part of the Marshall's circle there. But Tom would not allow himself to be discouraged by this. No, he must be sanguine in the belief that he could both win back Diana's esteem and prove himself to Mr. Marshall, for not only were Lady Athena and Iris convinced of his superiority to Reggie, but Mrs. Marshall had shown herself equally his friend, and with such women at his back, his chances of success were greatly increased. The misfortune of the ball and the argument this morning with Diana had hampered his progress, to be sure, but after his enlightening discussions with Mrs. Marshall and the other Goddesses, he felt sure he had correctly interpreted Diana's statement this morning, that she could not give her heart to one who was blind to another's virtues, to mean that she had all but chosen Tom as her object.

In light of this, it was imperative that he meet Diana again, and soon, to present an apology and to assure her of his intention to make a push toward friendship with Popplewell. She need not know that he further intended to try if he could expose Reggie's flaws to her in some way that would cause her the minimum of pain and prevent her being longer imposed upon. But even if he were unsuccessful in that, he would remain in the position of friend to Popplewell—for whatever good that may do either of them—and hope that he could resist whatever ill consequences might result.

The curricle entered Brighton two hours later, coming along the King's Road with the sea sparkling in the afternoon sunlight to the south, and sending up salty spray into the air as it crashed against the cliff. The town was in the throws of intense growth, with streets and houses in various stages of construction extending beyond the old town limits. This prosperity was almost entirely owing to the whimsical patronage of the Prince Regent who, finding in the seaside town a novel and pleasant escape in which he could secrete his illegal wife, had managed to broadcast her presence to the world by making the place into the retreat to which all the *ton* resorted for the summer.

At the Ship Inn, Tom bade farewell to Matthew, who was to take the evening mail to Hertfordshire and bring down the necessary clothing and other items for a protracted stay, including his master's favorite hack. Tom secured his room—a lucky thing at the busiest time of year, made possible by the sudden indisposition of a lady who had left incontinent only that morning—and ordered his dinner. In the certainty that he had a few days to kick his heels before the Marshalls arrived, he determined to see something of the town, and find out if perhaps he might enjoy himself as he plotted out his re-captivation of Diana's heart.

As dinner was some hours off, he went out to stroll along the Steyne, watching with some fascination the crowds of people who looked as though they had been transplanted directly from Hyde Park. That the greater part of them had, was surprising—Tom found it incomprehensible that so many persons should be so unexacting as to flock to wherever was most popular and to the same unvarying society as they had always enjoyed.

He had reached the head of the green when the Marine Pavilion swam into his startled view. It had begun existence, Tom knew, as a respectable farm house whither Prince Florizel had brought his Perdita. But the Prince Regent, tiring quickly of life as a sober gentleman, had transformed the house over the several years of his residency—even after his enforced separation from Mrs. Fitzherbert— into a fine Georgian mansion with three wings and many magnificent apartments. It seemed Prinny was still not satisfied, however, for workmen moved like a swarm of ants along a cage of iron bars that imprisoned the sober facade and extended up beyond the central dome in an oddly-shaped arch.

Tom joined a group of onlookers who gaped at the work, and was about to ask one of them if the cage was indeed more than scaffolding when an unwelcome voice said in his ear, "It's a fright, is it not? I believe His Royal Highness intends to create an Indian exterior, complete with minarets and onion domes, though the interior is wholly Chinese."

Tom turned to see Reginald Popplewell, his hands buried in the pockets of his breeches and his gaze fixed on the scene before him, and was obliged to suppress a strong sense of ill-usage that he was so immediately to be called upon to implement his plan, without even a day to himself.

"He has been at the interior for some years," continued Popplewell. "Have you ever seen it? No, of course, you have not before been to

Brighton. The Pavilion is something of a marvel, I suppose. But I am no expert. In fact, I have no opinion of the Oriental style." He turned a bland smile to Tom. "How come you to be here, Breckinridge? I'd no notion Brighton was in your way to Hertfordshire."

"I did mention I might come here," returned Tom amiably. "It seemed a shame to waste an opportunity when I was already so close by. How extraordinary that we should meet again so soon. I have only just arrived."

Popplewell shrugged, rocking back on his well-booted heels. "As have I. But it is not so large a place, as watering places go."

"Indeed? I know nothing of the matter, for I prefer Branwell to watering places in general."

"And I prefer Brighton to Ashurst in general. My estate seems always to need my attention and I have no head for estate business."

"Then we are very different men," said Tom. "I'd liefer be at home attending to estate business than kicking my heels in Society."

Popplewell's brow rose. "Then you will pardon my curiosity that you are here, rather than there."

"I was prevailed upon to try the sea-bathing," said Tom, without even a blush.

"Indeed?" Reginald cast him a speculative look but then turned his attention back to the Pavilion. "It is too bad that you have come when it is entirely unlikely that our dear Prince Florizel will host his drawing rooms this summer. He is generally depended upon to issue an invitation to every moderately genteel traveler who puts up at the Ship—you did find a room at the Ship Inn, did not you?"

Tom assured him that he had and Popplewell, nodding, continued, "It is not the only inn, but it is considered to be the best, for the Prince Regent has his eye on its guests. Though entirely unknown to

His Highness, you must have garnered an invitation, I am persuaded—if he had intended to hold his drawing rooms—simply by virtue of your freshness to the Brighton scene. Prinny is incurably enamored of freshness, you know."

"How interesting," said Tom, wondering if all these nothings were leading to something and deciding that he did not care to find out. He drew out his watch, and was relieved to discover an excuse to close the interview. "You must pardon me for abandoning you, but it is time for my dinner. I do not wish to make myself disagreeable to the landlord by being late. Perhaps we may run into one another again, Popplewell."

Reginald seconded this civility and Tom, pleased that his reputation and pride had survived this first meeting, made his escape. When at a reasonable distance, he shrugged off the shiver of tension that had come to accompany any interaction with his rival, reflecting that he must take pains to overcome this aversion or all his resolutions in befriending Popplewell would be in vain. He could not comprehend how so many of Reginald's acquaintance, including Diana, saw only his charm and friendliness. At least Tom had discovered there were others who doubted Reggie's perfections.

He ate his dinner and considered what he could say to Diana when next they met that would effectively banish her annoyance with him, but was unable to hit upon anything satisfactory. Therefore, he whiled away the evening with reading *The Turf Remembrancer*, a book on horse racing that had been left behind by a recent traveler. It proved to be exceedingly soporific, and after nodding off several times, he at last gave it up and went to bed. He enjoyed a much better rest that night than he had the previous night, waking with the intention to familiarize himself with his environs.

Asking of the waiter at breakfast the direction of the library, he presently set out across the Steyne to Donaldson's to procure himself a guidebook. Upon entering the portals of this popular establishment, he discovered that it was much more than a library, boasting articles for sale such as post cards and trinkets, subscription tables for various charitable organizations, discussion groups whose protestations often rose above the hubbub of the regular patrons, occasional bouts of music and singing, and an odd sort of game called a Loo, which was entirely inexplicable to him.

Overcoming his astonishment at the noise of the place, Tom made his way to the counter and paid the subscription fee—eight shillings for the month—and received in exchange a copy of *The Brighton Ambulator*, newly published that spring. Rejecting the notion of settling in one of the reading rooms—they being only nominally removed from the general clamor of the whole establishment—Tom took himself off down the street to a tavern and sat at one of the tables.

He was absorbed in the description of Brighthelmstone's history when a shadow fell over him.

"May I intrude upon your solitude, Breckinridge?" said Popplewell, pulling out the opposite chair.

Tom smiled wanly at his guest, resigning himself to his fate. "What brings you to this lowly establishment, sir? Are you not used to frequent—" he flipped through the pages of his guidebook, "the Brighton Club?"

"Yes," answered Popplewell, signaling to the waiter for a drink. "It was my father's club. I go there out of habit, I suppose, though in defense of my sheep-like inclinations, it is the only gentleman's club in Brighton."

Tom nodded, taking a sip of his Blue Ruin. "It was established by Raggett, was not it? Is the play there as deep as at White's?"

"Not hardly," said Popplewell, crooking an eyebrow. "Do you intend to play?"

"One need not be a card player to join a club."

The other eyebrow went up. "You do have singular notions. But that is perhaps why you are here and not requesting entry to the Brighton Club."

Tom shrugged. "You know full well I play at cards just as any other gentleman will, and I do not blush to say I have enough skill to display creditably in a card room, but I do not prefer it to other entertainments. My step-father sponsored me at White's, so I'd likely gain admission at the Brighton Club—if I sought it."

"But you do not intend to stay in Brighton long enough to make it worthwhile?"

"Perhaps not. Or perhaps I do not wish to become embroiled in politics during my stay. How Tory is the Brighton Club?"

Popplewell chuckled. "It passed out of Raggett's hands some years ago, so I really cannot say. I've not much interest either in politics. Though, since I came into my estate, I have been told that it behooves me to take an interest." He sighed. "It is enough to give one the blue devils."

Tom took another ruminative sip of his drink. "I fancy that it was Mr. Marshall who advised you."

"Astute, Breckinridge. Yes. I suspect that my dear Mr. Marshall hopes to instill in me his own zealous interest in politics. I scruple not to inform you that his hope is misapplied. Excellent man, Mr. Marshall, but imperceptive. Do not misunderstand me—I do not say so to disparage him. He was with my father at the end, you know. Rode over from Findon to watch at his deathbed with me. I suppose he is as a father to me now."

"I imagine he should be glad for you to think so," said Tom dryly.

"Perhaps," said Popplewell, tossing off his gin. Reaching over the table, he turned Tom's book toward him to read the title. "A guide-book—you don't want such stuff, Breckinridge! You must allow me the honor of taking you about town. I am something of a native here, and will undertake to show you everything of interest."

Tom wished for nothing less than to toddle about Brighton with his rival, but knowing this to be a perfect opportunity to forward his plan, he accepted. Reginald, declaring himself unutterably pleased, stood and tossed a few coins on the table, bidding his companion follow him out of the tavern and back up the Steyne. They walked past Donaldson's Library, Popplewell pointing out the Castle Inn, which held promenade concerts through the summer, but as it had recently been purchased by the Regent, it would be soon transformed to enlarge his palace. Having already taken in the wonder that was to be the Brighton Pavilion, they wasted no further time in speculation there but moved along up the Pavilion Parade.

Crossing to Marlboro Road, Reginald indicated the Prince's lodgings there—" just while the Pavilion is under renovation, of course." From here, they entered the lovely Pavilion Gardens, and admired the magnificent domed stables that looked fit to house much more fantastic beasts than mere horses. After Tom had got his fill of this monument to squandering the People's money, they wandered along the gravel paths between stately trees, listening to the cawing and occasional fluttering of the rookery above.

Exiting the gardens, Popplewell showed Tom the Post Office, the Chapel Royal, the Old Bank, and the principal coaching offices in Castle Square, then proceeded down Great East Street to the White Horse Tavern, where they sat at a corner table and were served fish pies and ale.

"Our interactions at Findon have given me to believe that you are strangely keen on farming," said Popplewell amiably.

"I do not see anything strange in it—indeed, I find great satisfaction in farming," answered Tom, in a carefully neutral tone. "There is nothing quite like a well-plowed field ready for seed, except perhaps that same field at harvest time, with the scythers marching along in a line, singing to keep time."

Popplewell looked nonplussed and Tom, rather than blushing as he had hitherto done, merely chuckled. "With your dislike for estate business, it ought not to come as a surprise that our ideas on farming also do not march."

"I fear so," replied his companion. "But I commend you for your enthusiasm. I've not the least turn for farming. Leave all that to the land agent. I'd much rather improve my stables than my estate."

Tom took a draw of his ale. "Not even your tenants' houses?"

Popplewell shrugged. "My father was a good landlord. I trust he kept the tenants in good shape. But the land agent manages all that. No need for my interference when I've no notion how to go on."

"You'd learn quick enough, I'd wager," opined Tom, but Reginald shook his head.

"No head for it, I'm afraid. I was raised to be a gentleman, not to grub about on the land," he said, gesturing with his mug.

It occurred to Tom that Reginald's dislike of estate business might be what had caught Mrs. Ridley's quick ear, for a gentleman who was so disconnected from his estate might easily be deceived as to its worth, either through inexperience or by the word of a dishonest steward. He was obliged to stifle a sense of triumph at this discovery, for it was only what Mrs. Ridley had hoped he would feel, and he did not intend to stoop to her suggestion that he use it to his advantage.

"Many gentlemen grub about on the land, Popplewell, and I'm proud to be one of them," said Tom. "I'd much rather jaunter about my estate than do the pretty in a stranger's drawing room."

Popplewell shook his head sadly. "Dashed waste of a pretty face, I say. Look at you—regular Adonis. I can think of a great many drawing rooms in which you'd display very creditably."

Tom raised an eyebrow, on guard for what Reginald may be trying to draw him into. "Whether I display well or not, it's dashed agonizing. Too much work by half. Allow me to know myself, man. If you've no head for farming, I've no head for society."

"Then you have set yourself a task, for how shall you manage in Brighton?" inquired Popplewell pointedly. "Not a farm in sight, but plenty of drawing rooms."

With a laugh, Tom admitted he had him there and, sensible that he must ingratiate himself, asked what his more knowledgeable companion would advise.

"There is more to society than drawing rooms, you know," said Popplewell, a speculative gleam in his eye. "If one knows the right people, one may often be quite at one's own disposal."

Tom opened his eyes at him. "Is that so?"

"Certainly, and I shall be delighted to show you how to go on. With a word from me, you shall have the best society in Brighton—amongst my set, that is. But I guarantee you will be snug as you could be in their company. You may still be called upon to do your duty in a few drawing rooms, to be sure, but there will be plenty of time to enjoy yourself otherwise."

Believing he had a fairly accurate comprehension of Reginald's notions of enjoyment, Tom knew a moment of hesitation. It would not do to be drawn into Popplewell's set only to get in over his head.

But Tom was no flat to be gulled—he knew what men like Reginald could do, and he flattered himself that he was well able to handle most situations. Besides, he could not very well reveal Reggie's flaws to Diana if he did not first discover them himself.

Popplewell had sat back in his chair to draw at his ale, his eyes never leaving his companion's face, until Tom reached out and lifted his mug of ale, saying, "Very well, sir, I accept."

"Good! Devilish excellent." Popplewell emptied his mug and set it on the table with a satisfied sigh. "Now, Breckinridge, I must leave you; however, we shall meet tomorrow to begin your introduction into Brighton society." He rubbed his hands together, standing and retrieving his hat and cane. "Meet me in the coffee room of the Ship at ten."

Chapter 13

POPPLEWELL WAS TRUE to his time and arrived in the coffee room of the Ship Inn exactly at the chime of ten on the fine old clock on the mantelpiece. He whisked Tom out upon the town again, taking him first to Donaldson's to return the guidebook—"They are all of them horrid moral treatises disguised to deceive the unsuspecting," he exclaimed with an eloquent shudder—and replacing it with a telescope, which he assured Tom would offer much greater enjoyment.

With this instrument they retired to the Marine Library, which boasted extensive views of the sea, and Tom perceived that several other gentlemen were stationed at the windows, possessed of telescopes. A pasteboard sign informed the reader that interesting and instructive views of various marine vessels and wildlife could be obtained through the use of telescopes, and Tom was at first astonished that so innocuous a pastime could appeal to such as Reginald.

But with an effort of charity, he allowed it to be possible that perhaps he had mistaken the tenor of that gentleman's interests.

As Popplewell trained the telescope on the beach that extended out from the cliff at the end of the Marine Parade, he gestured for Tom to take his place at the eyepiece. "A fine sight, on such a clear day, don't you agree?"

Tom pressed his eye to the eyepiece and saw not the rolling waves of the sea, nor the majestic flight of seabirds, nor even the worthy travails of fishermen upon their bobbing boats. The telescope was trained directly on a group of bathing machines that had been led out into the water to disgorge their fair passengers into the healthful waters to bathe.

That these females were clothed from neck to ankle in bathing suits, and had been taken far enough out into the water to be almost entirely immersed, was nothing; the power of the telescope allowed the viewer to glimpse, from the variation of the tide or the exertions of the bather, the emergence of various body parts from the water, enticingly draped in wet and clinging muslin.

"Good heaven above," murmured Tom, momentarily paralyzed by the sight.

Popplewell chuckled. "A feast for the sensations, and all part of the subscription."

This statement broke the spell, and Tom put down the telescope, casting a look of incredulity at his companion. "Does no one object to this pastime?"

"There is the occasional outcry," said Popplewell, plucking the telescope from Tom's nerveless fingers and bringing it to his own eye. "But it remains prodigiously popular, even among the natives."

Perceiving that he had in no way mistaken the tenor of his companion's interests, Tom informed Popplewell that he was more curious what else Brighton had to offer than to stand staring at unsuspecting and innocent female bathers. Reginald continued gazing for some minutes, however, before lowering the telescope and handing it back to Tom with a shrug.

"Do what you will. You have the loan of it for a week, sir," he said with a smirk and turned to lead Tom out of the library and toward the South Parade.

They entered the Brighton Club, where Popplewell vouched for him and led him to the card room, explaining that he must make him known to a few friends. "Ah! Here is Bentley! My Lord Bentley, allow me to make you known to Mr. Tom Breckinridge."

Lord Bentley, a distinguished-looking man some years older than Popplewell, ran an eye over Tom's person as he thrust out his hand. "How do you do, Mr. Breckinridge? You are not, by any chance, a relation of the late Bertram Breckinridge?"

With an effort, Tom kept his countenance passive, replying politely, "Yes, my lord. He was my father. Did you know him?"

"A bowing acquaintance," said Lord Bentley, with a look that suggested he knew more than Tom would have liked. "My condolences on his death, young man. Broke his neck on the hunt, did not he? Tragic. To leave behind a wife and young family, too. But I see that you have managed very well."

"Yes, my lord. Thank you."

The intelligent eyes ran up and down him again. "So you are Reggie's latest project, are you?"

Tom quirked an eyebrow. "I'd no idea of being a project, my lord, but I suppose I am."

"It's very well for you, I assure you," laughed his lordship, indicating that they join him at the table. "He's a devilish good tutor, if you've got the heart for it, which I'm bound you do. You look very much a cut above the strays he is wont to take under his wing."

Popplewell disclaimed any interest in strays, but Lord Bentley overruled him. "Country squires and bumpkins, the lot of them! It's your deplorably soft heart, my boy! You simply cannot stand to see anyone beneath the knocker." He turned confidentially to Tom. "He's such a fine gentleman himself that it bruises his sense of propriety."

Tom smiled perfunctorily, finding his lordship's expansive friendliness discomfiting. But he responded lightly, "Was he always so odd, or only since discovering he is heir to a viscountcy?"

"Oh, always," replied Bentley. "It is the greatest affliction to his friends, I assure you. Do you play, Breckinridge? I recollect that your father was an avid player."

Acknowledging this last with a curt nod, Tom admitted that he did play, and they called over a Mr. Dixon—fresh-faced but not so young as Tom—to make up a game of whist. Tom was paired with Popplewell, who scrupled not to disparage any mistakes Tom made, but in the bantering tone used by old cronies. Tom was not offended, nor was he taken in. He thought he knew exactly where he stood in this company.

"I assume you inherited your father's estate," remarked Lord Bentley as he laid down a card.

Tom corroborated this and his lordship said, "Fortunate for you. I hope you do not have any younger brothers to care for? No? Even better."

"Bentley has three younger brothers," supplied Mr. Dixon, chewing his lip over the arrangement of his cards.

"I never could comprehend the reasoning behind having more than one child," said Popplewell.

Lord Bentley laughed. "Then you have never known a woman! It is why I never married."

"Then your title and estate will devolve upon another relation," observed Tom.

His lordship waved this away. "If my brothers survive me— which I very much doubt will be the case—it will be some distant cousin or other—and a very deserving one, I am to believe. May he appreciate it."

"He's a nincompoop if he does not," put in Mr. Dixon. "Any estate is a honey-fall, particularly when it comes to you out of the direct line."

"Not every estate is a honey-fall," said Tom, laying down his card to take the trick.

Lord Bentley glanced at him. "Was not yours?"

"No, my lord."

His lordship took the next trick and said, "I fancy I heard that your father was not as dab a hand at estate business as he was at cards."

"You could say that."

"However," said Popplewell, taking the next trick with a trump, "This industrious young man has very prudently turned his estate to good use, and has quite reversed his fortunes, have not you, Breckinridge?"

As this was exactly the case, and he was generally pleased to make the fact known, it nevertheless grated on Tom that Reginald had told it to his cronies. "Yes, Popplewell, but it will be some time before I shall be living as a gentleman of leisure."

"How commendable," said Lord Bentley. "One does not often meet with such a determined mind in a man of your tender years."

Tom smiled. "I am neither so young nor so commendable."

"But so modest," said his lordship wryly.

Tom bowed in mock acknowledgment and they turned their thoughts to the game. The stakes were nominal, for though the Brighton Club was run along the same lines as White's Club in London, its rules were more flexible, particularly in private games. Even so, Tom played only four games, winning one and losing the other three.

As Lord Bentley shuffled the deck to deal again, Tom stood, removing his wallet to pay his losses. "You will excuse me, gentlemen. I must be going. It was a pleasure to meet you, Mr. Dixon, my lord."

"Surely you may play another game," insisted Popplewell, not wishing to lose his partner. "We will arise victorious, if only you do not abandon me, my friend!"

"I told you I am no card player."

"No card player!" Lord Bentley regarded him with eyebrow raised. "Not Bertram Breckinridge's son!"

Tom merely smiled politely. "I am told I take more after my mother in such things."

"You cannot, in good conscience, leave him to his own devices, Breckinridge," put in Mr. Dixon. "Very indifferent player, Reggie, but can't seem to leave the cards alone! He'll only take up piquet with Bentley and lose everything in his pockets."

"As long as my luck is in," qualified Lord Bentley with exaggerated humility.

But Tom was unmoved. "Popplewell may accompany me to the Ship, or he may try his luck with his lordship, but I know when I've been beaten."

Their further protestations were in vain, and Tom left Reginald—who declared that his luck was bound to change—to the mercy of his friends. That Tom's opinion of these friends was unfavorable was to be expected, for his father's friends had been just such a set—always jovially interested in his welfare, yet he had somehow been led from innocent games of whist at White's, to heavier bouts of Macao at Watier's, to very deep doings indeed at a snug little establishment in St. James's Street. Tom need only look in the mirror to be reminded of what his father had wasted.

As he left the club, he nearly collided with a gentleman entering, and as he stopped to make his apologies, he was startled to see it was Mr. Marshall.

"You, here?" said Mr. Marshall, glancing with furrowed brow from Tom to the door of the club and back.

Tom thought quickly, cognizant that Mr. Marshall must be unaware of his wife's invitation to him. "The Vapor Baths!" he produced, receiving a startled look from his companion. "Yes, sir, Mrs. Marshall spoke so highly of their beneficial effects that I fancied I might try them for myself."

"You will not be disappointed," said Mr. Marshall, still blinking in astonishment. "But you do not suffer from the rheumatism, I am persuaded. Could it be a skin eruption?"

Tom smiled weakly. "Something of the sort, sir. You may see how one would wish to find relief without delay."

"Then you must try the Shampooing treatment, my boy. Nothing better for diseases of the skin. I have rid myself of more distressing ailments than I can count by that means. But how come you to be at the Brighton Club? Are you a member? Can it be you have been to Brighton before?"

"Oh, no, sir, I am not a member," said Tom, grateful to move away from the subject of skin eruptions. "But Popplewell was kind enough to vouch for me. I am his guest during my stay."

Mr. Marshall's brow cleared. "Ah! Just so. Then he is within?

Fine young man, Reginald. Always bound to do the right thing by his friends. Well, good luck to you! And remember, you cannot do better than the Shampooing treatment!"

As Mr. Marshall strode toward the door, Tom could not help but ask, "Pardon me, sir, but as a member of Brooks', is not the Brighton Club too Tory for you?"

"Not in the least, my boy!" exclaimed Mr. Marshall. "Very tame here, I must say. Besides, only club in the city! Must go somewhere for a quiet game of cards." With that, he ducked inside, in quest, no doubt, of his favorite.

Much relieved that he had brushed through that meeting fairly well, Tom went on to the Ship, all his thoughts bent upon ascertaining without delay if Mrs. and Miss Marshall were also in Brighton, and whether it was safe for him to attempt a reconciliation with Diana. This was his whole object in coming thither, after all, and the sooner such a reconciliation could be effected, the sooner he could proceed to further his suit, and the sooner leave this place and return to his well-ordered life at Branwell.

Inquiries in the Royal Crescent—where Mrs. Marshall had informed him her husband had secured lodgings—produced the information that Mr. Marshall had come on ahead, in order to make the house ready for his wife and daughter, who would be joining him in a day or two. Tom had, therefore, no alternative but to kick his heels about town, and he resolved to try out the sea-bathing if only to be able to tell Mr. Marshall that he had done so.

His sentiments upon the experiment were tepid at most. Having grown up with a pond within an easy distance—and a mother who paid no heed to the warnings of the village tabbies against the combined evils of water sports and evening air—Tom had expected a trifle more excitement from the beating waves and the salty water. But as he was made to don the restrictive bathing attire he had seen through the telescope, and the movements of each bather was limited to the immediate area of the bathing machine from whence he descended, and the rise and fall of the waves tended to bring on a milder form of his seasickness, Tom emerged from the experience with no yearnings to repeat it.

Having very little of interest to occupy him, therefore, Tom dispatched a messenger boy from the inn to the Royal Crescent each morning after meeting Mr. Marshall, and thus had the earliest intelligence of Diana's arrival on the second day. His great relief was not unnecessarily mixed with anxiety, but he presented himself without loss of time at the house—only to discover that he was behind Popplewell, who seemed to have been more minutely informed than himself, and who even now was cozily ensconced on the sofa with Diana.

Mrs. Marshall, who welcomed Tom into the drawing room, followed the vexed line of his gaze and said quietly, "He arrived only minutes ago. It is a great pity, for she has been out of sorts, and I am persuaded it is on account of your disagreement, and to clear it up would do her a great deal of good."

Tom nodded, encouraged, but when he went forward to greet Diana, she would hardly look at him, and after the briefest of civilities, went on chatting brightly with Reginald. Taking a seat near Mrs. Marshall, Tom cast his hostess a look of frustration and she shook her head, merely beginning the subject of his travels and inquiring innocently what brought him to Brighton.

As Diana scarcely paid him any notice at all, Tom's visit lasted only the requisite quarter of an hour, and he took his leave while

Popplewell was still busily engaged with his hosts. Walking down the stairs in something like dejection, he was stopped by Mrs. Marshall, who had come after him to adjure him not to despair.

"She is merely embarrassed with Reggie here, Tom. She cannot know your mind, and so will not show hers just yet. Give it time, and come again."

Though the past fifteen minutes had made him reluctant to do anything of the sort, he yet saw the wisdom in her advice, and he soon resolved that he would not make the previous five days go to waste by giving up now. So he thanked her and said he would try again tomorrow, and went on his way to find solace in the local tavern.

Matthew arrived the following day with Tom's hack, his first question being, "Any luck with Miss Marshall, sir?"

Obliged by this to admit the circumstances, Tom decided to make a clean breast of it, and told him everything that had happened since he came to Brighton.

Matthew whistled. "Them coves as Mr. Popplewell has introduced you to sound mighty sly, sir."

"Not to worry, Matthew," said Tom. "I know what I'm about."

Matthew accepted this without demur. "Then you'd best go see Miss Marshall now, while I see to the horse's board for the week."

This Tom did, but he arrived at the house in the Royal Crescent in time to see Popplewell admitted, and not about to repeat yesterday's performance, he turned himself about and went back to the Ship to further refine his apology to Diana—should it ever take place. The next day he came prepared, and when he had got within view of the house, he stationed himself beside a protrusion in the sea wall across the street. Pulling the borrowed telescope out of his pocket, he trained it on the windows of the drawing room and attempted to ascertain who, if anyone, occupied the room. This was difficult, for the windows were on the first floor, and afforded the observer the tiniest glimpse of the room, and after ten minutes of seeing only vague shadows, Tom gave it up in disgust.

When he took down the telescope from his eye, however, he was horrified to find that Mrs. Marshall was coming across the street from the house, and he hastened to put the improper instrument back in his pocket, out of sight.

She smiled, however, as she came up to him, holding out her hand. "My dear Mr. Breckinridge! I hoped to see you today. However, I cannot say I imagined you would be peeping at us from out here, rather than coming up to the house like a civilized gentleman."

"Of course—I was about to—it is not what it seems—you mustn't think—" Tom stammered, red-faced.

But she laughed gently, taking his arm and pulling him with her toward the house. "Do not worry, sir, that you have offered me an affront. I believe I know exactly what you have been about, and I do not blame you in the least. How you could hope to discern anything through those windows, however, I do not know. As most persons sit on the sofas and chairs almost as soon as they come into the room, you know, there is not much walking about near the windows."

They came to the steps and she let go his arm. "Thank you for your support across the street. As a reward for that good deed, I will supply you with this information: Reginald is not in the house, but neither is Diana. They are not together, however, so you may get that wretched look off your face. If you care to walk up the street to the Clarke Music Library in German Place, you will find her looking for some music to play on the pianoforte, and I rejoice to inform you that she is in an excessively temperate state of mind."

With a great sigh, Tom took her hand and bent over it. "Thank you, Mrs. Marshall. You shall never know—"

"Yes, yes, my boy," she said, waving him away. "Off with you now!"

Chapter 14

T HE RELATIVELY SHORT walk to German Place was spent by Tom in preparing anew the speech he had been considering for days, that would both convey his abject humility and assure Diana of the strength of his conviction to fulfill her expectations. Upon arrival, he stopped short at the doorstep, having caught a glimpse of Diana at one of the counters there and suddenly finding it hard to breathe. The door to the library had taken on the proportions of a portal to an unknown universe, and Tom stood gazing dumbly at it a full five minutes, commanding his brain to stop being ridiculous and his heart to resume its natural beating. At last, the spell was broken by a patron exiting the building, and Tom, straightening both his spine and his hat, entered the library.

Going to the counter where Diana had been, Tom drew a blank, and was obliged to look about the room. It was bustling with patrons, but though he peered keenly after every dark-haired damsel in the place, none were Diana. He stationed himself, therefore, at the counter with a good view of the door so as not to miss her exit, but was obliged to wait thus some time, and the strain upon his nerves from every jangle of the shop bell had him on pins and needles by the time Diana reappeared, coming from the back of the shop, with her maid.

"Diana! At last!" he cried, then, recollecting that theirs was to be an accidental meeting, said, "That is, it seems an age since last I saw you—though it was but two days ago." He swallowed, only just keeping himself from tugging at his neck cloth. "How felicitous is this?"

Diana, covered in confusion, turned red and white by turns, stammering that she had not thought to see him here, and after many false starts, at last succeeded in inquiring his direction.

"I am at the Old Ship," answered Tom easily enough, but then silence descended between them.

After studying her shoes for some moments, Diana said abruptly, "It was good of you—"

But at the same moment Tom had begun to say, "You may wonder at—"

They stopped, each urging the other to speak first, until Tom managed to carry the point, insisting that he had nothing to say that could not wait.

Looking somewhat disappointed, Diana averted her eyes and said, "It was good of you to visit us the other day. I own I was entirely shocked to see you. I thought you in Hertfordshire, and fear I was too much astonished to greet you properly."

Having not considered this possibility, Tom was rather relieved. "Yes, well, it does not signify. I was excessively well entertained by Mrs. Marshall."

She glanced up with a quick smile then away again, looking about the shop as though to find a suitable subject for two people who labored under the burden of having too much to say and no words with which to say it.

At last she remarked, "I had not guessed that you are musical, Tom."

Tom opened his mouth to answer in the negative but, loath to own that he was there by the design of her mother in order that he may find her alone, he cast about for a rational explanation for his presence there, blurting at last, "I am not musical myself, Diana; however, you know well that Lenora is, and when I happened upon the library, I thought to look out some music for her to play."

"It is excessively thoughtful in you, Tom; however, this is a library, as you know, and unless you mean to have her send it back at the close of the loan period, she may be better served were you to purchase music for her."

Tom stood there gaping like a rather handsome fish until a happy thought occurred to him. "Oh—oh, certainly, but as I have very little to do in Brighton at present, I thought to come in an familiarize myself with what is on offer."

She smiled and nodded, blushing at her misunderstanding of the situation, and when silence threatened to engulf them once more, he added hastily, "Perhaps you will help me to choose?"

With a sigh of relief, Diana expressed herself very willing to assist him, and she joined him at the counter, where they were instantly attended by a clerk. The act of perusing the various songs and debating the value of each and explaining why one or the other was a favorite eventually restored Diana to something of her natural manner, and by the time the choice was made, she found herself able to look him in the face.

"I hope Lenora will like it," she said with a tentative smile.

"As do I," replied Tom, coloring slightly.

Diana looked down, as if finding her tightly clasped hands vastly interesting. "I suppose you must be going."

"Yes—no!" said Tom, desperately seeking for an opening for his prepared speech. He glanced quickly about and was struck with inspiration. "You came here for music, and yet I see you have none. I fear I have taken all your time with my own errand. May I now assist you?"

Diana peeped up at him, a blush tinging her cheek. "You are very obliging, Tom, but I have been all over the library, by myself and with a clerk, and I cannot find anything that I want. It is very disappointing."

"Were you looking for a specific piece, or simply a certain style of music?" he asked with becoming solicitude.

"I had hoped to find a piece by Mozart," she said, pleased. "His *Kleine Gigue in G*. It is one of my father's favorites, that his sister was used to play when they were young. She was an accomplished musician at only fourteen, but I resolved to learn to play it for him, for I shall have little else to do here." She blushed and glanced up at him, then down again at her hands. "I have been so often at Brighton, you see, that there is nothing new to me here. I had much rather be at home in the summer months."

"I know what you mean," said Tom feelingly. "There is nowhere I'd rather be than Branwell in the summer."

She looked curiously at him. "What is it that brings you to Brighton, then, Tom?"

"Oh—I thought perhaps I might try sea-bathing after all," he said, taking inspiration from his dialog with Mr. Marshall the other day. "You did give it a most excellent recommendation."

"And have you tried it?" she asked, incredulous.

He was pleased to report that he had, and the mischievous smile that came to her face on this revelation drove away every memory of the disagreeable sensations related to his adventure.

"I own I would not have believed it," she said. "But you must pardon my suspecting you—it is only that you are very prompt! You can have been here only a few days—but here I am, chattering on, while you must wish to order Lenora's music. There is a capital shop just on George Street."

"There is no hurry," said Tom truthfully. Then, recollecting that he was to be a perfect gentleman, he added, "Unless I am keeping you."

She blushed again. "No, not at all. Though I suppose I must be getting home."

"May I accompany you, Diana?" asked Tom, nearly succeeding in keeping the note of pleading from his voice.

She hesitated, but only for a moment. "Certainly."

Encouraged, Tom held the door for her and her maid, then walked with them to Marine Parade, the maid trailing behind.

"Beyond the sea-bathing, how do you like Brighton, Tom?" inquired Diana after some minutes.

They talked of the charms of the town, the sea, and the weather with great perseverance, until the Royal Crescent came within view. Then Tom, mustering courage, said, "Diana, when I visited the other day, it was not merely a social call. I had hoped to speak to you privately—with your mother present, of course."

"I thought you might," said Diana quietly. "I would have liked nothing better, for I, too, have something I must say to you. But as I told you, I was excessively surprised at your appearance, and Reggie was there, and I was sorry. That is, I was not sorry that Reggie had come to visit, only that he had come precisely then—you see."

Possessed as he was of Mrs. Marshall's information, Tom thought he did see. "Well, it is of no consequence, for now will do as well." He took a deep breath and plunged on, "I wish to apologize again for—for everything. For Mrs. Ridley—"

"Please, Tom," interrupted Diana, stopping to look imploringly into his eyes. "I believe what you said about what happened that night—and have done almost from the moment you told me. I was simply—" She resumed walking, and gazed out over the sparkling sea. "I was angry, Tom, and hurt. After you had told me what you thought of her, to find her locked in your arms—or so it seemed—I felt horridly used! It was impossible that my feelings should be easily subdued, even in light of the truth. However, it was stupid of me to allow them to linger, and silly, and I wish you will forget all about it."

"But—the other things," Tom pressed courageously on. "My abominable behavior, and—and Popplewell. I truly regret my jealous words, Diana, and I will change—indeed, I have changed. You will be pleased to know that we have met, here in Brighton, more than once, and we are something in the way to being friends."

She stared at him. "You are not serious! That is, I know you have met, for he was here at the house, but as far as your beginning to be friends—after so little time—" She stopped at his injured look and bit her lip. "Forgive me. I simply must be suspicious! You see, I am as much at fault as you—perhaps not quite so deplorably, but it is too true." She stopped again, moving in front of him and taking a deep breath. "I will make amends."

Smiling ruefully, she held out her hands to him. "Dear Tom, I forgive you for every horrid thing you said and did at the house party, for I know you did not mean to hurt me, and I believe that your intentions have always been honorable. Can you forgive me for acting so foolishly, and for imagining, even for an instant, that you could be capable of such odious behavior with Mrs. Ridley? And can you forgive me for distrusting you just now?"

Tom, gazing into her pansy-blue eyes and believing that she was a treasure amongst women, said, "There is nothing to forgive."

They stood there on the street, gazing into each other's faces as the sea breeze tugged at their clothing and the waves danced in the sunlight beyond the cliffs. Her eyes held such a melting look that Tom thought for an instant she might wish him to kiss her, but then he knew she would not, nor did he wish her to desire so improper a thing, out in the public view. It was enough that she cherished such amiable sensations toward him.

With a happy sigh, he tucked her hand in his arm and began walking again, believing this walk had become one of the most pleasant of his life.

"You say you have seen all there is to see in Brighton?" he asked after a few moments.

She huffed. "Indeed, I have. I could be employed as a guide, I daresay."

"Perhaps, if you truly have nothing else to do," he said carelessly, "you might show me the sights."

She turned her head to look at him. "Do you anticipate a protracted stay in Brighton then, Tom?"

He shrugged. "Long enough to ease your boredom by giving you something worthwhile to do."

"You are too kind. But what of Branwell?"

"It is in good hands, or so my retainers tell me often and often, while they are shooing me away in the same breath. They believe I am in need of a holiday, and so I am taking one."

"Then I will certainly lend you the benefit of my experience, sir, for it is suddenly my greatest aspiration to be a guide," she said, dimples peeping as she walked on. "We must only come to an agreement upon my fee."

Tom looked scandalized. "You could not stoop to accepting money—that is unless you are a very capital guide. But then, you have not yet begun, so how can you tell?"

"I shall be a famous guide, I will have you know, sir," she said, lifting her chin. "Better than any other you have had the pleasure to hire."

"Well, that is something, for I have never hired a guide." Tom looked at her askance. "But I wish to hire a capital guide, not merely a famous one."

"Oh?" she said, raising her brows imperiously. "Then you are exposing your ignorance, Mr. Breckinridge, for in Brighton a famous guide may ask twice the fee of a capital one."

Tom nodded. "I see I have mistaken the matter." They had reached her doorstep, and stopping, he withdrew his purse and peeked inside. "I fear I shall be pressed for funds. I don't suppose you should be willing to offer me a discount, on account of our long friendship?"

"I will give the matter some thought," she said, hesitating on the step. "Will you come in? Mama is at home, and I am sure she will like to see you."

Tom, admirably masking his delight at this unanticipated civility, bowed. "It will be my pleasure, ma'am, for we may discuss our arrangement further."

Diana giggled and ushered him into the house, up the stairs and into the drawing room, where Mrs. Marshall sat with her embroidery.

"Mr. Breckinridge!" she said, rising instantly and putting out her hand. "What a delightful surprise. I did not imagine we should have you here today."

Feeling rather boyish, Tom said, "Ran smash into Diana at the music library of all places, and there was nothing for it but to see her home."

"How positively providential!" was his hostess's unblushing reply. "Come, sit and tell me how you have been amusing yourself these two days."

"He has done some sea-bathing, Mama, if you can imagine!" said Diana.

Mrs. Marshall opened her eyes at this. "How singular! But then, everyone must try it at some time or other. I suppose the lure of the waves was too strong?"

Feeling slightly sick at the mere mention of waves, Tom only smiled wanly. "Diana has very kindly offered to be my guide while I am in Brighton. She claims to have seen everything there is to see."

"I fancy that is not too far from the truth, Mr. Breckinridge, for we are forever coming here, as you well know. But she will make a famous guide, to be sure."

Tom and Diana exchanged a look, which was not wasted on Mrs. Marshall. Smiling complacently, she said with a mischievous twinkle, "Diana, you must take him to the library and get him a telescope. There are ever so many things to see through the telescopes, Mr. Breckinridge—you cannot imagine!"

"Mama!" cried Diana. "Do not heed her, Tom, for she is only funning. It is scandalous what those telescopes are used for, when they are meant to be used for the enjoyment of the scenery."

Tom, whose neck had heated at Mrs. Marshall's speech, nevertheless understood that she was harmless and undertook to enter into her joke. Looking grave, he shook his head over Diana's words, evincing an admirable disgust for anything smacking of impropriety, and remarked that he did not know what the world was coming to.

Mrs. Marshall, wholeheartedly enjoying the exchange, commanded herself enough to say, "If Diana is to show you about, Mr. Breckinridge, you must take her driving, for though Brighton itself is full of wonders, the true sights are in the countryside."

"Certainly, ma'am," said Tom with alacrity. "I have my curricle, as you know, and shall be delighted to drive her about. And if Diana has brought her mare, I have had mine brought down from Branwell, and we may go hacking over the countryside together."

Both Diana and her mother approved of this scheme, and Mrs. Marshall, believing everything to be going according to plan, invited Tom to dinner the following evening and then retired behind her work basket and serenely allowed the young people to visit uninterrupted.

After half an hour, Tom rose to take his leave, and Diana accompanied him downstairs. As she gave him her hand, she said, "Do you attend the assembly Thursday at the Old Ship Rooms? They are not often held in the summer, as so many Society ladies hold their own private balls. It is an event when there is a public assembly anymore."

"I am partial to assemblies, but never more so when Miss Marshall is in attendance."

She colored prettily and assured him she would be there.

He adjusted the hat on his head and said, "That is well, for I am put in mind of an obligation you have to me."

Diana blinked. "What is that?"

"You promised me a dance—and a supper dance at that—which you never made good on."

She ducked her head with a rueful smile. "Of course, sir. Yet another odious omission for which I will now make amends. I will dance with you if you go to the assembly."

"I imagine I can bring myself to it, if you will engage for the supper dance," said Tom.

Having received her promise that she did, Tom bent to lightly kiss her fingers, and went away in a better mood than he had enjoyed for a month.

He was in such good spirits that an excellent thought occurred to him, and he betook himself back to German Place, entering the Music Library once more. At the counter, he inquired if he could order music from London, and after receiving the information that this was a common occurrence, and that such an order generally could be filled within a week if an extra shilling were paid on the subscription, he placed an order for Mozart's *Kleine Gigue in G*, requesting that it be delivered to Miss Marshall in the Royal Crescent, as soon as it had arrived. After paying the clerk, he exited the shop and went on his way to the Ship, firm in the belief that the Marine Parade was the pleasantest street, and the stretch of sea the pleasantest view, and Brighton the fairest spot in all the earth.

Chapter 15

THE FOLLOWING MORNING, Tom was met by Reginald while exercising his hack on the Steyne, and was induced to take breakfast at the Brighton Club. Here, they met Lord Bentley, who had evidently stayed up all night at cards.

"Lost pretty heavily, too, I see," said Reginald, triumphantly scooping up a pile of vowels that lay at the elbow of Bentley's competitor, who was sprawled, snoring, in his seat.

Bentley acknowledged this with a groan and rubbed his temples. "Never take brandy after four in the morning, sir. Fuddles the senses. Devil of a head I've got! What's the time?"

"Past ten o'clock, my lord," said Reginald brightly. "Will you join us for breakfast, or were you wanting your bed?"

His lordship declined their hospitality, declaring that the very idea of food nauseated him, and that he must be going home. Reginald watched him totter out with a grin, then signaled Tom to follow him into the dining room, where he introduced him to two more cronies, Mr. Trenton and Sir Humphrey Gosford. They all settled down to a table and ordered breakfast, which they devoured to the gleeful telling of Lord Bentley's defeat at the gaming table.

As the other men laughed over their friend's misfortune, Tom saw again in them the countenances of the men who had come often to his father's house when he was young, and whom he had watched through the rails of the banister as they milled about in the hall, readying themselves for the hunt or a race or a "friendly" game of cards. These men had proved themselves no friends to his father, and Tom had no wish to follow in his unwise father's footsteps—a gull to be gulled and a flat ripe for the taking.

It seemed, however, that this course was furthest from their minds, for they treated Tom with jovial bonhomie but did not press him, other than a brief and friendly inquiry, to play at cards. They did engage to take him next morning over the downs, and then regaled him with stories of the hunt, which threw off there regularly in the winter.

That evening, Tom dressed with care and presented himself in the Royal Crescent at ten minutes to six o'clock. He was ushered into the drawing room as usual but instead of Diana and Mrs. Marshall there to meet him, he received a welcome from Mr. Marshall that could only be described as grudging.

"Had no idea you'd been invited, Breckinridge," he said, shaking Tom's hand peremptorily. "Suppose I ought to have asked Mrs. Marshall, though, for you know what females are."

Blinking at this cryptic utterance, Tom thought it wise to simply observe the civilities, and asked his host how the Indian Vapor Baths had treated him. This was a felicitous choice, and filled the next five minutes with a monologue of healthful advice which ended only with the entrance of Mrs. and Miss Marshall into the room. But no sooner had they finished their greetings than the door once again opened, this time to admit the Throckmortons and Mr. Popplewell into their midst.

Tom's heart sank, but after a stern reminder to himself that he had nothing to fear from Reggie on Diana's account, he straightened his spine and determined not to fall for any of the scoundrel's tricks while under Mr. Marshall's observation.

This proved more difficult than he had imagined, for Popplewell seemed intent on destroying his credibility with every turn. Reggie's demeanor was all that was jovial and friendly, but in the five minutes that elapsed before Kittering announced dinner, Tom's hack, which he had bred himself, had been laughingly stigmatized as a slug, his groom as a wastrel, and even his curricle as shoddy. Throughout this volley, Tom stood firmly, suppressing his desire to plant Popplewell a facer— which he fancied would be easy to do to so frippery a gentleman—and shrugging everything off as the joke Reggie made it out to be.

As they entered the dining room and took their places, Mr. Marshall grumbled, "We are so crowded in this pokey dining room. Whyever did you choose such a place, my dear?"

"It was your choice, my dear," was Mrs. Marshall's placid reply.

To which her husband responded, "Oh! Yes, well, when one is aware of the limitations of the dining room, one ought to restrict the numbers at table."

"I thought I had, my dear, and if you had consulted me before inviting Reginald, I should have been in a position to warn you of the consequences. However, you did not, so we must make the best of it, mustn't we?"

This was answered with a huff and a muttering about never having a quiet family dinner, which was not very encouraging to Tom. As Diana had been placed at his side, however, he soon found much to console him in her smiles and bright conversation.

During the second course, the tables turned, as it were, for Popplewell thought to press his advantage as an old family friend and throw convention to the winds, conversing across the table to Diana as though Tom were not there. Tom could not long be affronted by this, for none of the Marshalls or Throckmortons seemed to mind it in the least, and he quickly gathered that any complaint he made on the matter would be looked upon as unreasonable. He was forced to be content, therefore, with snatches of conversation with Diana, had between the long reminiscences shared by all the others, to which he listened with a determined interest for the sake of not appearing put out.

After dinner, Popplewell did not put himself to any trouble to bring Tom into the political conversation Mr. Marshall instantly instigated, but here Tom was able to serve himself, interpolating comments on the issue of grazing rights in Exmoor forest that made Mr. Marshall look twice at him, and even listen with less than disapproval to his opinions. Popplewell, surprised at Tom's comprehension of matters he had assumed well outside the ken of a mere gentleman farmer, was unable to tease him any more than to accuse him of studying up on the newspapers since last he had seen him.

With this small victory under his belt, Tom joined the ladies in the drawing room with something like confidence, and greeted the announcement that Diana was to play for them as manna from heaven. Here was a situation that Popplewell could not manipulate against him, he thought, and he settled in to enjoy a peaceful interlude of delightful music.

But he soon found that he was mistaken. Popplewell sat sedately through the first piece, listening in evident enjoyment until the end, but as the second piece began, and before Tom knew what was going forward, Popplewell was at the instrument turning the pages for Diana, and bending annoyingly close to do so. There were innumerable smiles and gentle comments exchanged between them the while, and it was all Tom could do to keep the smile pasted to his lips and the irritation from his countenance until the song had ended.

But Popplewell was not done yet, for he next suggested a duet, and when Diana insisted she did not sing, he altered to a request that she accompany him as he sang. As he was possessed of a fine, rich baritone, his singing was inexpressibly odious to Tom's ears, but Tom bore the wretchedness of the interminably long ballad with fortitude, only shrugging once or twice during the performance.

When this was understood to be the last of the music, Tom felt some relief, but was wary of Popplewell's next move. Whatever this was to be, however, was happily prevented by Mrs. Marshall, who begged dear Reggie to indulge Mr. Marshall and the Throckmortons in a game of whist, which he could not very well refuse to do. As she then settled very quietly to her embroidery, this left Tom and Diana to amuse one another, and the whist game lingering long due to Mr. Marshall's frequent attempts at dialog wholly unrelated to the play, Tom's mood had ample opportunity to mellow, and he left the party at last with the sense that it had been a rather pleasant evening after all.

The following morning, true to their appointment, Popplewell and his friends met Tom with their horses at the Ship and led him out along Church Street to the Steyning turnpike, which would take them northwest out of town and across the downs.

"That's a fine nag you've got, Breckinridge," said Mr. Dixon, himself upon a large roan stallion that looked to be easily touched in the wind. "Get it at Tatt's?"

Before Tom could reply Popplewell said, "Nothing so unexceptionable. It's from his own stock, which any man calling himself a true horseman could see at a glance."

Taking this to mean Popplewell believed his horse to be inferior, as he had implied last night, Tom retorted, "A true horseman would be willing to prove those words."

"I beg your pardon," said Popplewell, "for I fancy I've struck you on the raw. It was only a joke."

"Must know better than to make game of a man's mount," said Dixon. "Bad form, Reggie."

Popplewell assumed a contrite expression. "A thousand apologies, Breckinridge. How may I make amends?"

Tom could think of many ways Popplewell could make amends—namely taking himself off to Ashurst and leaving Tom in peace, or finding another heiress to plague than Diana. But he said only, "Pit your nag against mine."

Popplewell laughed but eyed him with a speculative gleam. "What's the wager?"

"Need there be one? A race is enough for me."

"A race is a race, but a wager—Well, if you've not got the stomach for it," said Popplewell, turning away.

"Twenty guineas to the winner of a race, here and now," said Tom.

Popplewell turned back to him with a smug smile. "Very well. But for that price, it mustn't be too long. We have the ride yet to Devil's Dyke."

"Certainly," said Tom. "Dixon will choose the course and be the judge."

"Capital," cried Dixon, turning his horse to allow him to survey the landscape. "From the church to the Lewes turnpike. Good, level road and the horses will recover quickly."

By this time, Lord Bentley, Mr. Trenton, and Sir Humphrey had ridden back to inquire what was keeping them and entered instantly into the wager, Sir Humphrey offering odds.

"Two to one," he said, measuring up Tom's mount with a practiced eye.

This was enough to excite the rest of them, and they spent the next five minutes finalizing bets and jotting them down in Mr. Dixon's notebook. Then Tom and Popplewell walked their mounts up to the starting mark and awaited Dixon's signal.

It was given—a shout and a dropped hand—and the two were off, their horses' hooves pounding along the packed earth. This was no paved road like the New Road out of Findon, but a dry, dusty highway that thankfully had no potholes to speak of due to the unusually hot and dry summer thus far. Tom's chief concern was that the road was new to him, while Popplewell must know it like the back of his hand, and he was not so sanguine as to believe that Reggie—or Dixon for that matter—would not try to better their chances by foul means. But Dixon was true to his word, for the road was level and smooth and neither horse seemed at all distressed by it.

Tom was no jockey, nor did he breed race horses, precisely, but he had entered that business because one of the few instincts he had inherited from his father was how to judge horseflesh. When first he had seen Popplewell's showy chestnut he could tell at a glance that its back was too short for speed, and that its long, elegant legs were better for high stepping than racing. It was a fine animal, to be sure, and could be put to good use on the strut in Hyde Park or on a canter at Richmond. But Tom's horse, though bred for stamina rather than speed, had shown a surprising aptitude for racing when put to her paces at Branwell, and her master was much mistaken if she would not easily win a short race on level road in the cool of the morning.

Thus, Tom allowed Popplewell to pull ahead, watching the chestnut's motion and gauging the best opportunity to make his own move. When the course was two-thirds run, he judged it best to give his horse her head, and they leaped forward. Just as Tom had suspected, they flew to catch Popplewell, whose horse's stride could not match Tom's mare's, and passed him to win by a length.

Tom walked his mount for a minute or two, then led her over to the trough that stood before a small shed at the intersection of the turnpikes, where the others had gathered. After receiving various congratulations, he turned to Popplewell.

"Well run," he said, putting out his hand.

Popplewell took it with a grin. "I'd no notion you were such a knowing one, Breckinridge, with your horse at least."

"Knows his horseflesh, you mean, Reggie!" cried Mr. Trenton, accepting his winnings from Sir Humphrey.

"I'll even allow that," said Popplewell, shrugging.

"Don't know if I've ever seen a better finish at Newmarket," put in Mr. Dixon, coming forward to pat Tom's horse on the neck. "I've a mind to buy her from you. By the by, what's her name?"

"Fida," said Tom, attempting with tolerable success to keep the smugness he felt from his countenance. "And she's not for sale. However, I have four or five very promising colts in my stables at Branwell if you have a mind to make the journey to see them."

Dixon grinned and shook hands, saying, "I might just find it necessary to do that, after what I've just seen."

After the horses had adequately rested, they mounted again and rambled along for four or five miles, chatting jovially of hunts and runs which they had all enjoyed over the years. They pointed out where such and such hunt had thrown off in '15, and where so and so had overrun his hounds in '13, and where so and so nearly broke his neck in '17. Tom listened to it with amiable tolerance, not being inclined toward hunting himself, but mellowed by the lingering sense of satisfaction from having so handily put Popplewell in his place.

They at last came to the top of a long, slow climb that ended in an expanse of hilltop surrounded by a low berm, which had formerly been, Tom was informed, the wall of a Roman camp. Tying their horses at an available post, they walked north beyond the wall where they found themselves at a steep declivity called Devil's Dyke—so named for the legend that claimed the devil, intent upon drowning half of Sussex, had come by night to dig a monstrous trench but was surprised in his work by an intrepid old woman who scared him away with her candle, which he thought was the sun.

"Sounds an unlikely story," said Mr. Trenton, looking out over the steep valley.

"'Course it is, cod's head," replied Mr. Dixon. "It's a faerie story for children. This valley was dug by natural forces over hundreds of years."

"But that the devil should think a trifling old candle was the sun—"

"It wasn't the candle, precisely, but the light, for a cock crew and the devil took it to be the dawn."

"Well, it's my belief the devil ain't very wily."

"I tell you it's a nursery story, sapskull—"

Tom moved away from the bickering gentlemen and skirted around two groups of visitors, with which the hilltop was amply provided, this being a popular resort for summer excursions. There was even a small marquee that had been set up to dispense refreshments to those who had not thought to provide for themselves. Tom walked beyond these obstructions to the outermost point of the hill and looked out over the miles of downs that were visible from its great height.

"It's the tallest hill in Sussex," said Popplewell's voice from beside him.

Scarcely keeping from rolling his eyes at Reginald's continually popping up where he was least wanted, Tom turned to him. "So it seems. One could, I imagine, see the whole of the county from here."

"Very nearly," said Popplewell. "And if you walk around the hill to the south, you may see all along the coast, from Beachyhead to the Isle of Wight, and far out into the Channel."

"It is no wonder, then, that the Romans chose it for a camp."

Popplewell nodded. "They chose Cissbury for that reason as well. They could light a signal here and the guards on Cissbury could see it, and vice versa. It was a way to send messages to and from the coast."

"And here I thought it was merely the presence of faeries on these high places that made them so interesting."

This made Reginald smile, and Tom waited for him to come to whatever point he had followed him to make.

After an extended few minutes of gazing out over the valley, Popplewell said, "Diana and I grew up roaming these downs. We learned to ride our ponies between Findon and Ashurst, and when we were old enough to venture farther, we came as far as Bramber together. We were often on long rambles together."

"But then you were apart for some years," mused Tom. "And I am much mistaken if you did not grow somewhat distant."

Popplewell turned to him with a wry smile. "Oh, not distant, sir.

Whatever transformations Diana and I underwent over the past four years or so did not distance us, not materially. We are as close as ever we were, I assure you."

"May I know what is your point, Popplewell?"

His companion sighed. "I merely wish to make it plain to you, Breckinridge, that there is a deep bond between our families—the Popplewells and the Marshalls. It is one that will not be broken easily."

"If you imagine that my wish is to break your bond, you are mistaken, sir. On the contrary, my actions prove that my whole desire is to make a friend of you."

"How moving, Breckinridge. And here I had fancied myself generous in bringing *you* into *my* circle."

Tom laughed. "Think what you will, Popplewell. It is for Diana's sake that I have accepted your overtures."

Popplewell regarded him. "You hope to sway her by making up to me?"

"Not in the least. It pains her that we have been at odds." Tom turned to face him. "I would not injure her for the world, you see. Thus, I have put aside my own sentiments and done my possible to like you."

Popplewell digested this. "Very well, Breckinridge. I will take you at your word, for which I trust I will be recompensed. I, also, do not wish to give Diana pain, and so will do all in my power to allow our friendship to flourish. We must begin by ceasing to stand on ceremony. I beg you will call me Reggie. Everyone does, you know."

So saying, he put out his hand, and Tom, considering that Popplewell had no notion of what would cause Diana pain, and determining to shield her as much as possible from his inevitable lapses, shook it.

Chapter 16

THURSDAY CAME, AND the assembly at the Old Ship Rooms, which were not such as those at Almack's, for nothing could rival that great place. This did not injure them in Tom's eyes, however, for he was used to the smaller assemblies of Berkhampstead, and rather looked forward to a more intimate evening in Diana's company, without a crush of Town Beaux about her.

He had long ago accepted that Popplewell would be one of their circle at the assembly, which was not quite the ideal, but he faced the fact with fortitude, for only under such a circumstance would he be enabled to exhibit the burgeoning friendship between himself and his rival, thus proving his faith to Diana. He also expected that Diana's continued exposure to both himself and Reginald could not but bring to light their vast differences, and he trusted that she would inevitably begin to show her preference for himself in a way that would undermine Reginald's insufferable confidence in his superiority.

Tom also hoped to see and be seen by Mr. Marshall, for he had taken a notion to try what Iris had implied—if Mr. Marshall could not be swayed by the power of his own observation, he may be brought to change his mind through sheer force of repetition. With this in mind, Tom thought to be at the rooms when the Marshalls arrived, but not knowing when this would be, he presented himself at the opening of the rooms at eight. The Marshalls had no similar idea of punctuality, however, and he was made to wait some time, beguiling the half-hour by signing his name in the book and promptly being required by Mr. Forth, the Master of Ceremonies, to partner a shy young damsel in the minuet.

When the dance was over, he took refuge at the refreshment table under the musician's balcony, and was therefore privileged to witness Diana's arrival on Reggie's arm. He had time only for a small pang at this, for Diana perceived him almost instantly and came directly to him, plainly pleased to see him. His delight only grew as she proceeded to chatter to him with what he flattered himself to be many more blushing smiles than she directed to her old childhood friend.

Popplewell, unable to claim the supper dance, had taken Diana's first two dances instead, and when the set struck up, Tom availed himself of Mr. Forth's good offices to be introduced to another young lady, refusing to bolster Reginald's self-consequence by propping up the wall like a jealous beau. This arrangement having taken some minutes to effect, he was not in the same set with Diana, which he quickly comprehended was just as well, for he had much to do already—conversing affably with his partner and remembering the steps—without having Diana's smiling lips and bright eyes forever in his direct gaze. He was able to glimpse her progress from time to time, which was enough to see that though she enjoyed herself, it was not more than she was wont to do when dancing with him.

At last the dance ended and, Popplewell having been drawn away by another acquaintance for the interval, Tom found himself the sole beneficiary of Diana's smiles. Making the most of the circumstance, he procured for her a glass of lemonade and led her to a quieter corner where they could converse with more ease.

"We did not see you yesterday, Tom. Will you think me impertinent to inquire what, beyond sea-bathing and haunting music libraries, you find to do with yourself?" asked Diana, sipping her lemonade.

Tom shrugged. "This and that. I spend the majority of my time with Reggie and his friends."

"'Reggie?' Since when do you call Mr. Popplewell 'Reggie,' Tom?"

"Since he invited me to do so, Diana."

"You see?" she said, beaming. "He is no villain, just as you are not."

"No, he is not," he said amicably. "To own the truth, I might have bored myself to death by now without his good offices."

"Except when you had been sea-bathing?" she asked archly.

Tom answered truthfully that the sea-bathing was something he had not been privileged to repeat, but when she inquired if he had taken her father's advice and tried the Vapor Baths, he fell into a stammering explanation that of course he still intended to go.

Before he had got too much entangled, she laughed, saying, "Do not tease yourself, Tom. I am glad you have enjoyed yourself, whatever your entertainments, for otherwise you would never have been able to make a friend of Reggie. What has he done to amuse you?"

"We have gone riding over the downs and breakfasted at the Brighton Club and patronized the library—" But believing there was no occasion to increase Diana's estimation of Reginald's goodness, Tom seized the opportunity to turn the subject. "Do you know, Diana, the libraries are the most extraordinary places, nothing like in London. Such a rabble and rumpus, and the noise! There is too much going on in those places by half. But the most ridiculous thing—I must beg you, oh famous guide—pray explain to me the point of a Loo, for if you do not, I am persuaded I shall never know what the devil it is all about."

She laughed, setting down her empty glass. "I knew you could not go to the library for anything so ordinary as a book! But I will tell you about the Loos, for they are not so outlandish as it seems. They are sweepstakes contrived to replace the raffles, for those were outlawed—but I see you do not even know about that. The libraries, at least outside the very large cities, do not make enough money on subscriptions alone, it seems, for there is a shocking number of persons who take out books and never return them, and this is a great burden to the libraries. They began holding raffles to raise funds to replenish their collections, but these, as I said, were outlawed. Some years ago, they got approval to hold Loos, which have many features of the game of loo, but that operate entirely on chance, and can be a great deal of fun, too."

"But everyone acts as though they are in a farce, with the players taking up characters."

"Yes—but that is what makes the fun!"

Tom opined that one person's idea of fun was very different from another's, and Diana laughed again. "I suppose it would be, for now that I think of it, I cannot imagine you play-acting."

This was not precisely salutary to Tom's self-esteem, for he could only imagine her to be comparing him with Reginald—who did a great deal too much play-acting, in Tom's opinion—and he attempted to divert her thoughts once more. "But you still have not told me how the game is played."

"Oh! The play is simple enough—one lays down a shilling on a number, and when there are eight subscribers, the bidding is closed. Then the numbers are called out as the cards are turned over one by one, and the number that is called when Pam is turned is the winner. But the fun is the wit used to entice the observers to enter, and the clever names the subscribers give their characters. There is even some music involved to entertain the group. It is very droll, and an excellent way to raise funds."

Tom was doubtful, but as she engaged herself to show him how it worked one of these days, he accepted her offer, reasoning that even if the game turned out as weirdly as he fancied, he would at least have spent time with Diana. But before he could be carried away by this pleasant notion, Mr. Marshall emerged from the card room and bore down upon them.

"Diana, my dear, I see you are enjoying yourself. Capital! Capital." He then perceived Tom at her side and his delight diminished a trifle. Blinking, he began to look about the room. "Where is Reginald, my dear? Is he not to partner you tonight?"

"He was my first partner, Papa," answered Diana, "but he cannot claim my every dance. How singular it would look! You cannot wish me to be whispered about as fast."

Mr. Marshall harrumphed. "Nonsense! Reginald is like a brother to you—that is, like a cousin. There could be no question of impropriety in your standing up with such a well-known acquaintance."

"Perhaps not, Papa; however, I should not like to do so when there are so many other amiable gentlemen present, and as you see, Reggie has no notion of monopolizing me." She indicated Reggie, who was conversing animatedly with the pretty young lady who had caught his eye.

"Very well," said Mr. Marshall, though without much conviction. "As long as you are happy, my love."

With a bow to Tom, he returned to the card room, and Diana looked an apology at her companion. "He is very protective of my interests, as you may see."

"It is right and proper that he should be," said Tom magnanimously, fairly easily suppressing his recurring desire to send Reginald to grass. "I trust you feel no compunction in sharing my company."

"Dear me, no!" cried Diana, laughing. "I could stay all night in your company, without the least scruple." But no sooner were the words past her lips than she realized what she had said, and she pressed a hand to her mouth, her cheeks suffused with color. "Good gracious, my careless tongue!"

Blushing himself, Tom strove to keep the grin from his face, with indifferent success. "Do not tease yourself, Diana. I take your meaning."

Her wide eyes met his. "Do you?"

With a rush of comprehension, he blinked and felt the heat rise up his neck.

She turned away, her color deepening as well. "I am as bad as Iris! Dear me, what next will I say?"

Tom, valiantly making a push to regain his countenance for her sake, said gallantly, "It is a mark of your honesty and trust, Diana. I hope you will always say just what you wish to say to me." And taking her hand, he lifted it to his lips and kissed it.

Her fingers returned the pressure of his for a fleeting instant, then she recovered her hand, seeking in her reticule for her fan. Upon finding it, she plied it for some minutes to ease her burning countenance, as Tom, with some effort, wiped the rather foolish smile from his face and looked about with the utmost nonchalance.

At last, she recovered enough to peep up at him, saying, "You are a good friend to let such an impertinence pass, Tom."

"I would be the greatest clodpole in creation to hold such a thing against you," he returned.

She smiled, looking at the dancers on the floor. "I believe you to be in earnest, but even if you were not, there is nothing to be done about it now. The dance has begun and you cannot find another partner and enter the set. You are destined to remain a wallflower with me and listen to all the ridiculous things I may choose to say to you."

Tom planted himself more firmly beside her. "You do not frighten me, Diana! Do your worst; I am here to stay. At least until Mr. Forth commandeers me for the next dance."

She giggled, and the last vestiges of her discomposure vanished, enabling her to perform the steps of their dances, when they came, with style and energy. They went in to supper in a very good humor, and when Reginald claimed Diana for the next two dances, Tom let her go with a good grace, finding another young lady to stand up with whom he charmed unknowingly with his high spirits. He was the lucky man with whom Diana danced the final set and when Mr. Marshall came to collect her, he scarcely grimaced.

Tom went round to his rooms and prepared for bed in the belief that all was coming along nicely for, given enough time, he was confident he could bring Mr. Marshall around to a right way of thinking. As he laid his head upon his pillow, it occurred to Tom that Reggie did not seem to be in the least hurry to claim Diana for his own, a fact which Tom found both providential and incomprehensible. He meant to take every advantage of the circumstance, but he did find it strange that Reginald, who had Mr. Marshall's unalloyed approval and who believed himself to be Diana's preferred suitor, had not made the one move that would effectively end the game at once.

The following morning, Tom paid a correct call on Diana to see how she fared after the rigors of the evening. She greeted him with such glowing humor, hinting at her excessive gratitude for his forbearance at her gaffe, that when the butler announced the arrival of Mr. Popplewell, Tom felt only mild regret.

Reginald's presence brought the now inevitable change, and despite his equanimity, Tom was much tried to bear it with patience. Much as he had done at Findon, Reggie took the conversation into his own hands without the least putting himself forward, and subtly manipulated it to cast himself in a superior light to Tom, while inviting the ladies' attentions to himself. Tom held to the fast-receding triumph of the previous evening in vain, for he was encouraged, within a very few minutes, to feel that he had nothing to contribute, was far behind Reginald in everything—particularly Diana's affections—and that it would have been better had he never come to Sussex.

Inevitably, it was at this moment that Mr. Marshall came into the room.

"Reginald, my boy!" he boomed, bearing down on the young man to pump his hand. "I could not get near you last night. It's been an age since I spoke to you!"

Reginald laughed. "Unless I am Rosamund and have slept for a hundred years, I fear I must contradict you, sir."

Mr. Marshall laughed heartily and took his seat beside Reggie. "Have you given any thought to what we last talked of?"

"Well, sir," said Reginald, adjusting his tone and countenance to one of respectful consideration, "I hope I am always grateful for your advice, and have no doubt I would profit by following it. However, I must own I am persuaded this particular action would be precipitate. It is uncertain when I shall come into the viscountcy, after all. Lord Belstone is not so very old—it could be years."

"Hmm, just so," conceded Mr. Marshall, his brow furrowing. "However, as his heir you may have some sway with the old gentleman. Do you not think, perhaps, you could speak to him?"

Reginald flashed his most winning smile. "As I am only just acquainted with his lordship, sir, I must again demur. That sort of thing, I am persuaded, would require a longer-standing relationship, and I would hate the old man to think me coming, just as we are getting to know one another."

"To be sure, to be sure," said Mr. Marshall reasonably. "You are very wise for one so young. It could wait a month or two. Warm him up a bit, then make your wishes known—that sort of thing."

Reginald murmured something that could have been acquiescence, and Mr. Marshall took it as such. He stood, turning to shake hands again.

"I'm off to the Indian Vapor Baths," Mr. Marshall said. "The Shampooing treatment does wonders for the rheumatism. You don't have any ailments, do you? Not like Mr. Breckinridge, here? No skin eruption or lumbago? He will tell you, the treatment is wonderfully effective on all sorts of—no? But of course you would not. Not a healthy young man like you. Well, good day."

He kissed Mrs. Marshall and went away, while Tom, rigid and red-faced, endured a wickedly curious look from Reginald. Before Tom could wish to sink into the floor, however, Diana whispered in a dramatic undertone, "Good heavens, Reggie, what secrets can you have with my father?"

"Perhaps we should ask Tom what secrets he has."

Tom tugged at his neck cloth, which suddenly seemed too tight, but Diana persisted, saying, "Come now, Reggie! What was Papa speaking of?"

Sighing gustily, Reginald turned his eye away from Tom and said, "Only that he believes me to possess great political power, now that I am to inherit a rotten borough."

Tom was momentarily roused from his mortification. "Your viscountcy holds a rotten borough? Both seats?"

Reginald nodded. "It is a great bore, for I had rather not have them. What do I want with seats that everyone will fight over? The idea of making some money from selling them is tempting, I own, but I should never do it."

This was said with such an air of virtue that Tom was hard pressed not to roll his eyes. However, Diana nodded solemnly and inquired what good her father thought they could do him.

"He hopes to fill them with persons who are like-minded to him, but I do not know what good it could do for his bill. The seats will not be mine for years, perhaps."

"Dear me," cried Mrs. Marshall, throwing up her hands. "He has not been pestering you over that odious bill! My dear Reginald, you must pardon him." She turned to Tom and said, by way of explanation, "Mr. Marshall has a bill that he wishes to push through Commons, and he hopes, no doubt, to control the seats to secure the majority. He has no sense of moderation whatsoever when it comes to his politics. It is his passion, and he cannot see anything but his own ideals."

"We must be grateful that Papa's ideals are generally excellent," said Diana. "I confess myself shocked that he would think to press such an advantage, Reggie."

"Do not be over-anxious, I beg," said Reggie, with his caressing smile. "I do not care at all for politics. If I had those seats today, they would be his for the asking, and with my good wishes. I fear I am so backward in politics that I should only make a mull of things were I to involve myself. God help us if I elect to take my seat in the House of Lords."

Both ladies shook their heads over this, exclaiming that he was too modest, and that he had been formed for such a distinction. Tom, still smarting from the mortifying effects of Reginald's adroit handling, could not but agree that dear Reggie was formed for swaying the masses, and God help them if ever he was put in a position to do so.

But Tom's sentiments upon the matter went unexpressed, for he had been too struck by the implications of what he had just learned to ruminate long upon Reginald's fitness for the House of Lords. It was now apparent why his struggle to ingratiate himself with Mr. Marshall was all but vain, for though he possessed much virtue and character that Reggie lacked, he would never be in possession of two seats of Parliament that could be filled almost at will by the one who controlled them. Such an allurement would be almost impossible for a man of Mr. Marshall's inclinations to relinquish, even, Tom feared, at the expense of his daughter's heart.

Tom was also struck again by the wonder that Popplewell did not press his advantage, for it seemed as though nothing stood in his way. It was unaccountable, and Tom found it all too easy to suspect him of ungentlemanly motives, no matter how disinterestedly he attempted to look at the matter.

Chapter 17

Now that the principal cause of Mr. Marshall's preference for Reginald had been made clear, Tom was at a loss as to how to raise himself in the older gentleman's estimation, and wondered if it was even possible. Even had Tom an interest in politics, the greatest office to which he could ever aspire was that of magistrate. This, he knew, was nothing in the grand scheme of things, especially when contrasted with that of a lord with a rotten borough, and he despaired now more than ever of achieving what Mrs. Marshall and Iris had hinted was possible—the concession of Mr. Marshall to his suit.

With these thoughts still heavy in his mind the following day, he went to the Brighton Club where he had agreed to meet Reginald. He found him in the card room, at whist with Mr. Dixon, Mr. Trenton and Sir Humphrey Gosford. Lord Bentley stood over them, watching the game with no little evidence of boredom.

"Ah! Breckinridge!" he cried upon perceiving Tom. "Just the man I want. Play at piquet? If you do not indulge me then I fear that you, too, will be made to be a Woodpecker, and to watch what you cannot join."

Tom obligingly settled down to an empty table nearby.

Lord Bentley lost the cut and dealt the cards. "How long have you known Reggie, Breckinridge?"

"Only a few months. We met in London—he is the childhood friend of a mutual acquaintance."

Bentley inquired the name of the acquaintance and when Tom named Miss Marshall, he surprised him by saying, "Lively little thing, Miss Marshall, and pretty, too. If the lady were not too young for my taste, I might be tempted to have a touch at her myself."

"I'd no notion you knew of her," said Tom stiffly.

Bentley shrugged. "Reggie speaks of her from time to time. Finds her delightful company."

"Merely delightful?" Brows furrowed, Tom darted a look to Reginald, who played intently at a small distance, oblivious to their conversation. "I was persuaded he thought more of her than that."

Bentley suggested they declare—and they came up very evenly—before he answered. "Reggie's not in the market for a wife. At least, I do not think so. Too young—as are you. Still in your salad days."

"I suppose so," said Tom, looking intently at his cards but considering Bentley's words.

Lord Bentley cast him a knowing glance. "Have an interest there yourself?"

Tom glanced up quickly, realizing too late his slip. Lord Bentley whistled. "There's a romance for you! Friends and rivals, eh?"

"Perhaps not, if Reggie does not look for marriage."

Lord Bentley studied his hand. "Has a tidy fortune, don't she?"

"Respectable," Tom said nonchalantly.

They played on, and Tom won the first partie, though Bentley avoided a Rubicon. Tom dealt the next hand in silence.

"Wouldn't worry too much if I were you," said Bentley, watching Tom's face.

"About what?"

"About Reggie running a rig on you. Wouldn't think he could—not with your looks. Bit of a rover, Reggie," said Bentley, exchanging three cards. "I'd say he's unlikely to settle for years yet."

They declared and Tom took several tricks, saying carefully, "It does seem that Reggie is in no hurry to declare himself."

"It seems so."

Bentley dealt the next hand and they played it through. Tom earned a repique and, at the end of the partie, Rubiconed his opponent. With some confidence, he cut the deck and lost, earning the deal.

As Tom dealt the hand, Bentley mused, "Come to think on it, things have changed since the autumn. Bit of a catch now, is Reggie. What with inheriting his father's estate, which earns somewhere in the region of four thousand a year, and the viscountcy, moreover—" He whistled.

They exchanged cards and declared, and Bentley was the clear winner, earning a pique. Tom watched in silence as his opponent dealt the next hand.

"How much are you worth, Breckinridge?" asked Bentley conversationally.

Tom chewed his lip, choosing his discards. "Not as much as Reggie's viscountcy."

"Ah, well," said his lordship, regarding his hand. "One can't have everything." He smiled in a fatherly way as Tom declared and said, "I'm afraid you're not at all good, sir." He laid out his cards, with forty-one points. "I fear you are piqued, repiqued, and capotted."

Tom gazed at his cards, then at him and put down his hand. "Well done, Bentley. I felicitate you on an excellent game. Very well managed."

Reginald called over from the other table, "Has he scalped you, Breckinridge? Poor man. He does that from time to time. Not to worry, however; he can never keep a run of luck long."

"You'll get him next time!" added Mr. Dixon bracingly.

Tom forced a laugh, doling out Bentley's winnings at five shillings a point, according to club policy. "I had better, boys, or I shall be obliged to sell my fob."

They laughed and slapped him on the back, declaring that if the fob didn't cover his losses, there was always his horse.

Tom left all this jocularity after a few more minutes and exited the club with a grim and thoughtful brow. He was no skilled card player, but he knew enough to sink some of his combinations during that last hand, and thus was fairly certain that Bentley had cheated. His lordship would have won the partie in any case, even without the capot, so Tom could only imagine that Bentley had cheated out of habit. It was unsurprising with the sort of man Tom suspected his lordship to be, and it was disturbing that Tom had allowed himself to be received into the bosom of a whole ring of such men.

With an odd sort of detachment, Tom looked out over the ocean, where fishing boats bobbed on the gently rolling waves. A cool breeze fanned him, and he could smell the tang of salt spray. Digging his hands deep into his pockets, he considered what Bentley had revealed about Reginald—that he did not seem eager to marry—and wondered again why he should be so eager to hint Tom away from Diana if he did not mean to secure her for himself. As he ruminated, his only logical conclusion was that Reggie wished to retain Diana for some hazy future date, perhaps after he had exhausted any hope of making a better match with a wealthier heiress. It would only be of a piece with his carelessness, and Tom once more deprecated the blind affection that connected Diana—and her father—to such a man.

Diana's voice, calling from the direction of the road, roused him from contemplation. She was mounted on her chestnut mare but she swung down, handing her reins to a groom, and hastened over the lawn to him, smiling and holding her bonnet with one hand to prevent its flying away on the breeze.

"Tom! How good to see you. Do you like the view? It is a particular favorite of mine in Brighton."

"It is a good view."

She laughed. "It is magnificent! The roll of the waves, the tiny little boats moving up and down on the swells, the seabirds soaring as if they were pasted into the sky—it all makes my heart sing."

"It is lovely," allowed Tom, "though I must own my feelings are not quite so profound."

She pursed her lips, but her eyes danced as she regarded his grave countenance. "You are blue-deviled, and I will not allow it. What do you mean to do today?"

"Perhaps I shall stand here and grow more attached to the view, as you have done."

"Pooh! You will do nothing of the sort. Have you any objection to taking out your mare? It is a splendid day for a ride."

Even Tom's grim mood was not proof against such sunny attacks, and he managed a half-smile. "It is a splendid day."

"I was just wishing for a riding companion," she said coaxingly, challenging him with her bright eyes.

This was just the sort of balm his wounded pride wanted, and his smile grew to a grin. "Shall we send off your groom and take Matthew with us?"

Diana assured him this would afford her the greatest pleasure in the world and slipped her hand into his arm, walking with him to retrieve her horse and acquaint the groom with their plans.

"Have you seen the Chalybeate yet, Tom?" she asked as they led her horse toward the Ship. At his negative, she added, "It is the most delightful little spring outside town."

"You intend to prove that you are, indeed, a famous guide, I see."

"It is something that need not be proved," she said loftily.

"I'll be the judge of that," he replied, raising a cynical brow as he looked at her askance. "It is from my pocket that your fee shall come, after all."

"Well, if you are not entirely satisfied, sir, my services shall be *gratis*."

Tom readily gave his approval to this pleasing arrangement, and Diana waited in the coffee room while Tom ordered his mare to be saddled. When they were both mounted again and Matthew following behind, Diana led him up King's Road to West Street, then out of town about half a mile, passing several large stones that had tumbled onto their sides and lay in a haphazard fashion. These, his guide primly informed him, were the remains of druidical altars, and no one really knew why there were so many.

When he teased her that perhaps it was she only who did not know, she assumed a scholarly tone and said, "I expect they were either very religious people, or they had rival factions in their priests, for that is always the way with history, is it not? If it is not one person scrambling for power, it is another. There are barrows all around as well, but they are not very exciting to see, for they are mere mounds like any other."

They stopped at the bottom of a hill near the wall of a neat house belonging to the vicar, who owned the spring. Tom helped Diana to alight amid a plethora of waiting carriages and looked about for the delightful spring. When its location was not forthcoming, he turned to inquire of his guide and discovered that Diana was walking purposefully toward a small building nearby that he had taken for an outbuilding. She informed him in her most authoritative tone that this modest edifice, comprised of two rooms connected by a columned portico, enclosed the spring.

Leaving Matthew—who declined any interest in partaking of the waters—to walk the horses, they entered the building and, by the donation of a shilling, gained access to the spring. Upon entrance into the next room, they beheld a low brick wall that created a small reservoir, into which the spring bubbled, and from which one could dip a cup of the waters. A platform had been erected over the back half of the room behind and over the spring, upon which one could climb to reach some comfortable chairs arranged around small tables. Several persons were already there gathered, sipping the waters from small tin cups as though it were the finest tea in the land.

Tom, gazing about indignantly, muttered, "It's no more than a puddle in the ground."

"Tom!" remonstrated Diana in a low whisper. "How can you say such a thing? This is the Chalybeate—everyone comes to see the Chalybeate!"

He removed his gloves, nodding at a gentleman and lady who were just leaving. "That is as it may be, Diana, but I must feel myself completely taken in. Famous guide, indeed! From your description, I was prepared for something more—delightful." He gestured with his hand at the mundane little reservoir.

"Will it retrieve my reputation, sir, to inform you that this spring has excellent mineral properties, and is prized for its medicinal value—"

"I regret to say, ma'am, it will not," murmured Tom implacably. "I fear I am far from satisfied."

She was obliged to press a hand to her mouth to smother a peal of laughter. Commanding herself, however, she took his arm and led him toward the basin. "I suppose your opinion is reasonable. The spring is rather ordinary. But if you imagine it would be more delightful in its natural state, I assure you, it would not do."

"Dashed if I see how this could be better than nature," muttered Tom.

"Your sentiments do you credit," allowed Diana, moving forward to dip some water. "However, you know not whereof you speak. In its natural state, the surface was encrusted with so many mineral deposits that all the guidebooks say it was rendered quite disgusting. You could not, I am persuaded, prefer that."

She handed the tin cup to him as she spoke and he looked at the milky water, wrinkling his nose. "I fancy I comprehend your meaning."

This earned him a mischievous look, but though he complained that the water smelled strongly of metal, she insisted that they partake, "Otherwise, your shilling will have gone to waste."

As Tom grimaced over his water, Diana sipped serenely at hers. "It is a trifle strong, I suppose. But never fear, I am told one mustn't imbibe too freely, for the medicinal properties of this spring are far greater than those at Tunbridge, and one may find oneself in greater need of physick after taking the waters than before, if one is too eager."

"Or if one has no need of physick in the first place," said Tom, relinquishing his empty cup with a shudder. Their sampling complete, he gladly led her back out into the sunshine. "Where do we go now, oh wise Guide?"

Diana raised her brow. "It is daunting to make suggestions to one so high in his notions of the delightful, but I will endeavor to impress. My fee, after all, is in jeopardy." She considered for a moment, her brow wrinkling. "Shall we walk to the church? You may see it from here, and the view is, I am certain you shall agree, delightful."

After shading his eyes against the sun to look over the downs, which were covered in spring flowers, Tom pronounced the view to be, unequivocally, delightful.

Smiling, Diana said, "And I am in full confidence that you shall find the walk delightful—indeed, I shall stake my reputation upon it."

Finding this recommendation satisfactory, Tom offered her his arm and they returned to the horses, arranging with Matthew to meet them at the church. Then they proceeded down the drive to a footpath lined with bunches of scabious, scarlet pimpernel, ragwort, and eyebright, which Tom acknowledged to be excessively pretty.

"This path is one of Brighton's most popular destinations," said Diana triumphantly. "I have been here many a time with Reggie."

Tom paused for a moment, reflecting that the day Reginald did not intrude in their conversation would be welcome indeed. "Did he take the waters?"

"Once or twice. Oddly, he also did not care for them."

"Odd that he did not care for them, or odd that he and I think similarly on that subject?" inquired Tom.

Diana considered him. "You are not so dissimilar as you may think, Tom. I had hoped that you would have seen that by now, as you are friends."

"We shall likely see soon enough, for I have allowed Reggie to initiate me into the mysteries of gaming."

"What?" cried Diana, subjecting him to a startled and searching look.

"Reggie and his friends do more than breakfast at the Brighton Club, Diana. I have been often playing at cards with them there—they are far more absorbed in the sport than I own I believe is wise."

Diana huffed. "That is not gaming. Good heaven, Tom, you gave me a turn! Everyone knows that gentlemen play at cards at their clubs, and very often run up debts, but that is not so very bad."

"Only when they do not become so enormous that they cannot pay them."

Diana paused. "You are not suggesting that Reggie is profligate?"

Tom hesitated, choosing his words carefully. "He has been so obliging as to show me his style of living, and from what I have seen, it is very different from how I should choose to live."

"That is to be expected," said Diana reasonably. "Reggie is, after all, a man of the town, while you—you are a gentleman farmer."

For all it was true, the comparison was a bit of a blow, for it forcibly reminded Tom of his dream back at Branwell, wherein she had called him a dull dog. His inevitable reflections kept him quiet as they entered the churchyard and went about the grounds, and when she commented on his silence, he told her with forced humor that he wished to reclaim himself in her view by his respectful and thoughtful contemplation of the church.

"Stupid," she said gently, pressing his arm. "You need never reclaim yourself to me, Tom Breckinridge—in any way. You are a gentleman of honor, and have no need to excuse who you are or how you live."

Reflexively, Tom covered her hand with his own, looking gravely down into her upturned face. "Diana, is it very disagreeable to you—my being a gentleman farmer?"

"Indeed, no!" she cried instantly. "I should not have you think so for the world! There are few occupations more honorable than that of a farmer, and the gentleman who undertakes it only elevates both the position and his own character. We have enough gentlemen without occupation, I daresay, for when they are young they are forever in a scrape, and when they are old they are so busy about nothing that there is no doing anything with them."

Her sincerity of expression and of word was both soothing and enervating, and his spirits revived. Looking into her bright eyes, he determined that he must make a more concerted effort to overcome his feelings of inferiority to Reggie, for then he should be more likely to gain Mr. Marshall's respect, and could ask his consent to make Diana his wife, which would make him the happiest of men.

After more wanderings amongst the tombstones, the odd names of which they read aloud for their mutual enjoyment, they walked to the road to meet Matthew, and mounted their horses for the ride back to the Royal Crescent.

When Tom at last had deposited Diana on her doorstep and said goodbye it was nearly time for the daily promenade, and crowds of sea-goers and sight-seers thronged Marine Parade. Rather than take his country-bred horse through such traffic, Tom directed her up to the quieter St. James's Street and followed it back toward the Steyne.

As he approached High Street, he was obliged to pull up as a smart carriage whipped through the intersection and flew up the street. Following the carriage's progress with indignant eyes, Tom saw it draw up in front of a townhouse where a gentleman stood at the top of the steps, looking as if he had just been knocking at the door. The gentleman turned, and Tom recognized with a disagreeable sensation that it was Reginald, dashing in a bottle green coat and pale yellow pantaloons, and tipping his hat to the lady who had just alighted from the carriage and rushed up the steps to greet him.

The lady turned to address her driver, and when she did so, Tom started. It was Mrs. Ridley, and she took Reginald's arm and proceeded with him into the house. Tom, realizing that he was staring, and not wishing to be remarked by the driver, gave his mare the office and left High Street behind.

"That were Mrs. Ridley and Mr. Popplewell," observed Matthew when he had drawn up level with Tom again.

"It was," said Tom. "And that was not his lodging."

"I didn't think it was, sir," was all Matthew thought prudent to say.

Chapter 18

THE NEXT DAY being Sunday, Tom attended services in the quaint little church he and Diana had explored, for she had mentioned that it was where her family had always gone. He arrived too late to sit with the Marshalls in their pew, however, and though after the service Mr. Marshall was not uncivil in his greetings, he hurried his wife and daughter away with prognostications of rain. The sky was cloudy, but the summer still continued hot and what rain might have fallen did not touch the parched earth.

The following day, as Tom ruminated upon his ill-fated resolution to improve his acquaintance with Mr. Marshall, he was suddenly struck by an idea so brilliant in its simplicity that he was astonished it had never occurred to him before. Resolving to lose no time in implementing so excellent a scheme, he made his way directly to the Indian Vapor Baths and dawdled about the entrance until Mr. Marshall arrived to take his regular Shampooing treatment.

"Breckinridge!" cried Mr. Marshall upon recognizing him. "Here for the vapor bath?"

"I have observed its beneficial effects, sir," said Tom in perfect truth, as they entered and paid the fee. "I must thank you for bringing me here in the first place."

Mr. Marshall chuckled amiably, motioning Tom to come along with him to the reading room, where they would wait until a spa room became available. "I don't doubt your skin eruptions are well on their way to being healed."

"I cannot even recall their having been present, sir," was the glib reply.

They entered the well-appointed reading room, where ladies and gentlemen of all ages and situations sat perusing books or periodicals of various kinds. Mr. Marshall sat on a sofa and Tom settled beside him.

"Tell me, sir," said Tom in a tone of solicitous respect, "how long have you suffered from your particular ailments?"

Mr. Marshall looked grave. "Several years now, Breckinridge. It is a misfortune of age that brings on infirmity, but it is to be anticipated by all in the human family. Little did I know how various were the ills I was fated to endure, however. One hopes for the best, but one must, in the end, accustom oneself."

Tom murmured agreement, thinking that Diana knew firsthand of older gentlemen who had too little to do, of whom she spoke on their outing. "I hope you will pardon my curiosity, sir, but I ask in fellow-feeling—when did you deduce that your ailments would be benefited by these particular vapor baths? Are not there similar baths in London?"

Mr. Marshall opened his eyes, shocked. "Do not consider the baths in London, sir, for they are nothing but chicanery. Mr. Mahomed, whose baths these are, introduced the vapor baths at his workplace in London, but the proprietor quickly forsook Mahomed's excellent practices and developed his own methods, which are vastly inferior. Mr. Mahomed could not, in honor, remain in business with such a person, and brought his practice to Brighton. And you and I, sir, shall be forever grateful! Do not, I say, allow yourself to be deceived by charlatans."

"Certainly not, sir. I thank you for your wise counsel. As a young man, I am not always in the right way of things, and must look to my elders for direction."

This speech seemed to strike Mr. Marshall as very proper, for he removed his snuff box and offered Tom a pinch. As an attendant came to summon Mr. Marshall at that moment to the spa room, Tom's refusal was not unkindly remarked, and Mr. Marshall bade his companion a hearty and pleasant farewell.

Having not considered much past meeting and conversing with Mr. Marshall at the baths, it was now borne in upon Tom that he would be expected to undertake a lengthy and foreign treatment, of which he had little understanding and no real desire to partake. His first instinct upon this realization was to slip unobtrusively out of the bath house, but having no wish to outright deceive Mr. Marshall, he steeled himself to the consequences of his precipitate choice and waited anxiously for his turn to arrive.

It was not long before the Indian attendant returned to lead him up a pair of stairs and down the corridor, gesturing for him to enter a small, marble-lined room with a low, padded table and a chair as its only furnishings. Tom was instructed to remove his clothing and give it into the keeping of the attendant, who then handed him a towel and, bowing low in the Eastern style, closed the door and left him. Tom lay on the table, glancing in some curiosity at the vents that punctuated the facing wall, and at a strange type of curtain that looked much like a dressing gown that had been hung over a door.

To his surprise, a popping and hissing noise presently ensued, and steam issued from the vents, to fill the room with a pungent odor. The effect was heady and not unpleasant, and after recovering his surprise, Tom quite forgot himself and fell asleep.

He awoke to the shocking sensation of hands massaging his limbs, and he started, ready to defend himself, only to be told by a cultured voice with a trace of Indian accent—which emanated from behind the flannel curtain—not to be alarmed, but to relax and enjoy the Shampooing treatment. This proved to be a vigorous application of soothing oils to the majority of his body and lasted several minutes. The effect, when he came to reflect upon it, was exceedingly refreshing to muscles he had not known to be aching, and he wondered that he had not been put in the way of a Shampooing treatment before.

The whole of the experience left him feeling the gratitude toward Mr. Marshall to which he had earlier only pretended, and it was with real pleasure that he met with that gentleman on his exit from the bath house.

"Mr. Marshall!" he said, taking his hand and shaking it. "Allow me to thank you again for acquainting me with the Shampooing treatment! It has exceeded my expectations."

"Certainly, my boy, certainly," replied Mr. Marshall, gratified. Smiling, he clapped Tom's shoulder and said, "Best treatment in the world for all sorts of ailments. Now you've got rid of the skin eruption, no doubt you'll begin to imagine yourself free and clear, but do not believe it! Before you know it, some other irritation will creep upon you, and you'll wish you hadn't left off the Shampooing."

"Depend upon it, sir, it would take more than perfect health to make me forget such an experience," said Tom, which so impressed Mr. Marshall that he issued him an invitation to accompany his family to the theater the following evening.

"Just a small gathering, mind you. Only Mrs. Marshall and myself and some old friends—and Diana. Of course, I expect Reginald, you know. Maybe too many in the box, come to think of it."

Before he could talk himself round to negating the invitation, however, Tom assured him he did not mind a squeeze at all, thanked him profusely for his kindness, and took hasty leave, whistling on his way to the Ship in the happy conviction that he had made a very good morning's work.

Tuesday evening Tom met the Marshalls at the theater, a fine new building facing the Pavilion Gardens. It was hardly as big as Covent Garden Theater or anything of the kind in London; however, it was handsomely appointed, with a large gallery and two tiers of boxes, all decorated in white and pink with gold embossed woodbine and Egyptian ornaments. The Prince Regent's box, to the left of the stage, was set apart by a latticed grille, ostensibly to protect His Highness from the excessive adoration of his subjects.

The box Mr. Marshall had taken for the summer season was quite large enough for the party, for Reginald had declined the invitation and Mrs. Marshall had invited only two female friends. They arranged themselves in the grey-cushioned chairs much to Tom's satisfaction, as he was given a seat in the front row with Diana. She was very pretty tonight in yellow satin with scalloped sleeves and a fetching velvet and feather headdress, and Tom found it difficult to drag his eyes away from her and to the stage.

As they awaited the rise of the curtain, Tom inquired how she had been entertaining herself since last they had met and she turned to him with shining eyes.

"I have been practicing Mozart's *Gigue*, which very unaccountably arrived at the house yesterday. I wonder if you know anything of the matter, Mr. Breckinridge?"

"Nothing at all, Miss Marshall," he said, holding back a smug smile. "How do you progress?"

Her dimple pronounced, Diana told him of her pleasure in the music until the gas lights dimmed and they were hushed by their companions.

The play was a production of *Hamlet*, with Mr. and Mrs. Kemble in the lead roles, and Tom was heartily bored by the time the curtain closed for the interval. Had not Diana been there to remind him why he came, he may have slipped out then and there; however, he wanted only to see her impish smiles at his attempts to stifle his yawns to discover that the theater was a very tolerable place, whatever happened on the stage.

As the elder members of the group joined in commendation of the performance, Tom bent his head nearer Diana's and whispered, "You cannot make me believe you like that stuff."

She giggled, hurriedly covering her mouth with her hand. "You certainly cannot make me believe that you do. But no, I am not partial to tragedies, though neither am I very partial to farces. I suppose I prefer a little of both."

"A moderate, eh?" said Tom, brow raised. "What will your father say?"

Before Diana could respond, Mrs. Marshall asked him from behind how he liked the play and Tom, pointedly ignoring Diana's glee, turned to respond with pleasant mendacity when the curtain behind them parted and Reginald walked in, Mrs. Ridley on his arm.

"You will never guess who I found on High Street," he said, bringing his companion forward to receive the greetings of her friends in the box.

"How lovely to meet you again," gushed the widow, taking Tom's hand and pressing it meaningfully. "And so soon after we had parted. I never imagined I should be with you—all of you—so soon."

Tom extricated himself from her grasp as Mrs. Marshall introduced the widow to her companions, inquiring how long she was to stay in Brighton.

"Only a week or two, perhaps," sighed Mrs. Ridley, settling into a chair beside Tom. "You may well guess that I have come for my health. I fear I must try the efficacy of the baths for a trifling little complaint I have. Spasms, you know."

The elder ladies in the box did know, and joined in their general approbation of her course of treatment. Tom, drawn somewhat into the circle by Mrs. Ridley's continual glances as she spoke, listened politely until the subject began to run into avenues that, he was persuaded, no young man could ever wish to tread, and he turned to engage Diana in conversation more appropriate to the setting.

Diana, however, looked thunderous, and after he had recovered from his astonishment at finding her thus, he began to cast about in his mind for the cause. That it had something to do with Mrs. Ridley, he was fairly certain, for Diana had been nothing but sparklingly amiable up until the moment the widow had appeared on Reginald's arm. Whether it was the widow herself, or her relationship to Reggie that had done the business, Tom could not say, however.

Tom had gathered from the house party at Findon that Diana had no opinion of Mrs. Ridley though she was a relation—and perhaps because of it, for Mrs. Marshall had freely declared that the widow's questionable morals were well known to the family. Knowing Diana's extreme loyalty to Reggie, he suspected she disapproved the negative influence which Mrs. Ridley could exert upon her dear, high-spirited friend, but the unwelcome thought that Diana resented the widow for taking Reggie's fancy did intrude.

Before he could satisfy himself as to the cause of Diana's irritation, however, the lights began to dim and Mrs. Ridley rose. Mrs. Marshall pressed her to stay for the next act, and at first the widow declined, saying that she must return to her poor box alone, and that she had come simply because she could not pass up the opportunity to say how do you do. But after continued pressing from Mrs. Marshall's friends, and even a grunted "You're welcome at any time, Anthea" from Mr. Marshall, Mrs. Ridley was prevailed upon to stay. With a speaking look at Tom, she settled back into the chair at his side, while Reginald took the seat on Diana's opposite for the next act.

The proceeding hour proved a trying one for Tom, for he was precluded from engaging Diana by the daggered looks of various occupants of neighboring boxes whenever as much as a whisper was attempted, while the widow constantly obtruded herself upon his notice by little touches or movements or noises. At the fall of the curtain, the gas lights flared to life, and before Tom could turn to discuss the inferiority of the second act with Diana, Mrs. Ridley placed a hand on his arm.

"My dear Mr. Breckinridge! I cannot begin to express my astonishment and delight upon learning that you were in Brighton. And I being obliged to come here—it must not be a coincidence."

Tom smiled flatly. "Rest assured, ma'am, that it is. When last I saw you, I had no more idea of coming here than you did, depend upon it."

"Always so sensible," she said, with a sly smile. Lowering her voice, she bent closer to him and said, "Would it please you to know that I came to Brighton in the hopes of meeting you?"

"It would surprise me, ma'am," said Tom, stiffening, "for I cannot imagine how one could be astonished upon finding another exactly where one knew him to be."

She laughed that tinkling, opera-dancer laugh. "There is no flummering you, sir! But I mean what I say—the second time, that is. I came to find you, for I believe we have unfinished business."

With a meaningful glance toward Reginald, who was conversing avidly with Diana, she added quietly, "A certain person also suspects this, and has been making the most outrageous attempts to inveigle himself into my good graces."

Thus the meeting on your doorstep, thought Tom blandly. Aloud, he said, "Then I regret to observe that the pair of you have been wasting both time and resources, for I cannot comprehend what business I could have with you."

"That is not very gallant," she said, her lips in a pretty pout. "Come now, Mr. Breckinridge, I simply cannot credit that you are not the least bit intrigued by my proposal."

He was too much the gentleman to explain in so public a setting that it was her character that had decided him against her, he thought to choose his reply carefully, but was forestalled by Mrs. Marshall requesting Mrs. Ridley's opinion of the play, and it blessedly seemed his conversation with the widow was over.

As Reginald persevered in dialog with Diana, however, Tom was left to the musings of his own brain, which wondered not what Mrs. Ridley wished to do with him, but what she had conspired to do with Reginald. That they had met by design did not admit of a doubt, for even were she speaking the truth about having come to Brighton chiefly to do business with Tom, it was not he whom she welcomed into her lodging, but Reginald—not that Tom in a hundred years would consent to do so improper a thing, even were his sentiments warm toward Mrs. Ridley. But the widow, it seemed, could not be convinced of this fact, and insisted upon pressing her attentions upon Tom, hoping, no doubt, to wear him down just as she had any number of other gentlemen, with the intent to bend him to her will.

But Tom was not the bendable sort of gentleman, nor was he the sort who was easily worn down. He knew, if she did not, that if he could withstand the constant friction of Reginald's jibes and hints and slights, so he could withstand the widow's promises and allure. She would, he opined, have a hard job of it if she expected to turn him to good account.

As they moved out into the gallery to await their carriages, Reginald was his most charming self, dominating the party and engaging every female eye without ever actually excluding Tom or Mr. Marshall or giving himself cause to blush. It was all very masterfully done, as was Reginald's habit in such things. The misfortune was that Diana seemed utterly oblivious to it all, laughing and blushing along with all the other ladies, young and old. Occasionally, Tom thought he saw a glint of ice in her eye, especially when she turned toward Mrs. Ridley, but it was gone so quickly that he could never be sure it had been there at all.

When Mrs. Ridley's carriage was called, she sighed and with a speaking look to Tom and many promises to see them all as often as her short stay and her indifferent health would permit, she left the theater accompanied by the charming Reginald. Before they went,

Reggie issued a very civil invitation to Tom from Lord Bentley to make one of his party in an excursion of pleasure setting off next morning.

At last permitted to speak to Diana, Tom was again astonished to find her mood mercurially changed, almost sullen, and he inquired as to the cause.

"I am tired, merely," she said, not looking at him.

In an attempt at lightness, he said, "That play will have put anyone into the dumps."

"What a selfish creature you are, Tom, to be forever assuming that everyone thinks as you do," said Diana petulantly. "What if I enjoyed the play? You should not have known it."

Tom was justly annoyed by this, for after having gone to great effort and personal inconvenience to win the right to accompany her to the theater—though the vapor bath had ended up being quite wonderful—and then having been made to endure Reggie's snubs and Mrs. Ridley's insinuations without the balm of Diana's attentions, he felt that he deserved at least civil treatment from the object of his admiration.

A little tartly, therefore, he said, "I am persuaded all your chatter and laughter with Reggie has worn you down."

She darted a fiery glance at him. "And I am shocked to find that you are not prostrated by the effort of resisting the allure of my cousin all the evening. Perhaps such exertion is rendered less irksome by keeping her in a flow of spirits—though one should imagine that to be more of a bother, not less—but I know nothing of the matter."

Even as he opened his mouth to refute this, light dawned in Tom's mind, and it seemed to travel down through his body, infusing his chest with a soothing warmth rivaling that of the Indian Vapor Bath. With a slow smile, he took Diana's hand and pressed it, saying,

"Indeed, you know more than you imagine. There is nothing so vexatious as to be forced to resist the charms of a woman in whom one has no interest, while the lady one would far rather be obliged to resist sits conversing ceaselessly and animatedly with another man. It really ought not to be borne. I am nearly exhausted, and if I do not keep my bed for a week, I can think of only one other thing that could cure me of it."

In an instant, Diana's countenance had transformed from petulance to enlightenment, and she returned the pressure of his hand. "And what is that?"

"The assurance that you could never truly suspect me of flirting with Mrs. Ridley," said Tom gently.

Coloring, Diana averted her gaze, but did not remove her hand from his grasp. "Oh, Tom! You are a complete hand! But it is foolish of you to be so gallant, for I must be the silliest girl alive. What an odious evening we have had, and all from a ridiculous misunderstanding!"

"It was not odious until they came to disturb us, and even after that it has ended well, has not it?"

"True," she murmured, her pansy blue eyes bright.

Then the Marshall's carriage was called, and Tom, reveling in Diana's smile, kissed her hand and bade them all farewell, receiving a warm look from Mrs. Marshall and a handshake from Mr. Marshall to complete his victory.

Chapter 19

FOR ONE WHO prided himself on being a fairly percipient fellow, Tom was obliged to own that he had recently suffered significant lapses. With Reginald, he believed he was awake on every suit, undeceived as to that gentleman's loyalty, no matter how friendly they had become. With Mrs. Ridley, he knew quite well that he must keep her at arms' length—more if it were possible, though situations such as last night had proved that it was not so easily done. But with Diana, he had allowed his jealousy of Reginald to cloud his understanding to the point that he had completely misread her.

All this while, at Findon and at Brighton, he had imagined her annoyance at Mrs. Ridley to be unrelated to himself. Whenever she had expressed disapprobation of her cousin it had been, by Tom's calculation, when Reginald had shown too eager an interest in the widow's charms. Even when Diana had discovered Mrs. Ridley in a compromising situation with Tom during the ball at Findon—though the chief of her ire had been directed solely at him for his apparent perfidy—Tom had believed her distress to stem from her dislike of the widow's allure in general.

The revelation of Diana's true sensations had brought him great relief—not to mention a delightful sense of well-being—but it had also given him to think on the fragility of a relationship that was not completely and wholly transparent. Diana could not be easy in Mrs. Ridley's company because she had been given reason not to trust her, and they would never enjoy a bond greater than the ties of blood. It was similar with Reggie, for she was laboring under a misconception where Reginald was concerned, and it could only be a matter of time before his true character revealed itself and her confidence in him was shattered. It was borne in upon Tom now that he, also, was imposing upon Diana, in pretending to friendship with Reginald, and the realization did not sit well with him.

Though he had made much to Diana of his blossoming friendship with Reggie, he had never intended his efforts to prosper more than outwardly. He could not bring himself to trust Reginald, nor even like him. Reggie embodied much that Tom abhorred, including dandyism, careless stewardship, excessive gaming, and thoughtless flirtation. At every turn Tom was reminded of how dissimilar he and Reginald were and, despite his assertions to Diana and even Reggie himself, he had been as unwilling as he was unable to surmount this gargantuan obstacle to the possibility of their friendship.

So he had carried on the deception, justifying his position by maintaining that he did it for Diana's sake. He had even formed the conviction that he had never relinquished the hope of finding some concrete proof of Reginald's unworthiness only so that he may undeceive her. And yet, every day that passed was another that Diana believed him to be truly Reggie's friend.

He could no longer delude himself that upholding the illusion would save her pain or disappointment, any more than he could justify Reginald's position. But his clear duty caused him no little distress, and he spent many sleepless hours trying to find another way. No matter how he went round the matter, however, he was confronted by the same conclusion: he must come clean to Diana regarding the true state of his relationship to Reginald, and try again if he could disabuse her mind of the notion that he and Reggie could ever truly esteem one another.

But as the clock chimed the early morning hours, and he considered how his new resolution should affect his behavior toward Reginald, another idea occurred to him that at once resolved the issue and saved him from the probable wreck of a confession: he could try to be a real friend to Reggie. He could truly work to overcome his disgust of Reginald and try if he could make him see the danger in his path, not through disapproval or self-righteous tolerance, but through friendly discussion and advice. It was only what any other friend of Tom's would deserve, and what he gladly would have given—had it not been Reginald, who scoffed at every virtue, slighted at every turn, and scorned common sense.

However, Tom's soul-searching had made him recollect that he had been guilty of something very similar with regard to Mr. Marshall's views on health, and yet he had been made to repent it. His experience there proved that advice could be mocked and scorned before it was taken to good account—it might well prove to be the case with Reginald. If Tom attempted this course, he could fulfill Diana's expectations to befriend Reggie, and perhaps also reveal his flaws—but to Reggie, who would then be under his own obligation to make a transformation.

This virtuous notion had its risks, but they were not so great as they would have appeared to Tom only two days ago. Now that he had undeniable evidence of Diana's attachment to him, he was no longer fearful that her admiration of himself was mere liveliness while she cherished an infatuation with her dear Reggie. But as nothing was settled between him and Diana, there was nothing to prevent her changing her mind if Reginald improved to her taste. After very little reflection, however, Tom became convinced that if Reginald did materially change, it would merely make him the man Diana already believed him to be, which would not likely alter her affections a whit.

Indeed, if Tom's and Lord Bentley's observations were correct, Reggie was not anxious to secure Diana as his bride—at least not in the near future. It was even possible that he was not the rival he pretended to be, and all his hints to Tom were merely high-spirited attempts at a good hoax. As he at last drifted off to sleep, it seemed to Tom that there was no just cause preventing his suppressing his prejudices and pursuing a true friendship with Reginald.

That this would take a monumental effort, Tom was well aware, and it was with grim determination that he descended to the taproom of the Ship Inn a few hours later, where he found Reggie enjoying a mug of ale.

"Breckinridge!" Reginald cried, pushing away the mug and fishing in his pocket for a coin to toss onto the counter. "I thought you'd never come. They have nearly finished stowing the gear, and then we must be off."

"Without knowing to where we are off," said Tom, yawning, "I can only hope I'm ready. May I know what sort of excursion this is to be?"

"An adventure," said Reggie, eyes twinkling. "No need to trouble yourself; there's nothing you'll need that won't already be provided. Come along."

With that, he clapped Tom on the shoulder and led him out of the Ship and down onto the beach. Tom began to be uneasy when he spied two small boats moored on the sand and two magnificent yachts at anchor farther out to sea.

"Wait a moment, Reggie," he said, slowing to a stop. "This isn't a sea excursion, is it?"

"We must make haste," cried Reginald, waving him toward one of the boats. "Bentley is already aboard and if we miss the mark he'll have our heads!"

Tom, shaking his head, eyed the boats uneasily, believing that his new resolve could wait another day, and that they would be better off without him. But before he could voice a negative to Reginald's continued urgings, Mr. Trenton came up beside him and grabbed his arm, scrambling him into the boat. Tom was given an oar and told to "pull like the dickens" while Mr. Trenton took the other and did the same.

Already feeling the seasickness coming over him, he did not need to be told that he was rowing to certain disaster. He gritted his teeth and, focused on the movement of the oars rather than the water, he muttered, "What have you gotten me into, Reggie?"

Reginald laughed as he sat in the stern. "An adventure, Breckinridge! Just as I said. You are about to participate in a race."

"Good heaven," said Tom, forgetting momentarily to row. He was called to order by Mr. Trenton, whose exuberant efforts threatened to turn them entirely about, and he went back to work immediately. "I know nothing of seafaring, I tell you, Reginald, and you know my propensity—you know I do not do well—" He ground his teeth at the impossibility of it all. "I hope you have not doomed your team to failure."

"Devil a bit!" said Reginald cheerily. "You shall do famously, once you forget yourself for a bit. You are a capital oarsman, you know."

"You mistake my meaning," muttered Tom, a sweat breaking on his forehead.

"Oh, the sun shall not bother you if you do not look into the waves," advised Reggie blithely. "The sea just takes some getting used to, you'll see."

"I can already feel the slivers from the oars," Tom said testily. "I tell you, Reggie, I know nothing of seafaring and will not be responsible for the consequences."

"Buck up, man! You've a quick mind—you'll pick it up in a pig's whisper."

"Must," Mr. Trenton put in, with a significant look. "I've got a hundred pounds riding three to one on this race. It'll do for me if we don't win."

Tom snorted ungraciously and continued rowing, buffered momentarily from his sickness by the immense irritation he felt toward Reginald and his entire race. It did not bode well for his new resolve, and he knew, despite his inclinations otherwise, that he must master his feelings. He was not the man he hoped to be if he balked at the first obstacle set in his way. Swallowing down the rising queasiness in his throat, therefore, he pulled at his oars with spirit, and they reached the yacht to be helped aboard by Mr. Dixon and Sir Humphrey.

"Breckinridge!" cried Lord Bentley upon seeing him. "Reggie and the others have boarded *Luck's Lady* many a time—you are the guest of honor on this voyage."

"I hope it will not prove to be an inauspicious one, sir," said Tom, staggering a little with the dip and roll of the deck.

"Nonsense! You'll find your legs. Now come see the *Lady* and tell me what you think of her."

She was a lovely yacht, Bentley informed him, forty feet long with a tall mainmast and two headsails attached to the forestays—that at present lay on the deck awaiting the signal to start the race. All this terminology was lost on Tom, who was endeavoring valiantly not to lose his breakfast, but he nodded and admired, all the while suppressing the urge to jump overboard and try his luck swimming to shore. He was aided in his struggle by the solicitude of his host, who obligingly pointed out the cushioned benches that were arranged in the bow and the stern, and a comfortable cabin that held various forms of refreshment. These, however, were to be resorted to only after the race, Tom was told, in answer to his hopeful request for a good, stiff drink.

"Our time will shortly come," Bentley said briskly, consulting his watch. Then he left Tom to the care of Reginald while he issued orders to Mr. Dixon to weigh anchor.

"I shall do my best, Reginald, but this is madness," said Tom, pressing a hand to his stomach.

Reginald clapped him on the shoulder. "Courage, man! Not a sliver in sight. Now listen to me, yours is an easy task. Simplest thing in the world." He led Tom to one of the headsails and put a rope into his hands. "At the command 'raise the sails,' pull this and then tie it off. At the command 'lower the sails,' let it go—but with control. Never let the rope get away from you!"

Before Tom had fully assimilated this, a shot was fired, and Reginald clapped his hands together, exclaiming, "We're off!"

Tom had scarcely braced himself to begin when Bentley cried, "Raise the sails!" Setting his jaw, Tom obediently hauled on the rope and up went the headsails. There was a general cheer from all the crew as the boat began to flow forward, and he knew a moment of satisfaction to have been charged with something so important. Despite his sea-sickness, he experienced a surge of energy, believing that this was not so hard after all and that perhaps he would find his legs. But suddenly the boat, which had been hither-to running gently against the wind, pulled sharply to starboard and he was knocked off his feet.

He struggled to his knees, only to have the precious rope torn from his hands, and he panicked. Someone shouted "Man that blasted sail!" and Tom made a frantic grab at the rope that was undulating upward as the headsail came down. He missed, but caught it the second time, and hauled up the sail, then nearly lost his feet again as the boat vigorously picked up speed. Muttering an oath, Tom regained his balance, and as the rope fought his hold, he recollected that Reginald had told him he must tie it off. Bracing against the bucking of the boat, he likewise recalled that the obliging Reginald, who had since vanished, had neglected to show him how this was to be done.

"It cannot be so difficult," he told himself, looking about for something to tie it to, and found a raised rod fixed to the deck that would suit the purpose. Ignoring the protests of his unsettled stomach, he wound the rope in a figure-eight around the ends of the rod, then tied a knot around it. He stood up, admiring his handiwork, and was startled by a shout of "Tacking!" The yacht swung to port and he was thrown to the deck once more.

The sails flapped and fluttered, the mainsail sagging for an instant as the boat swung into the wind and then refilled again. From his vantage point sprawled on the deck, Tom saw his rope go taut, bounce once, twice—like a live thing—before the neat knot he had made popped loose and the rope slowly began to pull itself free. With a growl, he threw himself at the recalcitrant rope, grasping it tightly as it fought him for freedom, all while battling the inertia of the tacking boat and the threatenings of his stomach.

At last the boat ran true, and Tom retied the rope, making a double knot this time for good measure. His stomach heaved and he took several deep breaths, wiping his perspiring brow. He suddenly regretted that he had not listened more closely to old Captain Wardley, who had served twenty years in His Majesty's Navy and liked nothing better than to talk of life on a ship while drinking ale at the Hanged Man in Berkhampstead. But Tom had never dreamed he would be in the position he was now, and perhaps Captain Wardley had never divulged the magic of ropes and knots in his rambling talk, so it didn't much signify whether Tom had listened or no. Now, he simply must keep the rope—and his stomach—under control until the race was over.

When another shout of "Tacking!" rent the air, Tom was prepared; he planted his feet on the deck and seized the rope to keep from falling down again. The tension in the rope shocked him, and he held on with all his might, feeling the rope chafing at his hands as he held it tight. Then the boat straightened once more, the tension eased as all fight went out of the rope, and Tom experienced a thrill of triumph.

As he braced for another abrupt turn, Tom was bewildered by shouts of dismay that went up all around, and he looked up to see the other yacht racing ahead toward a third boat that was anchored not fifty yards away. It sped past *Luck's Lady*, cries of victory were heard on the wind, and Lord Bentley, with a few choice words, declared the race over.

"Lower the sails!" he shouted, stomping toward the cabin door in evident disgust and disappearing belowdecks.

Carefully, Tom loosened the rope, keeping a good hold on it as he fed it hand over hand back up. The headsails came down to crumple on the deck like discarded bedsheets, and the yacht slowed to a standstill beside the anchored boat.

Reginald appeared and clapped Tom on the back. "Capital work, my boy! Do you see! You're a natural."

"I'm obliged to you, though you neglected to mention we were going to zigzag like a dashed Borachio," huffed Tom, but he grinned. "I might have been thrown overboard and drowned. It'd served you right had I done so, and your precious sails had come down on top of you!"

"Or if you had cast up your accounts all over the deck!" laughed Reginald, slapping him on the back. "But never fear, now you may complain of the glinting sun all you wish, and none will blame you, least of all me. You've excellent bottom, Breckinridge!"

So saying, he went away to speak to a crewman, and Tom, shaking his head, gazed about at the now unimposing yacht, believing that seafaring was not so very bad after all. Mr. Dixon and Mr. Trenton came to commiserate with him over their loss, but as they did, Tom's queasiness returned and he felt the sweat break out on his brow. He breathed deeply of the salty sea air, focusing intently on his companions' talk of a review of the Brighton Militia that had been scheduled to take place on the Steyne that morning, and their debating whether the assembled crowd could have seen the yacht race from this distance.

After a few agonizing minutes, the winning yacht drew up alongside and hailed them, and as Dixon and Trenton walked away to the railing, Tom resolved that he had earned his good, stiff drink, and that it would do him some good to descend into the cabin and get one. It did not much matter if he was mistaken in this, he reasoned, for he had rather be out of sight of the others if he was so unlucky as to be sick, and the cabin seemed to be the one place that was not crawling with men. He managed to walk steadily to the wall of the cabin, and made his slow and careful way along it.

The voices of Lord Bentley and Sir Humphrey, laughing and cursing their luck in the race, stopped him as they stomped up the cabin stair, then they joined the others at the railing to exchange personalities with the winning yachtsmen. They took no notice of Tom who, grateful that he would now be well and truly alone, shuffled to the cabin door and stumbled down the stair.

Upon reaching the liquor cabinet, however, he was possessed of the certainty that alcohol was the last thing he wanted, and he leaned against the wall, willing his stomach not to expel its contents onto the floor. He pressed his eyes closed, trying to divorce himself from his surroundings, but a creaking noise scratched at his aching brain, and his eyes snapped open to search indignantly for what was making the offending sound.

A door in the side of the cabin was gently swinging open and shut with the swell of the waves, the latch not having been done properly. The cupboard was not empty, however; it was filled with casks, and an aroma of brandy wafted on the air. As the thought took shape in Tom's pained mind that such a cargo should not have been taken on a race, his stomach heaved, and he turned quickly, locating a bucket on the floor, and was violently sick into it.

Footsteps hurried down the stair and Bentley's voice smote his ears. "What the devil? Breckinridge—" He cursed and Tom heard him latch the cupboard door. "Breckinridge—been too much for you, eh?

Sorry, old boy. Get you up to the deck. Fresher air up there, and can cast your accounts over the railing."

As his lordship hefted Tom to his feet, the sufferer bent glittering eyes upon him. "Dash it, Bentley—that's a cargo of brandy—" But his stomach heaved again, and he was obliged to close his mouth or he would be sick all over the pair of them, and whether or not Bentley deserved it for having involved him in what was almost undoubtedly illicit business, Tom had no desire to spoil his own garments. He had decidedly had enough discomfort for one day.

Chapter 20

ALMOST THE MOMENT Tom was deposited safely on land again, the horrid seasickness left him and he found he was fully capable of both perambulation and rational thought. He was also starved, and after receiving again the congratulations of Reginald and his friends, he took himself off to the Ship to wash and eat. As he contemplated the events of the day over his dinner, he came to two conclusions: he would not soon sail again—indeed, he could not find out he wished to at all—and Lord Bentley was a smuggler.

Though he knew little of the sea, Tom had heard enough to know that free-trading, as it was euphemistically termed, was common up and down the Sussex coast. But Brighton seemed an unusual place for it, even without the militia stationed there, for it was growing more and more busy with the society brought in result of the Prince Regent's patronage. It seemed to Tom that it would be exceedingly dangerous for "the Gentlemen"—as smugglers called themselves—to propose work in a busy regiment town, but Lord Bentley had evidently risen to the challenge. Unless Tom was much mistaken, Bentley had used the yacht race as a front to transfer smuggled brandy from the boat at the finish line—a well-disguised free-trading vessel, to be sure—to his yacht. The cupboard must conceal a hidden port in the side of the boat that corresponded to one in the other vessel, through which the brandy was passed after the evident loss of the race. Bentley had descended into the cabin immediately as the yacht drew along-side, and Sir Humphrey had very likely been waiting to assist him.

Though Bentley and Sir Humphrey were undoubtedly co-conspirators, it was highly probable that all the sailing gentlemen had been in on the scheme. These men proved Diana's assessment of idle gentlemen: they were forever in a scrape, whether it was incurring gaming debt or participating in an adventure like today's supposed yacht race. Tom imagined that the excitement of free-trading—and the ironic association with the epithet of Gentlemen—would be a draw to all of them, Reginald included; however, it was not certain that they all had been in the know.

Two days ago, Tom would have needed no proof of Reggie's complicity to justify himself in taking the tale to Diana, for he had only agreed to Reginald's friendship in order that he may unveil his weaknesses. But now that he had made his new resolve, he knew he must force himself to consider his situation from the point of view of a true friend—one who cared that Reginald had entered into a risky scheme and wished to get him well out of it before it caught up to him—no matter how little he desired at the present moment to do so.

Tom had resented the cavalier manner in which Reginald had forced his participation in the race but had soon forgot it while facing the challenges of the adventure, and were it not for the inauspicious ending to the event, he might have looked back on the whole of the experience with a sort of fondness. As it was, however, Tom would require some time in which to dispel his annoyance at having been embroiled in an illegal activity, no matter how innocently it had been done. And while he felt he ought to make the attempt to alert Reginald to the evils of his situation, he was all but convinced that Reggie was perfectly aware of them, which made it unlikely that any interference of Tom's would do much good.

As he ruminated over his duties in the business, Tom dismissed the notion of laying evidence against Bentley with the excise officer, for his lordship was immune to common laws and regulations, and could easily resist a search until he had off-loaded his cargo. Indeed, he had likely already got rid of it, for it was rumored that one out of every ten persons in Sussex was in league with the Gentlemen in one way or another, and Bentley would laugh to scorn any attempt at an investigation. And even should there be something by way of evidence discovered, there was nothing to stop the other men from implicating Tom in the business as well, so there was no use in making himself disagreeable.

In the end, Tom determined that no matter the futility of it, he had best do his duty as the friend he had resolved to be and try to talk some sense into Reginald, and he had his first opportunity the following morning when that gentleman came to see him at breakfast.

"Good to see you fully recovered, Breckinridge," Reginald said, eying the rashers of bacon, fried eggs, kidneys, toast, and coffee with which Tom was regaling himself. "You were so green yesterday that I despaired of your ever being right again."

"Your despair was misplaced, Reggie," replied Tom. "You would have been better served to despair of my ever going on board a sailing vessel again—for that I believe I shall not."

Reginald chuckled, settling into a chair and accepting some coffee. "You must pardon me. In my excitement I convinced myself that your disinclination for the sea could be overcome. A gaping hole in my apprehension of the situation."

"You were lucky that it proved to be the case," said Tom around a mouthful of egg, "at least until the race was finished."

Reginald fiddled with his coffee cup. "Bad notion to go below-decks, my boy."

"On that vessel, or on any vessel?" Tom inquired with a significant look.

"On any vessel, when one is seasick. Makes it worse. However, you cannot have known that."

Tom smiled blandly. "No. A gaping hole in my apprehension of the situation."

"I suppose you only went down thinking you'd feel better?"

"I went down to get a drink, which I hoped would ease the unpleasant effects of an adventure I shall not soon forget."

"Ah," said Reginald, nodding.

Tom took a bite of toast. "But the overwhelming smell of brandy made me even more violently sick. Odd to take such a large cargo of brandy on a race. Bentley in the habit of grandiose celebrations after a victory?"

Reginald bit his cheek, regarding Tom. "What Bentley does with his boat is no concern of mine. I am only an amateur. A large cargo may well give an advantage, for all I know."

Tom wiped his mouth with his napkin and sat back in his chair. "Dixon and Trenton said there was a military review scheduled on the Steyne yesterday. I wonder that they were so keen on discussing it."

"I could not say," said Reginald, shrugging. "Once one has seen a review, one has seen them all."

"Their discussion got me to thinking, however, that perhaps Bentley specifically chose the day of the review for his little escapade. It is my belief that it was in Bentley's mind to have an audience, for there was a great crowd gathered—besides the militia."

A tiny smile lurked on Reggie's lips, but he denied Tom's assertion. "A yacht race is no oddity in Brighton, I assure you, Breckinridge. If it was remarked at all, it was with only passing interest."

"But this was no mere yacht race, Reggie, and I suspect you know it."

Reginald paused in pouring more coffee into his cup, but otherwise gave no indication of understanding him.

Tom regarded him. "It's a bad business, Reginald. You ought to be well out of it."

"I don't know what you're talking of, Breckinridge," he said, stirring sugar into his coffee.

"There is no honor in engaging in brandy smuggling in full view of the Brighton militia," said Tom inexorably.

Reginald's brows went up, and he surveyed Tom over the edge of his coffee cup. After a pregnant moment, he set the cup down. "I never imagined you to be such a gudgeon, Breckinridge. Have you any idea of what you are accusing me? Or more importantly, of what you are accusing Lord Bentley?" He looked down, fiddling with the handle of his cup. "Your reasoning is faulty, for you will recall that you also were on that boat, and if you are to go about accusing people, you must comprehend that you would bear scrutiny no better than any of the rest of us."

"Is that an admission or a threat?"

Reginald looked up and met his eyes before exhaling with a forced a chuckle. "You have excellent bottom, Breckinridge, and I give you credit, but I am only quizzing you. It is all a foolish misapprehension. A few casks of brandy in the hold, no more!"

Tom did not speak, and Reginald sipped at his coffee, saying, "Do you imagine Lord Bentley to be unable to procure such a load of brandy legally? He is a wealthy man, Breckinridge, as you ought to know. It is not as though he could not afford it."

"I do not imagine anything of the sort," said Tom, spearing a kidney and cutting it into pieces. "He is so accomplished a card player that he must have made a fortune from it."

"Now you are raving," Reginald scoffed. "Lord Bentley is a middling player at best. His luck fluctuates so wildly that one can never know when he will make you rich for a day, or win even the coat from your back."

Tom snorted. "Indeed, it is a most singular habit."

Reginald laughed and said, "Unnerving, I'd call it. One would think that a man of his age should have learned the ropes by now, but not he. As wild as a game cock." He stood, picking up his hat and gloves, which he had laid on the table. "Bentley will be happy to hear you are no worse for the experience yesterday. Indeed, he begged me to express to you his sincerest apologies, and hoped that you would do him the honor, if you have not had too much of us, of being his guest this evening."

Tom gazed evenly at Reginald. "I wish you will give up his acquaintance, Reggie."

Reginald stilled, the smile frozen on his lips. "But why should I wish to do that?"

"He can do you no good, and may do you great harm."

Reginald's brow furrowed in incredulity. "Perhaps you are not so well recovered as you profess to be. Doubtless you have taken a touch of the sun."

"Reginald," said Tom, with more urgency in his tone, "I have seen his kind before. He loves a challenge, and more particularly one that makes him rich, but there is no kindness in him, or loyalty. It is dangerous to associate with him."

"You are very kind to warn me, Breckinridge," said Reginald, shaking his head. "but there really is no occasion for it, depend upon it. You make a great deal out of nothing. Bentley is the best of good fellows, and would be excessively distressed to know of your disapprobation—especially after all he has done to welcome you into our circle."

"I very much doubt that," Tom said, and sighing heavily, played his last card. "There is more at stake here than your own comfort, Reginald. I am persuaded that the Marshalls would be vastly disappointed to discover you were involved in something so degrading as smuggling."

"Are you still on that, dear boy? I must beg you to desist before you become a dead bore."

But Tom was undeterred. "You claimed that you would not wish to give Diana pain for the world. Do you not see how your activities will injure her?"

Reginald pursed his lips and gazed at Tom. Then, after some moments, he recovered his smile and said, "My dear Breckinridge, I believe I comprehend you now. But I warn you that you are well and truly off, and will only make yourself foolish if you insist on pursuing this subject. I am the first to admit I am no saint, but neither are the Marshalls to be easily swayed against me. Has the experience of the past month taught you nothing? Mr. Marshall is so much my friend that, while well aware of many of my exploits, he looks upon them as merely high-spirited pranks. If you were to carry this tale to him—in the hopes, perhaps, of blackening my character in his eyes, and thus forwarding your suit—you would soon discover just how hopeless was your case. To him, you are a pestilential nuisance, for all your salt-of-the-earth airs; on the other hand, he thinks the world of me, no matter what I do."

"He thinks the world of your rotten borough seats, perhaps," said Tom amiably.

Reginald chuckled, gathering his hat and gloves and standing, "Even were that so, I am still the preferred suitor, Breckinridge."

"If, indeed, you intend to declare yourself in the near future."

Reginald hesitated, his lips tightening. "There is something to be said for deliberation."

"Just as there is something to be said for honesty."

Reggie's eyes narrowed a fraction, but he broadened his smile. "I suppose it will be up to Diana to decide."

"Oh, certainly," said Tom, returning his smile.

"Then may the best man win," said Reginald, saluting Tom and walking to the door.

Tom, gazing ruminatively into the depths of his coffee cup, said suddenly, "Tell Bentley that I bear him no ill-will, but I cannot accept his kind invitation for tonight."

Reginald regarded him meditatively. "He will be disappointed." And with a nod, he was gone.

As soon as the door had closed behind him, the smile vanished from Tom's features and he fell into a brown study. Dash Reggie's impudence! The man was so full of himself that he couldn't see beyond the shine on his own boots. He may have Mr. Marshall well in hand, but he was in for an unpleasant surprise if he thought to toss the handkerchief to Diana—or at least Tom fervently hoped so.

Even in anger, Tom could not congratulate himself on the outcome of the conversation. For all the good it had done, it seemed he would have done better to have remained silent on the subject of smuggling. It seemed only to have sunk Reggie further into his deception, and Tom was forced to own that any scandal arising from the yacht race would not reflect well upon himself. But all personal considerations aside, he had made a mull of it. His was such an upright character that he could not understand a wayward man's reasoning, and his imagination was not so open that he could place himself in the other man's shoes. It was all very lowering, for he had sincerely tried to do well by Reginald, if he could. But now he doubted very much whether it was possible. If Reginald insisted upon staying his reckless course, there was not much anybody could do, whether in the name of friendship or anything else.

As he contemplated what were his options now, he wandered out of the Ship and onto the Steyne, thinking perhaps to look in at Donaldson's. As he entered those noisy portals, however, he repented his choice, and would have turned about and walked away again had not he been hailed by a smiling gentleman behind a wide table.

"You, sir, are the very picture of number three," said the man, pointing in Tom's direction as the eyes of several persons nearby followed him. The man turned to the group for validation. "Is not he a perfect specimen of the male principle? Who better, sir, than yourself, to take up this number, and with it, perhaps, the name of Adonis?"

Bewildered, Tom gaped at the man until he recognized him as the conductor of the Loo, and realized that he had been singled out as a potential subscriber. It had not been his intention to play at this odd game—at least not without Diana's company—and he knew a moment of consternation; however, it would be horridly rude to decline and walk away when so many eyes were upon him, and after all, it would do no harm to play. Fishing in his pocket, therefore, he withdrew a shilling and laid it on the table.

"Number three, sir," he said amiably. "But I'll call myself A Man of Sense."

The conductor swept up the shilling with a smile. "Very sensible indeed, sir! And may we take this lady as an interested party? The female principle in number two being taken, we may assign her number five—for the male principle and the female principle being married gives us five."

Amid the general approbation of the crowd, Tom looked about for the lady in question, and was brought up short by the sight of Mrs. Ridley at his elbow. "No, sir, there is no interest here," he said quickly.

But Mrs. Ridley bent forward to lay a shilling on the table, saying archly, "A Man of Sense, it seems, has no sensibility. It is fortunate that I am a widow, and have done with marriage. But if I am not to take the number five, what other is on offer?"

The conductor gladly sold her the number eight, which he claimed, with a sly look at Tom, was a most auspicious one, and she took it up willingly. "The very thing for me. And I will be called The Widow's Mite, for it is all I am to have."

There were shouts of mirth and a smattering of applause from the crowd, and Tom felt himself color. But there was nothing for it but to see the thing through, and the number five being taken by a blushing young gentleman with red hair, the game commenced. The cards were dealt, and each player turned one up at a time, until the Knave of Clubs appeared in Mrs. Ridley's hand.

She placed it down with undisguised satisfaction. "There! My number was most auspicious, to be sure. And what is it I have won, sir?"

"A very special prize, ma'am," said the conductor, all but winking. "Your prize is the gift of luck. You will, no doubt, use it well."

She gave her tinkling laugh, bowing her head gracefully to the other players, and stood, putting her hand out to catch Tom as he turned away. "Will you not shake hands, Mr. Breckinridge? We have played a good game, you and I."

Mortified at the curious looks from his fellow players, Tom took her hand briefly, but she gripped his, bending close to whisper, "You mustn't fear me, sir. I will not eat you, upon my word."

"You mistake me, ma'am."

"I know I do not." She passed her gaze over his face. "It is excessively simple to read those handsome features. You do not like me, and I wish it were otherwise."

Grimacing at her forwardness, and in so public a place, Tom took a step backward, but she moved with him, retaining her hold on his hand.

"I know your heart is taken. Who could not love Diana? She is such a pretty thing, kind-hearted and good, and so lively that she has ten beaux on a string at any time. And she has ten thousand pounds—she really is quite perfect!"

"Yes, ma'am," agreed Tom coolly.

"But I fear your suit is in vain. Diana is so universally charming that she is, unfortunately, easily misread. Much as I hate to do so, I must tell you that Reginald is very much her favorite, and he enjoys Mr. Marshall's unqualified preference."

Annoyed by the baldness of her tactics, Tom said merely, "Then I must hope that my luck is as good as yours was today."

After another prolonged perusal of his face, she lowered her long lashes again and said, "Pray be assured, sir, that if events do not transpire as you should hope, there are other options open to you."

With that, she released his hand and took her leave, and Tom, flexing his hand in his glove, waited some minutes to go out onto the street, finding it necessary when he did so to take himself directly to the White Horse tavern to enlist the aid of Blue Ruin in completely erasing the taint of Mrs. Ridley's insinuations on his mind.

Chapter 21

Tom was convinced by this interview that what he had only suspected at Findon was true: Reginald and Mrs. Ridley had joined forces to discourage his suit. It seemed that the two of them, even while professing no affinity for one another, had settled on the same design of undermining and corrupting him, believing that in doing so they would separate him from Diana, and thus gain their own ends. Indeed, they both seemed to take for granted that Tom's natural inclinations were as bad as their own, and they need only apply their tactics with enough persistence to expose him. It was unfortunate for them that Diana had made her sentiments known to him, and that he was not so easily led as either of them supposed.

If truth be told, he was affronted by their continued assumption that he was a gull ripe for the picking. He had imagined that with the time spent in his company at Findon they would have come to understand him better, and given up any idea of his being one of their ilk. But he supposed that just as he had been blind regarding the truth of Diana's jealousy of Mrs. Ridley, Reggie and Mrs. Ridley were blind regarding Tom's intelligence and morality. He was upright and had simple tastes, he was forthright and generally honest; but rather than view him as a respectable gentleman, they had taken it as proof he was a flat. It was highly annoying.

However, if he could take one lesson from them, it was not to knuckle under. They had both given him to understand that they could not be diverted from their purpose—Reginald, he knew, wished to keep his hold over Diana, but whether he wished to marry her, sooner or later, was unclear. He did not seem to be trying to fix his interest with her, to be sure, for if he was, he was doing a very poor job of it. Mrs. Ridley, though having made her plan a little more clear this morning, was still a wild card. She very noticeably professed an interest in Tom, but he suspected she had her claws pretty deeply into Reggie, for whatever purpose. They had, after all, been alone together at her house, which did not bode well for virtuous intentions, either toward each other or toward Tom. Her exact motives, therefore, remained a mystery.

But Tom was not one to waste his day in ruminations over a pair of gadabouts, and being refreshed by his look in at the White Horse, he promptly pushed them from his mind, for he had pleasanter obligations. He had arranged to go driving with Diana that afternoon, and taking his curricle round to the Royal Crescent, he left it in the care of Matthew while he was shown into the drawing room to wait. Soon afterward, Mr. Marshall came into the room.

"Good morning, Breckinridge," he said, looking about as though he had expected someone other than Tom to be there. "Pardon me, I believed Reginald to be with you."

"No, sir," said Tom. "I called to take Diana driving. Were you expecting Mr. Popplewell?"

"Must speak with him. Bad doings in the Channel—must have those seats before all hell breaks loose!"

Startled, Tom asked if there was threat of another French invasion.

"No, no, my boy—smugglers! Here, at Brighton, and in broad daylight! Excise officer caught wind of some havey-cavey doings yesterday, but he's got no proof and little enough hearsay to go on. Extraordinary! The Gentlemen, landing right under the Prince Regent's nose!" Mr. Marshall shook his head sadly. "If such impudence is not checked, I know not where it will end. I drink brandy as much as any other man, and the tax is dear—very dear—but we must stand against this flagrant disregard of the law, before it undermines our great system!"

Pleased at this unequivocal proof of Mr. Marshall's sentiments regarding smuggling—which might well have astonished Reginald—Tom entered wholeheartedly into his feelings, and commiserated very articulately. They were deep in discussion when Diana appeared—very dashing in a brown pelisse trimmed with pink and a matching jockey bonnet—and Mr. Marshall turned to her, his face brightening.

"Well, you look a picture, my dear! Off driving with Breckinridge? Well, well, and a fine day for it, too. You must show him the Chalybeate, my dear, for he will appreciate its medicinal qualities. Take my word for it, Breckinridge, our Chalybeate waters beat Tunbridge Wells all hollow! You will see when you try them."

"Yes, sir, I have tried them only last week, and they are, as you say, quite—extraordinary."

Diana, suddenly finding the buttoning of her glove excessively absorbing, bent studiously to the matter, and Tom, a muscle twitching in his cheek, went on to inquire of Mr. Marshall whether he advised taking the Chalybeate waters frequently.

"Now there's a conundrum, my boy, for the more I indulge in the Shampooing Treatment, the more good it does me; however, the effects of taking the Chalybeate waters more than once in a fortnight are terribly distressing—terribly distressing. It is most perplexing—I cannot advise it."

On this sober warning, he wished them a pleasant drive and excused himself, looking more well-pleased with his daughter's companion than he had ever done. As soon as he had gone, Diana went off into a peal of laughter.

"Dear me, I thought I should die!" she said, wiping tears from her eyes. "How could you ask him so gravely about the waters? As though you would follow his advice! Shame on you!"

"Oh, I shall follow his advice," said Tom, grinning. "I shall not take the waters more than once this fortnight—which I have already done—and then I shall decide that I am cured and no longer need them."

"You are a complete hand!" accused Diana.

With a chuckle, Tom held the door for her and they descended to the curricle. As Tom handed her in, she said, "But what were you conversing so seriously about with my papa before I came in, Tom? Anything the matter?"

"He is concerned about smugglers having been rumored to make a daylight landing at Brighton."

"But surely they would not risk coming ashore in the daytime, and at so busy a place," she said scornfully. "It must be a mistake. There are hundreds of far quieter and more convenient places to try. Why, Brighton has no coves, and only the one small beach that is covered with bathing machines from morning to evening."

"It would be brazen indeed to attempt such a thing here," agreed Tom, settling beside her and signaling Matthew to let the horses go. They set off at a smart trot in the direction of the downs and Matthew swung up behind.

"To be sure," continued Diana, "they would get a scolding from the Duckers, who like to hold a monopoly on the rough handling of their charges."

Having had his own experience holding off the Ducker who operated his bathing machine, Tom nodded feelingly and said, "Perhaps that is how it could be accomplished: bribe a Ducker to let go their charge long enough to pass a barrel of brandy into their bathing machine. The poor bather would be submerged and could not be a witness to the crime, and only the horse would know the difference as it pulled a heavier load going back up the beach."

"Tom!" cried Diana, between admiration and shock. "What a clever notion! I declare, it is a good thing you are an honorable man, and unlikely to put your ideas into action."

Finding this observation not a little ironic, Tom chuckled and feather-edged the turning onto the Lewes turnpike.

"If there are smugglers here at Brighton, they could not be many," continued Diana, laughing. "Can you imagine a whole fleet of boats taking it at turns to deposit their contraband on our little beach? I fancy the Gentlemen would be obliged to live up to their name, and treat each other with great civility, only to fit everyone into the schedule."

As the Gentlemen were generally known to be gruff and uneducated persons, the vision of a group of them huddled around a desk while a harried secretary worked out when each was to sneak onto the lone Brighton beach was so comical to her that she could not stop giggling until they had got quite far away from town.

Tom, smiling at her innocent mirth, could not help saying, "Indeed, I am persuaded it would only take a few exceedingly clever persons to make quite a brisk trade in plain sight. Take, for example, the pleasure boats that go about all day long. How simple would it be to meet the Gentlemen out at sea and in the guise of a friendly chat, pass a few barrels of contraband between themselves?"

She looked at him, surprised. "Now you are worrying me, Tom. Where have you got all these ideas?"

He hesitated, unwilling to embark on a topic that he knew would inevitably wander onto unsteady ground. "I suppose all my admiration of the sea this past fortnight has suggested them to me."

"Nonsense! I have admired the sea all my life and have never had such notions. What have you seen, Tom?"

He chewed his lip, ruminating over his answer. He still wished to stand Reggie's friend if he could, but after the wreck of this morning, he doubted it was possible. To retain Tom's friendship, Reggie would be required to reform, which he seemed disinclined to do, and Tom would not support even a fast friend in shady dealings. Thus, it was tempting to acquaint Diana with the facts of the yacht race, but if he told Diana what he had seen in Lord Bentley's hold, would she even believe him? And if she did, would it change her mind about Reggie?

But his resolve to cease any deceptions rose up in his mind, over-shadowing his desire to keep her longer in the dark regarding her dear Reggie's flaws.

"Perhaps I saw just such a scene as I have described to you," he said at last.

Her brow furrowed and she regarded him suspiciously. "But how? To see such a thing, you must needs have been on one of the boats, and unless I am much mistaken, you have been out on the water only with Reggie, yesterday."

He was silent a moment too long and her aspect transformed from suspicion to hurt. "Tom! Oh, Tom." Slowly, she turned from him, gazing forward in consternation. "I thought that you had overcome this unreasonable dislike of Reggie. How could you deceive me so? Oh, I wish to go home."

Tom drew up his team, saying, "I only know what I saw, Diana. I did not say it was smuggling, nor that Reginald was involved."

"No, but you think it, Tom." She huffed, crossing her arms over her chest. "Even if he were as bad as you believe him to be, he would not be so lost to all propriety as to participate in illegal activities!"

"He told me it was an adventure," said Tom, becoming irritated.

"And you took that for an admission? I suppose that is all the proof you need of another man's guilt—a careless statement loosely tied to the situation."

Tom's jaw worked. "If that was all the proof I had, Diana, I assure you I should have dropped my suspicions entirely. But it was not all—there was a hold full of Nantes brandy that could not have been there at the start of the race, for who takes on a cargo of brandy when speed is necessary? And Lord Bentley was mighty disturbed at my finding it, for he got me out of the cabin double quick. And when I confronted Reggie about it, he made all sorts of spurious excuses and tried to fob me off!"

"And what were these spurious excuses, pray?"

Tom counted them off on his hand. "That Bentley had every right to carry brandy on his yacht, that such a sizable cargo was entirely reasonable for a gentleman to own, and that Bentley could easily afford to purchase so much Nantes brandy through legal means."

"And well he may," cried Diana hotly. "None of what you have mentioned is proof that Reginald is a bad man, Tom!"

"I did not say it was, Diana! But I have been doing my utmost to be a friend to Reggie these three weeks, and I can tell you that the company he keeps is doing him no good."

"Lord Bentley? Now you are being ridiculous. He is accepted everywhere, including, on occasion, my mother's drawing room!"

"That may be, Diana, but he and his cronies have the flavor of my father's friends—all of whom ran in the highest circles, and all of whom benefited from and encouraged my father's excessive gaming habits."

"But why would Reggie persist in friendship with such men?"

Tom made a helpless gesture. "He delights in adventure, I suppose. When I asked him to leave off the acquaintance with Bentley, he laughed at me."

She sat hugging herself and shaking her head for another few moments, then suddenly exclaimed, "It is too nonsensical! I cannot believe it of Reggie—nor of Lord Bentley! In your fear of becoming like your father—a very righteous and understandable fear, to be sure—you have misapprehended the situation—"

"That is not the case at all, Diana."

She raised her hands in frustration. "Then you have deliberately misread it! It is prejudice, Tom, barefaced prejudice and nothing more! You think you know these men, that you know their kind, but you have been in their company only a handful of times. You cannot judge them on so slight an acquaintance."

"Three weeks is not slight!"

"In the larger picture of things, it is, Tom Breckinridge, and you may depend upon it, once you have put away your horrid prejudice and afforded these men their due, you will repent these feelings. They are not saints, to be sure, but neither are they villains, as you are so willing to make them out to be."

Tom's fists clenched and he said in a strained tone, "If I have been so very wrong about Reggie and his friends, I wonder if I have likewise misjudged Mrs. Ridley?"

Diana sputtered, "Certainly not! She is plainly a hussy, and I do not scruple to say it! However, that is neither here nor there, sir, for we are not discussing my odious cousin, but my poor, dear friend, Reginald."

"I cannot fathom why you will persist in being blind to Reginald's every fault!" cried Tom, his slender self-control snapping at last. "He is an ugly customer! I have seen it from the beginning of my acquaintance with him. He colluded with Mrs. Ridley to make me look a scoundrel, and has met with her privately here in town—"

"The theater is not private!" exclaimed Diana.

"No, but her house in High Street is!"

She gaped at him, but he was too angry to stop. "He speaks to you with honeyed words that always manage to make him out to be the hero, and me the laughingstock! When I tried in good faith to be his friend, he led me into association with gamesters and card sharks, and then lured me out on a smuggling run, all in the name of entertainment! One of these choice spirits told me I am Reggie's latest project, and I do not doubt it, for I am a gaby if he does not intend to make me a fool!"

"He wants no help there, Tom Breckinridge!" cried Diana, bosom heaving. "You have allowed your jealousy of him to overtake your reason, and it does you no credit!"

Gritting his teeth, Tom set his pair to and they bowled down the road. He was fuming at her obstinate blindness, and she obviously believed him to be nothing more than an envious wretch. He took the turning onto the Preston road at a dangerous clip, earning himself a glare from Diana.

"There is no occasion for you to be jealous of him, Tom," she said coldly, "as I have been obliged to remind you time and again."

"No? You must tell him that, for he does not let a moment pass without reminding me that I do. I have no borough seats for your father to covet, I have not the long association with your family that he enjoys, I am not the preferred suitor for your hand—"

"For my hand?" she said indignantly. "There is proof of your ridiculous jealousy! He has no interest in my hand. He is my friend, almost a brother—"

"It seems to me that you speak nothing to the purpose during all those lively chats you have with your dear Reggie, Diana. He is evidently laboring under the misapprehension that he is very much interested in your hand."

"It is untrue! He has never even hinted at—"

"Perhaps not to you, my girl, but he has a thousand time hinted to me—tried to hint me away! And I am very much mistaken if he has not hinted to your father, as well, for Mr. Marshall seems exceptionally keen on your being friendly with Reggie."

She looked daggers at him. "You are odious. I refuse to listen to you. Vexatious and provoking—Oh! Take me home, Mr. Breckinridge, at once. I no longer desire to be in your company."

Tom was, at this point, only too willing to accede to her request, and he barely checked his horses to pass the carriages rattling sedately past the Steyne, and to take the turning onto the Marine Parade. They reached the Royal Crescent in smoldering silence, and it wasn't until Matthew came to the horses' heads that Tom realized, with a sinking feeling, that the groom had been a witness to the whole of the argument with Diana.

She seemed to recognize it at that moment, too, and it was with flushed cheeks and a tone of utter mortification that she thanked Tom for the drive and allowed him to hand her out of the curricle. She begged him not to see her to the door, and after she had gone into the house, Tom turned with gritted teeth to face his loyal servant.

"I beg your pardon, Matthew. I entirely forgot myself."

A sad smile tugged at the corners of the groom's mouth. "Seems you likewise forgot me, sir. But no harm done."

They climbed in and set the horses to, and after a few moments of heavy silence, Matthew said, "That is, no harm done to me, sir. Might be considerable harm done. Happen you'd do well to beg the lady's pardon."

Tom cursed him, his cheeks flaming, and Matthew sat back in his side of the curricle, a satisfied smile curling his lips—such as that of a loyal retainer who has yet again put his master in his place.

Chapter 22

Tom was mortified. He had deserved almost every bit of censure Diana had flung at him—excepting that against his judgment of Reggie of course—for he had been a boor to cut up at her as he had. It really was unaccountable, for until Reginald had appeared on the scene, he had never had a disagreement with Diana, nor even felt the least inclination for one, in the whole of their acquaintance.

In a black mood, Tom slammed into the coffee room of the Ship Inn and ordered his dinner, descending into a brown study at his table. From the looks of the serving wench who brought his meal, he gathered that this state was becoming all too frequent, and not wishing to bring down even more disapprobation upon his head, he ate his dinner as quickly as possible, taking himself off afterward to the White Horse Tavern to recruit his spirits with Blue Ruin.

Over his second glass of gin, it became clear to him that all his misfortunes were Reginald's doing. Reginald had demoted him in

Mr. Marshall's esteem, Reginald had put him in an impossible place with Diana, and he was very much mistaken if Reginald had not encouraged Mrs. Ridley to make her insensible proposal. When he came to reflect upon it, Tom found he could even lay the blame for his seasickness at Reginald's feet, for he may never have got on a boat in his life if it were not for that gentleman.

What to do about it remained the problem, however, for whichever way his muzzy mind looked at it, he could not simply rid the world of Reginald. Murder, as he and Iris had discussed previously, was unfortunately out of the question, for once perpetrated, the killer must flee the country or die himself—and besides, even in his slightly foxed state, Tom could not imagine that Diana would look kindly upon any such course. A tantalizing vision of setting upon Reggie in a dark alley and trussing him up to be thrown in the hold of some ship bound for parts unknown danced before his mind's eye for a moment, only to be dismissed. Tom should be required to board some sort of sea-going vessel in order to ensure his prisoner was properly disposed of, and that was not to be attempted for any consideration.

But after some deep cogitating, Tom determined that none of this would be to the purpose at any rate, for his fuddled brain deduced that even were Reggie made to disappear, Diana would only mourn him as the heroic figure she thought he was, and never be made to understand how handily she had been deceived, and thus how terribly she had wronged Tom. As this could never be permitted to come to pass, Tom could see nothing for it but to persevere in his resolution either to bring Reggie to a comprehension of the error of his ways, or in the hope that Diana would somehow be brought to recognize his true character.

This conclusion, bringing him as it did right back where he had started, did nothing to improve his mood, and he was still laboring under a dangerous mixture of ill-usage and guilt when Lord Bentley came upon him.

"My dear Breckinridge! I had not thought to meet you here. May I join you?"

Tom's grunt was invitation enough, and his lordship sat down. "You have had a rough go of it, I apprehend, if what Reggie tells me is true."

Tom huffed a laugh. "And what does dear Reggie tell you, my lord?"

"That you suffer from seasickness, my dear boy. I tell you, I was shocked and grieved when he owned to having known of it before yesterday. I should never have asked him to invite you onto *Luck's Lady* had I the least grasp of the situation."

"I am much moved, sir."

His lordship called for a drink and turned a sympathetic eye upon Tom. "You need not blush for your performance, you know. The task we laid you was a Herculean one in and of itself—to one of no experience that is—but to have done so well while so very ill—It begs repeating: you need not blush. The best of us suffers from weakness of some kind."

"How very true, my lord," said Tom, gazing blandly at him.

Lord Bentley chuckled. "I trust I know that look. No, our dear Reggie is not immune to weakness, to be sure. Though an excellent fellow, he is far too excitable, particularly when it comes to defending his friends. I fear he was a trifle offended by your—ah—intimations regarding the purpose of our voyage."

"He said something of the sort."

"He was terribly shocked," said Bentley, sighing. "Reggie was wounded enough on my behalf that he told me the whole. My poor boy, I fear your illness affected your mental acuity—that, and you undoubtedly had a touch of the sun. It is not uncommon for inexperienced sailors to become delusional in such conditions, and I fear that is precisely what happened in this case."

"Is that so, my lord?" inquired Tom with evidently keen interest.

His lordship smiled indulgently, taking a sip of his gin. "It was not a cargo of brandy you saw, my boy, but a few casks only. Your affliction, I have no doubt, affected your vision and multiplied them tremendously. But you need not be embarrassed—I understand perfectly."

Tom blinked slowly at him. "Very obliging of you, to be sure, sir."

Lord Bentley smiled. "There, now. I knew it was all a mistake, to be cleared up by a little honest dialog. But my dear Breckinridge, how comes it you are here—alone, and in obviously depressed spirits—when you could be with friends?"

"Perhaps I was under the misapprehension that I no longer have any friends, my lord."

"Ah, but you do, Breckinridge! I assure you, we mean you no ill-will! Yesterday's misunderstanding is a thing of the past—whooosht! Gone! We are not so unreasonable as to hold it over your head for even a moment. Come, do you have plans for this evening?"

"It seems I do not."

Bentley opened his arms. "Then you must come to my little party. Reginald told me you could not join us, but I apprehend that is no longer the case. Indeed, you must want jovial company at this present, when you are so evidently cast down."

"I am cast down, sir, to be sure; however, I do not believe I am equal to jovial company."

"Nonsense! A gloomy old tavern is no place to recover your spirits, certainly not when you could be with friends, Breckinridge!" said his lordship expansively.

Tom gazed stormily at him, and the sight of his adversary's mentor, so smoothly speaking of friendship, wound him up still higher, to a point almost of recklessness. He was tired of being made to look no-how, and even more tired of being underestimated. It seemed very clear to him that he had a point to make, and it would serve them all right if he made it.

He made a decision. "I *could* be with friends, couldn't I?"

His lordship slapped a coin on the table. "You could, and you shall. Walk with me. I am on my way home, to preside at my little card party. I only stopped here to meet with an associate, and I am glad of it, for it has enabled me to come to your rescue! You would be most welcome in my home, Breckinridge. Will you not say you will come with me?"

"Why not?" Tom said, tossing down the rest of the gin. He stood, gathering his gloves in his hand and placing his hat on his head at a rakish angle. He laid his coin carefully on the table and, setting his jaw, followed Bentley's lead out the door.

They had not far to go, walking along Ship Street to Duke, and stopping outside a smart-looking residence with lights blazing in all the windows on the ground and first floors. At Bentley's knock, a respectable-looking butler opened the door and ushered his master and his guest into the house. Bentley led Tom up to a saloon on the first floor, where Reginald, Mr. Dixon, Sir Humphrey, and Mr. Trenton awaited them.

Reginald whistled. "Well, look what the cat dragged in!"

Bentley shepherded the latecomer over to the others to shake hands. "Our dear Breckinridge has come after all. You see that

Reginald did not deceive us—he looks fit as a fiddle!"

Mr. Dixon slapped Tom on the back. "No lasting harm done, I trust."

"None, sir," said Tom with a glinting smile. "Never felt better in my life."

This brazen mendacity was lost on his companions, who joined in a chorus of good-natured taunts as to the likelihood of his ever attempting another voyage. They bantered for several minutes over the events of the race, how their speed was adversely affected by having such a greenhorn as Tom among them, and what losses they had sustained from their ill-advised bets.

"Never bet on yourself, m'father used to say," observed Mr. Dixon sadly. "Ought to have listened to him."

"Hard to know when to start listening to the old man, eh?" said Mr. Trenton. "Mine talks incessantly it seems, and never to the purpose."

"Ought not to listen until you're an old man yourself, I say, or you'll turn into an old woman!" said Sir Humphrey with a guffaw.

"No use for old women here," said Trenton, blanching. "Only old woman I know is m'Aunt Josephine, and she terrifies me!"

Mr. Dixon shuddered. "Your Aunt Josephine terrifies everybody!"

"Then perhaps I'll engage her to come preside at my card parties, to even up my losses," remarked Lord Bentley, going to the sideboard to pour out drinks. "What'll you have, Breckinridge? Madeira? Port?" He paused, his back to Tom. "Brandy?"

"Brandy will do fine for me, thank you, Bentley," answered Tom without hesitation.

Glancing over his shoulder at him, Bentley poured the drink and brought it to Tom. "Fine vintage, this. Excessively glad I came across it."

"I'm certain you are," said Tom, his eyes overbright.

Lord Bentley smiled benignly on him and ushered everyone to

the gaming table. "Macao is the order of the day—or, rather, night. Shall we say pound points? That should afford us some fine sport. We're here until someone's pockets are to let, and some of us have pretty deep pockets."

"Not after that race," Mr. Trenton mourned, as Bentley dealt the cards. "If only m'father would pop off, then I could kiss my fingers to his paltry allowance."

"Not fond of the old man?" inquired Tom amiably.

Sir Humphrey guffawed again. "He's a brimstone saint, is Old Mr. Trenton. Rains hellfire and damnation over his poor, wayward boy's head every time they meet."

"Regular jaw-me-dead," agreed Trenton, staring bleakly at his card.

Tom picked up his card—it was the four of spades.

"Better leave off Old Trenton, boys," advised Reginald, his eyes on Tom's slightly flushed countenance. "Wouldn't wish to shock Breckinridge, here."

Tom looked calmly up at him. "Not to worry. I wasn't overfond of my father, myself."

"Were you not?" inquired Bentley. "I should not have guessed it."

"He was not very wise," explained Tom.

Bentley nodded. "Ah, yes. So I have heard. But you, my boy, are far wiser."

"Time will tell, I suppose," said Tom, smiling grimly.

Reginald, drawing a card, said, "Time has a way of revealing things."

"Or of burying them in obscurity," replied Tom, gazing pointedly at Reginald.

Reggie's eyes scanned Tom's face for a moment before they flicked back to his own card laying face downward on the green baize. "Nothing to fear from Breckinridge," he said, turning over his card for all to see. It was the nine of diamonds.

"No," said Tom, smiling beatifically at them all as he revealed his losing card. "Nothing to fear from me."

There was a shout of laughter at this, and then the others revealed their cards, groaning or chuckling according to their luck. Points were tallied and money was exchanged, drinks refreshed and the cards dealt again. They played the game into the night, and Tom lost spectacularly the first few rounds, won a round, then lost another. He was quizzed for his fickle luck and Lord Bentley congratulated him on being a kindred soul.

But near midnight, Tom's luck seemed to take a dramatic turn, and he began to win almost every round. Lord Bentley, as banker, remarked often on Tom's skill, but Reginald blandly remarked that Macao was far more a game of chance than of skill, "unless one fuzzes the cards."

All eyes turned to Tom who, blinking, asked what was the matter.

"Wasn't your father some sort of card shark, Breckinridge?" demanded Trenton.

"Yes!" cried Sir Humphrey, "I remember—Bentley said he was a notorious card player. Always playing high, and had the devil's own luck!"

"Only if the devil had bad luck," said Tom. "My father scarcely ever won."

"Met a bad end, didn't he?" pursued Trenton, narrowing his eyes at Tom.

"Certainly he did," said Tom, gazing back with a furrowed brow. "Bad end for a bad man. Everyone knows it."

"But what we don't know is whether his son takes after him!"

declared Trenton.

But before anyone else could fling aspersions at Tom—or Tom could decide to fling civility to the winds and draw some claret—Lord Bentley called them all to order, pouring another glass of Madeira for Trenton and quelling him with a stern eye.

"I will thank you to recollect that this is an exclusive establishment, gentlemen. I do not invite just anyone to enter into these hallowed portals. We are civilized men, and will not stoop to allegations of cheating—especially when they are utterly unfounded. Mr. Breckinridge's luck has been middling at best! A mere half-dozen rounds of winning. Even Reggie can boast such a paltry run as that!"

This remonstrance was met with snorts of derision and laughter, and the jovial mood returned—assisted by liberal doses of wine—and carried them well into the morning. The play ended only when, about three o'clock, Trenton, perhaps succumbing to grief over his mounting debt—or to the terror of his father's certain wrath—put his head down on the table and promptly began to snore.

"That is where I draw the line," said Bentley, gathering the cards into his hand. "I will brook no guests slumbering in my saloon. Count your losses, gentlemen. Unless I am much mistaken, I believe Breckinridge to be the clear winner."

Tom, who after the brief altercation had played with the intensity of one who has something to prove, looked down at the pile of vowels and bills before him. There were several hundred pounds-worth there, if his eyes were not, as Lord Bentley had this evening assured him they had on the boat, multiplying his vision out of impairment. But he had not, as the others, drained his glass more than a few times, and his hands, as they rummaged among the papers, remained single, and so he could only conclude that the papers and bills were all real. His only concern was that he could not recall writing a single IOU himself, though he had come with only a hundred pounds in his pockets.

"Whashou make it, Breckinrish?" asked Sir Humphrey who, having imbibed very freely of the brandy, was three sheets to the wind.

Counting the bills and vowels, Tom discovered that he was richer by over two thousand pounds, but mistrusting this figure, he counted again. He had made no mistake. He sat blinking at the scrawled handwriting in the blazing candlelight.

"Dixon, your vowels amount to three hundred; Trenton, two; Sir Humphrey, two; and Reginald, five." Lord Bentley had been the sole player with the means to pay all his stakes in cash.

"All part of the sport," mumbled Dixon with a sigh, getting up and shaking Trenton awake.

Trenton, swaying a little as he stood, gloomily promised to pay on quarter day, and the others told Tom they would wait on him in the morning, after they had visited the bank. They made their rather haphazard way to the door as Tom carefully folded the IOUs and put them in his waistcoat pocket, then placed the bills in his pocketbook.

"If I did not know better, sir," remarked Lord Bentley, watching coolly as Tom tucked away the pocketbook in his coat, "I'd say you have an illustrious career ahead of you."

"What do you know better, my lord?" asked Tom, feeling slightly light-headed.

"I know you are not interested in cards. I suppose it comes of having a father who was all too interested. Very sensible, but a pity. I'd give a fortune to have your luck."

Tom smiled a little foolishly. "You just gave a fortune, sir."

"That I did," said Bentley, laughing and rising to usher his guest out. "It is not every player who can win so well. I stand by what I said earlier: you have considerable skill, my friend—more so than your father. He was a dab hand at cards, but had the most devilish runs of bad luck! You don't take after him, I am persuaded. If you take my advice, you will give serious consideration to using your skill more often."

Tom, feeling the weight of the bills and vowels in his pockets, smiled again. "I will, Bentley. They say once one's luck is in, it is in."

"Yes, for luck is lazy, and doesn't like to turn," said his lordship, smiling broadly. "Mine has been belly down for a month or more. But you shall see for yourself. Come tomorrow night for another party and we will prove the strength of that maxim."

Tom returned his grin and shook hands, thanking his host for a most enlightening evening. Then he went out into the night.

Chapter 23

SLEEPING SOUNDLY, TOM nevertheless awoke betimes, and lay in his bed gazing at the ceiling above him. The plaster was cracked, and had the smooth lines of a lady's face turned partially away, and he was put forcibly in mind of Diana. She had turned away from him several times yesterday, and with good reason. Though he had only spoken the truth, he had been harsh, even churlish at times, and deserved that she should never wish to see him again. The thought pained him dreadfully, and he wondered if he would be able, a third time, to earn her forgiveness.

He sighed, for now that all his spleen had been spent feverishly playing cards, he wished nothing more than to be right with her. But at this moment he felt that he had only compounded his iniquities by throwing in his lot with the very set of persons he had deprecated to Diana, and participating in an activity which he had professed to abhor. He had reason to hope, however, that all would yet turn out well, for his motives had been pure—at least to his own mind—and though he had courted disaster, it had all come off as he had suspected.

He had more than two thousand pounds to his credit—a thousand in bills and twelve hundred in vowels. He shook his head. Unwise, to write vowels. He had never stooped to it, though he had rashly resolved to do so last night if the necessity arose. But it had not arisen, and that was a singular circumstance for an unskilled player at a select card party. Tom had learned quite a bit about runs of luck from his father's sad experience, but contrary to Lord Bentley's assertions last night, Tom knew such a one as he had enjoyed happened only under unusual circumstances. He also knew that though Luck was a fickle lady, the sort of luck Tom had enjoyed last night never lasted more than a day. Of that, he was certain.

He arose at noon and dressed, taking his breakfast in the coffee room, where Dixon found him and duly presented his three hundred pounds.

"I'll get it back, Breckinridge," he said, with as wicked a smile as he could muster. This was difficult, as his rounded countenance made him resemble a cherub. "Just you wait—at Bentley's tonight, your luck will abandon you for me. It must, or I'm for it."

Tom looked sympathetic. "I hope it will."

Trenton also came, handing him one hundred in bills as an advance and challenging him jovially to stake it all in one go the next time they met at cards.

"It's a Martingale—best thing to do, you know, to make the luck hold," he said with a knowing wink.

Tom returned the look—but not the wink—and said, "I believe I've heard of that. Fascinating."

Reginald, however, did not show his face at the Ship, and tiring of waiting, Tom went off to see if his tremendous luck would hold long enough to make Diana listen to his abject apologies. It seemed it had not, however, for he got only so far as the Steyne when he saw her, walking arm in arm with Reginald and looking up into his face from time to time, as if deep in conversation. That she was not as animated as usual was a small comfort, for when she glimpsed him, there was no warming of her smile or brightening of her eyes—only a continued look of discomfiture.

"Good morning, Breckinridge!" said Reginald, as soon as he was within polite hailing distance. "I must explain my tardiness to you, it seems, though I had hoped to avoid the chopping block a few more days."

"I see you were more pleasantly employed, Reggie," said Tom, tipping his hat to Diana, who still had not shown him anything near her usual welcome.

Reginald turned his beaming smile upon her. "Very pleasantly, but that is not the whole of it. I fear I must beg your indulgence for a few days—a trifling misunderstanding with my bootmakers that it became necessary I address. Tiresome creatures, tradesmen, but I suppose it stands to reason one must pay them some time."

"Certainly one must pay them," said Diana, looking up at Reggie with a troubled expression. "Their work is done in good faith, and must not be disregarded."

Reginald chuckled indulgently. "To be sure, Diana, and in general I am very prompt. However, it seems these things have a way of getting out of hand, particularly when one is so very busy with good company and pleasant entertainments, and the bills do have a nasty habit of coming due at times that are not in the least convenient. It is paid, however, and I must now trust in Mr. Breckinridge's patience."

Diana cast each of them a questioning look, which pressed Reginald to further explain, "We were both of us at Lord Bentley's for a game of cards last night, which lasted quite until four this morning, which accounts for my sleepy head, upon which you have so kindly commented. Breckinridge, here, had the most unaccountable run of good luck—beat us all to flinders! He was the only one who left with anything in his pockets. I was unfortunate enough as to be obliged to write him several vowels for, thanks to the aforementioned bootmakers, I was cleaned out before midnight."

"Good heavens!" exclaimed Diana, clearly shocked. She included Tom in her look of disapprobation and then said, "And yet you continued to play, Reggie?"

"Nothing for it, my dear girl. Mustn't leave a party early—bad *ton*. You recollect so from your time in London, I daresay."

"Yes, but that is entirely different. No guest at a respectable card party would be expected to continue to play upon credit. Indeed, it could not be necessary, for the stakes are so trifling."

Reggie gave another indulgent laugh and cocked a brow at Tom. "Useless to attempt to explain it to a female, eh, Breckinridge?"

Diana did not seem to appreciate this remark and turned to Tom. "But you will certainly allow him more time to pay you, Tom. It cannot be more than a few pounds, I daresay."

Tom cast Reginald a significant look and he coughed, his gaze carefully averted. Diana's brow furrowed again.

"You have been playing deep, I apprehend." She looked from one to the other, her consternation visibly growing. "Then you must simply forgive the debt, Tom. It is ridiculous, after all, to be owing so much money among friends—money which has been so unjustifiably gained."

"Not for the world, Diana," Reginald said hastily, causing her to look troubled again. "For all you think it ridiculous, I must and will pay him, for it is a matter of honor."

Tom said diffidently, "Nonetheless, I shall return your vowels, if you desire it, Reggie."

"You shall not!" cried Reginald sharply, then recollected himself. "Pay no heed to Diana, Breckinridge. She means well, we both know, but she knows nothing of the matter."

At this, Diana bit her lip, letting go Reginald's arm. "I must be going. My mama will be finished at Donaldson's and will be looking for me. Thank you for the walk, Reggie." She nodded curtly to Tom, and with a stormy look at each of them, hastened away.

Watching her progress across the green swathe of the Steyne, Tom said, "She's quite right, you know, Reggie. It is nonsensical to be owing so much money between friends. My offer stands."

"I'll not take it," snapped Reginald, glaring at him.

Tom shrugged. "Heaven knows I don't need the money, and it was just a card game between friends. It does seem harsh to make you pay such a sum simply because Bentley set the stakes so high."

"Do not dare play virtuous with me," Reginald growled, stepping menacingly toward Tom. "Diana may think much of you for it, but I will not be made to look ridiculous. I won't let you do it." He clenched his jaw and looked away, shoving his hands into his pockets. "Just give me time."

"As you wish, Reggie," said Tom, and he turned away.

"In any event, I mean to win it all back from you tonight," said Reginald.

Tom, bending upon Reginald a quizzical smile, said, "I daresay you do," and resumed his walk in the direction of Great East Street.

On his way, he came upon Sir Humphrey Gosford, who was looking haggard and heavy-eyed as he slumped over a mug of porter outside a tavern.

"The devil," muttered the gentleman, patting his waistcoat in a bleary manner. "Was coming to see you. Where the deuce did I put that pocketbook? Oh, here it is." He plucked out a stack of bills and thrust them at Tom. "Take it, you dog."

"A fine night's work," said Tom, grinning. "I suppose that is why so many men make it an occupation of sorts."

Sir Humphrey grunted and said, "Scorched us properly. But don't let your luck go to your head."

"I am convinced it was not luck," rejoined Tom.

"Of course it was!"

Tom gave him a significant look. "I am informed it was skill."

Sir Humphrey barked a laugh. "Is that what Bentley told you? I'd advise against heeding him but he knows what he is about. Born with cards in hand—a Don if there ever was one, I'd say."

"How odd that you should say so, Sir Humphrey, for Reggie is forever telling me that his lordship's understanding of cards is middling at best," said Tom, sitting down beside him.

"Devil a bit," said Sir Humphrey, drawing at his porter.

"To be sure, if I were to make my assessment of his skills from last night, I should consider his a very indifferent ability. Even he has no very high opinion of it."

Sir Humphrey gazed owlishly at him and then, blinking rapidly, he seemed to reconsider. "Oh, yes, yes, very true. I meant to say that Bentley has been known to have as much good luck as the next man. But the fact of the matter is that he has been in somewhat of a slump since your arrival. But then, the trumps all seem to be in your favor."

Tom smiled, nodding. "Perhaps I am more a knowing one than you realize. Such a sensation, to be at the top of one's game. One feels such power over one's opponents, it is quite impossible to believe it will end."

"Your sun will set tonight, pup," said Sir Humphrey, drawing himself up. "See if we do not cut you down a notch or two."

"Ah, but that I could," said Tom, rising with a regretful look.

Sir Humphrey slewed to look narrowly at him. "What's that? You're not coming?"

"No sir. If you will be so kind as to give my regrets to Lord Bentley—"

"But you must come, my boy," said Sir Humphrey, pounding the table with his fist. He started, looking at his fist and then turned again to Tom with a winning smile. "It will not be the same without you! The boys, you know—all the boys!"

Tom shook his head regretfully. "The prospect does strike me as delightful, but I simply cannot come tonight. You will have to do without me."

"But that's infamous, my boy! We cannot do without you. You must come!"

Unmoved, Tom gave him a sympathetic pat on the shoulder and bade him good morning, going on his way to the bank in rather a good humor. The conversations of the morning had been excessively revealing, and now he was certain of what he had only suspected last night.

He had fancied from the start of the evening that his luck had run rather too well, after the first few rounds. But that was the way it always was with such games, run by such men. Tom had heard of it time and again from his mother—who had witnessed her husband's own spectacular entry into the world of sharps and flats, and gone on to see his steady decline, which ended only with his sudden demise. A poor flat found himself welcomed with open arms into the bosom of a masculine family, treated to every sort of friendly inclusion he could wish for, and made to feel as though he was part of something familiar and comfortable.

Then, once his skill had been tested and found wanting, he was brought to a select gathering where his luck became so superior that it was deemed something between magic and skill, and the enormity of his winnings and the congratulations of his friends combined to set the seal to his self-consequence. Tom had felt the smug power of that position this morning, as the shock of it wore off and his opponents made all sharply real by delivering to him what they owed. As he had gazed over his winnings at the breakfast table, he had recognized that this was the most dangerous point of the game. Now he was at the crest of the hill, the top of the cliff, and he need only be led along to the edge where he could then be pushed over, never to regain his footing.

It was unsurprising, therefore, that Tom had not gloated over his riches, but had promptly taken them to deposit in the bank. And he would forget them. It would be easy, really, with Diana's troubled blue eyes in his mind's eye, and his conviction to regain her trust. His fantastic luck and incredible winnings had already been relegated to the back of his brain, only to be considered as a cautionary reminder against any future temptations.

Sir Humphrey's urgency only confirmed Tom's suspicions. His winnings were an investment only, and he was meant, as they each had so obligingly taken pains to inform him, to return it all tonight, with interest. They knew full well that his incredible run of luck would not last another evening, for they would not allow it. But they were destined for disappointment. Tom smiled at the thought—and fancied it was even more satisfactory than having attained the 'top of his game.' He had seen the flick of Bentley's wrist as he had dealt the cards last night and had no doubt he had fuzzed the cards in Tom's favor; he was as certain his lordship would not be so kind tonight. Therefore, Tom would not give him the chance.

What Reginald's part was in all this he thought he knew. Reggie must be what was known in vulgar circles as a Beau Trap, lying in wait for likely victims and pulling them into the fold. Then, along with Lord Bentley and the others, he was to set the stage—to pretend at mediocre play, to be surprised when the luck fell his way and to be resigned when it did not, to talk up their latest victim's prowess and to downplay his own and Bentley's. All this to execute the Dead Set—the game that would seal the victim's fate and eventually defraud him of every penny to his name. It did not surprise Tom that Reggie should play his part so well, for had he not witnessed his excellent playacting at Findon?

But Tom must believe—if not for Reggie's sake, for Diana's—that Reggie was not so irredeemable as Bentley, or Sir Humphrey for that matter. The two latter were older men, seasoned and set in their ways, while Reginald was still young enough to make a change—if he so desired.

For this cause, though he still could not like Reggie and was not convinced he deserved it, Tom had offered to return his vowels. It was an olive branch—an invitation to leave the game, or at the very least, a signal that Tom was not to be gulled, for he did not hold the same reverence for gaming as most men did. That this offer had been rejected was unsurprising, for it would be humbling indeed for Reggie to stoop to accept grace from his intended victim's hand, even if nobody discovered it beyond themselves. That he had rejected it so emphatically merely confirmed in Tom's mind that there was yet more to be played.

Thus, after thwarting all morning the attempts to get him to Bentley's again that evening, Tom suspected that he would be sought out again by his lordship, and he spent the remainder of the afternoon galloping over the downs with Matthew as his companion. This was an enjoyable pastime, as he knew from years at Branwell, for while Matthew was apt to speak freely, he was always to the point, and never short with praise where it was due. When Tom had regaled the groom with the tale of his exploits over the past twelve hours, Matthew was duly impressed, and counseled Tom to stand buff and give those Hawks a taste of their own. But Tom could not stay forever on the downs, and returned to take his supper at a tavern Matthew had discovered, before creeping up the back stairs to his room, prohibiting the chance that Lord Bentley should find him in the taproom of the inn.

The next morning, Tom ordered breakfast in his room and then slipped out of the inn to partake of amusements he imagined Reginald and the others would never consider: viewing an exhibition of glass works in St. James' Street, and admiring the workmanship of French prisoners of war who had created a likeness of the Palace of Thuilleries and the Bastille in bone. These curiosities engaged him much of the day, and then he indulged himself with another Shampooing Treatment, which lasted until it was time to dress for dinner. As he was to spend the evening with some friends of the Marshalls whom he had met at the assembly, he was thus saved his erstwhile friends' importunities for another day.

Sunday morning, when Tom slipped out for an early ride on the Steyne, he encountered Reginald on his chestnut, cantering toward him. As he had little to fear from an invitation to cards this evening, and was quite refreshed from a day and a half of intrigue and evasion, Tom greeted him manfully.

"You're out early, Breckinridge," said Reginald, in his usual carefree manner. "I made sure you were ill or something, for I have not laid eyes on you for an age."

Reminding him that they had spoken only the day before yesterday, Tom assured him he was quite well and thanked him for his solicitude.

"Good to hear," replied Reginald jovially, "for we have all been impatient to meet again at cards. I laid a monkey against Trenton that your luck, when we meet, will be quite out."

"Dear me, how uncomplimentary of you," said Tom. "And he took the bet? Poor Trenton seems to be alone in believing my luck will hold. Does he never have such luck himself?"

Reginald chuckled. "Occasionally. He is, unfortunately for himself, quite often a flat."

"He lost the bet on the yacht race, I recall. And it was a large one."

"It was," said Reginald, smiling wryly, "but then so did we all. And then there was our disgraceful performance Thursday night."

"I thought your performance masterly," said Tom, and smiled benignly at Reginald's sharp look. "You played directly into my hands, you see, and I could have asked for nothing more satisfying."

With a scornful huff, Reginald gave him to understand just what he could do with his flattery, and they both laughed heartily.

"We will see who is the better card player tonight, at Bentley's," said Reginald, turning his horse to go.

But Tom said, "No, I cannot come tonight. Give Bentley my sincere regrets, would you?"

Reginald's horse pranced impatiently as he turned him back. "What? No, you cannot fail! Breckinridge, it is the devil of a thing to do, when we counted on your coming two days since! Why, we are all eager to show you down!"

"I am certain you are," said Tom, smiling. "But I simply cannot come. I never play cards on a Sunday."

Reginald pressed him to no avail, and they parted, Reginald to convey the sad news to his co-conspirators and Tom to ruminate on the satisfaction of having principles upon which to cast oneself.

Chapter 24

IN ADDITION TO abstaining from cards, Tom's custom on Sunday was to go to church, and thence he went after breakfast, walking the half mile to the church near the Chalybeate, where he had attended services the Sunday before. He saw Diana there, as he had expected, but he was not prepared to find her looking eagerly over her shoulder at everyone as they came in the door. When her eyes met his, he wondered for an instant if she would turn away again, as she had on Friday on the Steyne, but then her eyes brightened and she looked such an entreaty that he nearly stumbled into the lady and child walking in front of him.

His feet carried him of their own accord, it seemed, to the Marshall's pew, and at Mrs. Marshall's kind invitation, he joined the family, feeling all the privilege and delight of sitting beside Diana, knowing that she wished it and rejoiced in it. So pleased was he that his spirits were unaffected when Reginald appeared and sat on the other end of the pew beside Mr. Marshall.

After the service, as they milled about greeting friends, Tom half expected Reginald to appropriate Diana, and he did make the attempt, but Diana was firm in rejecting his advances, recommending he talk to her papa while her own steps carried her unerringly toward Tom. The determination on her face at once made him quail, for he thought anxiously that she meant to give him a set down once and for all, perhaps demanding that he leave Brighton and its vicinity forever. But this was not to be, for she stopped in front of him, dropped her eyes to her hands which wrung together before her, and asked if he would be so obliging as to walk out with her to the Chalybeate and back.

Tom agreed with alacrity, offering her his arm, and they went out the door and through the lych gate to the well-worn path to the vicarage. Diana clung so to his arm that he dared not be the first to speak, and he was kept in suspense until they were well away from the bustle of the church. Then she took a breath, as though preparing for some momentous announcement, and Tom steeled himself.

"Oh, Tom, I am so thankful that you are willing to walk with me, for I must speak with you," she cried, clasping both hands about his arm and looking earnestly up at him. "I could not sleep a wink all night, because at last I know how dreadfully I have wronged you—can you ever forgive me?"

Taken aback by the intensity of this confession, Tom nevertheless found words to reassure her in the joy that leapt up in his breast. "There is nothing to forgive, Diana. It is I who must beg your forgiveness. I acted most ungentlemanly when last we were together, using a tone no one should be subjected to. I regretted it instantly, but was too angry to moderate my feelings, and went on out of sheer obstinacy."

"Perhaps your tone was harsh, Tom, but I needed to hear your words. Oh, how I needed to hear them! It was the only way to open my eyes. Tom, you were right!"

Her emotion was strong but it was not high; she was in perfect command of herself. She did not weep or even tremble in her voice, but spoke with conviction and deep, deep sadness. Tom covered her hand on his arm, drawing her toward the Chalybeate path.

"Oh, Tom," said Diana, in obvious distress, "You are so kind, and yet I have been so blind, and have heaped upon you such unjust censure!"

"Not all of it was unjust," Tom assured her, and would have gone on, but she forestalled him.

"Do not pardon me, Tom, for I will take the blame that is due me. It is only right, as you have tried so faithfully to meet my unpardonable requirements." She closed her eyes as though on a painful thought. "After we fought, the very evening, Reginald came to dinner, and he brought a cask of brandy with him from Lord Bentley. He presented it very properly to my father, saying that Bentley found himself with a surfeit and would take it as a favor if Papa would accept it as a gift. But as he did so, Reggie seemed so very self-satisfied—gleeful even— talking on about duties being so dear and what a fine thing it was to receive so generous a gift, and I began to suspect him. At first I set it down to your assertions that had got into my brain, and I tried to reject my suspicions, but all through dinner my papa commented on the excellence of the brandy and Reggie wore such a smile—oh, I could not let it go!

"Then as we were waiting for the gentlemen at their port, my mother requested that I bring her shawl from the drawing room, and as I passed the dining room door, I distinctly heard my father say how he should like to have those horrid seats, and then Reggie—Reggie! Oh, I can hardly credit it now—he said that if he could call Papa his father in truth, then it would be a settled thing."

She looked at Tom, her incredulity writ on her face. "He could mean only one thing by that, Tom! You were not mistaken, and he does wish to marry me! But there is more—I was so shocked by this revelation that I could not move, and I heard him go on to say that he could not feel himself ready to marry at this time, but that he foresaw it in the near future. I was astonished at his impertinence! To all but expect my father to keep me for him, waiting for him to drop the handkerchief, as it were! And for what? So that he may live out his salad days with the promise of ten thousand pounds at the end of it? Oh, I could box his ears!"

Tom concurred, but she was not finished, and he let her go on. "From then on it was only natural that I should suspect his every word, so when he joined us in the drawing room, I saw the trifling little signs of his deception, just as you said, but I could not believe it—or I was too injured to do so—and I resolved to rest on it and see again on the morrow."

She looked up at him again, wearing the same troubled expression she had worn the day following the card party. "Reggie found me at Donaldson's with my mama and carried me off, and was the same as he had been the previous evening. I was nearly horrified, Tom. His every word and glance was practiced and calculated to arouse my admiration, and I was aghast that I had not seen it before. I could only wonder that I had never seen it as flirtation, for that was what it was, and I knowing all the while that he did not mean anything by it but to fix his interest with me, so that I might be held in reserve for some far off, misty future! What if he should meet a richer heiress than myself during the interval, I ask you? Did he ever consider my feelings if that should happen? I think not!"

Her jaw worked. "It is not surprising, is it, Tom, that when we met you, and he spoke so slightingly of his bootmakers, it made me nearly ill? To treat so cavalierly those to whom he owes his comfort and respectability! Who rely upon him for their livings! But the final blow was when he owned to playing so recklessly at cards."

Here, Tom felt it incumbent upon him to admit that he, too, had participated in the card game, but Diana would not allow it.

"I must own, Tom, that I was inclined to blame you at the time, but after a very little reflection, I saw that I was unjust. You told me when we fought that Reggie had led you into bad society, and this was the proof. If anyone was to blame for your playing in that horrid game, it was I, for I harried you to be more in Reggie's company, more in his friends' company, and that is precisely what you did."

"Diana, if I were to lay blame beyond myself, it would be upon Reginald, for he, as I told you, promoted my entry into that circle. But he did not force me to play—I made that choice, and so the blame is solely my own."

Diana was quiet for a moment. "Do you intend to continue in their company, then, Tom?"

"Not for the world," he said, with enough conviction that she exhaled in relief. "It was horrid, Diana—as near to a reenactment of my father's worst moments as I can imagine. I could almost feel them coddling me along into their clutches, and I could not bear it. They made me lose at one moment, and let me win at another, all the while encompassing me about with suffocating bonhomie. I shall never play cards with them again. And in future," he added earnestly, "I will take care not to be even in their company, if I can help it."

"Please do not, Tom," said Diana. "I should feel so ashamed if you were to keep up the acquaintance in any form, for it would be from my prodding, and would do you no good at all, I am persuaded."

"Even with Reggie?"

She sighed. "I suppose you must not, if he is to be with them. Oh, Tom, when you said that Reggie was a bad man, I was so angry—but not because he is an angel. I confess—that is, I believe I have suspected for some time, somewhere in the recesses of my brain, that Reggie is not quite—that he is lamentably—" She sighed again. "But I would not heed it. I suppose that when he took you under his wing, I took it as proof that my doubts were unfounded. He is like a brother to me—that is, he was when we were children, and it is prodigiously hard to forget it. Indeed, he takes great care that I do not! But I can no longer pretend that things are as they once were. My eyes have at last been opened, and I must admit that Reggie was always unsteady, and he has only grown more so. It is very lowering."

"Indeed, for as his near-sister you would wish him to be happy, and you know that he cannot be in his present pursuits."

She acknowledged this with gratitude, but he saw that she was, indeed, very sad.

"I am sorry to have brought you pain, Diana. It is what I most wished to avoid, but I made a pretty poor job of it."

"It was not you who brought me this pain, Tom, for you merely wished to warn me of it. It is Reginald's doing, and he must answer for it someday." She lifted her chin. "But I am no longer his dupe, and I shall take great care that my father and mother are not either."

"I believe your mama is pretty well aware of Reginald's true character," said Tom, smiling encouragingly.

She looked a trifle annoyed, but said, "Well, I am glad of it.

Between the two of us—three, counting you, Tom—we ought to be able to protect my papa from further deception."

Tom declared his willingness for the scheme and they walked on, turning back at the Chalybeate grounds and retracing their steps along the path to the church.

"It is all very distressing, Tom." She sighed. "I do not yet know how to go on, for it is not as though I may cut an acquaintance with whom I have been friends all my life. But there must be a change. Either Reggie must renounce his present course, or I must simply become used to his being a scoundrel, I suppose."

Feeling it wiser to keep his own conclusions to himself, Tom merely suggested, "You must speak to your mama. She is a very sensible woman, and I fancy will have some good advice for you."

To this Diana was quick to agree, and Tom, fatigued with such a heavy subject, regaled her with a story he had heard of a vicar who had no notion his church was being used to store smuggled contraband on the weeks he preached at another parish—until he mistook his day and came to find not penitents but casks and bales in the pews. Diana was able to recover much of her usual liveliness, and he returned her to her parents in much better spirits than she had left them.

The reconciliation with Diana at last accomplished, Tom returned to his normal occupations, driving out with her almost daily and attending other social events to be near her. His only alteration was to avoid interaction with any of Reggie's set, and not to enter the portals of the Brighton Club. Two days passed, therefore, before he met Reginald again, exercising his horse on the Steyne. Reggie greeted him with excessive pleasure and inquired where he had got to these many days.

Tom laughed. "Only to the point at last, Reggie."

Reginald regarded him a trifle stiffly. "You will pardon my sense of ill-usage if I am to understand that you require my felicitations."

"No, no, not as much as that," assured Tom. "Only my fortunes have improved significantly since last we met."

Reginald hesitated for a moment before beaming at Tom. "Capital! We must celebrate by having you at Bentley's once more. He has settled upon tonight for another game, if you will join us."

"Very obliging of him, but I am promised to the Marshalls for dinner tonight, as are you, if I do not mistake."

"Well, certainly I am, but dinner does not last all night."

Tom gazed innocently at him. "But it is not only dinner. Recollect that Lady Lyons gives a ball tonight, and I will not miss the chance to dance with Diana. Indeed, I should have imagined you, too, would not miss it."

"I do not intend to, but we may count ourselves excused by midnight and join the card party."

"Oh, no, I will not be so rag-mannered. I have yet again been so fortunate as to engage Diana for the supper dance, and simply could not get away until afterward."

"I know it too well, you lucky dog, for she would not promise it to me. But I will explain the matter to Bentley, so he will not look for you until one or two," said Reginald with aplomb. "We will await you with eagerness, but do not blame me if they all roast you for putting romance before friendship."

Unable to suppress a chuckle at this audacious persistence, Tom said, "Nothing of the sort! But your eagerness will be wasted on me. I shall be far too fatigued after dancing to stay up all night at cards, I assure you."

Reginald would not give it up, coaxing him in every way imaginable to say he would come, but Tom remained unmoved—and highly diverted.

"I know what you are about, Reginald," he said sapiently, earning a wary glance from Reggie. "You think to cozen me into fulfilling your prediction of my downfall, for if I give in to you, it will only be so that I may lose everything as I fall asleep over my cards. If my weariness does not see to that, Bentley's excellent brandy will, I am persuaded."

"You cannot be so poor-spirited, Breckinridge!" cried Reginald, pursuing to the last.

Tom turned his horse away and urged it to a canter, laughing over his shoulder, "See if I cannot!"

He was so successful in this challenge that over the following few days none of Reggie's circle could get more than a few moments speech with him, and always with the vexatious conviction that Tom had become mighty slippery.

So provoking was this, apparently, that Thursday morning Tom found Reginald lying in wait for him when he came into the coffee room at the Ship to order breakfast. Tom's mood was elevated by several excessively agreeable days in Diana's company, and he greeted Reginald brightly, shaking hands and inquiring where he had been.

"For I declare I haven't seen you in days, Reggie!" he said ingenuously.

"No," agreed Reginald, his smile a trifle strained. "You're a hard man to run to ground, Breckinridge. Worse than an old fox on the downs."

Tom laughed heartily. "Poor Reginald! And here I have been laboring under the misapprehension it was you who were avoiding me. But sit down and take some breakfast. You look hagged to death! Allow me to recommend the buns—they are excellent. Yes, Mr. Timms, the usual for me."

Reginald, declining sustenance of any kind, sat down. "Seriously, Breckinridge, what have we done to offend you? Was the yacht race so traumatic that you have given us up?"

"Race? You mean the free-trading expedition, do not you?" asked Tom sweetly.

Reginald exhaled, rubbing his nose. "Very well, it was free-trading. And it was infamous of us to drag you into it all unawares. But you must believe me that it was just a lark—nothing more than something to do."

"Such as peeping at unsuspecting females as they bathe."

"Yes!" cried Reginald, but at Tom's raised brow he sighed. "I can see that you are determined upon holding your grudge. I am disappointed in you, Breckinridge. I thought you were a better man than this."

Tom barely contained his admiration. "Dear me. I am desolated, I assure you. What can I do to redeem myself?"

"Mockery does not become you," said Reginald, annoyed.

"You are very right."

Reginald strove against what Tom hoped was a violent urge to plant him a facer, but whatever incident threatened, it was forestalled by the arrival of Tom's breakfast, borne by the landlord. By the time that worthy had gone away again, Reginald was in command of himself.

"Breckinridge," he said, with brotherly tenderness, "come back to your friends. You are greatly missed."

Tom dropped his eyes, taking a bite of bacon and chewing. "I know I am."

"Then come see us. Let us make things right."

"I would like that," said Tom, frankly meeting his eyes.

Reginald smiled disarmingly. "You owe us a game."

"I? Owe?" said Tom, blinking at Reginald. "No, no, you have it all wrong. You owe me, Reginald. I have your vowels, recollect. A great many of them, in fact."

"You agreed to give me more time, Breckinridge."

"My offer still stands, Reginald. Say the word and I will consign your vowels to the fire."

Reginald hesitated, but then looked away. "You have a very poor idea of my honor if you imagine I should accept such an offer."

"It is because I have a very poor idea of your honor that I make the offer, Reggie." They held gazes until Tom sighed, putting down his fork and regarding his companion gravely. "Drop the acquaintance with those scoundrels and put your attainments to better use. I have seen where your present path will lead you, and it is no very honorable course, I assure you."

Reginald's lips pursed. "Your solicitude is disarming, my dear Breckinridge, but as I have told you before, you are mistaken in Lord Bentley and the others."

"Very well," said Tom, picking up his fork. "Do what you must to redeem your vowels. I have all the patience in the world, depend upon it."

"It would be a simple matter if you would but trust us."

Tom chuckled, surveying his plate. "I do not doubt it."

Reginald's eyes hardened. "You do not know what you are about, Breckinridge. This is a very dangerous game you are playing."

"Forgive me for contradicting you, Reginald," said Tom amiably, "but I am not playing. Or did the fact escape your notice?"

Reginald's hand clenched on the table and he stood. "Have it your way, Breckinridge. But do not say I didn't warn you."

Tom watched him go, taking a forkful of eggs in his mouth and chewing ruminatively. Battle, it seemed, was joined.

Chapter 25

THE BATTLE WAS not to begin as Tom had imagined however, for that very afternoon he was ambushed by Mrs. Ridley in Clarke's music library.

"Mr. Breckinridge!" she cried, smiling up from under a dashing bonnet of green velvet made to set off her eyes perfectly. "What a lucky chance! I had just thought, only this morning, that it would be a shame to leave town without meeting you once more. I am to return to the country tomorrow, you know."

"I did not know," said Tom with utmost civility. "I wish you Godspeed."

She chuckled, taking his arm. "But how adorable you are! You must escort me home. You are finished here, I perceive."

Having come into the library only to evade Lord Bentley—whom he had noticed browsing a shop window nearby and was now gone— Tom was obliged to acknowledge that he was, indeed, finished there, and led her out onto the street.

"Brighton is so very exciting, is not it, Mr. Breckinridge?" declared Mrs. Ridley brightly as she hugged his arm close to her bosom. "I do believe this view of the sea to be the most lovely in all of England. I wish I could stay out the season, but my poor purse cannot allow it. You, however, have been very lucky recently, I hear, and could stay any number of seasons, and in a very fine style."

"I have known some luck here," allowed Tom, "but it will not enable me to stay longer than I had planned."

She looked up in astonishment. "You do not mean you have lost it already? No, I do not believe it! How could such a thing happen? For you are not so foolish, I am persuaded."

"I hope I am not, Mrs. Ridley. No, I have not lost it, but I do not choose to alter my style of living by so handsome a sum as I have come by. I have a much better use for it."

She seemed pleased at this, and eyed him with something that could have been respect but which was more hungry. "Mr. Breckinridge, you are a most singular gentleman—quite out of the common way! I cannot help but contrast your perspicacity with that of poor Reggie, who, I believe, had the misfortune to contribute to your luck."

"You have very good information, ma'am," said Tom blandly.

"Did not I tell you I run in a well-informed circle?"

"I had no notion your circle had come with you to Brighton."

She chuckled, a husky sound that made the hair on Tom's neck stand on end. "All of London converges on Brighton in the summer, sir. Naturally, many of my acquaintance are here. But it is of no consequence, for I did not require their information to convince me of Reggie's inferiority."

They had reached the steps of her lodging, and Tom bowed, taking the opportunity to stand away from her. "I am flattered, ma'am, but can only say that Mr. Popplewell and I are so dissimilar that one cannot compare the two of us with any fairness. Now, I wish you the best of luck on your journey and in your future life, and—"

"You are absolutely correct, Mr. Breckinridge," she interrupted, grasping his wrist. "You are nothing like Reggie, and I will tell you why. He is an impostor!"

Tom narrowed his eyes at her. He knew Reginald to be unscrupulous, selfish, and prone to deception, but an impostor? "How so, ma'am?" he inquired.

She leaned forward and in a confidential tone said, "Our dear Reggie is not the heir to the viscountcy—at least, he is very likely not, according to my information. There is a rumor even now circulating London that the soldier—the one who was next in line and was supposed to have died on the Continent—is very much alive, and is expected to arrive in England any day!"

Tom stared at her. "Does Reggie know this?"

"The rumor has, no doubt, reached his ears by this time, for his circle is quite as large and as well-informed as my own."

"Then he must be exceedingly disappointed."

"Undoubtedly," she said, stepping closer to him and running a finger over the folds of his neck cloth, "and it seems to have driven him to be very unwise. The loss of several hundred pounds at the gaming table would be distressing to him at any time, but it must be nothing to his sensations now, on the verge of discovering that he has lost the viscountcy and all that it entails."

Shaking his head, Tom edged away. "It is a fine mess, all of his own making, and I pity him."

"But you could do so much more," she said with a triumphant smile. "Think of the power you have over him, Mr. Breckinridge. You hold in your hands—" Her eyes slid to his waistcoat— "or in your pocket, hundreds of dollars' worth of vowels that Reginald would give—oh, I imagine he would give anything to have them back."

She advanced as she spoke, and Tom backed away, only to find he was up against the steps of her house. "My inclinations do not run with yours, ma'am. Rest assured that I do not wish to drive Reggie—or any man for that matter—to desperation. I have already offered to return his vowels, but his scruples forbid it. Nevertheless, I have made it plain that he may redeem his vowels whenever he is in cash again."

"But where is your imagination?" she said, a pretty pout on her lips. "Come into the house, Mr. Breckinridge, and hear me out. I am persuaded you and I could deal extremely together."

She put her hand up to grasp his lapel, but Tom, perhaps inspired by his recent moralistic discussions with Reginald, decided it was high time that he got him out. Unwilling to waste a good coat, however, he twisted to the side to evade her grasp, and without another word, took to his heels down the street.

Reaching St. James's Street in safety, Tom slackened his pace and strode toward the Steyne, ruminating upon Mrs. Ridley's offer. He was unable still to resolve whether Mrs. Ridley was on Reginald's side or her own, and his mind was in a whirl of speculation. Doubtless Reginald and she were enjoying an *affaire*, but this disturbing news may have changed the lady's mind regarding any long-term continuance. Her information on Reginald's uncertain prospects could well keep him in her pocket, for if he was as imprudent in general as he had hinted at last week, he would not wish for such news—be it true or false—to get about to his creditors.

But it was not, after all, such information as could keep him in her power forever. Tom deduced she had been playing a double game all along, with her talons sunk into Reginald and her eye out for any possibility of richer game. Tom's "luck" had struck her as a perfect opportunity, and believing him to be either as unprincipled as herself or a countrified simpleton, she had made this offer to him, no doubt hoping to form a partnership that would bleed him dry while extorting what she could at the same time from dear Reggie.

Tom could guess how she would take his patent refusal. There would be no more caressing attempts to win him over, and not even a civil cut direct. No, he knew her well enough to conjecture that she would not remove to the country before she had had her revenge, and he was a cod's head if she didn't join forces with Reginald, who already had cause to wish him ill.

Reaching the Ship, Tom went up to his room to change for dinner, which he was taking at the Marshall's. Mrs. Marshall had made a habit of inviting him nearly every evening of late, and Mr. Marshall had begun to grumble less regarding the small size of the dining table and a surfeit of guests. He did, however, tend to invite Reginald whenever he could get him, and such was the case tonight.

Despite circumstances, however, the evening went off very well, owing greatly to Mr. Marshall's need to expostulate on the shocking state of morality among smugglers— "how dared they violate the Prince Regent's favored summer home?"—and finding in Tom a responsive listener. Mr. Marshall was so gratified that he attempted to draw Reginald, who had been quieter than usual, into the conversation; however, Reginald's responses were not warm enough for him to continue the project, and he spent their quarter of an hour over port almost entirely engaged in receiving Tom's commiseration.

After dinner they attended another private ball, where Tom enjoyed the supper dance with Diana.

"You have risen in his estimation," observed Diana as they danced. "I heard him remark to Mr. Pennyweather the other day on your acuity in matters of the law."

"I hope Mr. Pennyweather will not think it expedient to examine me," said Tom with a grimace.

Diana laughed. "He will not, though I fancy you should be quite capable of impressing him with your understanding were he to trouble himself. Do not scoff! I overheard much of your discourse with Papa, and you exhibited very well."

"Yes, one might even believe I knew of what I was speaking!" said Tom in self-mockery. "It was only what any country parson might sermonize on every Sunday."

"Well then, Mr. Breckinridge," said Diana archly, "we now have proof that you are not irreligious, for you must have been listening."

Tom laughed, and they went down the dance in excellent spirits. At the end of the first set, Reginald came to take his leave of Diana, asking if she would convey his regrets to her father. This she gladly agreed to do, but expressed a wish that he would stay and enjoy the dance.

"For you do not look at all the thing, Reggie," she said, eying his slightly haggard countenance with concern. "It is my belief you have been pushing yourself too hard."

"Yes, stay and enjoy yourself, Reginald," said Tom. "It will do you more good than wherever you are off to, I am persuaded."

Reginald grimaced at Diana, casting a daggered look at Tom. "However, I have obligations that must be met, and dancing will not do the job. Pray excuse me."

They were, therefore, obliged to let him go, but as Tom led Diana in to supper, they were accosted by Mr. Marshall, who demanded to know if they had seen Reginald.

"He had another engagement, sir," supplied Tom helpfully. "He asked us to convey his regrets."

Mr. Marshall huffed. "That's a devil of a nuisance, for I could not find hide nor hair of him in all this dashed house, though I went over the whole of it, and even made a spectacle of myself walking into the ladies' withdrawing room by mistake!"

Diana did what she could to soothe him—which was much, and her mother's subsequent ministrations proved very efficacious—and he soon was able to sit and eat a plate of cold meat and fruit. And though he did mutter to himself from time to time, he did not more than once gaze in irritation at his daughter's laughing interaction with Tom, and when she danced with Tom a second time at the end of the night, he only pulled out his pocket watch and remarked on the lateness of the hour.

When the ball had ended, Tom returned to the Ship and made his way to his room. To his astonishment, his door was open and Matthew stood in the center of what looked like a maelstrom had hit.

The groom, looking gravely at his master, said, "It seems to me someone wants something of yours, sir."

Tom, gazing in wonder at the mess, said, "It does seem that way."

They moved about the room, picking up pieces of clothing and sundry toilette articles from the floor and replacing them properly.

"You wouldn't know anything about it, would you, sir?" asked Matthew conversationally.

Tom grimaced. "Indeed, I do have a notion what they were after, but as I have placed it in the inn's strong box like an intelligent man, I cannot conceive of what they can have hoped to achieve by this."

"Mayhap that didn't occur to them, sir, whosomever they may be."

Lost in thought, Tom merely shook his head and desired Matthew to call a maid to help them put his room to rights. It did not take a great stretch of the imagination for Tom to conclude to whom he owed this upheaval, and as the chaos was reversed and the damage assessed, he struggled between grim amusement and a sense of very ill-usage. He simply did not believe he merited such treatment.

He had been nothing but tolerant of Reginald and his pranks, and had only gone along in whatever that gentleman had seen fit to involve him. He had been often annoyed, to be sure, but in all he was persuaded he had been quite amazingly patient. He was under no obligation to continue the card parties with Reginald and his friends, and he had been entirely civil in refusing the innumerable invitations. And he had offered to return Reginald's vowels without comment. Reggie had only himself to blame for landing in this pickle, and it irritated Tom excessively that he would stoop to something as vulgar as petty thievery.

But as he lay in bed that night, Tom found he was glad that Reginald had made so impudent a move, for Tom was impatient to see this thing through. The games of words were amusing, to be sure, but the rifling of Tom's belongings had advanced the battle into the realm of the physical, and the rules had been changed. But this notion only put a smile on Tom's lips, for upon reflection, he was made to own that he had cherished a desire for a good set-to with dear Reggie for many weeks.

In light of this, Tom felt it prudent to be on his guard for whatever might come his way, and it was with a feeling of suppressed excitement that he attended the promenade concert at the Castle Assembly Rooms with the Marshalls the following evening. As the concert commenced without Reginald or Mrs. Ridley putting in an appearance, Tom expected at any moment for an unknown person to slip into the row behind and attempt to do him an injury. An avid pupil of Mr. Jackson whenever he was in London, Tom rather hoped they would do their worst.

The sacred precincts of the Castle Inn were not to be so desecrated that night, however, for the only murder attempted was of a poor lady's heart, and brilliantly—if a trifle extravagantly—executed in Italian. At the moving climax of this song, Tom, thrilling with expectancy, was startled almost out of his wits by a sudden touch on his arm, but as it was Diana clinging to him in her emotion, he very composedly—and with not disagreeable sensations—allowed her to do so.

After the concert, the Marshalls offered Tom a place in their carriage, but as he was by this point a veritable powder keg on the verge of explosion, he graciously declined their offer and wished them a very pleasant evening, electing to walk to the Ship by the darkest route possible so as to encourage Reginald—or whatever thug he may have hired to do his business—to attack while his victim was in top form. His plan worked to admiration; he was walking down the alley between Black Lion Street and East when a burly figure in black hove into sight, swinging a cudgel at his head.

Tom ducked, lunging forward and burying his shoulder in the man's gut. The man was solid—smelling of coal dust and fish and other unpleasant things—and he no more than wheezed at the unexpected impact before bringing the cudgel down on Tom's back. The angle of the blow was not optimal, however, and Tom sustained it with only minimal pain. Whether this was from the excessive energy that pumped through his veins or the fitness of his body was inconsequential; he took the opportunity to step between the man's legs and throw him cross-buttock to the ground.

The man hit on his side, and he rolled to his back, bringing the cudgel up and swinging it at Tom, who had stepped forward at the ready. Tom danced to the side, aiming a kick at the man's bicep and stunning it. The cudgel dropped and Tom kicked it away. When he turned back, his assailant had regained his feet and looked to be as mad as fire.

The man was large, but Tom was taller and younger, and had the quickness of a trained boxer. The first attack—a bear hug—Tom slipped and countered with a left hook to the ribs, earning a grunt of pain. But his assailant recovered quickly, pulling his elbow backward into Tom's head—which wasn't there. Tom, anticipating this move, had ducked and come up with an uppercut, hearing the sickening crunch on impact of a breaking rib.

This slowed the man down, and Tom thought he saw a gleam of fear in his eyes. Smiling grimly, he stood ready, fists up, but the man only watched him in wary indignation.

"She said you was a soft cove, and wouldn't be no trouble," the thug abruptly pronounced.

Tom hesitated in his bouncing on his feet. "Who said?"

"Flash mort what snabbled me for this lay. Said you was green at the gills, weak as a kitten. Done humbugged me, she did."

Precisely the course for Mrs. Ridley, Tom thought. Aloud, he said, "My apologies for your inconvenience. Perhaps you have learned a lesson."

The man rubbed his side where Tom had cracked his rib. "Aye, that I have! To be leery of a swell mort what makes ducks and drakes with the ready."

Tom blinked, swiping the sweat from his forehead. "What precisely did she hire you to do?"

"Clobber you and swipe the gewgaws. But this here mort, she gets the scrips you got on you. Dicked in the nob, I say."

Frowning in an effort to comprehend this speech, Tom said carefully, "You say she wanted papers from me? And you could keep the valuables?"

"Aye! And five megg she'd of dropped for it, too!"

The man muttered something that Tom took to be animadversions on the morals of so-called gentlewomen and turned, looking about for his cudgel. Tom darted between him and where the weapon lay on the flagstones, but the man simply raised his hand in surrender.

"Stow it, cully, I'll knuckle under. It ain't you I got a crow to pluck with. It's that flash mort what wants a chivey."

"I couldn't agree more, though it wouldn't do, my good man," said Tom, lowering his fists a bit as the man continued to grumble. As it appeared that his attacker truly had no intention of pursuing the fight, he said, "See here, you can't go about roughing up a lady, no matter how she has wronged you. But there's no sense in your being stiffed for giving your best go either. What if I paid you double what she offered, and you tell her I had no papers on me?"

His erstwhile assailant considered this a moment. "Double the muck and diddle the prig—that's a rum bob!" He smiled, revealing a missing tooth, and stuck out a grubby hand. "Aye, all's bowman!"

Forgoing an attempt at translation of this, Tom shook on it, giving the man ten pounds, after which they each went on their way, the man with his cudgel toward Black Lion Street and Tom to the Ship. As he walked, Tom rolled his shoulders and flexed his fingers, musing that a good set-to was always excellent for the relief of tension, even if one were bloodied and bruised at the end of it.

Chapter 26

WHEN TOM REACHED the Ship, he was met by the landlord, who informed him he had visitors. "A gentleman and two ladies, sir. Come ten, fifteen minutes ago. I've put them in the private parlor."

Tom, non-plussed, thanked him and asked him to bring hot water and bandages and some basillicum powder to the parlor. Then he ascended the stairs and opened the parlor door to find Mr. and Mrs. Marshall and Diana sitting together in the room.

"Tom! We have been here this age!" cried Diana, coming smilingly to meet him. "We have just been wondering what had become of you."

Tom bowed to them and said, "To what do I owe this pleasure?"

Diana giggled. "How very proper. This is no social call, silly. Only you left your gloves behind at the Assembly Rooms. A porter found them and brought them out just after you had left us—Oh, good gracious!"

Tom had reached to take his gloves, but at sight of his bloodied knuckles Diana dropped the gloves and took his hand, examining it in horrified astonishment.

"Oh, Tom! What has happened?"

By this time, Mrs. Marshall had hastened forward and taken Tom's other hand to examine, and Tom cast a despairing look to Mr. Marshall.

"Now, now, my boy," Mr. Marshall said, shaking his head, "best cut line. The females always find us out, no matter how cleverly we try to fudge things."

The ladies added their protestations to his and Tom at last sighed. "I was set upon as I walked."

Their horror was entire and eloquent until Mr. Marshall quieted them with his own expostulation. "I am shocked and grieved. What can this world be coming to? First smugglers and now marauders in the streets of Brighton. Brighton! Were you robbed, lad?"

Tom satisfied them on this point, saying that he had had his wits about him enough to avoid such a calamity.

"Your face tells the tale well enough, my boy," said Mr. Marshall with satisfaction. "Not a scratch! Do you look at him, Mrs. Marshall— sported himself handsomely, I'd wager."

Mrs. Marshall did look—as did Diana, who had not wanted her father's admonition to do so. As they were wondering over and admiring him, a knock on the door admitted the landlord, with water and other supplies for Tom's comfort. Mrs. Marshall took these in hand and bade the curious landlord goodnight, assuring him that she would minister to his guest's needs.

"Well," said Mrs. Marshall, settling to bathing Tom's left hand while Diana tended to his right, "I, for one, do not believe it was any common cutthroat who assaulted you tonight. You were far too excitable this evening to have wished to walk home for nothing."

Tom hesitated—wishing he had taken even longer to return to the Ship, and so avoid this scrutiny—but Diana seconded her mother's statement, adding, "Pray, do not keep secrets from us, Tom."

"Very well," he said, never proof against those blue eyes. Thinking quickly of what best to disclose, he said, "I won a large sum at cards several nights ago, and several interested parties have been very urgent with me regarding a number of vowels in my possession."

Diana cried out, a hand going to her mouth, but Mrs. Marshall said, "But you are no gamester, Tom."

"No, I am not," he said firmly, "which is why I suspect they let me win on the expectation that I would fancy myself either very skilled or lucky enough to repeat the occurrence. I can only say they have been deeply disappointed."

"Enough to have you set upon! Oh, it is wicked, wicked!"

"Smugglers, marauders, and Dead Setters!" muttered Mr. Marshall, taking an agitated turn about the small room. "I never thought to see the day. I shall not and will not stand for it! Mrs. Marshall, Diana, we are leaving this place tomorrow."

"I am glad to hear it, my dear," said Mrs. Marshall complacently. "I wish to be home in time for the blackberrying."

"But what of Tom?" cried Diana.

Tom smiled. "Do not worry for me, Diana. I shall go home as well." He lowered his voice and his eyes. "After you go, there is nothing to keep me here, after all."

The ladies, who had tenderly bandaged Tom's hands, stood, pressing them gently in their shared sympathy and esteem for his ordeal.

He thanked them, bowing low over their hands, and gingerly shaking Mr. Marshall's.

As they filed out the door, Tom wondered with a sinking feeling if, after all, his efforts had been in vain, and Mr. Marshall would carry Diana away from him again without any promise of seeing her until next Season in Town. But his spirits instantly recovered when Diana said quietly as she passed him, "Come to the house tomorrow, early. Do not fail!"

This, Tom found no difficulty in agreeing to, and after an excellent night's sleep, he rose betimes, breakfasted and requested Matthew to pack his bags and ready the horses for a journey.

"Home, sir?" asked the groom, eyebrows raised.

"Not certain, Matthew," replied Tom. "Either there or Wrenthorpe Grange, if I am fortunate enough to have good news at the end of the morning."

Grinning, Matthew wished his master good luck and went away to his work, while Tom set off down the Marine Parade toward the Royal Crescent. He arrived to find the house in a bit of an uproar, maids and footmen scurrying here and there with trunks and parcels and piles of clothing and other articles, and the butler and housekeeper calling out directions and instructions.

Flagging down the butler, Tom inquired for Miss Marshall and was directed upstairs to the saloon, where Miss was entertaining Mr. Popplewell. Tom's brow furrowed, and he took the stairs two at a time, throwing open the door to the saloon with rather more force than was civil—or necessary, as it turned out, for Diana was alone in the room, huddled on the sofa and dabbing at her reddened eyes with a handkerchief.

Tom went instantly to her. "Diana, pardon me—I understood you to be with Reginald."

"Then of course you would come crashing in," she said, but as she did so with a pathetic little smile, he did not take offense, and sat down beside her, taking her hand.

"What is the matter? Was Reginald here? What did he say?"

Her hand gripped his. "Oh, Tom, do not speak to me of Reggie—I wish never to see him again, or even to hear his name!" She paused to blow her nose defiantly. "He tried to make love to me—I, who have ever been as a sister to him! It was just as you said—he would have me believe that he has been violently in love with me these many months, and has only been kept from speaking by his extreme sense of delicacy. What utter claptrap! He doesn't know the meaning of the word—he never has!"

Tom did his best to show sympathy, uttering soothing noises and patting her hand while inwardly he alternately seethed and rejoiced. That Reginald had had the temerity to press his suit upon Diana when he almost certainly wanted only her fortune—it was enough to make Tom's blood boil. Reginald evidently was hard-pressed enough for money that he had found it expedient to forward his plans of marriage to the nearest heiress at hand. That he had not succeeded—not by even an inch—filled Tom with joyous relief and not a little smug satisfaction.

"But that is not all, Tom," continued Diana stormily. "After I had refused him—and I was obliged to do so repeatedly, for he did not cease to importune me, even when I told him how it pained me—he tried to trick me into going with him in a carriage! Tom, he had a post-chaise and four ready outside! I never was more incensed in my life! He said that I must think, and that a drive would clear my head, and wouldn't I like to drive along the King's road with him? I went to the window to see his precious carriage, and when I saw the postilions, I knew instantly what he was up to—for no one wants postilions but for a long journey—and I hit him."

"Good girl, Diana!" said Tom warmly, unable to refrain from kissing her hand.

She sniffed. "Then he went away, and I am very glad that he did, for I was so angry that I knew I would cry, and I was determined not to show him any sort of weakness." She dabbed at her eyes again. "Do you think that he has left Brighton? For I am certain he is in want of money, if he wished so desperately to marry me."

"I fear you are right, Diana," said Tom, patting her hand to keep himself from kissing her temptingly indignant lips.

She glared at him askance. "Do you mean you know I am right, Tom? For it was he who lost all that money to you—so it must have been he who set those horrid thieves on to attack you. I was not born yesterday, Mr. Breckinridge! It is clear as day that Reggie was behind that attack!"

"Perhaps not, Diana," Tom's honesty required him to say. "I have reason to believe my assailant was hired by a woman, in which case—"

"A woman!" cried Diana. "But who—Oh, good gracious! Could it have been Mrs. Ridley?"

Tom did not know whether he was pleased at her quickness of mind or amused that she would think so readily of her cousin in such a circumstance, but he answered, "I truly do not know. Mrs. Ridley is not in charity with me at the moment, but neither is Reggie."

"It does not admit of a doubt! She has been so cozy with Reggie that I daresay he put her up to it. Well, it is just like them! But Tom, I do not suppose—" She bit her lip, then tried again, "I do not suppose all this could have been avoided if you had given his vowels back."

"I fear not, Diana, for I did offer to do so, multiple times, but he would not allow it."

Her countenance filled with annoyance and she snapped her fingers. "That for his honor! What use is honor if it will not allow the reasonable forgiveness of a burden while it smiles upon cheating at cards and smuggling brandy and setting thieves on to attack an innocent person—"

She blinked very quickly, then her face crumpled, and Tom put his arms about her as her shoulders shook. "Hush, Diana! My dear Diana, I beg you—it is not certain that Reggie was involved, you know, for even he may draw the line at such violence—"

"It is not that!" she wailed, turning in his arms so that she wept into his neck cloth. "Oh, Tom, it is my fault that you were almost killed last night! If I had not insisted that you befriend Reggie, he would not have introduced you to his odious friends, and they would not have tried to take you in, and you would not have won all that horrid money, and you would not have been set upon!"

Overwhelmed by many sensations—most delightful, but one resentful of her poor opinion of his skill in self-defense—Tom simply held her until they both had regained some command of themselves.

When she pulled away, he took her hands in his and said gently, "Diana, your instinct was virtuous and right, and I am glad I followed your advice. Though he is a scoundrel, he deserved the chance to act decently, and to mend his ways. He chose poorly and I am none the worse for it, for God in his wisdom provided me with an excellent mother who scrupled not to own my father's deficiencies. And when it came to it, I was saved from any physical harm through the exercise of—I say this in all humility—my own various and not inconsiderable skills."

"Tom, you are a complete hand," said Diana, her mouth twitching despite her tears.

"A knowing one, up to all the tricks," he said, grinning and gazing into her bewitchingly blotched face.

She returned his gaze for several moments, then the humor left her eyes. "Tom, why do not you kiss me?"

He blinked. "Forgive me, Diana. When I was so improper as to give in to the temptation to kiss you before, I paid dearly for it."

"But I did not want you to kiss me then—that is, I did, but—" She blushed rosily, her breath coming quickly as her gaze flicked from his eyes to his lips and back again. Then she uttered, "Oh, hang it all!"

To Tom's complete astonishment—and not inconsiderable delight—Diana reached up to take his head and pull it down, planting her lips squarely and firmly on his own. His brain needed only a moment to assimilate that reserve was no longer required, and his arms went around her, holding her to him, and his mouth returned her rather blunt kiss with greater imagination. The softening of her lips on his told him that this was entirely acceptable, and he abandoned himself to the enjoyment of—if not the first kiss—the most memorable kiss he had yet enjoyed with the woman he loved.

Abruptly, the door opened, and Mr. Marshall came in on the words, "You'll not believe it, my dear, but Reginald's lost his viscountcy!"

He stilled on the threshold, arrested by the sight of his daughter locked in the arms of a young man whom he had only recently come to acknowledge as a sensible boy with considerable bottom, but whom he was by no means convinced was an eligible *parti*. The guilty start with which the couple jumped to their feet confirmed him in this suspicion.

"What the devil?" he exclaimed, raising a hand to point at Tom. "How dare you, sir—"

"Mr. Marshall! It's not—I can explain," stammered Tom, blushing red. "I should like to ask for your permission to pay my addresses—"

Mr. Marshall's brow lowered. "A strange way to ask permission, sir!"

Diana took Tom firmly by the hand and led him forward, stopping determinedly before her father. "Papa, I am in love with Tom—you must know this. There is no one else to whom I wish to be married. Indeed, there is no one else to whose addresses I should pay any heed. Will you not give your consent?"

He sputtered for a moment, but the precipitate entrance of Mrs. Marshall into the room checked whatever protest he would have formed.

"Good heaven, what a morning," she cried, pulling at the strings of her bonnet and removing it. "Hello, Mr. Breckinridge! I am so glad you are here. How are your hands today? Better? Good. But I perceive I have interrupted you. Forgive me, I am full of news; however, it can wait."

She looked expectantly at the couple before her, but Mr. Marshall turned to her, saying blankly, "My dear—she loves Breckinridge, here."

"Yes, my love."

"But do not you mind it? What of Reginald?"

She took his hand and patted it. "I own I never did like the notion of our Diana married to dear Reggie. But it does not signify, my dear, for I fear Reginald has gone away. It is not all that bad, however, for I have just discovered that he has taken Mrs. Ridley with him, so it seems he plans to marry her—at least, I sincerely hope so, for that would be a great weight off your mind, would not it? He can be of no better use to you now, after all, for he has lost the viscountcy."

Mr. Marshall blinked, recalling the paper he held in his hand. "So he has! The most extraordinary thing! The true heir—that soldier supposed to have died of consumption in Paris—is alive! He appeared in London yesterday, and we have just had news of it today. So Reginald hasn't got the rotten borough, and I shall not get the seats."

He was so truly consternated that Mrs. Marshall kissed his cheek and said gently, "No, my dear, but perhaps it is wiser that you discuss your bill privately with other members of parliament, and thus gain their support."

"A deal of work, that," he said testily. His eyes alighted once more on the happy couple, whose hands were still tightly clasped. He harrumphed. "Yes, well. I suppose I must give my consent to this match. Very irregular, sir, to propose to my daughter before asking my consent. I do not like it, but it is all of a piece with the world nowadays. Everything going sideways, and I never knowing if I am on my head or my heels."

"Oh, Papa," said Diana, stepping forward to kiss his other cheek. "It is not so bad as that. He did not propose, precisely—he merely kissed me, which is perhaps the same thing, but I forced him to it, I assure you—he should have asked you presently, as he told you. Say you will hear him."

Mr. Marshall's countenance softened, and he said, "Well, if you wish me to so very much, my dear, I will." He cleared his throat. "Well, what have you to say for yourself, my boy?"

Tom, feeling much as though he had been through another madcap voyage on a racing yacht, pulled himself together. "Sir, I am in love with Dia—that is, Miss Marshall, and should be honored if you would allow me to pay my addresses to her."

"And what do you fancy you have to offer her, sir," replied Mr. Marshall in a businesslike tone, "or do you flatter yourself that you will be able to repair your fortune with hers?"

"Frank!" interjected Mrs. Marshall. "How can you suspect Mr. Breckinridge of such a motive?"

"It's quite alright, Mrs. Marshall," said Tom manfully. "It is true that my estate is not quite profitable just yet, sir, but my finances are in an excellent train, and I do not require anyone's fortune to repair my own. I am fully prepared to explain my circumstances to you, if you wish."

Mr. Marshall nodded, looking his prospective son-in-law up and down. "You've not got political weight, by any chance, have you?"

"None, sir."

Grimacing, Mr. Marshall turned away, but Diana took his arm and said coaxingly, "My dearest Papa, you will not be so odious as to sacrifice my happiness to your political aspirations! For I have not the smallest desire to be wedded to a politician, and I declare I will be heartbroken—indeed, I shall most certainly go into a decline—if you do not consent to our marriage."

Mr. Marshall looked startled at this and, turning to his lady for confirmation, received a very speaking look.

"She is not like her mother, you know, my dear," said Mrs. Marshall, "For I am as persuadable as a lamb. But Diana takes after her father, who will not be moved for anything."

Mr. Marshall cast her a deprecating look, but then he huffed, then chuckled, and his eye twinkled. "I suppose you are right, my love. After all, she could do worse, now that Reginald has turned tail. Breckinridge at least has shown himself a sensible fellow, and game as a pebble."

Then, losing all that was left of his gravity, he tossed the newspaper aside and grasped Tom's hand, shaking it. "Very well, you may marry my daughter, sir, since it seems you've no need to address her.

Come to think of it, I kissed Diana's mother before I got her father's consent, so I've only got my own again. Well. Why are we all standing about like dullards? This calls for celebration! Kittering! Kittering! Where is that butler? Kittering, there you are. Why are you running about like a madman? Fetch us the brandy—the good brandy, I tell you, that we got from Lord Bentley. There's a good man."

Epilogue

THE CURRICLE, DRAWN by a fine pair of greys, swept up the drive of Wrenthorpe Grange, stopping smartly before the front door. Matthew jumped down from his perch on the back and went to the horses' heads as a footman came forward to collect the portmanteaux strapped behind, and Tom, leaping out to hand Diana down from the vehicle, took the opportunity to kiss her hand and receive yet another of her brilliant smiles.

He had been basking in those smiles almost continually over the course of their several days' journey from Brighton to Wrenthorpe, having determined on bringing the news of their engagement to Sir Joshua and Lady Stiles themselves, and without loss of time. Mr. and Mrs. Marshall had accompanied them as far as London, eager to put the business of Reginald's defection behind them and to celebrate the satisfactory disposition of their daughter's future. They had stopped in Town for a few days, where Tom had once more proved his worth to Mr. Marshall in choosing for him a broad-chested black hunter at Tattersall's, and where Diana and her mother had enjoyed a week of shopping and ordering wedding clothes. Then the happy couple, eager to be on their way to Hertfordshire, took Tom's curricle with Matthew, leaving Diana's parents to follow them in a few days' time upon the conclusion of business and social engagements in Town.

Leading Diana up the steps, Tom watched her delight as she admired the symmetrical beauty of Sir Joshua's house, then as she gazed about in approval at the entry hall.

"It is lovely, Tom!" she said, beaming and relinquishing her hat and pelisse to the butler. "I can only imagine that Branwell will be every bit as lovely and welcoming."

Before Tom could corroborate this, his mother's voice hailed them from the staircase, and they turned to greet Lady Stiles as she descended toward them. Her gait had become somewhat ungainly, owing to the enlargement of her belly as her condition progressed, but her countenance glowed and her eyes sparkled with pleasure as she held her hands out to Diana.

"My dear! How wonderful to see you here at last!" she said, embracing her future daughter-in-law as firmly as her condition would allow. "And I do mean it is a cause for wonder, for I declare if it was not two months ago that we despaired of the event!"

"I never despaired of it, Mama," came Lenora's voice from the library, from whence she glided into the hall, embracing her friend and brother before looking smugly upon the latter. "But Tom, gudgeon that he is, was certain you had developed a tendre for Reginald, of all persons. How is dear Reggie, by the by?"

"Reginald," said Diana, becoming somewhat prim, "has shown his very poor judgment by taking my cousin into his protection and absconding, and we know nothing more of the matter."

Any attempt by Lenora to inquire further was forestalled by the arrival of Sir Joshua, who hastened down the staircase, tutting at his wife for putting herself to the great and dangerous effort of ascending to the first floor without his assistance.

"But how am I to move about the house if I am forever to wait upon your convenience, my dear?" was Lady Stiles' very reasonable defense. Sir Joshua, however, was not to be dissuaded, and he took her by the hand, his other arm about her waist, leading her at a snail's pace up the steps. The three young persons quickly outstripped them, entering the drawing room as they chuckled amongst themselves at the anxious ministrations of the father-to-be.

"I had not imagined Sir Joshua to be so nervous a man," Diana observed, her brow furrowed over laughing eyes.

Lenora bent her head near to her friend, saying *sotto voce*, "I fear that the discovery of my mother's impending confinement has transformed Sir Joshua from a rational, staid man into something more resembling a mother hen."

"It is not so surprising, I suppose, seeing as this is his first experience of fatherhood," said Diana kindly.

"Perhaps not," said Tom, "but you may wish to revise your opinion once you have been privileged to witness the full and nauseating extent of his clucking and hovering."

As Sir Joshua and Lady Stiles then entered the room, they were obliged to turn the subject, and the conversation devolved upon Lady Stiles' plans for a new pleasure garden and Tom and Sir Joshua's descriptions of their latest farm machinery—a subject encouraged, to Lenora's amusement, by Diana.

When the housekeeper came to report that Diana's room was

ready, Lenora went with her, shooing out the maid as soon as she had finished unpacking Diana's portmanteau and settling onto the bed for a comfortable coze.

"You appear to be entirely taken in by my brother, Diana," she said archly. "I should not have believed it, but you must know what you are about. Tell me, and do be serious, how you like being engaged to him."

Diana smiled. "It is the most wonderful thing imaginable, to be sure, Lenora. But you must have guessed as much, knowing him as you do."

"But it is of the utmost interest to me to know how you see him, particularly, Diana."

Diana sat on the edge of the bed and considered blissfully. "He is lively and humorous, yet steady and careful. And he is very attentive, and so capable. And so much the gentleman—at least," she blushed and averted her eyes, "sometimes he forgets himself."

"Gracious," said Lenora, eyes wide with mock horror. "I should hope that he is suitably remorseful after such lapses. That is, unless you do not particularly wish for him to be."

This was said with a sly look, and Diana and Lenora collapsed into sympathetic giggles on the bed.

"Oh," said Diana, when she could once again breathe, "I never imagined the deliciousness of being in love—well and truly in love! For though I have watched my parents ever more closely as I have become aware of such things, I am persuaded that my intimate knowledge of their faults and foibles has held me back from believing that they could cherish anything so exciting for each other as the passion I hold for Tom. But the experience of these past months has thrown my views contrariwise, and I now believe that only a lasting passion—a strong and abiding love—could hold two people together through thick and thin."

"Through better and worse, rich and poor, sickness and health, 'til death do you part?"

Diana dimpled. "Well, yes!"

Lenora sat up. "It is the same with my parents. I love my mama and Sir Joshua dearly, but they are imperfect beings, after all. I am grateful beyond words that they have found one another, for their marriage has made all the difference to our present and future happiness—I should never have met my dear James if Sir Joshua had not brought us here, you know—but I do not believe I should be willing to put up with either of their quirks—not for a lifetime, at any rate. Do you know, ever since my mother disclosed her suspicion that she is carrying twins, Sir Joshua does not leave her alone for longer than an hour or two each day for fear that some unknown evil will swoop upon her and carry her off? I should run mad under such constant hovering, I declare."

"It does seem a trifle suffocating. However, you must admit, if it were your dear James..." offered Diana with a teasing smile.

Lenora's gaze flew to hers and they exchanged a sparkling look. "Yes. Somehow, the thought of James' undivided and unceasing attentions does not fill me with repugnance." She laughed and stretched luxuriously, contemplating the many delightful interactions she had enjoyed with her betrothed since they had declared themselves. She glanced at Diana. "Is it the same with you and Tom?"

Diana giggled and nodded.

Lenora regarded her intently, suddenly serious. "Are you sure, Diana? I do not wish to discredit your understanding, or wrong my brother, for I have the highest opinion of both of you—each in your own way, of course. But I do know you both very well, and I cannot help but wonder at your satisfaction in his attentions—your complete satisfaction. Are you certain you wish to share a lifetime with him? Are you certain you will not grow weary of his steadiness?"

"Dear me," said Diana, coloring a little. "When put so bluntly, it does seem a great risk, but so it would be with anybody, I daresay. When two persons from different families, with differing experience and views, come together in marriage, there is bound to be dissonance of some kind, and even occasional dissatisfaction. But where there is mutual affection and respect, where there is a real interest in the other's welfare—where there is true love—I am persuaded it will overcome any obstacle."

"But he is not romantic, Diana," pursued Lenora.

Diana smiled. "Recollect that you have, yourself, discovered the value of romance to be highly exaggerated. What of evil Dukes and stammering heroes and abductions and rescues?"

"All that is not romance, Diana," said Lenora, dismissing such notions with a wave of her hand. "That is all stuff and nonsense, and is best confined between the covers of a novel. What I speak of now is real romance—the sweet yearnings of a man for a woman, and she for him. The desire to love and cherish. I am not at all certain that Tom, who strides about his acres in buckskins and top-boots and discourses on the breeds of sheep and cattle to anyone who will listen, knows the meaning of the word 'cherish,' or how to show it if he does."

"Oh, I think he does," said Diana, blushing knowingly. "At least, he has done so to my satisfaction, and not infrequently."

Lenora, watching her closely, felt a slow smile spread across her face. She nodded, contented that her dear friend had made the choice that would make both her and Tom as happy as they deserved to be. When she left her friend to dress for dinner, she thought she heard retreating footsteps in the corridor, but when she looked up and down, there was no one in sight and, believing that she had imagined it, she went on her way to her own bedchamber.

Lord Helden dined at the Grange that night, and was glad to renew his slight acquaintance with Diana, whom he had met briefly in London the previous Season. There was much laughter and reminiscence over the two courses, as well as inquiries after the progress of renovation at Helden Hall, Lenora's future home. The enjoyment of the hour was only augmented by Sir Joshua's solicitude for his wife, which revealed itself in his watching zealously the prudence of her portions and taking into his own hands the cutting of her meat into harmless-sized pieces.

When the ladies left the gentlemen to their port, they were not long kept waiting in the drawing room, for there was little to entertain three besotted gentlemen without the objects of their affection present, whether or not the port was the very finest Sir Joshua's cellar had to offer. All the company was very soon reassembled, therefore, and they settled to talking, playing, singing, and otherwise contemplating their various states of joy.

Tom, finding himself alone with Diana on the window seat, bent his head to ask her what she had found to discuss so long with Lenora that afternoon.

"And how do you know we discussed anything very long, sir?" she asked archly. "Was your meeting me in the corridor just as I emerged not an accident, after all?"

Tom shrugged, not meeting her eyes. "It stands to reason that two women who are such friends and have been apart for some months would talk incessantly when given the chance."

Her brows rose. "Or you might have loitered about outside my room, listening at the keyhole."

Tom made some blustering noises disclaiming this, but Diana stopped him with an indulgent smile. "Pardon me for rallying you, Tom, for I know very well that if you had been listening at the keyhole, you should not be so curious as to the subject of our conversation. Besides, you have simply proved what Lenora and I came to acknowledge: that real romance is demonstrated by simple acts rather than unreasonable ones."

"Then loitering in the corridor outside your room is romantic?" inquired Tom, unable to keep the incredulity from his voice. "Lenora tried once to explain romance to me, but I fear she failed miserably—either that or I failed miserably to comprehend her. But it is all of a piece, or so I am told. Romance, according to my sister and mother, is beyond my understanding."

Diana chuckled. "Certainly not, Tom. That is what we came to understand—that you *are* romantic, at least to me."

"You think me romantic?" inquired Tom, a rather foolish grin transforming his handsome countenance. He took Diana's hand and turned fully to face her, stroking her fingers with his thumb. "I fear you must explain, my love, for I am at a loss as to how in the deuce I am romantic."

She proceeded to enumerate the ways in which she found him romantic, the ways he showed her he cherished her, from his glowing looks, to his alacrity in looking after her comfort, to his eagerness in making Branwell Manor her home in every sense of the word—until they both became aware that the others in the room had fallen silent. They glanced up to find themselves the center of a very avid and gleeful attention.

Tom cast each of his relations a challenging glare. "What is the meaning of this?"

Lady Stiles turned to her husband, murmuring loud enough for all to hear, "I prophesied this very circumstance, you know."

Lenora crossed her arms. "And he accused us of being nauseating."

Tom stiffened, his gaze flitting to his betrothed, who was blushing furiously. With a swift movement, he stood, pulling her also to her feet and declaring, "Diana has expressed a desire to see the garden. We intend to explore it now, before we lose the last of the light."

This pronouncement was met with dubious gazes, but Tom, majestically ignoring them all, swept an astonished Diana along with him out the door. As soon as they had gone, Lord Helden gave it as his opinion that Tom was in for a rude awakening if he thought to avoid any such emotions as he had just been caught displaying for the benefit of his relations. And Sir Joshua expressed his delight that Tom was, indeed, capable of foolish and irrational behavior.

Tom led Diana down the stairs and into the parlor, exiting through the French doors onto the veranda. His pace did not slow until they had reached the trimmed hedges of the formal garden, through the opening of which he pulled Diana. Once within, he took a stabilizing breath, offering her his arm and proceeding at a more sedate pace along the walks.

"Forgive me for exposing you to such impertinence, Diana," he said. "I am ashamed of them, and will make them beg your pardon before they are much older."

"It was not so bad, Tom," she said soothingly, having recovered her countenance. "They were simply rallying us."

"But it ought not to have happened!"

Diana looked conscious. "There was no impropriety, I am persuaded, so we need not blush for ourselves. We were merely talking together, after all."

Tom stopped, turning to face her. "Yes, but there ought not to have been any occasion for them to rally us. Our conversation was—we were— overcome by sentiment." He said the word as though it tasted foreign.

Diana blinked at him, then laughed. "We were, were not we? However, I am certain that they were only delighted by it, for it is not something that you are used to, though they have often wished you to be. Lenora said as much to me—while you loitered in the corridor outside my room."

"It is not what I am used to," repeated Tom, but then he paused, momentarily fascinated by the loveliness of her features when she laughed. He pulled her closer, furrowing his brow. "Why is it that I am unable to be rational when I am alone with you, Diana? I assure you, it is quite against my character to become lost in a lady's eyes, or wish to forget everything else but her, or go into a jealous miff at the mere mention of another man's good qualities. And yet you have made me do all of these ridiculous things and more. I am beginning to believe that something is gravely wrong with me."

"It is nothing of the sort, Tom," said Diana, lifting her hands to smooth the shoulders of his coat. "I daresay it is the most natural thing in the world to do ridiculous things, when one falls in love—at least at first. I am persuaded that, with time, you will grow so used to my proximity that you will be once more fully capable of rational thought, no matter the circumstance."

He gazed at her, a smile growing on his lips. "I highly doubt that, Diana, and upon reflection, I cannot find out that I regret it at all."

So saying, he gathered her to him, brushing a stray lock of hair away from her cheek with one hand and rubbing a thumb along her jawbone. She lifted her chin, her eyes sparkling, and the bewitching dimple appeared in her cheek. Tom's heart beat fast, and for the hundred-millionth time since she had agreed to his proposal of marriage, he thought himself the luckiest man in the world, and decided that sense and reason—at least in this case—could go to the devil.

It was at this moment that Tom perceived four pair of dancing eyes watching them from the window of the drawing room. Lenora hid behind the curtain with Lord Helden gazing smugly over her shoulder, but Lady Stiles stood openly at the sash, arm-in-arm with Sir Joshua and smiling down upon her unromantic son and his chosen bride.

When Diana perceived them, she blushed, pushing away from Tom with a murmured exclamation. But Tom was not about to let her go after having so dearly won her at last, and he pulled her back to him, his gaze never leaving the window.

"Tom!" she protested, her forearms pressing against his chest. "They are watching!"

"And well I know it, my love," he said, glaring pointedly at each pair of eyes in turn before turning back to her. "I say we give them what they are waiting for."

She gasped, but as her eyes glinted as much as his own at the thought, Tom felt no compunction in tightening his embrace and capturing her mouth in a kiss—not a chaste kiss at all, but a long, lingering, breathtaking and emphatic embrace that left no doubt in the minds of any observing it that Tom had well and truly lost his head along with his heart.

The eruption of cheers, claps and laughs in the drawing room was unheard and unheeded by the couple, but their ardor was both appreciated and emulated by the two other happy couples who rejoiced with them over a most satisfactory conclusion of events.

If you enjoyed this story, please consider leaving a review on Goodreads, Bookbub, or the store site where you purchased this book. Reviews are greatly appreciated by the author, and help others to find their next great read.

Thank you!

To find out more about The Branwell Chronicles series, go to judithhaleeverett.com or scan the QR code below:

Author's Note

I OFTEN END UP going down rabbit holes in pursuit of esoteric facts pertaining to my books. They are sometimes surprising, but more often only validate what I already know. Whatever the case, they are always fascinating to me—and I hope to you, too!

The Fens are a marshy area on the coast of eastern England that was drained during the 17th century to create more land for farming. The drainage caused unforeseen problems, however, because the peat shrank from lack of moisture and the fields sank below sea level and were re-flooded. Draining was again attempted in the late 18th century, with the same result, but in 1820 powerful steam pumps were installed which were finally effective in keeping the fields dry. On higher ground, fields could still be wet due to poor drainage, but because the encroaching sea was not the problem, different methods could be used that were effective. One technique was bush drainage—the practice of trenching heavy clay fields and lining the trenches with brush, then burying them again, thus creating a sort of natural underground filtration system. The brush would eventually deteriorate and the trenches would need to be redone, but the practice was nearly as effective as using perforated clay pipes—which were expensive and still got clogged or broken and needed to be replaced—so it persisted beyond the Regency into the Victorian era.

Gambling in the Regency was like drinking: everyone did it, but there were various levels of acceptability. People in Society were expected to be able to play various card games: loo, whist, piquet, etc. (for rules and game play, see *Historic Card Games* in Sources below), and every social gathering had a card table set up after dinner. Except in family gatherings, where it was up to the players to decide, people always played for real money, and the average wagers at such card parties were pennies or shillings. To keep things simple, people sometimes used counters called "fish" that worked a lot like poker chips today, to be purchased or traded at the beginning of the game and exchanged for winnings at the end. As with every social indulgence, men had their own rules in gaming, and it was easy to break even those. Gentlemen's clubs offered card games at all hours and set minimum stakes that were anywhere from five shillings to a pound, with the idea that play would remain within what any reasonably wealthy man could afford. Since there were no limits, however, some men—nicknamed Flats—were led by unscrupulous friends—Captain Sharps—or their own hubris into addiction and ruin. The practice of writing "vowels" contributed greatly to this, as a vowel—an IOU—was treated just like money, thus prolonging both a man's ability to remain in the game and the likelihood of his running up his debt. There were certain clubs, called "hells," that allowed and even encouraged very high stakes, and it was not uncommon for entire fortunes to change hands in a single night of card play. At least Society frowned upon men who frequented these hells, considering them "gamesters," like George Wickham in *Pride and Prejudice*, and looked down upon them as profligate and undesirable.

The parliamentary system in England was established during the Middle Ages, and representative seats were assigned to political boroughs based on voter density (a voter was generally any male who owned land). However, by the 19th century, town growth and industrialization had caused voter populations to drastically change. Several towns that had once been small, like Manchester, had exploded in population, while areas that had been highly populated during the Middle Ages, like Old Sarum, had significantly dwindled in size until the need for representation was little to none. These over-represented areas were called "rotten boroughs" because, rather than reassign the seats for these areas, government gave the ruling lord of the area the right to fill them however he saw fit, and he even was able to pass that right down to his heirs, or sell it off to the highest bidder. This system negated the voice of the people and allowed men who might otherwise not have earned the majority votes to attain public office, including Sir Arthur Wellesley, the future Duke of Wellington. Obviously, these rotten borough seats were very popular among nobility, and they fought all efforts to dissolve them, maintaining that they preserved "the state of property as it is." Because of this opposition, measures to discontinue rotten boroughs weren't successful until the Reform Act of 1832.

Steam baths and spring bathing had been a custom in England for a hundred years by the time of the Regency, but it wasn't until 1808 that Dean Mahomed, a native of India, brought the idea of mixing fragrant oils and massage into the mix. He first introduced Indian Vapor Baths in London at the bathhouse of his employer, but after a parting of ways and a failed restaurant attempt, Mahomed wished to have his own bath house. In 1814, he moved to Brighton, a fast-growing spa town full of invalids and pleasure-seekers, and opened a very successful bath house there. His "shampooing" method was merely an aromatic steam bath followed by a massage using fragrant oils, and was extremely popular among sufferers of skin complaints to rheumatism to muscle cramp, and it was soon hailed as a kind of miracle cure for them all. These Indian Vapor Baths might well have been the precursor to the popular Turkish Baths of the Victorian era.

High duties on French wines during the Napoleonic Wars only served to increase an already lucrative trade on the Sussex coast: smuggling. Euphemistically called Free-trading, smuggling of all kinds of goods including lace, jewelry, silk, tobacco, and especially European liquors had become the staple of many coastal families' incomes. Whether they participated actively in the free-trade or not, most residents benefited from it in one way or another, and so were willing to assist smugglers, whether it be simply turning a blind eye or physically protecting them from the Excise men (coastal police). Thus, the job of an Excise man was not an enviable one—they were constantly slighted, tricked, and thwarted by most of the residents, while the smugglers—referred to as The Gentlemen—were enabled, sheltered, and pardoned. Almost every town on the Sussex coast was a landing site for smuggling at some point during the Regency. Worthing was a high-traffic smuggling port for most of the 18th century, until the town decided to transform itself into a spa town rivaling Brighton and stopped making smugglers welcome. Brighton, too, was a main port for smuggling before its rise as the Prince Regent's resort, but smugglers still found plenty of support amongst the residents there to continue their activities well into the 19th century.

Sources:

Turner, M. E. *Farm Production in England 1700-1914*. Oxford University Press. 2001

Williamson, Tom. *The Transformation of Rural England: Farming and the Landscape 1700-1870*. University of Exeter Press. 2002

Sickelmore, R. *The Epitome of Brighton*. W. Fleet. 1815

Parlett, David. *Historic Card Games*. https://www.parlettgames.uk/histocs/

Hoyle, Edmund. *Hoyle's Games, Improved: containing practical treatises, etc*. George Long, New York. 1825

Lathan, Sharon. "Gaming Counters." https://sharonlathanauthor.com/gaming-counters/

Simkin, John. "Rotten Borough." https://spartacus-educational.com/PRrotten.htm

Kumar, Anuradha. *Across the Seven Seas: Indian Travellers' Tales from the Past*. Hachette India. 2015

Mahomed, S. D. *Shampooing: or benefits resulting from the use of the medicated Indian Vapor Bath*. Creasy and Baker. 1826.

Zarr, Gerald. "The Shampooing Surgeon of Brighton." https://www.aramcoworld.com/Articles/March-2018/The-Shampooing-Surgeon-of-Brighton

Platt, Richard. "Smuggler's Britain." http://www.smuggling.co.uk/gazetteer_se_18.html

Evans, John A.M. *Picture of Worthing*. C. Stower, London. 1805.

Sandrawich, Chris. "In Search of Jane Austen—Guest Post: A Tour of Worthing." https://janeausteninvermont.blog/2012/05/10/in-search-of-jane-austen-guest-post-a-tour-of-worthing-by-chris-sandrawich/

Acknowledgments

$\textbf{E}$VERY BOOK IS a delight to finish, and this one is even more so—probably because it was the hardest so far to write. Since Tom has been a staple character in each of the previous books, I got into the way of thinking that he didn't need his own story, but near the completion of Book 3 I saw the light and planned this book. Perhaps because I had never thought about his story before, however, I just couldn't get it going for the longest time, but thanks to the vibrancy of the Sussex coastal scene it finally unraveled itself and turned out pretty well. I hope you agree!

Thanks as always to my fantastic beta readers, Diane Paredes, Emily Menendez, and my Auntie Laurie, who are always so willing to help me out no matter how busy they are.

To my friends, neighbors, and family members who are so supportive and excited to share my successes, no matter how small, you are the best!

To Rae Allen, my amazing book cover designer, you wow everyone with your talent and vision.

To Clare Wille, the fabulous narrator of my audiobooks and to Paul Midcalf, the wizard at Audio Sorcery Recording Studios, your incredible artistry brings my work to a whole new level. I cannot adequately express my gratitude.

Thanks a million to my boys, who deal with my inattention, listen to my books even though they aren't into Regency romance, and barely grumble when I tell them they're on their own for dinner. Again.

And to my husband Joe, who is my candid and thorough Alpha reader, listens to all my rantings, comforts me when I'm frustrated, rejoices with me when I've broken through a block, and always believes in me. I love you forever!

This book was launched in part with the proceeds of a Kickstarter campaign, and I am everlastingly grateful to all the generous backers who made it possible:

Alicia	Jenny Connolly
Casey Allen	ElBin
Rachel Allen	Valerie Erpelding
Zack Applewhite	Callan Everett
Amy Benson	Chad and Tanya Everett
Christopher Bradford	Rebecca Everett
Charlotte Brothers	Marina Fournier
Shanon M. Brown	Victoria Fulford
Ruth Bybee	Gabh
Carol	Karl Hale
Chloe	Kat Hale
Rachel Christensen	Laurel Hale

The Harkness family
Marianne Hales
Kurtis and Mary Jane Hansen
Marianne Harris
Wendy Hendry
Karrie Hyatt
Seth Jackson
Johan
Sergey Kochergan
Valerie L
Lauralee
Maria Mejia
Emily Menendez
Jessica H. @lovelybookishdelights
The International Heyer Society

Alisse Metge
Diane Paredes
Elizabeth Prettyman
PunkARTchick *Ruthenia*
T. Rodriguez
Emily Stanford Schultz
Katherine Shipman
Shauna Ludlow Smith
SnoozieQ
Nichole Van
Emily Wiebe
Stephanie Wollman

Thank you so much!

Judith Hale Everett is one of seven sisters and grew up surrounded by romance novels. Georgette Heyer and Jane Austen were staples and formed the groundwork for her lifelong love affair with the Regency. Add to that her obsession with the English language and you've got one hopelessly literate romantic.

You can find JudithHaleEverett on Facebook, Twitter, and Instagram, or at judithhaleeverett.com.